TAMAR

MAL PEET

WALKER
BOOKS

First published 2005 by Walker Books Ltd
87 Vauxhall Walk, London SE11 5HJ

This edition published 2012

2 4 6 8 10 9 7 5 3

Text © 2005 Mal Peet
Cover © 2012 Walker Books Ltd

The right of Mal Peet to be identified as author of this work has been asserted
by him in accordance with the Copyright, Designs and Patents Act 1988

This book has been typeset in Fairfield and Americana

Printed and bound in Great Britain by Clays Ltd, St Ives plc

British Library Cataloguing in Publication Data:
a catalogue record for this book
is available from the British Library

ISBN 978-1-4063-3913-0

www.walker.co.uk

TAMAR

By the same author

Keeper
The Penalty
Exposure
Life: An Exploded Diagram

For Tony Langham and Plym Peters,

and in memory of former SOE agent

Paul Peters (1924–2003)

PROLOGUE: LONDON, 1979

I N THE END, it was her grandfather, William Hyde, who gave the unborn child her name. He was serious about names; he'd had several himself.

Cautiously, when he and Jan were alone in the neglected little garden, William said, "Son, about this name. If the hospital is right and the child is a girl."

Jan was watching a tiny silver speck cut a white furrow in the blue sky. "Oh Gawd. Forget about it," he said wearily. "We'll sort it out eventually. There's still seven weeks before the baby's due." Then he looked across at his father, perhaps sensing the old man's gaze on his face. "Why? You got a suggestion?"

"Yes."

Jan's eyebrows went up. "Really? What is it?"

"Tamar."

"How do you spell that?"

William spelled it out and Jan said, "Is that an actual name? Is it Dutch, or something?"

"No, it's the name of a river. It separates Devon from Cornwall. Rivers are fine things to be named after, but that's not what matters. As a word, as a name, what do you think of it?"

Jan thought about it, the shape and the sound of it. "Yeah, it's rather nice, actually. Now tell me why. Why *Tamar*?"

His father took a while to answer. It was his way; Jan was used to it. He waited. From the open French windows, a scrap of his mother's voice, then Sonia's laughter.

"It has to do with the war," he said.

This was interesting. Jan knew that his parents had been with the Dutch resistance during the Second World War. When he was a child, fussy about his food, Marijke had told him stories of rationing and hunger and people who would kill each other for a chicken. His father, though, had said almost nothing about those years. Not voluntarily. And now this.

"You know that I was an SOE agent."

"That's about all I do know. You've never told me much about it."

"I've never wanted to. Psychologists tell us that keeping things buried inside is bad for us, makes us sick. Maybe it does. But I happen to think there are certain things that are best left buried, that we should take to our graves with us. Terrible things that we have witnessed. I'm sure you disagree. You belong to a liberated generation; you believe in freedom of information. But I am sure that one day you will change your mind."

Jan didn't know what to say. This was startling stuff, coming from his old man.

"SOE agents were trained in groups," William Hyde said. "Each agent had a code name; these were chosen by the British, not us, and they were quite eccentric. Early in the war there was a group named after vegetables, if you can believe that. Several men and women went to their deaths having to call themselves things like Parsnip and Cabbage. So I was relieved when the code names chosen for my group were the names of rivers in the west of England: Severn, Torridge, Avon."

"Ah," Jan said. "And Tamar, of course."

"Yes. And Tamar."

"So," Jan said, after another pause. "What you want, what you're asking, is… I'm not sure how to put it. You'd like your grandchild to, what, *commemorate* you. Is that right? You'd like this code name to continue after you've…"

"I would consider it an honour."

Jan almost laughed at this stiff and formal phrase.

"But only if you are sure you like it," William said.

"I like it. But aren't you forgetting something?"

"No. Sonia needs to agree, of course. But you'll discuss it with her?"

"Sure. Don't get your hopes up too high, though. If I say I like it, she'll probably hate it. That's the way it is."

His father considered this. "In that case," he said, "it might be best if you didn't tell her why I suggested it."

"What do you mean?"

"Well, she might not like the idea of a name which is connected with … well, with war. With that period of time. She might think it is…"

"What? Sinister, or something?"

"Something like that, perhaps."

"I don't see why. You were fighting on the right side, after all."

His father nodded. "True."

Jan studied his father's face for a second or two. It was so damned hard to know what the old man was feeling. He was like one of those office blocks with tinted windows; you could only see in if you happened to look from a certain angle when the light was right.

"It's not a problem for me, Dad," he said. "Anyway, it's the name of a river, as you say. Come on, let's go inside."

*   *   *

The following day, Sonia and Jan went to his parents' house for lunch. It was a monthly ritual that Sonia, in her present condition, found challenging. Marijke's Sunday lunches were no-holds-barred affairs.

While they ate the first course, William Hyde kept darting glances at his son and daughter-in-law. They seemed a good deal happier than they had the day before, but that meant nothing in itself. It was not until Marijke was serving the roast beef that Sonia reached out and put a hand on her husband's arm.

"Oh, come on," she coaxed. "Don't keep your poor old dad in suspense. Tell him."

"Aha," Marijke said, sliding a thick slice of red-centred meat onto Sonia's plate. "What's this? Some good news?"

Jan put his hands palms down on the table and leaned back, grinning. "It's a miracle," he said. "Sonia and I actually agree on a girl's name. Thanks, Dad. Well done."

Marijke was pouring gravy onto Sonia's plate. She looked up, puzzled. "Name? What name is this?"

Sonia said, "Tamar. It's perfect. I love it."

Marijke dropped the jug. It fell onto Sonia's plate, snapping a chunk off the rim. Gravy ran across the table and, before anyone could react, spilled onto Sonia's distended belly.

ENGLAND, 1944

THE AIR SHOOK; you could feel it. And the noise was unbelievable. It is probable that humans had never heard anything like it, since it was perhaps the sound of the planet giving birth to its mountains, of raw young continents grating together. In the fields of southern England, animals panicked and continued to panic because the noise would not stop. At a stables in Buckinghamshire, every horse kicked out the door of its stall and bolted. Near Mildenhall, in Suffolk, a line of military vehicles came to a halt and men tumbled out of the trucks to stare at the sky. A doctor, driving with his head out of the window to look upwards, ran into the back of the convoy and was killed instantly.

It was Sunday 17th September, the middle of the morning. People were in church. The pulsing downward beat of the noise overwhelmed their hymns. Choirs gave up. In Westminster Abbey the vast sound of the organ was drowned by it. Men, women and children went into the streets and gazed up, speechless, at the vast migration of mechanical birds that filled the sky. You could not see where it began, nor where it ended.

An army had given up the earth and taken to the air. It was flying to Holland to end the war. The aircraft – bombers, paratroop transports, gliders swaying at the end of three hundred foot cables, fighter escorts – set out for Europe in enormous columns ten miles across and a hundred miles long. One of the pilots who survived said later that the air was so packed with planes it looked like you could climb out onto the wings and walk all the way to the Dutch coast.

On a crescent-shaped lawn, part of the grounds of a large country house just north of London, about sixty people watched the vast airborne armada pass. They were a mixed bunch, men and women, some young, some not. Some wore uniforms; others were in civilian clothes. Few were known by their real names. Towards the middle of the lawn, close to a tarnished bronze statue of Eros, two young men lay on their backs watching the spectacle. The Special Operations Executive had given them the code names Dart and Tamar. Although both men were fluent in English, they spoke in their native Dutch.

Dart said, "I think we are witnessing the beginning of the end of the war."

Tamar saw a heavy glider swing into the path of another and then somehow correct itself. In Holland, flights of German fighters would be taking off. They couldn't miss so huge a target. He was watching men being flown – being dragged – to their deaths. My God.

"We'll not go in now," Dart said. "They've been wasting our time. The codes, the parachute jumps, the wireless stuff, all that shit. It was just a damn cover. They were planning this all the time."

Tamar turned onto his right side. "Listen – even if those poor bastards up there drive the Germans out of our country, that won't be the end of it. The Nazis have broken everything. There is no organization. There is no trust any more. Some of our people are collaborators; some are heroes. I'm almost as afraid of liberation as I am of anything else. So don't imagine there is nothing for us to do, that we have been wasting our time."

He rolled onto his back and watched the infinite planes cross the sky. "One way or another," he said, "we'll be in Holland soon. I'd bet my life on it."

Dart was arrested in the early hours of the morning. He was awakened by a Luger pistol pressed against his temple and a torch blazed into his face. There were two men, a sergeant and a private in Waffen-SS uniforms. He received some rough assistance getting to his feet and then a bag or hood was pulled over his head. The Germans half marched, half dragged him along a corridor, the pistol barrel at the base of his skull. They went through three sets of doors and made four turns. Dart tried to retain his sense of direction, but lost it. He half fell down a long flight of stairs and at the bottom found himself standing on cold stone. A door closed behind him and he was forced onto a hard wooden chair. His arms were wrenched behind his back and his wrists cuffed. The hood was removed.

He was in a windowless room that smelled of mould and something else – paraffin, perhaps. A shelf ran along the wall to his right and one of the things on it was a large toolbox, the kind a carpenter or electrician might use. It was open and Dart could see the implements it held. The hard light from three unshaded bulbs made the room seem colder than it was. Dart felt his skin contract.

The two SS men went to stand against the wall behind the thin bespectacled man who sat at a table studying Dart's false identity papers. He wore the black uniform of a major of the Gestapo. When he looked up, his expression suggested that he disapproved of Dart coming to this inter-view in his underwear.

"Good morning," he said.

Unnerved, Dart said, "Good morning," and by the slight downward shift of the Gestapo officer's mouth realized he'd already made his first mistake.

The major switched to Dutch. "Who recruited you into the British secret services? Was it Colonel Nicholson? Neave? Perhaps the persuasive Mr Clements?"

Dart kept his face blank. "I don't know any of those names. I am a doctor."

The major, without taking his eyes from Dart's, tapped the identity papers. "Not exactly. Not according to these. You are not fully qualified, it seems."

"True," Dart admitted. "The war interrupted my studies."

"In other words, you are merely pretending to be a doctor."

"I have a licence to practise under the emergency regulations. It is attached to my identification, as you see."

The major pushed Dart's papers away with his fingertips as if they were a particularly grubby work of pornography. "When did you arrive in Holland?"

"I do not understand the question."

"Yes, you do. You understand the question, and, as a matter of fact, I know the answer."

Dart was silent. The major shrugged, a dismissive gesture. "I am slightly interested in finding out which resistance organization you are attached to, even though they are all useless. What are you: a royalist, socialist, communist, or some other kind of *ist*?"

Dart said, "I am a doctor. I have no interest in politics."

The major leaned back in his chair. "Let me tell you something, my friend. The British are, as they themselves might say, taking the piss. You know that expression?"

Dart said nothing.

"Of course you do. The British send us rubbish like you to waste our time. They persuade you that you are doing

20

something important. That you have real secrets which you must go to your death before revealing. Their idea is that people like me, who have useful things to do, will waste our time in conversations like these." He rose and went to stand behind Dart, who, despite himself, twitched.

"Let me tell you something else, Mr so-called Lubbers. We know your real name. In fact, we know a great deal about you. One of your colleagues gave us this information just before he died. There is nothing for you to protect, except yourself. It would save us both a great deal of time, and it would prevent me getting very, very irritated, if you were to cooperate. Do you understand?"

After an hour, the Gestapo major yawned and looked at his watch. He turned to the SS sergeant behind him and said in English, "Williams? You still awake? Get the cuffs off our friend here and offer the poor sod a cigarette. Give him a blanket too, before he freezes to death."

Grinning, the sergeant released Dart. "You did all right, boy," he said. His accent was liltingly Welsh.

Dart said unhappily, "I was lousy."

The Gestapo major, rubbing his hands together for warmth, said, "Well, not too bad, Dart. Six out of ten, I'd say. Maybe seven. An extra mark for bladder control."

His real name was Franklin, and for SOE purposes he held the rank of captain. "We'll talk it through at ten o'clock. I'll tell canteen to hold a breakfast for you. I expect you might fancy a bit of a lie-in."

"Thank you, sir," Dart said. He was dog-tired.

Dart was mopping the grease from his plate with a slice of greyish bread when Tamar came in and sat down opposite.

"I hear you got the early call. How'd it go?"

"I was crap. The first thing he said to me was 'Good

21

morning' in bloody English, and I said 'Good morning' back to him in bloody English. Christ."

Tamar grinned. "Franklin. What do you think he was, before the war?"

Dart thought about it. "A solicitor," he said. "A solicitor with a passion for amateur theatricals."

Tamar threw himself back in his chair dramatically. "Hey," he said admiringly. "That is sinister! That is exactly what he was. You are a dangerously good judge of character, my friend. You should work here."

"God forbid."

"Amen to that," Tamar said. He took a folded newspaper from his jacket pocket. "What time's your debriefing?"

"Ten."

Tamar looked at his watch. "Twenty minutes. Do you fancy trying to crack the code of the incredibly insane *Times* crossword? I reckon two down is an anagram of *early bat*, don't you?"

As far as the locals were concerned, Ashgrove House was a convalescent home for Allied officers injured in action. It was odd that no civilians were allowed in, that all deliveries had to be left with the armed guards at the lodge, that the patients were never seen walking the lanes or footpaths. The accepted explanation was that these poor chaps were so badly damaged that it would be bad for civilian morale if they were seen in public. Stories went about of horribly disfigured characters glimpsed in the grounds, and the Special Operations Executive was happy to let these rumours circulate.

Officially, Ashgrove House was known as ST73. Agents, and the officers who sent them there, knew it as "the finishing school". It was the last place of safety. From here, on a moonlit night, SOE agents would be taken to an airfield in East Anglia, put into the belly of an RAF bomber and flown across the North Sea to parachute into Nazi-occupied Europe. With any luck, the reception committees that awaited them would not be German.

During the months before their stay at Ashgrove, Tamar, Dart and the other members of the Rivers group had been put through a training programme that was like a tour of the stately homes of England organized by dangerous psychopaths. At a succession of very grand houses – great echoing places commandeered for the war effort – they had practised concealment, stealth and sabotage. In splendid drawing rooms they had been taught to lie and to believe absolutely the lies they told. In deer parks and landscaped gardens they had practised killing: silently, with knife and wire garrotte; and noisily, with both British and German firearms.

They'd gone to Manchester for parachute training, dropping – if all went well – into the elegant grounds of Tatton Park. Dart found them exhilarating, those steppings-out into the empty air, and was interested to discover that Tamar was afraid, even though he was already an experienced parachutist. He'd never detected a trace of fear in the man until then.

Back in London, in an anonymous office building just off Baker Street, the group spent arduous days practising codes and cryptography. Their instructor was a cocky, brilliant and very young man who usually had an enormous cigar sticking out of his face. He introduced himself as DCY/M. They never discovered his name. He instructed them in the use of one-time pads. These were squares of silk, about three times the size of a handkerchief, printed with pre-set codes. He pulled them out of his briefcase and displayed them to the class like a salesman showing off a new line in underwear. He spoke of the strength of these silks and the ease with which they could be concealed. As a last resort they could be folded until they were no bigger than a square of chocolate and swallowed. Tamar put his hand up and asked, straight-faced, whether they might emerge intact "at the other end". Equally straight-faced, DCY/M assured the class that the inks were designed to dissolve in digestive juices.

During a lunch break Tamar said, "You know, the best thing about these one-time pads is something our boy with the cigar hasn't mentioned."

Dart looked up from his minced beef and mash. "Which is?"

"They make torture less likely. For you wireless operators, anyway."

Dart placed his knife and fork on the table, keeping his hands steady. *Torture* was a word that threw a shadow across his brain, one that he did not like to look at.

"Do they?"

"Sure," Tamar said. "Because you use a different line of code for each transmission, right, then you cut that line off the silk and burn it, or eat it, or whatever. You don't memorize anything. So there's no point in the Gestapo torturing you."

"Unless they just happen to enjoy it," Dart said.

"Yes, there's always that." Tamar looked at his watch. "Come on. Just time for a smoke before the boy wonder starts messing up our brains again."

Later the group divided. The WOs, the wireless operators, were sent to yet another stately home for an intensive ten-week course. Tamar and Dart didn't see each other again until the group reunited at Ashgrove House, six days before the sky filled with aircraft heading for Holland.

The agents became aware that something was wrong a couple of days before they found out what it was. There was a shift in the atmosphere at Ashgrove, like a change in the weather. Officers who were usually good at smiling seemed to have forgotten how to do it. The busy female clerks flirted less.

At the breakfast table, Torridge said, "You know what I think? I think something extremely bad has happened at home and they don't want us to know. There's been a major cock-up and they are embarrassed to tell us."

"They'll have to tell us," Tamar said, "but they'll wait until they've worked out how. You know what the British are like: 'It's not what you say, it's the way that you say it.' But you're right. Something has happened, definitely."

He pushed his crossword aside and tossed the pencil on top of it. "Shit."

Tᴀᴍᴀʀ ᴀɴᴅ Dᴀʀᴛ were summoned to the library three days later. There were two men waiting for them: Colonel Nicholson, who had been driven up from London just before dawn; and a middle-aged civilian called Hendriks. Tamar and Dart were told to sit in two of the large armchairs.

Nicholson paced as he talked. "I am going to speak to all teams separately; I can spend only thirty minutes with each. If at any time you wish to ask me a question, make sure it's a good one."

He went to the big bay window and stared out at the morning mist lifting from the lawn.

"The airborne forces that you watched pass overhead twelve days ago were part of a major offensive code-named Operation Market Garden. The objective was to seize certain key bridges over the Rhine, which would allow Allied troops to cross from the south of Holland into the occupied north, and from there advance into Germany. I regret to tell you that this operation has failed. You will be briefed on the details later. A decision has been taken that the attempt will not be repeated. Not in the foreseeable future, anyway."

He turned round, expecting a question, and got one.

"Are you saying, sir, that there will be no effort to liberate the rest of Holland?" Tamar's voice was hard-edged.

Nicholson's reaction was fierce. If he were a cat, Dart thought, his fur would be standing on end.

"Damn it, Tamar. The casualty figures aren't in yet, but I can assure you that a serious bloody effort was made last week. A lot of people died making what you call an effort!"

Silence. Hendriks shifted uneasily in his chair.

Dart cleared his throat. "Colonel, I think my colleague was trying to ask what our roles will be now. We have been trained to assist an Allied advance into our country. You seem to be saying that this will not happen. Is that correct?"

Nicholson put his hands in his trouser pockets and leaned against the wall. "I understand your concerns," he said. "We all do. Your fellow countrymen have endured appalling suffering under the occupation. We are deeply concerned for the Dutch people, believe me. But what we are now thinking about is the liberation of Europe. *Europe*. Not individual countries. We will defeat Germany. There's no doubt about that. And there's a race on. The Americans want to get to Berlin and drag Hitler kicking and screaming out of his bunker before the Russians do. Which means that pockets of the German army will get left behind to be mopped up later. In Denmark, for example."

"And Holland," Tamar said quietly.

"And northern Holland, yes."

"So what will we be doing? Sitting here on our highly trained arses doing crosswords?"

Nicholson almost smiled. "Oh no," he said. "You're not that lucky. You'll both be in Holland in less than a week. You, Dart, will be doing what you expected to be doing as Tamar's WO. Your cover story remains unchanged. You're still Dr Ernst Lodders."

"Lubbers, sir," Dart said.

"Sorry, Lubbers. So your medical training will still be useful. However, you'll be operating from three transmission stations, not two. It means you'll have to move about a bit more, but on the bright side it'll make it harder for German radio detectors to pin you down. You'll be given your new schedules and ID codes this afternoon."

Tamar said, "I get the feeling that I'm the one with the problems. Do you want to tell me what they are, Colonel?"

"You'll get an intensive briefing beginning this afternoon at 1500 hours," Nicholson said.

"Am I still to organize strategic acts of sabotage?"

"No."

"Am I still Douwe Schoeten, the railway maintenance engineer and Nazi sympathizer?"

"No."

"Christ," Tamar said. "I've been him for three months. Who the hell am I now?"

By three o'clock the room was full of sunlight. Nicholson sat looking out of the bay window, apparently watching a game of tennis that Tamar could hear faintly but not see. The man called Hendriks sat at the table. He was rather overweight and unhealthy in complexion; the flesh of his face looked as if it had been moulded out of dough by a baker with dirty hands. He took an ID booklet from his briefcase and slid it across the table to Tamar.

"Christiaan Boogart," he announced. "Taken into Germany as forced labour in 1941. Contracted tuberculosis winter '43. Failed to make a full recovery, therefore of no further use to the Third Reich. Repatriated. Now an itinerant farm worker."

Tamar didn't look at the ID. He didn't need to. "Again? I'm Boogart *again*?"

Nicholson said, with his back to the room, "We thought you might be pleased. A bit less homework for you to do."

"But, sir. Boogart? He's an agricultural labourer. What would he be doing in Rotterdam?"

"You're not going to Rotterdam," Hendriks said calmly. *"What?"*

Nicholson glanced round, his face inscrutable against the light.

"You're not going to Rotterdam," Hendriks repeated.

As Tamar gazed at him blankly, Hendriks leaned forward on his elbows, his plump hands clasped. "In your opinion," he asked, "would it be fair to describe the Dutch resistance as fragmented? Disorganized?"

"What? Er ... no. It would be fair to describe it as a bloody shambles."

"That's perhaps a little harsh. But, yes, the different resistance organizations have been mounting operations without any central planning. A bomb here, an ambush there, a train derailed, a telephone exchange blown up. Fine things in themselves, but not adding up to anything really useful. And the Germans are taking terrible reprisals for such actions. Their jails are packed with what they call *Todeskandidaten*. You know what the word means?"

"It translates as 'death candidates'," Tamar said.

"That's right. It's a system they were beginning to operate when you were last there, a year ago. Every time there's a so-called 'terrorist outrage' the Gestapo drag a dozen or so poor bastards out of prison and shoot them in the street. Making sure the locals are watching, of course. We don't think it's worth it. Do you?"

Tamar didn't answer immediately; then he said, "It's a complicated question."

Nicholson interrupted again. "Not to me, it isn't," he said. "Several of our people – your colleagues – are death candidates right now. Austin is. So are Holvoet and Dubois. Thijssen too."

Tamar looked at the colonel. "Thijssen? Jan Thijssen?"

"Correct," Nicholson said. "Your old boss. He's banged up in Apeldoorn."

"I thought he was dead."

"No. They kept him alive, poor sod. I don't much fancy his chances if we don't get a grip on things."

Hendriks cleared his throat officiously. "The point is that these hostages will be sacrificed if we do not establish discipline. For this and other reasons it is now an absolute priority to get all resistance groups to bury their differences and work together. You would agree that this is desirable?"

Tamar made an unnecessary sign of agreement.

"Therefore," Hendriks said, sounding proud of himself, "what we've done is divide Holland into sixteen zones. Each of these zones will have a commandant who will persuade – at gunpoint if necessary – the various resistance groups to unite under his control. Once that is achieved, the resistance will only conduct operations authorized by Delta Centrum in Amsterdam. You, Tamar, are to be the commandant of zone six. Now, I want to show you this."

The file he plopped onto the table had a brown cardboard cover with a thick red band running diagonally across it.

"This contains everything we know about your area as it is at present. It is as detailed as we can make it. We cannot guarantee that the information regarding the positions of German troops is entirely accurate. It was accurate last week, but…"

Tamar put up a hand, palm out, the way you might shield light from your eyes. "Please," he said, "tell me something simple. Where are you sending me? What is zone six?"

Nicholson turned away from the sunlight and the tennis and said, "Your old turf. Where you were last time."

Tamar's heart stumbled like a happy drunk.

"You got out clean," Nicholson continued. "You know the geography. And we need someone good near the front line. That's why we're resurrecting Mr Boogart. It's a largely rural area. Who else but an itinerant farm worker would be roving about?"

Hardly daring to, Tamar asked, "And where will I be? What are the safe houses?"

Hendriks tapped the file impatiently. "The information you need is all in here. At the moment, we believe that the Maartens farm is the best option. You do remember the place?"

Tamar lifted his face to the window, dazzling his eyes with the sun that now burned directly through the smeared glass. Praise God. "Yes," he managed to say. "I remember it."

An unfamiliar feeling grew huge inside him. Then he recognized it: joy.

Something in the dazzle moved: Nicholson lifting his arm to look at his watch.

"Now then, Tamar. Here's the drill. You've got this room for the next twenty-four hours. Learn everything in that file, and then lose it in some remote part of your brain. As if you've completely forgotten it. Do you understand? Right. You'll be here again at 1500 hours tomorrow, when Mr Hendriks will test you on your prep and answer any further questions you might have."

"Sir."

At the door, Nicholson paused. "This is Dart's first time," he said. "Did you know that?"

"I guessed."

"That worry you at all? A bit of a moody bugger, is he?"

"I don't think so. He'll be fine."

"Good. But I don't want you nursemaiding him, hear me? That's one reason we're tucking him away in Albert

31

Veening's nuthouse. We don't want him near you all the time. We can just about afford to lose him, but we can't afford to lose you as well. If we do lose him, you might have to be your own WO for a while. For that reason, you'll have your own set of silks. Now, get your nose into that file."

"Sir? May I ask when Dart and I will be going in?"

"There's a three-quarter moon in four days' time. The weather forecast looks reasonable. That's the timetable we're looking at. Is that soon enough for you?"

TAMAR AND DART sat in a dingy, blacked-out brick shed that contained a table, four chairs, a telephone and a good deal of cigarette smoke. Tamar wore a scuffed leather jacket over a high-necked sweater and grubby denim dungarees. Dart looked rather more respectable in a dark tweed overcoat and corduroy trousers. Outside, at the edge of the bleak airstrip, a Stirling bomber was warming its engines, and every time they faltered Tamar's heart faltered with them. The surface of the table was covered by a map of Holland brightly lit by the big lamp suspended from the ceiling. The young SOE officer was called Lennon and he had a heavy cold; the edges of his nostrils were raw. He would have preferred the two agents not to smoke, but didn't think it was reasonable to ask them to stop. He wiped his nose with a crusty handkerchief and tapped a pencil on the map.

"We last used this dropping zone seven weeks ago," he said. "It is, as far as we know, quite secure. There are small German garrisons here and here." He drew faint crosses with his pencil. "They might look uncomfortably close, but it seems they are lazy buggers who don't like going out at night. It's mostly marshy ground out there. Ponds and so forth. So you might get your feet wet. On the plus side, there aren't many roads good enough for German armoured cars and whatnot to pootle about on."

Pootle, Tamar thought. God, these British.

"The plane will make two passes over the DZ. Five of the containers will be dropped first. If there are Germans there and all hell breaks loose when those go down, we'll bring you back and try again at a later date. All right?"

"All right."

"On the second pass, the sixth container, the one with your stuff in it, will go first, then you. There'll be a big reception committee, so don't get confused. They all know what to do. When everything's been sorted out, you'll be taken in two separate vehicles to the Maartens farm. You, Dart, after checking the radio there, will then be taken to your base, which is, um, here." He poked his pencil at the map. "It's a shade less than three kilometres outside Mendlo."

Lennon gasped and threw his head back so violently that for an instant he appeared to have been shot. He sneezed explosively into his handkerchief three times, and then, as if nothing had happened, continued. "Good. Next thing. The weather people tell me there's a fifty-knot headwind tonight. That means the flight will take approximately two hours and twenty minutes. You're going to get bloody cold sitting in the belly of that Stirling. So I've brought you these."

He reached into his coat pocket and took out two flat metal flasks. "Whisky. Not enough to get you squiffy, but it'll help keep the heart rate up to scratch."

"Thank you, sir."

"Not at all. Now then. These damn things." Lennon took an ordinary brown envelope from his inside pocket, opened it and tipped two signet rings onto the map. They were rather chunky, similar in design, and didn't look new. One was engraved with the letters CB; the other, a touch more fancily, with the letters EL.

"You'll know what these are. Here's how you open them." He picked up the EL ring. "Just slip your nail in here, see? And then a little twist…"

The engraved panel swivelled to reveal a tiny compartment. A capsule of cyanide nestled snugly inside. Dart leaned forward to examine his suicide pill more closely.

Lennon cleared his throat and said, "Apparently, the best thing to do is just lick it out with your tongue. It's a bit fiddly to get at with your fingers. Don't forget to crunch before you swallow, of course."

He snapped the ring shut and wiped his nose again. Tamar slid his ring onto the second finger of his right hand; Dart found that his fitted best on the third finger of his left hand, where normally a wedding band would be worn.

"How's that feel?" Lennon asked. "Comfy?"

The door opened and an RAF man lugged two parachutes into the room.

Looking at Dart, Lennon said, "We need a signal from you at 0648 hours tomorrow, confirming that you are both in place. We must get that signal. Otherwise, we'll have to assume that things have ballsed up. If that happens, you are out there on your own. And I think you know what that means."

He stood up. "Right then. Flight Sergeant McKay here will help you on with your chutes and check them for you. Take-off in how long, Rory?"

"Soon as we're on board, sir."

"Super," Lennon said, rubbing his hands together. It seemed he had something more to say, but he paused, awkwardly. "Um… Any letters, at all?"

Puzzled, Tamar said, "Letters, sir?"

Lennon hid his discomfort in his handkerchief. He busied himself with his nose and then said, "Well, you know. Some of you, some of your colleagues, have left letters with me.

35

For me to deliver. To loved ones, nearest and dearest, that sort of thing."

Tamar and Dart looked at him blankly.

"No? Fine. Excellent. That's it then, I think." He held out his hand, and Tamar and Dart got to their feet and shook it in turn. "Good luck. You'll be fine, I know it."

"Thank you, sir," Tamar said.

Lennon picked up his briefcase, buttoned his coat, and left. Outside, he began a long bout of violent sneezing punctuated by curses, all clearly audible inside the shed.

Two hours later the farm worker and the doctor were semi-rigid with cold and numbed by noise, so they were startled when they looked up and saw Flight Sergeant McKay leaning over them, supporting himself on the steel ribs of the plane.

"We're about to cross the Dutch coast. The skipper will start to bank and weave to avoid anti-aircraft fire in about five minutes. You'll get chucked about a bit. Try not to puke, okay?"

They nodded, dumb.

McKay leaned closer. "Did Lennon give you a spot of whisky apiece? Aye, I thought so. He pays for it out of his own pocket, you know. Now would be a good time to take it. I'll be back in a while. All right?"

They nodded again. McKay went away and the plane began to lose height. Bubbles of pain formed inside Tamar's ears. Then the world began to rock and buck and tilt.

Some time later McKay came back, paler in the face, followed by a crew member the agents hadn't seen before. The containers, metal cylinders the size of corpses, were stuffed with guns, ammunition, medical supplies, radios, explosives, food and money. The two airmen began to free them from their fastenings and slide them along the parachute line towards the hatch. The sound of the engines wavered and the plane tilted then straightened. The two RAF men hauled the hatch door open; working very fast, they shoved five containers out into the howling dark.

Almost immediately the Stirling banked steeply. Dart and Tamar, strapped into their seats, were tipped backwards at a forty-five degree angle. Whisky-flavoured vomit rose in Tamar's throat and he forced it back down. The plane levelled then banked again; Tamar and Dart lurched forward. Tamar felt that his guts had come loose from their moorings. His breath came out of his lungs in ragged gasps. Seeing his terror, Dart reached across and gripped him by the forearm.

Then McKay was signalling urgently. The two agents unclipped their belts and stumbled across the jolting steel floor. McKay hooked their chutes to the line and checked the clasps. The sixth container went out, then Tamar was at the hatch. The inrush of air sucked the breath out of him. He gaped at McKay, who was holding up his right hand with the fingers outstretched: *wait*. The hand closed. Then one finger lifted, then two, then three. McKay's mouth formed words that Tamar could not hear.

Then he was where nothing could be felt or heard other than the dwindling sound that might have been the plane or his own screaming. Drowning, he tried to swim but he had forgotten how. He thought he saw below him a pale eye reflected in broken glass. Then something that might have been God grabbed him by the collar.

Dart heard McKay shout, "Go, Tamar, and good luck!"

Then he was himself braced at the hatch, and next he was free of everything. Like Jonah, he had been in the belly of the beast for a long time and now this was beautiful. It was not like falling. He stretched out his arms and the air ran through

37

his fingers like water. He was almost disappointed when the jerk came and he heard the unfolding bang of the parachute.

He looked down and saw his legs swinging out of control above a swaying world of dark and complicated mirrors. He saw, too, Tamar's chute sink like a jellyfish into the water of a deep well, then shrivel and fade. At almost the same moment, he realized that the black scribbles that divided the mirrors below him were trees with hard fingers waiting to seize him. He began to haul desperately at the lines of his parachute.

Tamar had not been able to drift clear of the surface of the water that rushed up to meet him. He was already fumbling with the harness release when he felt the cold shock of contact; he was terrified the chute would drag him under. He was thigh-deep before he felt something more or less solid – a mass of sludge and submerged branches – beneath his feet. With a moan of relief he got free of the chute and saw it settle onto the black water like a gigantic water lily. Then he began to struggle towards the denser shadow of the bank. His flailing right arm struck something hard and he grabbed at it. It shifted in the water. A boat? Yes.

He was pulling himself along it, looking for where it must be moored to the bank, when he heard someone speak.

"Welcome to Holland, Tamar."

He looked up. On the bank, distinct against the lesser darkness of the sky, was the unmistakable silhouette of a German soldier. The long field service coat, the jackboots. Cold moonlight glinted from the steel helmet and the snout of a sub-machine gun.

Even before fear took hold, Tamar was filled with a great and bitter disappointment, a sense of ridiculous failure. He stood away from the boat, feeling broken, and raised his arms above his head.

A short bark of laughter, then the dark figure spoke again. "Put your hands down, man. Don't be fooled by the fancy dress. It's Koop de Vries. I'm in charge of your reception committee."

Blindly, and in squelching boots, Tamar followed Koop along the labyrinth of paths through the marshes. Koop murmured greetings to dark figures holding Sten guns or rifles. The night was full of muffled business. Shadows moved and spoke in low voices. At a rough landing stage, two containers were being unloaded from a punt. Someone swore; someone else laughed.

"Wait here," Koop said, and dissolved into the night. Then he came back, a pale grin in the darkness. "We've got Dart," he said. "He's fine, more or less. This way."

Dart materialized out of the dark and Tamar embraced him. "Are you all right?"

Dart let out a long shaky breath, an attempt at laughter. "Yeah. No. Christ! I'm hanging from a tree and I look down and there's this bloody Nazi hanging onto my legs. I think I died. I really think I died for a second or two."

"No you didn't," said the Nazi. "You gave me a right kicking. I'm going to have the grandmother of all black eyes in the morning." He reached out to shake Tamar's hand. "Eddy Dekker. Glad you made it."

"Hello, Eddy. Are there any more of you SS men waiting to scare the crap out of us?"

"Just two. Oskar's keeping an eye on the transport. Wim is helping carry your stuff up."

Koop was twitchy. "We need to get moving," he said. "The sky's clearing. There's getting to be too much light for my liking."

In single file the four men emerged onto a narrow causeway between reed beds. Beyond the reeds, on both sides, a glittering track of moonlight lay on black water. They were very exposed now, and Tamar was relieved when the causeway began to rise towards a long line of willows. The agents followed Koop and Eddy through the trees and found themselves standing on a roughly paved road. A rich stink hung on the night air.

They were at the rear of a convoy. The last two vehicles in the line were big horse-drawn trailers piled high with manure. Up on the nearest one, two figures were pitchforking the stuff over one of the containers.

"Don't worry," Koop said, "that's not the way you two will be travelling. Come on."

He led them past the trailers. The horses stood silently, their faces in nosebags, their hooves muffled in sacking. Next in line was an ambulance, of sorts. It was, Dart now saw, an ageing pick-up truck that had been given a canvas roof, a coat of white paint and a stencilled red cross. He was horrified. It wouldn't have fooled anyone.

Koop saw the look on his face and laughed softly. "I know what you're thinking. But this is a one hundred per cent genuine ambulance with one hundred per cent genuine licence papers. It belongs to the asylum, and you're damn lucky to have it, if you ask me. Eddy will drive. Me and Tamar will be in the car ahead. If we stop for any reason, do exactly what Eddy tells you, right?"

Koop moved on. Eddy squeezed into the cab of the ambulance. Dart reached out and put a hand on Tamar's shoulder. "Good luck."

"And you. See you at the farm."

Dart might have been about to say something else but Koop called, impatiently, and Tamar moved up the road to join him.

Koop made a sweeping gesture with his arm. "Our transport for this evening," he announced.

"Dear God," Tamar said.

The vehicle at the head of the line was an armoured SS staff car. Camouflage paintwork, big black and white crosses on the front doors, swastika pennant flying from the wing.

"She's a huge great pig of a thing, isn't she?" Koop said, grinning like a skull.

"How…" Tamar tried again. "Where the hell did you get this? Where do you keep it?"

Still smirking, Koop said, "Do you really want to know?"

Tamar looked at him, considering both the question and the smirk. "Perhaps not. Not for now."

Heavy footfalls came out of the darkness: an SS sergeant and a trooper, shouldering their Stens, hands outstretched to shake Tamar's.

"Oskar."

"Wim. Good to meet you. Shall we go?"

Wim climbed into the driver's seat and Oskar sat beside him. Tamar got into the back with Koop. In the confines of the car he became aware of the rotten smell rising from his sludge-filled boots and filthy dungarees. Koop fussed with the skirts of his long coat and then settled back with a satisfied sigh, as if he were an elderly aunt being taken for a Sunday drive.

"There," he said. "Three gallant SS men taking a naughty terrorist to headquarters for a chat. What could be more normal?"

I T HAD A name – Sanctuary Farm – but the few people who knew it called it the Maartens place. For a long, long time the farm had clung to the landscape by its fingertips. It had no right to be there, so far from the good farming country to the east. At its back was a wilderness – the Veluwe, a great expanse of harsh grassland, bog, gorse and flinching trees. But they had been stubborn, those outcasts or runaways who first settled there and refused to run any further. Their soil was poor but they drained it and fed it and hung on. Loneliness and occasional starvation couldn't shift them. Plagues and wars passed them by. Eventually they acquired the name Maartens.

Seasons and centuries came and went. Then in 1724 the clan had a rush of blood to the head, a burst of energy that lasted two generations. What brought it on was the building of a new canal. It joined the wealthy towns to the north with the IJssel River and passed within two kilometres of the farm. The Maartens were slow-speaking but not slow-thinking. They got busy, and businesslike, and got what they'd never had before: money. The barges that carried their pigs and sheep to market returned laden with bricks and lime and sawn timber. The Maartens hauled it all back to their farm and went on a building spree.

They built, first, a barn with a thatched roof that sloped down close to the ground. They gave it big double doors like a gaping mouth. It had two storeys; in winter the animals lived on the ground level while the Maartens, or some of them, lived above, snug in the breath and odour of their livestock. They called this building the big barn, and when it was finished, they immediately set about another. It was pretty much identical to the first but slightly smaller, so they called it the little barn. The two buildings formed two sides of a courtyard.

The Maartens paused to get their breath back, which took twenty years. Then they demolished their ramshackle medieval cottage and built a sensible, plain-faced brick and thatch farmhouse. It formed the third side of the courtyard. These three buildings remained the heart of the farm for ever after. Later generations added bits and pieces: sheds, a porch, a wash-house. In 1899 the family imported a huge, elaborate Belgian stove and rebuilt the kitchen around it. This alien extravagance was the talk of the district for many weeks. In a last spurt of energy, the Maartens built a dairy; they started milking their cows in there two months before the start of the First World War.

Dart caught his first moonlit glimpse of the place when Eddy followed the German car down a gently sloping track. The shaggy thatch of the three main buildings put him in mind of beasts sleeping in a field. At the bottom of the incline Wim and Eddy jolted the cars into gear and headed for the black mouth of a great brick barn. At the last possible moment the headlights of the staff car came on and both vehicles passed safely through the doors and rolled to a halt.

"Wait," Eddy said.

Dart heard the scrape and slam of the barn doors. Eddy

got out of the ambulance, so Dart did too. He looked back, hearing heavy bolts sliding into place. An oil lantern threw grotesque shadows onto the walls. The person at the doors was a young man, perhaps a boy. He wore a black coat, rubber boots and a cloth cap too big for his head. Dart was expecting a greeting but didn't get one. The boy stared past him, lifting the lantern. Dart saw a smooth face dominated by large dark eyes, eyes that closed briefly when Koop and Tamar climbed out of the staff car. Now Wim and Eddy switched on big electric hand lamps and began to unload the boot of the staff car.

Amid the jittery shadows, Koop said, "Tamar? We'll stack everything here in this stall, and chuck straw over it. How long do you need to set up, Doc?"

"I've no idea," Dart said.

Tamar took the lantern from him and said, "Ten minutes. Fifteen at most."

The boy opened a small door cut into the main doors and Tamar and Dart followed him through it and along the yard to the little barn. Inside, the boy lit a second lantern then led them up a wooden staircase and along the length of the upper storey. In the swaying light, Dart could just see that the space on either side of the aisle was divided by wooden partitions into small rooms or pens. Ten paces from the end wall the boy stopped and reached above his head, feeling along a beam. A trapdoor swung down from the ceiling. Tamar stretched up, groped, pulled down a ladder. He climbed up, taking his lantern. Dart heard him say something like "Pah!"

"What?"

"Cobwebs. Wait a second. Okay, come on up."

Dart climbed into a room tucked under the thatch. Much of the floor space was taken up by junked and dusty furniture. Tamar had stood the lantern on an ancient dressing table with a blotched mirror. Now he set an upturned chair on its feet and placed it against the table.

Turning to Dart he said, "I sent my last transmission from here almost exactly a year ago. I never expected to come back."

"How does it feel, being here again?"

Tamar's eyes shifted to the yellow light shining up through the trapdoor. He seemed about to answer, then merely shook his head. "Let's check the equipment."

He went to a lopsided chest of drawers that was shoved into the angle of roof and floor and dragged it a little way into the room. On his knees, he rummaged in the exposed thatch and produced a small tan suitcase, a car battery and a metal box wrapped in lengths of green and black wire. He set all three things on the table. The suitcase transceiver was thick with dust. Tamar wiped it off with his sleeve and opened it.

"Look," he said, pointing to the beams overhead. "See those six hooks? For your antenna." He unwound the black wire and handed it to Dart. "The battery should be charged up. Now, are you all right to check this out while I go and see how Koop's doing?"

"Sure," Dart said, unravelling the power leads. "Shouldn't take long. I'll come and find you."

The boy led Tamar down to ground level. At the foot of the stairs he turned to face the agent and stood his lantern on a ledge. Having done that, he didn't seem to know what to do with his hands. Eventually he folded his arms and shoved his fingers under his armpits. He looked up at Tamar; below the peak of the cap his eyes were dark pools reflecting the lamplight.

"They told us only 'Tamar'. I prayed it would be you. I begged God to let it be you."

Tamar said, "There was no way I could let you know."

"No. But when I saw you get out of the car with Koop, I almost fainted."

Tamar let go of the stair rail and came down the last step. They were very close now.

"Has anything changed?"

Tamar smiled. "Many things."

"No. You know what I mean. Between us. Do you—"

"Yes," Tamar said, and something inside him opened, something he'd kept locked for a long time. "I still love you. I haven't stopped thinking about you. It's been like living with a part of my body missing."

He reached out and gently removed the cap, releasing a fall of dark hair that came almost to the narrow shoulders, framing the pale oval face in which the eyes now closed. He put his hands under the hair, cupping her head. He tried to say her name, but his throat was tight and he had to try again.

"Marijke. Dear God. Marijke." It was the first time in almost a year he had spoken the word.

Their two monstrous shadows, thrown by the lamp onto the far wall of the barn, merged into one and became motionless. Then Marijke spoke, but her face was pressed into his chest and he could not make out the words. He held her away from his body slightly. "What?"

"I didn't even know if you were dead or alive," she said, almost angrily.

"Nor did I."

From above them came a muffled creaking. Marijke pulled away, taking the cap from Tamar's hand. "I must go to the house," she said, glancing up to where light was brightening at the head of the stairs. "My grandmother will be very anxious by now."

"How is she?"

"The same. She will probably cry when she sees you." She stepped away from him, then paused. "Are you still Christiaan Boogart?"

"Yes."

She smiled for the first time. "Good. I liked him."

She was across the barn and through the door by the time Dart began to descend the stairs.

"Tamar? Tamar, are you all right?"

Tamar drew in a long breath, as if he were about to dive into cold water, then turned to look up at Dart. "Yes. Fine. Is the set up to scratch?"

"It works perfectly. I thought you were going to see how Koop was doing." The upward light from the lantern he carried turned Dart's face into a yellow and black mask that was both comical and sinister.

"Yes. I just stopped to get my breath."

"Well, it's been quite a night, one way or another."

Tamar almost laughed. "That is something of an understatement, my friend."

At the door of the barn, Tamar hung both lanterns on nails hammered into the wall. Then he extinguished them. The two men stood, invisible to each other, waiting for their eyes to adjust to the darkness.

THE JOURNEY TO the Mendlo Mental Asylum took twenty minutes, but seemed much longer on the narrow back roads. Dart saw a line of massive plane trees just before the car swung right between two tall brick gateposts. Then an impression of dark windows in a long brick wall. Ahead of them, the ambulance turned right again and vanished. Wim brought the German car to a halt beside what looked like a greenhouse. Koop was now very anxious about the nearness of dawn. Like a vampire, Dart thought. He even looks a bit like one.

A glass door was opened by a nun. She called softly, "Dr Lubbers?" Dart went up two steps to the door and shook the hand she held out to him. "I am Sister Agatha. Please come in."

She led him into a conservatory where silvery-green plants cast complicated moon-shadows. Oskar followed them, carrying two small black suitcases which he set down on the floor.

"Dr Veening is catching up on some sleep," Sister Agatha said. "He asked me to wake him when you arrived. You'll probably be more comfortable waiting in here."

She opened a door. Dart followed her through into

complete darkness. Then there was the scratching of a match and a sudden blossoming of pale yellow light. He was in a large room containing nothing but an assortment of dilapidated chairs. He sat down on the one nearest him and instantly felt unbelievably tired. Sister Agatha fiddled with the lamp until its flame was steady. In the yellow light her face looked as if it had been carved out of wax. Then she melted into the darkness.

Dart had been sitting for less than a minute when he heard the German car start up and drive off. Once again he felt that events were out of his control. His reception committee had gone, and he had not been able to say good-bye or wish them luck. He fought against an aching desire for sleep. The muscles in the back of his neck could hardly hold his head up.

He woke when he heard a chair scrape on the bare floor. He was being studied by a pair of ice-bright blue eyes set in a crumpled and stubbly face. The man was about sixty. He wore a grey dressing gown over a shirt and dark trousers. Wire-framed spectacles hung from a cord around his neck and rested on his chest.

"Good morning."

Dart straightened up in the chair. "Dr Veening?"

"Do you know," the other man said, "I think I would commit murder for a cigarette."

"What? Oh, right…" Dart fumbled in a pocket and produced a creased pack. The older man took a cigarette, ran it under his nose for the aroma, then lit it from the oil lamp. He exhaled a sigh of pleasure in a blue cloud.

"It's over two weeks since I had a smoke," he said. "Scrounged it off a bloody German while he was checking my papers. He knew damn well who I was, too."

"You are Dr Veening?"

"We are colleagues, so naturally we will use first names. You are Ernst; I am Albert." He extended a hand and Dart shook it. "Welcome to the madhouse, Ernst Lubbers. Since you must be out of your mind, doing what you are doing, you should fit in very nicely." He drew on his cigarette. "You look almost as tired as I feel. When I finish this I'll show you to your room. It's on the first floor, well away from the wards. The wailing and so forth won't reach you there. Sleep as long as you like. I imagine you've had an eventful night."

Dart shook himself out of his dazed state. "Dr Veening. Albert, sorry. I can't sleep yet. I have to make a transmission in" – he checked his watch – "Christ, in just less than an hour. I have to set the equipment up." He looked about the room anxiously. "Where's my stuff?"

"Sister Agatha took your kitbag to your bedroom."

"Is that where I set up?"

Albert Veening looked almost hurt. "Certainly not. We've got a special hidey-hole for that. We've made a rather neat job of it, though I say so myself. I hope you'll be impressed. And if you're not, I hope you'll pretend you are."

He put his cigarette out under his foot, then bent and picked up the stub and dropped it into the pocket of his dressing gown. He stood and lifted the lamp. "Your, er, technical equipment is already up there. Shall we go?"

They went through a panelled door into an impressive hallway. Its three tall windows were barred on the inside. Dart saw that the sky was paler now, a blue-grey slate sprinkled with chalky stars. Veening led him up a wide zigzag staircase with a dark mahogany banister. On the second landing they turned right, through a reinforced door. A corridor, more stairs, two turns. Dart remembered an earlier night walk with a Luger pressed against his skull.

Veening said, not looking round, "I know what you're

thinking. Bloody maze, this place. The architect must have been a lunatic. Right. Here we are."

They were in a passageway that ended at a black panelled door. Veening produced a large bunch of keys attached to his belt loop by a length of string. With some difficulty he separated one key from the rest and handed it to Dart. "Don't lose it," he said. "It's the only spare. Go on, open up."

Dart put the heavy key into the lock. There was some resistance, but eventually the door swung open.

"This is the old dispensary, where they doled out whatever weird and wonderful potions they hoped might do some good a hundred years ago. It hasn't been used for God knows how long."

The room, with its counter, resembled a shop. An elaborate set of scales had gathered equal amounts of dust in its tarnished brass pans. Behind the counter, along two walls, were many rows of small drawers, each labelled with flaking gold lettering. Along the third wall, dusty-shouldered flasks of coloured glass sat on shelves. Next to these shelves was a door, its varnish like diseased skin. Veening lifted a hinged section of the counter and Dart followed him through it. Veening opened the scabby door to reveal a walk-in cupboard. Dart's two black suitcases sat on the floor next to a rusty bucket and a broom. Four iron hooks were screwed to the back wall.

"Now then," Veening said. "Watch." He went into the cupboard and tugged the third hook from the left. It came away from the wall, attached to a short length of cord. He leaned his shoulder against the wall and it swung open. "*Voilà!*" he said, unable to keep the pride from his voice. "Do come in."

It was a room about three metres square, containing an ancient bureau, a chair and a sort of couch covered in a green blanket. In one corner, close to a small leaded window, stood a gadget that looked like a bicycle converted into a device for torture. It had neither wheels nor handlebars; the saddle was perched on top of a triangular metal frame. The chain connected the pedals to a dynamo, from which dangled two electrical cables with crocodile clips at their ends.

"A battery recharger," Dart murmured. "My God." He raised the lamp and looked around the room. "This is fantastic, Albert."

"It's acceptable, is it? This used to be the dispenser's office. The fake cupboard is something Sister Agatha and I cobbled together. Carpentry is one of her many skills, I've discovered."

"You must have worked incredibly fast. I'm amazed."

Albert Veening looked slightly embarrassed. "Actually," he said, "we did most of this six months ago. For another young man like you. But he didn't make it."

"What happened to him?"

"I've no idea. Now then, there's a battery under the bureau, see? And just outside that window there's a lightning conductor. I understand that the kind of antenna you'll be using can be hooked up to it."

"You seem well up on these technical matters, Albert."

"Not at all. I had a call from a mutual friend the other day. We discussed what you would need. I'm glad that it's suitable."

Dart fetched in the two suitcases. He lifted one onto the bureau and opened it. From the left-hand compartment he took out the headset, the Morse key and the leads. He looked at his watch again.

"Albert, I don't want to seem rude, but it's probably best if you're not here when I do this."

"Of course. I'll wait outside. I imagine you'll want me to guide you back."

"God yes."

"Fine," Veening said. "I'll take the lamp. There are two just like it in the right-hand bottom drawer of the desk, along with notepads and pencils." He turned to go.

Dart said, "Albert? You said just now you'd had a call from a mutual friend. Do you mean a telephone call?"

"Yes."

"You've got a phone here? One that works?"

Veening grinned. "Oh yes. I'll show you tomorrow. It's a work of art." He closed the concealed door behind him.

Dart found the lamps and lit them both, placing one either side of the transceiver. He connected the Morse key and the battery leads and clipped the antenna to the lightning conductor. He switched the set on. The voltage meter lit up, its needle swinging across the dial all the way to fifteen. From his coat pocket he took a crystal disguised as an ordinary two-pin electrical plug and slotted it into the transmitter. Then he tuned the aerial, using the most delicate of touches. Good.

He switched off, removed his wristwatch and put it on the desk. He took a second watch from his trouser pocket and laid it next to the first, checking that both gave him exactly the same time. After a bit of anxious fumbling he found the loose stitching in the hem of his coat and pulled out the squares of silk. He studied the one headed TRANS-MISSION PLAN and tuned the crystal to twelve megacycles. Using a notepad, he covered all but the bottom row of letters on a second silk and used them to encode his brief message. He double-checked it, then took from the inside pocket of his coat a small wallet made of scuffed crocodile skin. It contained a comb, tweezers, nail scissors and a file. He used the scissors to cut off the bottom line of the silk, then held the strip of material with the tweezers and set light to it with his cigarette lighter. He rehearsed the Morse in his head. At six forty-seven he switched the set on and made tiny adjustments to the transmitter. Then he rubbed his hands together vigorously with his fingers extended, like a pianist about to begin a recital. When the second hand of both watches touched twelve, he placed the second finger of his left hand on the Morse key and tapped out his identity checks, followed by a sequence of five-letter groups.

Ten minutes later, in London, a young woman in a blue uniform tiptoed into an office where a man was sleeping on a camp bed. She placed a sheet of paper on top of a pile of folders on his desk. Her note read: *River 3 in place. Checks okay. Delta Centrum not yet informed. Please advise.*

By the time Nicholson read the note, Dart was deeply asleep in a room in a building where mad people were starting to struggle free of their dreams.

THE BED HAD shifted and groaned slightly when she left it, and Tamar's hand had moved instinctively towards the pistol under his pillow. But Marijke had taken hold of his wrist and hushed him, and he had slipped back into the dream of slow-motion falling through endless plates of silently shattering glass. When he was at last fully awake, he groped on the floor for his watch and swore softly when he saw how late it was. Then he realized he was happy, and lay back on the pillows making sure that he had remembered everything accurately. Making sure his reasons for being happy were good ones. Which they were.

He became aware of voices from the yard below. When he swung his legs out of the bed, he was ashamed to notice that the spaces between his toes were still rimmed with dried mud. He went naked to the window and peered through a narrow gap in the curtains. Marijke was talking to a woman with copper-coloured hair who was holding a bicycle by the handlebars. The bike had a little trailer attached to the back of it, in which a small child was sleeping.

Tamar found his sweater and put it on. The scruffy leather jacket was hanging from a peg on the back of the bedroom door. His other clothes had disappeared, and for a moment he was at a loss. Then he saw that faded but clean cotton trousers and a pair of woollen socks had been left on the chair beside the bed. He put them on, went to the bedroom door, then remembered the gun. He took it from under the pillow, put it in his right-hand trouser pocket, and moved quietly towards the stairs. Marijke was waiting for him in the hallway outside the kitchen door, looking up at him. When he reached her, she put her arms around him and he held her head against his shoulder, stroking her hair.

After a while she pulled away from him and said, "Your courier is here. Come and say hello."

In the kitchen, the visitor was trying to interest her child in what looked like porridge. When Tamar came in she put the spoon down and stood up, hoisting the child onto her hip. She smiled and held her hand out. "I'm Trixie Greydanus."

"Christiaan Boogart."

Trixie raised her eyebrows and glanced at Marijke, who bit her lip to hide a smile and turned away. "And this is Rosa," Trixie said.

The child studied Tamar through chestnut-brown eyes and then buried her face in her mother's shoulder.

"She's beautiful," Tamar said, meaning it.

"She's still sleepy. She always drops off in the trailer. It's the bumping that does it."

Trixie Greydanus had a wide suntanned face scattered with darker freckles; with shorter hair she would have looked like a boy who had spent a long happy summer at the seaside.

"Trixie was at the asylum this morning," Marijke said.

The asylum, Tamar thought. Dart. Christ, I haven't so much as thought about him since he left last night. What the hell is wrong with me? He said, "Did you meet our friend? He got there safely?"

"I didn't see him, but he's fine, apparently. He was asleep. I spoke to my aunt. She's the head nurse there."

"Did she say anything else?"

"She said that he was a good-looking boy with lovely hands." Trixie grinned. "Aunt Agatha didn't become a nun until she was forty. She still takes an interest." Trixie turned to Marijke. "She also pointed out that she now has another mouth to feed, and that Dr Lubbers doesn't have a ration card yet."

"I've put a parcel together," Marijke said. "A loaf, eggs, dried sausage, a jar of Oma's raspberry jam, some other stuff. But make sure you keep some for you and Rosa."

"Bless you," Trixie said. She turned to Tamar. "I hope you realize how lucky you are to be sent here, Christiaan. You'll get home comforts that other men would kill for."

Her smile was innocent, but was that a wicked twinkle in her eye, Tamar wondered? And was he blushing? To cover his confusion he said, "Tell me about your routine, how you get about."

Trixie became businesslike. "Right. I visit my aunt at the asylum two or three times a week. Then I either go back to my place in the town or come here, visiting my 'cousin', Marijke. I can do it more often, if you need me to."

Tamar thought about this. "That's quite a trek on a bicycle. How long does it take you?"

"About an hour each way, usually. Less, if I haven't got Rosa with me. I'm used to it. It's why I've got legs like a carthorse."

"And how will you carry stuff, when we need you to? Other than messages, I mean."

"Rosa's trailer has a false bottom. It'll take a radio, one of the smaller models. Or a Sten, if it's in three pieces."

Tamar nodded. "What about the Germans? Do you get stopped very often?"

"On the country lanes, hardly ever. There aren't many motor patrols away from the main roads. There are checkpoints on the way in and out of town, of course, but I'm a familiar face. They don't even look at my papers most of the time. Some of them try to feel me up, but they don't usually go too far, maybe because I have Rosa with me. One or two of them are quite soppy about her."

And you are a very cool customer, Miss Greydanus, Tamar thought. "So," he said, "tomorrow morning. You'll call at the asylum at about nine o'clock, pick up the other transceiver, take it to the Grotiuses' house in Mendlo, and stand watch while Dart – Ernst Lubbers – sets everything up and makes his test transmission. Is that right?"

"Yes. I thought I might walk to town with him."

"Is that safe? We don't want the two of you seen together."

"Sure, but the chances of us meeting anyone on that road are next to nothing. Besides, what could be more natural than me escorting the new doctor to town to make his calls? I'd be going that way anyway."

Tamar considered this. He also thought about Dart making that lonely walk for the first time. "All right. But split up well before the checkpoints."

"Of course." There was a hint of impatience in her voice. "Do you have any messages for Dr Lubbers?"

"No. Just tell him that everything is okay here, please."

"I'll do that," Trixie said. "And I bring him here the day after tomorrow?"

"Er … yes, that's right."

"At what time?"

Christ, Tamar thought, I can't remember. Get a grip! "Ernst will confirm that when you see him tomorrow," he said. "Now, if you'll excuse me for half an hour or so, I've got some things to sort out in the barn."

When he'd gone, Trixie Greydanus leaned back in her

chair and regarded Marijke ironically. "Well, well, well," she said. "This Tamar turns out to be none other than the famous Christiaan Boogart. Would that by any chance explain the extra colour in your cheeks this morning, Miss Maartens?"

Giggling, Marijke cuffed her on the back of the head. Rosa looked up, wide-eyed.

The wind was easterly with a cold bite to it, and it sent falling leaves on ragged flights like yellow butterflies. At the corner of the house Tamar caught sight of Marijke's grandmother working in the kitchen garden. The old woman was swaddled in an oversized dark coat and an apron fashioned from a sack. She was harvesting beetroot, thrusting her spade into the ground, levering, stooping to lift them by their purple-veined leaves, dropping them into a heavy wooden wheelbarrow. When she saw him approaching, she straightened and wiped her hands on the coarse apron, smiling.

"Good morning, Oma. The garden is looking good."

Julia Maartens went into an elaborate mime: a sorrowful gesture at herself, another at the garden and the fields, a stoop as if under a heavy burden, a shrug, a prayerful gesture at the sky. Tamar understood. She was old, the work was too much, the farm was falling into ruin, but what could she do, other than hope that God would be kind to them.

"I'll help when I can," he said. "We'll be all right."

She reached up and touched his cheeks lightly with the fingers of both hands, careful not to soil his face. Her eyes were wet, perhaps because of the chill wind.

"I have some stuff to sort out, Oma. When I've finished, you must tell me what jobs you want me to do."

He turned to go, but she began another mime, this time silently mouthing the words as if she knew her gestures were inadequate. She pointed at the house and then at Tamar. She

59

hugged herself. She pressed her palms together and held both hands to the side of her face, closing her eyes. Finally she placed both hands over her heart, nodding and smiling.

Tamar stared at her. Was she really saying what he thought she was saying? That she was happy Marijke's lover had returned, happy her granddaughter was sharing his bed? Embarrassed, he turned his face away and watched a squadron of rooks wheel above the orchard. When he turned back, Marijke's grandmother was nodding again, tears falling onto her cheeks. Not knowing what else to do, he took her face in both hands and kissed her forehead. Then he left her and went to the barn.

He pulled away the straw that Koop's men had strewn over the contents of the container and began sorting, thinking of hiding places as he went. Two Sten guns, which he assembled and laid on the floor with their ammunition clips. Four bundles of second-hand clothes with pre-war Dutch labels. Two pairs of well-worn leather boots and a pair of black shoes. A metal drum, which he prised open to find sugar, tea, coffee, flour, powdered milk, powdered egg, tinned meat, English cigarettes in Dutch packets, candles, lard, several boxes of matches, and three slabs of something in plain brown paper. He tore the corner from one of them. Chocolate! He broke off a piece and put it in his mouth. It tasted like a lost childhood. A tin case containing medical supplies: dressings, penicillin powder, ampoules of morphine, syringes, disinfectant, iodine, three rolls of bandages wrapped around transceiver crystals. And a bottle labelled ASPIRIN. The white pills inside were, in fact, Benzedrine, little tablets of mental lightning for exhausted wireless operators.

At the bottom of the pile was a canvas satchel. Inside it Tamar found a set of maps, two German military compasses, a pair of binoculars and several rolls of Dutch banknotes, used, and not forged. Something else too, right at the bottom. A well-fingered ID booklet embossed with an eagle clutching a swastika in its talons. He flipped it open. It belonged to Gertrud Berendts, an auxiliary nurse. The photograph was one of Marijke, taken perhaps two years ago.

Tamar leaned back against the side of the stall. London knew everything, he realized. He felt foolish. "The Maartens farm," Hendriks had said. "You do remember the place?" And they'd known all along. They'd known that this time he wouldn't leave without her. They'd faked her an ID to make it possible.

He was still staring at the photograph when he heard the barn door open. He stuffed the booklet into the satchel and scrabbled around in the metal drum for the chocolate.

"I don't want to see anything you don't want me to," Marijke said, "but Trixie needs to go soon. You should come and say goodbye to her."

"I will. But come in here a minute. I want to kiss you."

When their lips were together he forced hers open gently with his own and slid the little chunk of chocolate from his mouth into hers. He watched her eyes fill with amazement then close; watched her taste a pleasure she'd almost forgotten.

Marijke held Rosa and Tamar held the bike. Trixie lifted the cushions and the blanket from the trailer and then pressed her fingers against its base. It swivelled up, revealing a hollow compartment. She put in the things that Marijke had given her.

Tamar said, "You have to hide food too?"

Trixie looked up. "You've been away a while, Christiaan. Food's getting scarce, and the Germans are nearly as hungry as we are. Some of them would slit your throat for a jar of jam."

Marijke and Tamar watched her leave. She had to stand on the pedals to power the heavy machine up to the road.

"She's good," Marijke said. "I'd trust her with my life. I *do* trust her with my life."

"And mine?"

"Without question. Why do you ask?"

"Because she lied to me," Tamar said, watching the receding bike.

"What? What do you mean, she lied to you?"

"She said she had legs like a carthorse, and nothing could be further from the truth."

Marijke took his chin between her fingers and forced his face towards her own. "If I ever catch you looking at another woman's legs again, Christiaan Boogart," she said, "I'll scratch your eyes out."

DART SAT HUDDLED inside his overcoat on a cast-iron bench on the terrace of the Mendlo asylum, watching the lunatics. One of them, a middle-aged man wearing a long cardigan over his uniform of white tunic and trousers, was trying to trap the shadows of clouds as they moved across the leaf-strewn lawn. His method was to stamp his foot down hard on each shadow as it reached him and use his weight to hold it there. He did not seem at all disappointed when the shadow escaped him, but turned and waited eagerly for the next, poised like a goalkeeper. Dart admired his attitude.

Albert Veening lowered himself onto the bench beside Dart and inhaled deeply. "I love these late afternoons at this time of year. There's a smell in the air that reminds me of tobacco."

Dart felt in his coat pocket and found his cigarettes.

When Albert had lit up, Dart said, "That one, there. The old lady. What's she doing?"

"The one with Sister Joanna? Her real name is Elena, but she will only answer to the name Sidona. She thinks she's a stranded angel. She may well be right."

The angel was wearing a man's cap and coat over her long white dress; her feet were bare. She was having an animated discussion with an invisible person.

"Who's she talking to?"

"Another angel," Veening said. "Probably the one she calls Michael. She says he has blue wings and hard shiny skin like a beetle. I hope it's him, anyway. If it's the one called Trago, we'll be up half the night. He upsets her."

"Tell me what you do for these people."

"Bugger all, frankly. We feed and protect them. There are drugs that would help, but we've no hope of getting hold of them. Before the war I had a colleague who used to wire patients up and shoot a dose of electricity through their brains. That would see off the demons for a day or two. And the angels, of course. But he joined the Nazi Party and went off to Germany to do 'research'. He made the right decision, seeing as how we're lucky to get electricity one day a week, at best."

Dart said, "But it's a miracle, isn't it, that the Germans haven't shut you down? The Nazis don't have what you would call a kindly attitude towards the mentally ill."

Veening watched the plane trees lose a few more leaves before he replied.

"We used to have a large number of inmates who were mentally handicapped, rather than mentally ill. I'm sure you understand the difference. Many of them were the kind of people who get called village idiots. Perfectly harmless. In 1941 the Germans came and took them away. Rounded them up and piled them into two trucks. Some of them were in mortal terror; others thought they were being taken out for a treat. It was a lovely summer day."

He stubbed his cigarette out and pocketed it.

"I don't know what happened to them. I think that if I did know, I'd be wearing a white uniform and trying to trap shadows with my feet, like Gerard over there. Now there are just twenty-four patients, and seven staff, including me. We rattle around in this huge great place like dried peas in a bucket.

But, as you say, it's a miracle that we are here at all. Perhaps Sidona's angels are watching over us."

He turned to face Dart. "Sorry. I tend to ramble. Now, come with me to the office. I promised to show you the telephone."

Dart stood. "Albert," he said, "I hate to correct you, but it's not seven staff. It's eight, including me."

Veening bowed his head, a gesture of apology. "Of course, Dr Lubbers. I get forgetful sometimes. I find it helps."

The asylum superintendent's office had once been rather grand. The leather-topped desk was the size of a bed, but there was nothing on it except a stained cup, a novel and dust. A large statue stood at the back of the room: a white marble woman, her upper body naked, one arm outstretched in a caring gesture. Veening had hung his coat, hat, scarf and umbrella on it. The ceiling was covered in fancy plasterwork, and the walls were dark oak panelling. Dart glanced around.

"Over there," Veening said.

In a corner, half hidden among a heap of unwanted furniture and old files, was a huge and ancient contraption mounted on a thick slab of mahogany: a pair of round bells with a little hammer between them, a brass winding handle, a handset on a brass hook. The mouthpiece looked like a black cup and saucer. It was connected to the rest of the machine by what looked like frayed grey rope.

"You're joking," Dart said.

"I found it in one of the cellars, a week after the Germans took our proper phones away. Dates from about 1900, at a guess. It's a beauty, don't you think? The wires run up behind the panelling. As I said, we are connected to only two other phones, one in Apeldoorn and one in Amersfoort, but there's a relay system. You have to wind it up with that handle thing before you can use it."

Dart ran his fingers through his hair. There were things he hadn't been briefed on, he realized. "London didn't say anything about this."

"I don't suppose they know. It's a local thing. Something we put together ourselves. And it's only for emergencies, mind. It usually only rings when some new kind of hell breaks loose."

"Albert, may I ask you something? How long have you been working for the resistance?"

"Since the day the Germans took my village idiots away," Albert Veening said.

Tamar propped himself up on the pillows so that he could see Marijke's face more clearly in the weak candlelight.

"Are you tired? Do you want to go to sleep?"

She shook her head. "I want to talk."

"We have lots of time."

"Perhaps. Listen. There, did you hear it? The owl again."

"Tell me about the Germans coming here," he said. "When was this?"

"A couple of weeks into the new year. We were half expecting them. A boy from one of the other farms ran over here to tell us that German soldiers had been at his place. We hoped they would pass us by, like most people do. But they didn't. They came the next day. Eight of them, in two trucks. We'd had time to hide quite a lot of food. They managed to catch about half the chickens, but the rest ran off into the orchard. Two of the Germans chased them, shooting at them with rifles. Can you imagine? It was almost funny. They were lousy shots."

"That's encouraging," he said.

"I suppose it is. But they took the tractor and both the horses. I bribed one soldier with a jar of butter not to take the bike or the tyres. They took most of the hay and half our firewood, the bastards. They took the sheets and blankets from our beds. Lots of stuff. They looted us."

"Did they…" He hesitated, not sure how to ask the question, or if he wanted to. "Did they hurt you, or anything?"

She reached up and touched his face. "No. They looked at me, you know? But nothing happened. I was well wrapped up against the weather, anyway; they probably weren't sure if I was a woman or a man."

"So they were stupid as well," he said, kissing her.

A little later, she said, "Don't worry. We'll survive. We've worked hard on the garden. That's all we can do now. We should have enough food to last until spring, if we're careful. After that—"

"After that," Tamar said, "the Americans or the British or the Canadians will be here. It'll all be over."

"I'd love to believe that."

"I'm sure of it. Believe me."

In the hidden room at the asylum the wind moaned softly at the gap in the window, but Dart couldn't hear it. He was wired to the transceiver, the headphones clamped over his ears. His right hand wrote fast, translating the stuttering Morse into meaningless sequences of letters. His pistol lay on the desk. At one point a moth crash-landed on Dart's notepad and his hand brushed it away without pausing in its writing. Now and again he danced his feet against the floor, warming them.

When London signed off, Dart removed the headphones and massaged the tense muscles in his neck. As he went to disconnect the antenna, he heard something calling on the wind. An owl, perhaps. Or a lunatic. He spread the silks on the desk and began the laborious task of decoding.

DART WAS FINISHING his meagre breakfast in the asylum's huge kitchen when Sister Agatha walked in holding an infant.

"This is Rosa." She made it sound important.

"Ah," Dart said, getting to his feet. He hadn't known that a child would be involved in his mission and he was rather puzzled.

"My niece. Well, actually she's my sister's daughter's daughter."

"I see," Dart said, untruthfully. The little girl regarded him with gravely suspicious eyes.

"You'll be seeing quite a bit of Rosa, I imagine," Sister Agatha said. "Her mother is Beatrix Greydanus. Trixie."

"Oh, right. Our, er…"

"Your courier, yes. Come and meet her. She's outside, talking to Sidona."

"The lady who has conversations with angels?"

"That's right. She's giving Trixie the latest news from heaven. Things aren't going too well up there, apparently."

Trixie and Sidona were sitting in a rather sorry-looking summer house at the rear of the building. When the old lady saw Dart approaching, she clamped her hands over her mouth and fled. Agatha handed Rosa to her mother and set off in unhurried pursuit.

Dart shook hands with Trixie. "I seem to have upset Sidona," he said.

"She'll be fine. She worries about strangers overhearing her when she's reporting on angels. She's quite security-conscious in her own way." She smiled. "Now, if you want to get your things, we'll walk to town. We're expected at the Marionette House at ten o'clock."

The road into Mendlo was not in good condition. It had been hastily patched up, here and there, with rubble or concrete. In several places the verges had been crushed down into the ditch by the caterpillar tracks of German tanks. At one point, the road had been reduced to half its width by a British bomb; fifty metres off to the right, a second bomb had exploded in a field and the crater was now a small pond. A single moorhen trailed ripples across it. Dart and Trixie took turns to push the bike and its trailer. Dart's medical bag with the pistol in it was slung over the handlebars. He was worried about what the jolting might do to the suitcase transceiver concealed below Rosa's slumbering body.

Trixie glanced sideways at him. Was he good-looking? Well, yes. Nice hair, a profile like that American movie actor whose name she could never remember. In fact, the two of them, he and Christiaan, looked similar. This one was tense, though. You could see all the muscles in his jaw standing out under the skin.

"So then, Dr Lubbers," she said, "tell me what you know about the Marionette House."

Dart thought back to his briefing at Ashgrove. Only six days ago. And a world away.

"It's at the corner of two small streets that run down

69

from Old Church to the market square. The building is wedge-shaped, with the narrow end facing the square. It's got three floors. The ground floor is the shop, with a workshop at the back. The living rooms are on the first floor. There's a single attic room at the top of the house, which is where I'll be operating from. It has a shuttered window overlooking the square. The shop entrance is on Church Lane, but I can come and go via the workshop if I need to. The owners are Pieter Grotius and his wife, Barbara."

"Bibi," Trixie corrected him. "No one calls her Barbara."

"Bibi. Thank you. They're in their sixties. Used to run a travelling puppet theatre called the, er … Blue Moon Theatre. Toured all over Europe during the twenties and thirties."

"All over the world," Trixie said. "America, everywhere. They were quite famous."

"Okay. They bought the Marionette House in … 1936, was it? They make, repair and sell puppets of all sorts. I don't suppose business is very good right now."

"No. You're not going to be disturbed by hordes of customers. Actually, the place is more like a museum. Pieter and Bibi collect all kinds of stuff. Books, toys, all sorts. It's a crazy place."

Dart saw that the morning mist had condensed on Trixie's auburn hair. It was coated in beads of moisture, tiny glass pearls.

"Bibi suffers from a terrible ulcer on her leg," she continued. "The dressings need to be changed every few days."

"Ah," Dart said. "That's why I am a frequent visitor."

"Of course. It's also why Bibi spends long periods sitting in her parlour, keeping an eye on the square. She's resting her leg."

So that's my lookout, Dart thought. An old woman with a bad leg. "What about German radio detector cars?"

Trixie drew in a long breath. "Well, the nearest ones are in Apeldoorn. We've positively identified two of them – a dark blue delivery van and a black car that used to be a taxi."

"There's got to be more than that. It takes at least three to get a fix on a transmitter."

"I know. We think they use ordinary army vehicles as well."

Trying to keep his voice level, Dart said, "And what's the procedure if they show up in Mendlo?"

"While you're transmitting, I'll be hanging around in the square with a girlfriend of mine, chatting and so forth. A couple of lads called Douwe and Henk will be kicking a ball about over on Kuyper Place; any traffic from Apeldoorn is almost certain to go through there. We have three other people as well; if any of them see the cars, they tip me off. Then I take my shoe off and shake it, like this. Like I've got a stone in it. That's my signal to Bibi, who'll be watching me. She'll run to the stairs and warn you. Then you shut down immediately and leave through the workshop. Pieter will be out the back, making sure the coast is clear."

Dart had stopped walking. Trixie turned and looked at him. He had thrust both hands into his coat pockets and was staring at the ground.

"Ernst? What is it?"

He looked up. "Mrs Grotius will run to the stairs? This is the same Mrs Grotius, I assume? The elderly woman who has trouble moving about because of the ulcer on her leg? Are you serious? Do you realize—"

He shut up because Trixie Greydanus had a big grin on her face. He was astonished when she slipped her arm inside his and squeezed it.

"Lord love you, Dr Lubbers," she said, "for being such a trusting soul. Bibi hasn't really got anything wrong with her leg. It's just bandages. She's as fit as a flea." She smiled up at him. "I wouldn't mind betting she's a faster mover than you are."

The open road became an avenue between scarred and wounded trees. Now buildings appeared on either side, many of them broken and abandoned. Then, ahead and off to the left, the humped outline of the town itself emerged: a looming church tower, wet light on grey roofs, smokeless chimneys like rows of teeth.

Trixie said, "Right. We're nearly there. Now then, the quickest way to Pieter and Bibi's is to turn left at the first crossroads after the station and then go over the bridge by New Church."

"Yes."

"But we're not going that way. We're going to go straight on, through what they call the Merchants' Gate."

"Why?"

"Because there's always a German checkpoint there."

Dart looked at her. "What?"

"The Germans are used to me coming and going," Trixie said. "Nine times out of ten they just wave me through. Unless it's the skinny one on duty, the one that likes to feel my backside. And they need to get used to you too. They need to get to know your face. This morning, they are going to check you out, have a good look at your papers, all that. Next time, the next few times: the same. After a while, they won't bother. You'll become as familiar to them as I am."

Dart forced a smile. "Do I have to let the skinny one feel my backside too?"

Trixie laughed, a little snort of delight. "I don't think he's that way inclined. But you never know."

In the shelter of the last trees Trixie stopped and Rosa, as if by arrangement, began to stir. "We need to split up here. You go ahead. I'll wait a few minutes, then follow you."

Dart could only nod. The fear was on him suddenly, like a thin coating of ice over his entire skin. Trixie unhooked the medical bag from the handlebars and handed it to him. When their hands touched she gripped his fingers briefly. "You'll be fine," she said. "Really. Try to look as if you're in a hurry, okay?"

The Merchants' Gate was a medieval tunnel of stone and brick. From a slanting flagpole above it the red flag of the Third Reich hung like a big wet rag. The arched entrance to the tunnel was barred by a fat coil of barbed wire slung on a wooden beam. One end of the beam was hinged to the wall; the other had a metal wheel, allowing it to be trundled open. There was a gap just wide enough for a man to walk through. Two German troopers, rifles slung over their shoulders, stood inside the gate, talking. Dart heard one of them, the older, thinner one, laugh. He had to force his legs to take him towards the barrier. He found himself praying, absurdly, that the Germans would not see him at all, that he would simply pass through the checkpoint invisibly. But they turned and watched him approach, and it took everything he had to keep walking.

He thought, My God, this is real. These are real Germans. I can't do this. He had a mad desire to burst out laughing, to confess, to be forgiven, to be allowed home. Then he remembered that he had no home; and, strangely, the thought gave him a little strength.

"Your papers, please."

It was the younger one, facing him at the gap in the wire. Dart looked down and saw his left hand move to his coat pocket as if someone were pulling it on a string. The hand emerged, holding the little booklet. The German took it. To Dart it seemed that the booklet had the word FAKE stamped all over it, but the sentry didn't seem to notice. He turned the pages slowly, twice. He looked at the photograph and then at Dart and then at the photograph again. He lifted his steel head.

"Dr Lubbers? Ernst Lubbers?"

"Yes."

The young German had pale grey eyes. Dart made himself imagine what they saw: a dark-haired, narrow-faced man wearing a slightly shabby overcoat with a red cross armband on the left sleeve. A man carrying a leather medical bag with a false bottom concealing a gun. An agent. A spy.

"I don't think we have seen you before, Dr Lubbers."

Dart heard words come out of his mouth. "Probably not. I was transferred here recently." His hand went out and turned the pages of the booklet. "You see? The authorization from the Department of Internal Security."

It was a flimsy piece of paper forged in England. Obviously. The German flipped the booklet shut. Dart held out his hand to take it back, but the young man turned away and went to confer with his older colleague. They spoke together, looking at the identity papers. They both looked again at Dart. The young German soldier returned to the barrier.

"What is the purpose of your journey?"

Dart gazed at the man. "I have a number of patients to visit," he managed to say. Remembering, he made a show of looking at his watch. "Now, if everything is in order, I—"

"The names and addresses of these patients, please."

"I... Well, I..." Dart attempted to make his stutter sound indignant. "Really, I do not think that it's any of your..."

Then Dart realized that the German's gaze had shifted. Something behind Dart had taken his attention, and he jerked his head in a signal to the other soldier. Dart turned to see Trixie shoving the bicycle up to the checkpoint. She looked hot and bothered. She had opened her coat so that the sentries could see her breasts tipping forward inside the threadbare summer dress. Rosa was crying. The expression on Trixie's face was apologetic, as if she were late for an appointment with the Germans and was relieved to see them still waiting. The thin sentry shouldered his rifle and shoved past Dart, grinning. Dart had to attract the attention of the younger German.

"Er… My papers? Is everything in order?"

The man barely looked at him. "You may go."

Dart squeezed through the now unguarded gap in the barrier. From the darkness under the gate he looked back briefly. The two Germans were crowding in on Trixie, who was smiling and shaking her head. Dart turned away. The icy film on his body had turned to sweat. He walked as steadily as he could into the town. The last thing he heard was Trixie's laughter.

THE SQUARE WAS almost deserted when Dart entered it. One or two women and girls hurried across, perhaps to take their places in the hopeless queue outside the bakery on De Kooning Street. He saw the Marionette House immediately, at the forefront of a wedge of ancient brick houses backing up towards the church. Its sign, crackled gold lettering on a dark green board, spanned most of the narrow front wall.

Dart pushed open the shop door and set jangling a cheerful little bell. Instinctively he reached up and muffled it with his hand. Because the shop window was packed with dangling puppets, the light inside was dim. He closed the door behind him and waited for his eyes to adjust. It was not a large space, and so crammed that he could not imagine how more than one customer at a time could squeeze in. The longer wall, opposite the window, was completely taken up with shelves and cabinets. One shelf supported the severed heads of clowns, kings, fabulous beasts, ogres, demons; another was filled with silent musical boxes, frozen figurines perched on their lids. A glass cabinet contained a galaxy of glass eyes. Tables and showcases crowded the floor. A host of marionettes hung limply from hooks in the ceiling like dead parachutists.

There was, Dart now saw, a narrow route through these obstacles towards a curtained doorway at the rear of the shop. Just in front of it, half a dozen ventriloquists' dummies perched on a counter, staring at Dart as though he had dared to interrupt a private conversation. He was seriously alarmed when one of them – the one with a head sprouting white hair like dandelion seeds – opened its mouth and said, "Dr Lubbers, I presume?" When Dart didn't manage a reply, Pieter Grotius took his elbows off the counter and straightened up. It didn't make much difference to his height; he was a very small man. He moved nimbly through the maze of the shop and held out his hand. Dart shook it; it felt like a clever contraption made of sticks and cords covered in skin.

"I hope you had no trouble getting here?"

"Um, no. Not really. But I am worried about Trixie. The Germans at the checkpoint—"

Grotius made a gesture, like waving away a fly. "Ach, don't worry about Trixie. She's an unstoppable force, that one. People with freckles lead charmed lives, have you noticed?"

"Er, no, I—"

"But you have noticed that she has freckles?"

"Yes," Dart said.

"Good," Grotius said approvingly. "Now, let's go through to the workshop. Trixie will be coming in the back way in just a couple of minutes."

Pieter Grotius's workplace was a complete contrast to the confusion of the shop. It was a long narrow room full of cool light. Two workbenches and two stools stood below the frosted glass windows. Carpentry tools hung in precise order on racks attached to the wall. An immense number of paint pots filled a shelf, arranged in a strict colour sequence like a stretched and flattened rainbow. On one of the benches, a small wooden torso was clamped in a vice.

77

Just as Pieter Grotius had predicted, Trixie appeared, shoving open the back door with the front wheel of her bike. Trixie stooped to kiss him on both cheeks, then turned and hoisted Rosa from the trailer. The child was snivelling quietly and her cheeks were wet with tears. Grotius locked and bolted the door and went to stand in front of Trixie, his eyes almost level with Rosa's. He put his hand into his trouser pocket, and when he pulled it out again it was wearing a white glove with two black buttons sewn onto the forefinger. He closed his hand and flexed his thumb, making a bug-eyed face that spoke with the voice of Groucho Marx.

"Hey, kid! Yeah, you! Wha's the madder? Looks like water on your ugly face. Is it raining in here, or you got water on the brain? Need a tap on the head?"

Rosa's wet eyes stared at the glove face.

"Yeah, I know what you're thinking: what's a girl godda do to get a drink in this joint? I was thinking the same thing myself. Waiter! Waiter!"

The hand looked around the room, recoiling in horror when it saw Grotius. Rosa thrashed her arms and legs delightedly.

Trixie glanced across at Dart and saw that his smile was forced. The tension showed through it. He felt, she realized, excluded from this familiar routine.

It seemed that Pieter Grotius also understood this. "Forgive us please, Ernst. It's our little ritual. Rosa enjoys it. And so do I, to be honest. She's the only audience I have these days."

"No, no," Dart said, a little too earnestly. "I enjoyed it too. You're very good, Mr Grotius. You've got the voice perfectly."

"Thank you. Call me Pieter, please. And time is passing, yes. Come."

Trixie lifted the transceiver from the trailer, then they all filed back into the shop and up a flight of dark and narrow stairs. The walls of the landing were covered in masks from

Japan, Africa, Italy, Java. They leered and grimaced at the passers-by. Pieter Grotius led the procession into the parlour, where his wife was standing, waiting to greet them.

Bibi Grotius was a good six inches taller than her husband, with a heavy upper body but slender legs, so that she seemed to have been put together from mismatching parts. Her hair was a smoky blonde with no traces of grey. A pair of spectacles hung from a cord around her neck, and Dart wondered how good her eyesight was. She was barefoot. Her left leg below the knee was wrapped in bandages. After she had kissed Rosa and Trixie, she stood in front of Dart and looked at him seriously. He had the strange feeling that he was being assessed, like someone auditioning for a part in a play. He put his bag down on the floor and held out his hand. Bibi ignored it. She placed her hands on his shoulders and kissed him on both cheeks; then, still inspecting him, she said, "Well, we must be grateful they've sent us a handsome one, at least."

To hide his embarrassment, Dart looked around the room. The walls were almost entirely covered with framed posters, most of them featuring a blue crescent moon with a laughing face. He saw the names of cities: Moscow, Chicago, Berlin, Venice.

The stairway to the attic was even narrower than the previous one – not much more than a ladder. An oil lamp with a glass chimney sat on the bottom tread, and Pieter lit it and adjusted the flame. Holding the lamp, his wild white hair lit up, he looked to Dart like some creature from a dark fairy tale.

The walls of the attic sloped steeply, giving the room the shape of a long tent. There was no daylight; the lamp illuminated an infinite jumble of stuff: suitcases, tea chests, bundles of paper, boxes filled with books, empty picture frames, theatrical costumes.

"I've tidied the place up a bit," Pieter Grotius said. He

carried the lamp deeper into the chaos. "Here, see, I've made a workplace for you."

He had shoved two tea chests apart and bridged them with a door taken from a wardrobe, making a rough desk. The chair had a woven seat and had once been painted bright yellow; it would have looked at home in some sun-lit farmhouse bedroom. Dart went to the shuttered window, following a thin shaft of sun in which dust swam. It came from a small peephole in the wood; he had to stoop to put his eye to it. He had a circular view down onto the square. On the far side, Trixie stood in a shop doorway talking to an older woman wearing a headscarf. Then two German soldiers on bicycles crossed his line of vision, and he shrank back from the hole automatically.

He rubbed his hands together in a businesslike way, forcing a grin. "Excellent, Pieter," he said.

"It will do?"

"Of course." Dart peered around. "Er, one thing, though. My power supply?"

"Ah, yes," Pieter said. "It nearly broke my back, carrying those damned things up. Over here, next to the desk."

There were two car batteries inside a cardboard box under a layer of theatre programmes. "I know someone who can recharge them, no questions asked."

"Excellent."

Dart sat on the yellow chair and unlocked the suitcase. Grotius put the lamp down but made no move to leave. Dart made a show of checking his watch. "Thank you, Pieter. I'd better get on with it."

Grotius said, "How scared are you, Ernst?"

Dart busied himself, fussing with the Morse key, the headphones, the cables. "Pardon?"

"I was wondering how scared you are. I ask only because I am very scared indeed. I have not done this before."

Dart clasped the corners of the suitcase and stared at his hands. He did not know what to say. Fear was a whole country he did not want to visit. A place he wanted no signals from.

Grotius said, "Have you done this before?"

"No."

The little man was standing with his hands in his pockets, staring into the darkness. "It's not myself I'm scared for." He stopped, tried again. "No, that's not true. I fear the Nazis and what they might do to me. They are … robots. They are puppets, and hate pulls their strings. They have lost control of themselves. I have seen them do terrible things, here, in this town. I have sat at night, in the workshop, painting smiles on dolls' faces while hearing the screams from neighbouring streets. I have sat holding my breath, waiting for the sound of their boots to pass our door. But that isn't it. Not really."

He turned and looked at Dart. "It's Bibi that I am scared for. Truly scared for. She's Jewish, you see."

"My God," Dart said. "Jesus Christ, Pieter."

"Yes, quite. So you will be very, very careful, won't you, my young friend? Look after us, please."

He turned to go, and when he reached the stairs, Dart said, "Pieter? Why did you agree to do this? You didn't have to."

Grotius lifted his hand, and it was wearing the glove puppet. This time its voice was Winston Churchill's. "There comes a time in human affairs," it growled, "when even the smallest man must stand up and say, 'Enough of this shit.'"

Dart almost laughed. "Did Churchill really say that?"

"No," Pieter Grotius said. "I did."

The transmission that Dart made at ten fifty-nine was very brief, really just a signal test: his security checks, followed by a short sequence of letter groups which told London that he was on station. When he'd finished, he switched to receive. He was startled when, through the wobbling static in the headphones, the acknowledgement he'd expected was followed by the code for *stand by*. He scrabbled in the medical bag for his notebook and pencil.

When he went down to the parlour, Rosa was propped up in an armchair gurgling, fumbling at a cloth doll. Bibi Grotius stood at the window. When she saw Dart she moved a house plant to the other end of the sill.

"There," she said, "Trixie will know that you have finished your work now." Without turning away from the window, she said, "When Pieter and I first came here, that square was packed, twice a week. Stalls and barrows selling cooked meats, cheeses, fish. There was a big fat lady who sold sweet pickled herring from a barrel. They were delicious. I can close my eyes and taste them, even now." She did so, sighing. "I can't tell whether dreaming about food makes it better or worse. Sometimes the dreams are so real that I feel as though I have actually eaten. At other times, well..." She stopped herself and looked at him, smiling. "Shame on you – isn't that what you're thinking, Dr Lubbers? People are having to endure much worse than a craving for pickled herring."

"No," Dart said, "I wasn't thinking that at all. I hadn't realized the rationing was so bad. I've already started to think about food a lot of the time myself."

Trixie was already back in the workshop when Dart came down. Pieter was at his bench, working on the little wooden torso with a fine chisel. He glanced up.

"Everything okay? No problems?"

"No, none. Thank you."

Dart took Trixie by the arm and led her to just inside the back door. "There was an incoming," he told her quietly.

"A what?"

"A message from London. I wasn't expecting it. I haven't deciphered it, but the third group was the standard code for *urgent*. I know we're going to the farm tomorrow, but…"

Trixie drew in a long breath and let it out slowly. "All right. I'll leave Rosa here. If I go now I'll be able to get back well before dark."

"No. Don't worry, I'll go."

"What, alone? Are you sure? Do you know the way?"

"I think so. No, wait. You'd better draw me a map."

He took the notepad and pencil from the leather bag. Trixie went to the workbench and began to sketch. "Oh God," she said, biting her lower lip. "I'm not very good at this sort of thing."

Wonderful, Dart thought. He said, "Pieter, I understand that you have a bike for me. Is it here?"

"It's outside. Come."

The back door of the workshop opened onto a small paved yard. A woman's bicycle was propped against the wall of the privy.

"Bibi's contribution to the war effort," Pieter said. "Her pride and joy. Well, it used to be. She hasn't been out on it for a long time now, of course. I've oiled it and tightened the chain up. Be careful with the brakes; I had to make new blocks out of wood. You can't get rubber ones any more."

Trixie came out and handed Dart the notepad. "Here, see? This cross? It's a little chapel with a burnt-out roof. Don't forget to turn left there." She took the lapels of his coat in her hands. "Listen. I'm really worried about this. Let me come with you. It would be better."

He faked a smile. "No. I'm going to have to do this alone sooner or later. It's something else I have to get used to."

Grotius opened the yard door and poked his fluffy head out, looking right and left. Dart jammed the medical bag

83

into the wicker basket on the handlebars, and when Pieter gave the thumbs-up sign he pushed the bike out into the lane. He shoved one foot down on the pedal and slung his other leg over the saddle, forgetting that it was a woman's bike without a crossbar. And because this made him feel foolish, he didn't look back.

Dart rode north, keeping to backstreets until he caught sight of the tower of New Church, then headed for that. When he was within a hundred metres of the church, he took a left, praying there wouldn't be a checkpoint at the bridge. His prayers were answered. He slowed and checked Trixie's map. He took the next turning eastwards, and within ten minutes was in open countryside again. He began to feel almost cheerful. The bike was heavy, but it rode well. The roads were deserted, and the sun, a flat brilliant disc, burned through the mist. It flickered like Morse whenever there were lines of trees on his left. He was moving, he was moving, he was out!

Dart was peering forward, looking for the burnt-out chapel, when a dark shape materialized on the road far ahead. He braked, too hard, and juddered to a halt. He was on a long straight stretch where the threadbare tarmac was hardly wide enough for two vehicles to pass. There was no obvious place for concealment. A low hedge ran down to the road just ahead of him, but met it at right angles; any-one looking that way would be sure to spot him if he took cover there. A long way off to his right there was a copse of tobacco-coloured trees; to reach it he'd have to lug the bike across a sticky-looking ploughed field.

His indecision became feverish. He needed to pee. Then he realized that he couldn't hear an engine, and the distant shape was approaching very slowly. Slightly reassured, and not knowing what else to do, he rode to meet it.

It was several long moments before he recognized the dull clatter as hoof beats. Instantly the riddle of the oncoming silhouette was solved. He could now make out the sway of the horse, the shape of the farmer perched high on the wagon, his head and shoulders slightly higher than the load behind him. Dart sat more upright on the bike and breathed out, relaxing. Seconds later his heart lurched as if he had taken a heavy punch to the chest, and he almost cried out loud. A glint of sunlight had struck the driver's steel helmet; then two others appeared, lifting themselves above the canvas-covered cargo to look forward. To watch Dart draw nearer. He saw the driver's head turn, then the two Germans in the wagon bend and straighten, lifting rifles.

Dart's mouth went dry. They would shoot him just for the hell of it, to have something to talk about, to enliven the day. He reached forward with his left hand and tugged at the leather bag, then changed his mind. He would have to dismount and use both hands to get the pistol out, and it was too late for that. The odds against him were hopeless anyway. His legs continued working the pedals as if they were nothing to do with him. The wagon, he now saw, was built of olive-green steel and had big rubber tyres. The horse was huge, black, with tufts of white hair almost covering its hooves. It lost its rhythm when it saw Dart, lifting and swivelling its great head. The driver called out and jerked the leather traces. A Schmeisser machine pistol was slung across his chest.

Dart felt certain that he would faint. He wanted to. Shakily he steered the bike over to the right-hand verge, so that the Germans would perhaps see the red cross on his armband. When the wagon was almost upon him, and when he could almost feel the bullets tear into his chest, Dart raised his right forearm in a vaguely Nazi gesture.

"Guten Morgen!" he cried, and when they were alongside

he aimed his smile straight into the muzzles of the German rifles. One of the soldiers was a scrawny youth with bad skin. The other man was much older and wore steel-rimmed spectacles. One of the lenses was cracked. There was a harmonica sticking out of the breast pocket of his tunic. These details slid past in frightful slow motion.

Dart turned his face back to the road. He could not unlock the smile. The muscles in his back stiffened, waiting for the shock of the bullets. He passed through a patch of air that stank of horse sweat. Behind him, one of the Germans called out *"Heil Hitler!"* in a way that made it sound like a question. Dart raised his right hand higher, his arm rigid, but he could not repeat the phrase because his mouth wouldn't work.

Five minutes later Dart more or less fell from the bike and stood bent over, bracing himself, his hands on his knees. After a while he walked shakily to the side of the road and emptied his bladder, splashing his left shoe and trouser cuff. He smoked a cigarette, gazing blankly at the brightening fields.

THE UNUSED SITTING room at Sanctuary Farm belonged to the past. The stiff upright chairs had been designed a hundred years earlier for stiff upright gentlemen who wore long-tailed coats and ladies who wore vast stiff skirts. The sofa had a surly look to it, as if it knew it was there for sinners who fancied sitting comfortably and was determined to frustrate them.

Tamar had opened up the gateleg table under the window and spread a map on it. He sat staring at it with a pencil between his teeth, glancing now and then at the two silk squares close to his right elbow. Unlike the other silks, these had nothing to do with radio transmissions. If you knew how to combine them, these two grids of jumbled letters and numbers would reveal the code names and locations of agents and resistance organizations in zone six. Nicholson and Hendriks had been reluctant to provide these silks, but Tamar had convinced them that although his memory was good, it wasn't *that* good. DCY/M had devised them at very short notice. There were no other copies.

Tamar had two big problems. One was that the resistance in his area was divided into numerous organizations known by their initials: the LO, the OD, the KVV, the KP and so on. Sometimes these groups worked together, sometimes they overlapped confusingly, and sometimes they were at each other's throats. In addition, there were freelance groups, like the one run by Koop de Vries. These were often bound together by relationships that had nothing to do with anybody else. Maybe they were old school friends, or had worked in the same factory. Until recently, there had been a very busy bunch of sabotage enthusiasts in Amersfoort who had been members of the same church choir. Such groups weren't always keen to take orders from Amsterdam, let alone London.

That, though, wasn't the problem Tamar had spent the morning in the gloomy sitting room thinking about. It was the map itself. There were too many empty spaces in it. Zone six was a rough triangle formed by five towns, one of which was Apeldoorn, the German army headquarters. According to the map, the area inside the triangle was more or less empty. But it wasn't, and Tamar knew it. The great expanse of heath and forest that loomed beyond the farm occupied a big part of it. It was webbed by a labyrinth of narrow lanes and tracks and paths – none of which appeared on the map. Further west, the heath dissolved into a complex patchwork of woodland, farmland and marsh. It looked to Tamar as if the map-maker had given up on this area. He or she had marked the few villages and the minor roads that connected them, and then filled in the gaps with patterns of dots and dashes meant to represent ... well, a messy sort of landscape.

He studied the silks again, running his finger down and then across the grids, jotting the results onto a scrap of paper. There was a resistance man code-named Banjo who operated from an abandoned chicken farm five kilometres south of a village called Elim. Tamar looked at the map and, sure enough, south of Elim there was ... nothing. So, if he wanted to get to Banjo – and Tamar was fairly certain he would – he'd have to be guided there by a relay of contacts and couriers, any one of whom could be a collaborator or Gestapo double agent. Or he'd have to get himself over to Elim and then ride around looking for this blasted chicken farm. Not good. Not good at all.

Tamar shifted his backside on the uncomfortable chair. The simple fact was, the maps were just not good enough. And that meant the coded map references were pretty damn useless too. He'd come up against the same problem the last time he was here, and when he'd got back to England he'd passed the time between debriefing sessions by dreaming up ways of pinpointing places more accurately. He'd decided it should be possible to guide someone to within less than a hundred metres or so of a certain place by using a code of ten, maybe eight, letters and numbers. The system would be based on identifiable landmarks, on cities and towns, rather than dodgy maps. He'd explained it to a major from Military Intelligence one evening. The man had listened carefully, despite the whisky they'd both drunk.

"I tell you what, old chap," the major had said, "that's bloody clever. Trouble is, it would take years to work out. And there's a war on, don't you know."

Months later, at Ashgrove, Tamar had shared his idea with Dart. Dart, who was quicker at codes and ciphers than Tamar, had been intrigued by it, and had spent several hours with maps and code books trying to make it work. Then other things, in the shapes of Nicholson and Hendriks, had distracted him.

It was as if thinking about Dart had conjured him up. Tamar heard Marijke's footsteps in the hall, heard her whistle the little tune that meant *no danger*.

"Ernst Lubbers is here," she said.

"What? Has something happened?"

"I don't know. He looks a bit ... wild-eyed." She smiled.

"Maybe that's because he's talking to Oma. Should I bring him in?"

When the two agents were alone together Dart said, "It was her, wasn't it? The boy."

"What?"

"Miss Maartens. The boy with the lantern who was here when we arrived. It was her." Dart sounded almost indignant, and Tamar couldn't help grinning.

Dart's face reddened slightly. "It's all right for you to smile," he said. "I feel a bit of a fool. I just stood there staring at her when I realized. She must have thought I was simple." He glanced at the door again. "But she's a looker, isn't she? Lovely. I hadn't imagined..." His voice trailed away. Then he wagged his finger at Tamar in mock severity. "I hope you're keeping your mind on your work, my friend."

Tamar made an awkward gesture towards the table. "Of course. Now, talking of work..."

"Right." Dart was suddenly all business. "I got an urgent from London. I decided to bring it myself."

"This came when? This morning, at the Marionette House?"

"Yes."

"What about getting here? Did you have any problems?"

"I... No, it was fine."

Dart picked up the medical bag and emptied its contents onto the table, then reached inside and felt around for the catches that released the false bottom. He took out the revolver and the sheet of paper, shoved the gun into his coat pocket and spread the paper out on the table.

"I haven't deciphered it. I thought if we did it together, we might be able to code a reply straight away." He looked up at Tamar. "If that's what you need to do."

* * *

When they'd finished, Dart dropped the pencil onto the pad and stared blankly at the message. "Well," he said, "that makes as much sense to me now as it did before. I hope it means something to you. What's Operation Pegasus?"

Tamar stood up. The light from the window had shifted now, and the sitting room had started to gather darkness. "It's a bloody headache, that's what it is. Come on, let's tidy up in here and go outside. Bring your coat."

Tamar led him to a rough bench at the end of the wash-house. The level landscape in front of them was still blurred, but the autumn light was now strong and golden. Dart caught the scent of fallen apples.

Tamar said, "When Operation Market Garden screwed up, a lot of Allied troops went missing. They weren't among the dead, and they weren't captured. Somehow they managed to sneak through the German lines and hide. Some are with our people; others are God knows where. Some are in a bad way. The British would like them to go home for a nice cup of tea. That's Operation Pegasus. And someone has to make it happen."

"And that someone is you."

"Yep. Hendriks briefed me for it, among other things. There are about two hundred men out there, maybe more. Julius, the head of the resistance in Ede, and a guy called Banjo are the only people who know where most of them are."

"Do you know either of them?"

Tamar shook his head. "No."

"And London say they haven't been able to make contact with Julius for eight days."

"That's right."

"Great. And you've got to get these people back across the Rhine at … what's the place called?"

"Renkum," Tamar said.

"Do you know it?"

"Not really. I was there just once. It's right on the front line, though. It's a fair bet that the Germans will be dug in along the river. I have to hope that the local guys know exactly where."

"So what are you going to do?"

Tamar squinted at the sun. "I'll have to go to Renkum, I suppose. Talk to people. See what's what."

"When?"

"Soon. In the next few days. I'll talk to Trixie tomorrow. I'll need guides. Albert Veening should be able to give me some names. Don't worry, it'll be fine. Come on, I'll give you a quick tour of Sanctuary. It looks better in daylight."

In the little barn, Tamar went to one of the stalls that had once housed the farm's horses and dragged a couple of bales of rotting straw away from the boards that formed the rear wall. He jiggled and pulled at two of the boards and lifted them away, revealing a narrow space between the woodwork and the outer brick wall. He reached down into it and produced the tin case of medical supplies.

"Take as much of this as you can carry. I suggest you leave some of it here, as a reserve. Take the bandages, though. And these." He held out the brown bottle labelled ASPIRIN. "You know what they are?"

Dart took the bottle. "Of course."

"Go easy with them, though. Okay?"

"Sure," Dart said, and put the bottle in his pocket.

Tamar thrust his arm into the gap again and produced a fat wad of guilders. He handed them to Dart. "Money."

Dart riffled the notes and whistled. "Hey, I'm loaded. I've never had my hands on this much cash before."

"You'll need it," Tamar said, rummaging once more. "Sister Agatha will be having to shop on the black market soon enough, and it's not cheap. Now, here's a box of ammo for your revolver. And some tea. This is coffee. Can you get that lot into the bottom of that magic bag of yours?"

"I think so." Dart grinned. "Sister Agatha will think another angel's arrived at the funny farm."

"What?"

"Nothing. It doesn't matter."

Tamar jammed the boards back into place. "There's more food and clothes and other stuff you should have. I'll get Trixie to bring it to you a little at a time. Or you could drive the ambulance over, if you feel up to it. You can sort that out with Albert."

"Talking of Dr Veening," Dart said, "were there any cigarettes in the canister? He's getting through mine like there's no tomorrow."

Tamar laughed. "I bet he is. You'd think he'd know better, wouldn't you? Anyway, there's plenty."

The two men stood looking at each other as darkness filled the corners of the barn.

Tamar said, very quietly, "I know what you're thinking. It's crazy, isn't it? This. What we're doing." He laughed softly. "Like kids playing at shops: here's your tea, Mr Lubbers; here's your coffee."

"Here's your bullets; here's your Benzedrine. Try not to get killed on the way home."

Tamar studied his friend's dark eyes. "Exactly," he said. "Let's not get killed on the way home."

The lowering sun had spread a long narrow carpet of light on the barn floor. When they reached the edge of it, Dart stopped and said, "Tell me about Miss Maartens."

"Marijke? Tell you what?"

"Well, you know. How come she lives here alone with her grandmother, for a start."

Tamar looked at the brilliant doorway. "Her parents are dead; she never knew them. They died within a week of each other when she was a few months old. The flu epidemic of 1921. Marijke shouldn't have survived, but she did. Her grandparents brought her up. She's lived here all her life."

"I thought she might be adopted, or something. She doesn't look … well, she could almost be Spanish. Or Italian."

"I suppose so. There's a story that the original Maartens were gypsies. Marijke rather likes the idea." He took a step towards the light, but Dart had another question, the one Tamar had been expecting.

"And there's no husband, boyfriend, anything like that?"

"No."

Dart looked at Tamar, raising his eyebrows suggestively. "Really? I find that surprising, don't you? You'd think the local men would be like bees round a honeypot."

Tamar was brusque. "There's a shortage of men in this country, didn't you know that?" He tried to soften it into a joke. "Well, apart from the ones in German uniform."

Perhaps it was shame that made him consult his watch and say, "Look, it's getting a bit late. Stay here tonight and eat with us. We'll work out a reply to the London signal and you can go back tomorrow after you've sent it. It'll be safer."

"Sounds great. I'm bloody starving, as a matter of fact."

"Good. Come on." Tamar stepped through the doorway, and had to screw up his eyes against the late sun's scrutiny.

They ate in the kitchen, in the mellow light of a tall lamp. Beetroot soup with coarse bread, then rabbit stew with wild mushrooms, mashed potatoes and cabbage. With some difficulty – the stove was cooling – Julia Maartens made pancakes and served them with jam. Dart had to force himself to eat slowly, heaping praise on the old lady's cooking between mouthfuls. No one else spoke much during the meal, and it dawned on Dart that this must be a house of silence most of the time. Although Oma – he'd started to call her that because Tamar did – wasn't deaf, Marijke frequently communicated with her wordlessly, using her grandmother's system of signs and gestures and facial expressions. It was fascinating to watch, this speechless dialogue. And Dart noticed that Tamar was already starting to use it. He'd make a little gesture to tell Oma that something was delicious. He'd look at Marijke in a certain way, probably to check that she felt comfortable about having these two dangerous outsiders at the table. And she would reply with a quick smile, a tilt of the head. Dart decided that this meant, "Yes, I'm worried, but it's okay. We are all in this together."

Dart was surprised that these silently shared conversations didn't make him feel excluded. The lamp had turned the table into a warm yellow island, and he was on it with the others, not a castaway in the surrounding dark. He felt ... *safe*. He had to examine the word in his head to make sure it was right, because he couldn't remember the last time he'd used it to describe himself. And in time he would learn the wordless language that the others used. In time he would do that. Because he wanted very much to share the secrets of Marijke Maartens's night-black eyes.

When Marijke began to gather up the used plates and dishes, Oma lit a candle and went down into the cellar. A few minutes later she returned, carrying an earthenware bottle of jenever. She poured a good measure into four little blue and white china tumblers, making a small shy ceremony of it.

Tamar grinned at Dart. "This is in your honour, my friend. A special treat. I wouldn't want you thinking that we live it up like this every night."

The gin burned going down, but it left in the mouth a trace of dark fruits gathered long ago. It also loosened Dart's tongue. He found himself talking about the Marionette House and giving fairly hopeless impersonations of Pieter

Grotius's glove-puppet routines. Julia Maartens, in a flurry of gestures which Marijke translated, told them all how, on market days before the war, Bibi and Pieter used to put on little shows outside the shop to attract customers. Her hands danced invisible puppets on the table top.

Later, after more gin, Dart told tales of the asylum. He got to his feet and enacted the lunatic called Gerard trying to trap cloud shadows with his boots. At one point he looked at Marijke and saw her smile. He felt as if he had conjured the sun to come out at night. He flopped back into his chair and lit a cigarette, and then immediately launched into an account of the mad old lady who called herself Sidona and talked with angels. Tamar stirred himself and joined in. Soon the two men were inventing ever crazier conversations between the madwoman and various messengers from above. Julia Maartens listened to these fantasies with a sort of horrified delight. Once, when Dart and Tamar were being especially outrageous about the goings-on in heaven, she crossed herself. Dart noticed this; were the Maartens Catholic, then? Marijke's eyes moved from one man to the other, fixing on Dart longer than on Tamar, watching him.

The evening died gently, like a torch with an exhausted battery. The four of them sat slumped around the table, full of food and laughter, staring into the black-edged flame of the oil lamp. When Tamar stood up, the sound of his chair on the floor tiles startled them all. He put his hand on Dart's shoulder. "Time for a security patrol, I think. You'll need your coat."

Dart smiled up at him happily. "I'm not cold."

Tamar leaned down and spoke softly into his ear. "Get your coat. I think your gun is still in the pocket."

Dart struggled to his feet. "Ah. Right."

When he returned from the hall, the two women had

gone and Tamar was lifting a Sten from the chest beneath the blacked-out window. Dart was dumbfounded: how could things change so quickly? His spirits dimmed.

They walked around the farm silently, checking the buildings. When they reached the bench outside the wash-house, Tamar sat, the Sten angled across his chest, his legs stretched out in front of him. Dart remained standing, his hands in his coat pockets, gazing at the moon. It was high and almost full now, with the familiar startled expression on its face. Below it, against the level black horizon, distant orange and white lights flickered and died, again and again. Faint booms reached them, soft as footfalls on a bedroom floor.

"Good night for a drop," Dart said. "Do you think there was that much anti-aircraft fire when we came in?"

"I don't know. Must have been, I suppose."

Tamar's voice was flat. Obviously this was not what he wanted to talk about. So Dart tried again.

"I'm beginning to work out what Oma is saying. Sorry, that's a stupid way of putting it. You know what I mean. I suppose that after a while it becomes natural. It must have been hard for Marijke, though, don't you think? No parents. Growing up with a grandmother who couldn't speak."

"She didn't." Tamar crossed his legs and clasped his hands over his knee. He didn't look up. "Julia wasn't born dumb," he said. "She stopped speaking just over two years ago."

"Really? What was it, cancer or something?"

"No. Shock, trauma, whatever the proper word is. Nothing physical, anyway." He lifted his face now, looking past Dart, half his face in moon-shadow. "This is something you should know, I suppose. The Maartens have relatives, sort of cousins, who've got a farm near Loenen. The two families always helped each other out at busy times of the year. So in late September '42 Johannes, Marijke's grandfather, took his wagon and one of the horses over there to help bring in the sugar beet crop. The field they were working in was a fair way from the farm, and by the time they'd picked up the last load it was almost dark. Johannes and a boy who was on the wagon with him were about halfway back to the farm when they ran into a German ambush."

Dart waited, silent, while Tamar lit a cigarette, cupping the flame in his hands.

"The Germans had intercepted a signal from London about an arms drop. They were reading all our radio traffic back then. Christ, they were sending most of it. But you know all about that. Anyway, they'd set up this ambush for the reception committee. They were expecting our men to move the guns on a couple of farm carts, probably under a load of sugar beet or whatever. Which is exactly what happened, as a matter of fact. But unfortunately for Johannes, the Germans had read their maps wrong. They should have been on a road three kilometres to the east. When Johannes came along, they didn't bother asking questions. He took a bullet through the throat and another in the right lung. When the horse panicked, the boy was thrown onto the ground. He broke an arm and a leg. He was still screaming when a German shot him in the head."

"Shit," Dart said. He reached over and took the cigarette from Tamar's fingers, dragged on it, and handed it back.

"Johannes's cousin, and his daughter and another boy, were on their own wagon a way back down the road. They took off into the fields when they heard the shooting and screaming. The Germans didn't find them; I don't suppose they were that keen on looking too hard. They still thought they were dealing with armed members of the resistance, I imagine. The Germans didn't find any guns, of course, so they cleared off, leaving the bodies where they'd fallen.

"The three people hiding in the fields stayed there a

long time. They suspected a trap, which was fair enough. When they eventually crept up, they found that Johannes was still breathing. They carried him to the farm and the daughter cycled over here to fetch Julia and Marijke. It was the early hours of the morning before they all got back to Loenen. Johannes was still alive, just. They'd had to lie him face down on a table with his head over the edge to stop him drowning in his own blood. He managed to hang on long enough to see his wife for the last time. He died ten minutes after she got there."

Tamar flicked the remains of his cigarette into the dark.

"Marijke says it wasn't until the following afternoon that Oma let them wash his blood from her hands and face. She couldn't speak. When she still hadn't managed to say anything a month after the funeral, Marijke began to think she never would. It looks like she was right."

Dart found that he had nothing to say either.

Tamar stood up and slung the Sten gun round onto his back. "These people matter to me. More than they should, probably. I would like to think that I can protect them, but the truth is that by being here I'm putting them in danger. I suppose when Nicholson told me where I'd be based I should have said no. But—"

"But you don't argue with Nicholson," Dart said.

Tamar nodded as though Dart had hit on the right explanation. "Exactly. No one argues with Nicholson. That's right."

An hour later Tamar stole barefoot into Marijke's room. The curtains were pulled back and the room was full of moonlight. She was sitting upright against the blue-white pillows, the blue-white sheet pulled around her; her face was divided in two by the shadow of the window sash. He sat sideways on the bed, then lowered himself so that his head rested on her shoulder. He felt the hardness of her collarbone against his cheek. She put her right hand to his face. They spoke in whispers.

"You haven't told him about us."

"No," he said.

"I don't understand."

Tamar sighed, but didn't speak.

She said, "It was so difficult tonight. I thought you must have told him, but then I watched his face and saw that he had no idea. I wanted to touch you but your eyes kept telling me not to."

"My love, I'm sorry."

"Oma actually told him, did you see that? And Ernst didn't understand. He thought she was still talking about the puppet shows, and I didn't translate. She looked so … confused."

"Marijke, I—"

"Is it against the rules, our relationship?"

He let his breath out: a sigh, almost a laugh. "Probably. I don't know."

"Don't you trust him?"

"Of course I trust him. Of course I do. It's not that."

She turned and let his head fall gently onto the pillow. She looked down at him, leaning on her elbow. "But this is all about trust, isn't it? Are you afraid that if Ernst knows about us, he won't be able to trust you? He'll start to think you'd put me first, rather than him?"

And he wondered how he could have forgotten how clever she was. Sooner or later she would work out what he was actually afraid of. It wasn't exactly a matter of trust, or lack of it. It was something more dangerous than that: envy. In English just a little word, but in the sound of it there was something green and grasping and wormy.

He said, "I just don't want anyone – anything – to touch us. There are things I want to …. keep out."

Later, when Marijke was asleep, he kissed her again and eased himself from the bed. Then, reluctantly, he went to the cold spare bedroom.

Dart had fallen into deep sleep so quickly that when the nightmare woke him he felt panicked and confused, completely ignorant of where he was. The strange gargling noise was coming from his own mouth, he realized. Someone had stabbed him in the throat with a pen and his windpipe was filling with black ink. He was so certain this had happened that his hand flew to his neck to feel for the wound. After a while, he was calm enough to realize that he was cold. He felt on the floor for his sweater and put it on, then spread his coat on top of the thin quilt. The gun slipped from the pocket and clattered onto the bare floorboards. He groped around for it and laid it on the cabinet next to the bed.

Moments later there was a light tap on the door, then a creak as it opened.

"Dart, are you all right?"

"Yes, I … I'm fine. Really."

Tamar was merely a shadow deeper than the others. "I thought I heard something fall," he said.

"The bloody pistol fell out of my pocket. Stupid of me. I'm sorry I woke you up."

"That's okay. I'm a light sleeper."

"I guess that's a good thing to be. In our line of work, anyway."

"Yes, I suppose so. I'll see you in the morning."

"Goodnight."

Dart heard a floorboard creak. He did not hear Tamar's door close. He must sleep with it open, Dart thought. And with his ears cocked, like a gun.

Comforted by the thought, he was asleep again in less than a minute.

ENGLAND, 1995

From the West London Post, *12th May 1995*

TRAGIC DEATH OF WAR HERO

An inquest yesterday recorded an open verdict on a man who died after falling from the balcony of his sixth-floor flat. William Hyde, 74, was found dead in the car park of Maris Towers, Hammersmith, on 19th March. The coroner, Dr Rose Lambert, said that although there was some evidence that Mr Hyde may have deliberately taken his own life, that evidence was not conclusive. Mr Hyde may have been suffering from depression; however, there was no suicide note and a post-mortem had revealed that he had been drinking.

Mr Hyde was Dutch by birth, but at the time of the Nazi invasion of his country in 1940 was a graduate student at Imperial College, London. He was recruited by the Special Operations Executive, a branch of the British secret services, and trained in sabotage and secret warfare techniques. He was parachuted into occupied Holland in October 1944, and became a key figure in the reorganization of the Dutch resistance, surviving the Hunger Winter of 1944–45, when thousands of his countrymen died of starvation. In the spring of 1945 his group was betrayed to the Gestapo, and he was forced to flee for his life with a female member of the resistance, who later became his wife. The couple escaped across the Rhine, under German fire, shortly before Holland was liberated.

Mr Hyde was awarded the DSO in 1946, and became a British citizen in 1947. He worked for the security services for five years, and then joined the Post Office, with whom he enjoyed a distinguished managerial career. He was a leading member of the team that developed the computerized postcode system which has revolutionized mail delivery.

His daughter-in-law, Mrs Sonia Hyde, told the inquest that Mr Hyde was a very intelligent and thoughtful man, though emotionally scarred by his wartime experiences. He had enjoyed a "deep and caring" relationship with his fifteen-year-old granddaughter, Tamar. However, in the weeks before his death he had become "noticeably withdrawn and depressed". Mrs Hyde told the inquest that her mother-in-law, Mrs Marijke Hyde, currently in a nursing home, had been diagnosed as suffering from a degenerative mental illness, and that Mr Hyde had "coped very badly" with the situation.

That was it, start to finish. I've got the clipping here in front of me now, but I could've written it out without looking. I know it by heart, word for word. At the time, when I read it, I felt all sorts of things. Proud of him, I suppose. Embarrassed. (At school: "Was that your grandad jumped off the balcony then?") A bit ashamed of myself – I didn't know what DSO stood for. Postcodes: boring. Now when I look at it, all I see is the spaces between the words where the truth might have been. But I've kept it anyway, along with some of the things that were in the box he left me. The box I refused to open until long after he died, because I was too angry with him. All those other feelings were wrapped up inside a thick layer of anger that stayed with me long after the grief had gone.

Because he had jumped, definitely. It wasn't an accident. He wasn't the kind of person who had accidents. He was the most careful man I've ever met. He thought about everything, even the simplest thing. You'd say, "Fancy a cup of tea, Grandad?" and he'd think about it. You could almost see him turning the question in his hands, like a squirrel looking for the best way into a nut. The coroner knew that, I think, when she said there was some evidence he'd committed suicide. I know what that evidence was. He was naked, for a start; and there is no way, no way at all, that he'd walk around the flat, let alone go out onto the balcony, like that. Not if he'd been in his right mind. He'd taken his false teeth out, and his glasses were on the living-room table. He couldn't see a thing without them, so he must've felt his way onto the balcony. But the clincher, for me, was that he'd shaved his moustache off. Such a strange thing to have done. It was the first thing Mum said, poor Mum, when she got back from identifying the body. "He'd shaved his moustache off," she said. "I hardly knew him."

I didn't understand it at the time, but I do now, I think. It was a sort of ritual. The clothes, the teeth, the specs, the moustache – it was as if he was stripping himself down to the bare minimum of what he was, removing all those disguises at last. And there *was* a suicide note; it's just that no one realized it. How could they? It was this box, and the things in it.

So it wasn't an accident, open verdict or not. He'd jumped, and he must have bloody known what that would do to me. He'd have known that it would open up the wounds my dad had left me with. And it did.

Dad had disappeared five years earlier, when I was ten and a half. We'd just moved to a bigger house near Ravenscourt Park, ten minutes from Gran and Grandad's. The upstairs seemed a lot further away from the downstairs than in the old house. There was a landing and a turn in the stairs and then a long walk along the hall to the kitchen. My bedroom was nice, but the wallpaper had a pattern that sometimes turned into faces, and I'd have to get out of bed to turn the big light on to get rid of them. The new school was okay, but I spent a lot of break times sitting on my own. I wasn't much good at making new friends. I suppose I thought that if there were friends out there, they'd find me. I'm still a bit like that.

I had a lot on my plate back then. I'd been sent to an orthodontist, who said I needed braces. My new teacher told my mum that I might be a bit dyslexic. Mum was always messing with my hair. It seemed like everyone was always wanting to do something to me, change me in one way or another. So what with all that, and the move, and the new school, I was a bit slow noticing how strange Dad was getting.

My dad worked for the DTI, the Department of Trade and Industry, and he was away quite a lot, abroad. We were used to it; it was okay. But then he was away a lot more, and it seemed to me that Mum was on the phone all the time, getting emotional. I had no idea why. He never came back from one of his trips without a present for me: a cowboy hat from America, a pair of clogs painted with flowers from Holland, a beautiful little wooden horse from Czechoslovakia. When he was home, he read to me at bedtime, nearly always from our favourite book, *The Wind in the Willows*. It's in my head, that story. I could recite you bits, like when Ratty takes Mole out in his boat for the first time:

"I beg your pardon," said the Mole, pulling himself together with an effort. "You must think me very rude; but all this is so new to me. So – this – is – a – River!"

"*The* River," corrected the Rat.

"And you really live by the river? What a jolly life!"

"By it and with it and on it and in it," said the Rat. "It's brother and sister to me, and aunts, and company, and food and drink, and (naturally) washing. It's my world, and I don't want any other. What it hasn't got is not worth having, and what it doesn't know is not worth knowing."

But then when he'd turned my light off and I was trying to dive into sleep, I'd hear him and Mum rowing downstairs. Their voices came and went in waves: loud, quiet, loud, silent. I never went down, though. Not because I thought I'd get into trouble if I did. I never got any serious grief from my parents. What I was afraid of was that I'd walk into the room during one of their silences.

And then the rhythm of his coming and going just stopped. He simply stopped coming back. He didn't phone. I waited for a long time, then one day I got in the car to go to school and I asked her.

"Mum? When's Dad coming back?"

And she said, "Put your seat belt on, love. Have you got your lunch box?"

And I said, "Mum? *Is* Dad coming back? Has he gone?"

We were at the traffic lights on Goldhawk Road. Mum

leaned on the steering wheel with her head on the back of her hands. "Christ," she said, "what have I done to deserve this?" She wasn't crying, exactly, but her throat was going in and out as if it was hard for her to breathe. Then there was a blast of car horns from behind, and I said, "Mum? Mum, the lights are green."

William and Marijke – Gran and Grandad – took it very hard, of course. Gran was already getting a bit "ditzy" – Mum's word – but I'm sure it was Dad's vanishing that sent her sliding down to the edge of darkness. At the time, though, she was the more practical one.

"Sonia, we must inform the police," she said.

I don't think this had occurred to Mum, because she said, "The police? Do you think so?"

"Of course," Gran said. "Jan is a missing persons." She held up three fingers. "There are two things here. Missing persons is a police matter and we must report it. Next, we can do nothing ourselves. Are we to drive all over the place looking for him?" Gran gazed at her hand, puzzled for a moment that she was still holding up one finger. Then she curled it down into her fist and said, "He is not dead, I believe."

That was when Grandad moaned softly and cupped his hands around her face. "I am so sorry, my love," he said.

Marijke said something in Dutch which Mum and I couldn't understand. I didn't say anything because I don't think I was supposed to be in the room.

The police came three times. They talked to me once, but they asked funny kinds of questions and I couldn't have been much help. The day after the first police visit, Tweedledum and Tweedledee turned up. That's what Mum called them, because they looked so alike: both Dad's sort of age, round

110

faces, glasses, suits. I answered the door, and they said they were friends of my dad's from his office, and could they speak to my mum? Mum took them into the living room and shut the door, so although I lurked on the stairs for a while I couldn't hear anything. They stayed about half an hour, and when they'd gone I asked Mum what that was all about, and she said, "Oh, work stuff, money, you know." But I could tell from the thoughtful look on her face that there was more to it than that.

They came back a few days later, around teatime, and asked if it would be all right if they had a look in Dad's "study". Mum wanted to know what for, of course. Tweedledum said that "the department" was having trouble tracing some of the papers to do with "the project" Dad had been working on, and perhaps he'd brought them home. Mum wasn't too happy about it, but she took them upstairs to the back bedroom where Dad had his desk. When they got there, Tweedledum – or it might have been Tweedledee – said, "Thank you, Mrs Hyde," and shut the door in her face. When they came back down, they were carrying two cardboard files. They gave Mum a receipt for them and off they went. Some time later, Mum discovered that a load of old bank statements and phone bills had disappeared as well, but I don't think she did anything about it. She had a lot on her plate too.

I'm ashamed to say that I started eavesdropping on her phone calls. But then, what else could I do? Nobody was telling me anything, and I was aching, aching for ... I don't know. Big things, I guess, like certainty, hope, understanding; things that ten-year-olds aren't supposed to concern themselves with. Things that are hard to replace once you've lost them. Things you aren't supposed to lose in the first place. Our phone was in the hall, in the recess under the stairs, so it was easy to hear her from the upstairs landing, driving myself crazy trying to imagine the other half of the conversation.

"Oh, hi."

So it wasn't Gran or Grandad.

"No, nothing at all. Well, sort of numb, really… Pardon? I don't know. Very quiet a lot of the time. Up in her room, yes."

In a lower voice, talking about me.

"I know you do, Andrew. That's one of the reasons it's always a comfort talking to you."

Ah, Andrew. Oily Andy, her boss.

"I know. Yes. Sometimes I think … I dunno, a letter from Brazil, or somewhere. A call saying they've found his clothes on a beach in Dorset…"

I wanted to run down and cry *"No!"* but I stayed still, clutching the banister.

"Yes, I know, I know. But it's a melodramatic bloody *situation*, Andrew… Well, of course I've thought about that, but… No. Funnily enough that's the one thing I'm fairly sure of. I'm certain I'd have known if anything like that was going on. Yes, I know, still waters run deep and all that, but no, I really don't think so. That's what the police think, though. Well, they would, wouldn't they? It's the usual reason."

There were quite a few calls to and from Andrew, and fairly soon Mum started working full-time. She had to, I dare say. So I started spending more and more time at Gran and Grandad's. I'd go there most days after school, because Mum was never back before six or half past. Then she started going away for a day or two, for work, or to conferences at the weekend, and I'd stay over at their flat. They made their spare bedroom into my room, and bit by bit I took a lot of my stuff over there. Pretty soon I was living with them as much as I was living with Mum.

Looking back, it must have been hard on her. It was a big house to be alone in. I remember one time when I was there with her, watching *Coronation Street*, and she said, "I've been thinking about your birthday, love."

It must have been my thirteenth.

"I thought you might like to do something on the Saturday, perhaps. Have you thought about it at all?"

And I said, "It's okay, Mum. It's sorted. Gran and Grandad are taking me and Lauren and Emma to the cinema. Then we're all going out for pizza and Lauren and Emma are sleeping over at the flat."

"Oh," Mum said, and then I looked at her, thinking, Uh-oh!

So I said, "I'm sure it would be okay if you came too. You can, if you like."

"Um, well, I'll see," she said. "Seems like you've got it all worked out anyway. Sounds great."

Then we went back to *Coronation Street*. I felt bad, but I knew it was okay really. Mum was probably thinking that she could spend the weekend with Andrew after all. Cynical little cow, wasn't I? But then, why not?

I'd put Dad away by then. He wasn't lost or gone or dead. In my head (or maybe my heart) I'd put him somewhere safe. He was tucked up in a tiny drawer which was one of hundreds of tiny drawers in a great big chest of drawers inside a great big cupboard, and the cupboard was in a locked secret room at the end of an endless corridor which was one of hundreds of endless corridors in a great big house. And that was fine. Until Grandad jumped into the sky and sent me back along those half-forgotten corridors, and I found myself standing in front of the little drawer labelled DAD wondering if it was full of nothing but dust and bones, or worse.

I must have hated him, surely.

I SUPPOSE YOU'D SAY that Gran was heart and Grandad was head. At first, he didn't do much except help me with my homework. Gran did everything else. She wasn't what you'd call a great cook, but she had a talent for conjuring something out of nothing. She'd had to learn to do this during the war, she said. I'd always been a picky eater, and I was worse after Dad went. I'd got a bit skeletal, to tell the truth. Mum worried and nagged at me about this, but Gran didn't; maybe that's why I started to eat, and then enjoy, the strange little meals she invented for me. She gave me a human shape again.

If I was ill, Gran would sit with me and fetch me things and watch daytime TV with me. When my periods started, it was Gran who went to the chemist's and got me the things I needed and talked to me about it all, very straightforward, very Dutch. It was Gran, not Mum, who went with me to Marks & Spencer and bought me my first bra. But all the time she was slipping a little bit further away. She was like sunlight on a cloudy day or shadows on a lawn: here, then gone, then back again. In the shady patches her two languages would get thickly entangled, and I'd have to appeal to Grandad to explain what she was saying; but sometimes he couldn't, or wouldn't. Sometimes she would sit in her armchair with a book or watching the telly and I'd look at her and realize that she'd gone. Often when she was like that the only thing she would say was my name.

"Tamar."

And I'd go and kneel beside her and hold her hand and say, "Yes, Gran?"

"Tamar."

"I'm here, Gran. Do you want something?"

"Tamar."

Grandad would just watch, not saying anything, his eyes wet and magnified behind his glasses.

He loved her. It was dead simple, the way he loved her. Seamless. His love was like a wall that he'd built around her, and there wasn't a chink or flaw in it. Or so he thought. But then she started to float out of the real world, his world, and he was like a little boy trying to dam a stream with stones and mud, knowing that the water would always break through at a place he wasn't looking at. There was nothing desperate about the way he did it, though. He was always calm, it seemed. Expecting the worst and determined not to crack. She started to get up in the night and turn on all the taps, and he would get up too and stand quietly beside her watching the endless flow of water as if he found it as fascinating as she did. Then he'd guide her back to bed before turning the taps off. One night I heard something and went into the living room and saw the two of them standing out on the balcony. He'd wrapped his dressing gown around her, and I heard him say, "Yes, you are right, Marijke. The traffic is like a river of stars. Would you like to watch it some more, or go back to bed?"

When the calls started coming in from police stations, he handled them as if it were just business, something that happened in the normal course of things. He'd call a taxi, get his coat, rescue her and return the stolen goods to the supermarket. (Usually it was exotic fruits, sometimes just bags of rice or potatoes.) I never once heard him complain or curse, not even so much as sigh. At first I thought he was being pig-headed stubborn, refusing to recognize the reality of the situation. Sometimes I thought he was just too distant from the world, not really grasping what was going on. But it wasn't like that at all. He and Gran had gone through terrible things when they were young, during the war. Bravery – endurance, all that – was a deep part of him. In other words, he was being heroic. It took me a long time to see it.

It's a very private thing, losing your mind. And all sorts of people, complete strangers, get involved. It was that, the invasion of his privacy, that started Grandad crumbling. And the fact that all those people – the social workers, doctors, police, psychiatrists – were younger than him, and not as clever, but more powerful. He felt – he must have felt – control slipping away. And what he did was build the wall higher, work harder to dam the stream, fight even more fiercely to keep the world at arm's length.

Mum and I both knew that Gran would have to go away sooner or later. Mum was good; she treated me like a grown-up; we talked about it all. But with her it was the practical stuff. What if this happens? Do you think we should do this or that? What about the flat? And so on. Which was missing the point, really. It was a small thing that made me realize. I went to the flat after school one day and got out of the lift, and Grandad was standing there in his coat. He couldn't hide the fact that he was hoping to see Gran, not me. She'd gone wandering. He looked straight past me at the empty lift and his face just collapsed. I understood then that his walls had fallen at last. That while we'd all been focusing on Gran, he was the one desperate for support, for love.

Standing there by the lift, looking up at his desolate face, I realized that there was only one person who could provide it. And it scared me. I didn't think I was up to it.

He was not what you'd call a lovable man, my grandad. It wasn't that he was cold, exactly. It was more as though he had a huge distance inside himself. There's a game I used to play with my friends. One of us had to think of someone we all knew, and the others had to work out who it was by asking questions like "If this person was a musical instrument, what would it be?" or "If this person was a place, what would it be?" I used to think that if Grandad were a place it would be one of those great empty landscapes you sometimes see in American movies: flat, an endless road, tumbleweed blown by a moaning wind, a vast blank sky. And after Dad disappeared, he withdrew even further into this remote space.

It was a funny thing, a surprising thing, that brought him back to me. It was algebra.

I collided with algebra in my first year at secondary school and it sent me reeling. The very word itself seemed sinister, a word from black magic. *Algebracadabra*. Algebra messed up one of those divisions between things that help you make sense of the world and keep it tidy. Letters make words; figures make numbers. They had no business getting tangled up together. Those *a*s and *b*s and *x*s and *y*s with little numbers floating next to their heads, those brackets and hooks and symbols, all trying to conceal an answer, not give you one. I'd sit there in my own little darkness watching it dawn on the faces of my classmates. Their hands would go up – *"Miss! Miss!"* – and mine never did. The homework reduced me to tears.

"I don't see the point of it," I wailed. "I don't know what it's for!"

Grandad, as it turned out, liked algebra, did know what it was for. But he sat opposite me and didn't say anything for a while, considering my problem in that careful, expressionless way of his.

Eventually he said, "Why do you do PE at school?"

"What?"

"PE. Why do they make you do it?"

"Because they hate us?" I suggested.

"And the other reason?"

"To keep us fit, I suppose."

"Physically fit, yes." He reached across the table and put the first two fingers of each hand on the sides of my head. "There is also mental fitness, isn't there?"

Behind us, Gran was watching a comedy game show with the sound off.

"I can explain to you why algebra is useful. But that is not what algebra is really for." He moved his fingers gently on my temples. "It's to keep what is in here healthy. PE for the head. And the great thing is you can do it sitting down. Now, let us use these little puzzles here to take our brains for a jog."

And it worked. Not that I ever enjoyed algebra. But I did come to see that it was possible to enjoy it. Grandad taught me that the alien signs and symbols of algebraic equations were not just marks on paper. They were not flat. They were three-dimensional, and you could approach them from different directions, look at them from different angles, stand them on their heads. You could take them apart and put them together in a variety of shapes, like Lego. I stopped being afraid of them.

I didn't know it at the time, of course, but those homework sessions were a breakthrough in more ways than one. If Grandad had been living behind an invisible door, then algebra turned out to be the key that opened it and let me in. And what I found wasn't the barren tumbleweed landscape that I'd imagined. It was not like that at all.

I'd known for a long time that he was fond of puzzles. When I was younger he used to send me letters with lots of the words replaced by pictures or numbers. They always ended 02U, which meant *Love to you*, because zero was "love" in tennis. He was often disappointed when I couldn't work them out. Or couldn't be bothered to. Now I discovered that Grandad's world was full of mirages and mazes, of mirrors and misleading signs. He was fascinated by riddles and codes and conundrums and labyrinths, by the origin of place names, by grammar, by slang, by jokes – although he never laughed at them – by anything that might mean something else. He lived in a world that was slippery, changeable, fluid.

He lured me into the weirdness of crosswords. He bought two newspapers, the *Independent* and the *Guardian*, every day, glanced at the news without too much interest, and then settled down to do both crosswords. At first I simply sat and watched him fill in the grids by some mysterious process. I watched as the tip of his pen moved from one white square to another, not forming letters, almost hearing him think. Then, in a flurry of writing, he would fill the squares and I would have no idea how he did it, how he locked one word into another. But he didn't try to explain it until I asked him to.

"Okay. Look at this one: nineteen down. It's quite easy. The clue says *Artist up for prize*, six letters. So what this tells us is that we have to find a six-letter word for artist that means something else when we write it backwards."

"Does it?"

"Yes, because in a down clue, *up* tells us to turn the word upside down, which is the same as writing it backwards."

"I see," I said untruthfully.

"Okay. Can you think of another word for artist?"

"Um … painter?"

"Does that make a word when you write it backwards? Here, have the pen. Write it out. Is *retniap* a real word?"

"I don't think so."

"No. And it's got seven letters, so it wouldn't fit anyway. What might an artist do, as well as paint?"

"Draw?" I said.

"Ah! Good. Someone who draws might be a drawer, yes?"

I was confused, maybe thinking of the drawer I kept my dad in.

Grandad said, "Write *drawer* backwards. What do you get?"

"Reward."

"Good! Now look at the clue again. What's another word for prize?"

"Reward! Is that the answer?"

"Of course."

He taught me that language was rubbery, plastic. It wasn't, as I'd thought, something you just use, but something you can play with. Words were made up of little bits that could be shuffled, turned back to front, remixed. They could be tucked and folded into other words to produce unexpected things. It was like cookery, like alchemy. Language hid more than it revealed. Gradually I became a crossword freak.

"These people who make them up," Grandad said, "the compilers, they all have their own little codes. You can learn these codes, break them, and that can lead you to the answer."

"Show me. Give me an example, Grandad."

"Okay. This one here," he said, tapping the *Guardian* with his pen, "he is fond of using the language of maps. When he says *going north* in a down clue, it means the word is written backwards from the bottom to the top. Because north is always at the top of a map."

"Like *drawer* and *reward*," I said, remembering. "That could be *Artist going north for prize*, yeah?"

He leaned back in his chair, faking amazement. "Hey, that's right. Well done. PE for the head, yes?"

Then he took off his glasses and rubbed his eyes. "It seems to me," he said, "that your grandmother is talking to us in crossword clues these days. And unfortunately I am not clever enough to work many of them out."

When there was no longer any choice, they took her away.

It was a bright, sharp October day, a month or so after my fifteenth birthday. When the social worker buzzed the intercom, Grandad made an awful wounded noise. I had to answer; he couldn't. We eased Gran away from the cookery programme she was watching. In the lift Grandad kept taking deep breaths and I could hear them catch in his throat. Gran was serious-faced and excited because she knew that today she was the centre of attention and it had been a long time since she had gone anywhere special. Looking at her lit up like that, I was struck by how beautiful she must once have been. She still was, really, with that perfectly straight silver-white hair and those big, deep black eyes.

I was on half-term holiday, and the arrangement was that Grandad would go to the nursing home with her, and I'd go back to Mum's. Grandad would come and have dinner with us when Gran was settled. But it didn't happen like that.

The social worker and the driver met us in the lobby. Gran seemed to think they were friends that she'd forgotten. The driver put the suitcase in the boot of the car and got behind the wheel. When I opened the back door for

121

Gran, I could see that she'd decided something wasn't right. Her eyes were flickering from side to side, a distress signal I recognized. So I held her hands and told her that everything was all right, feeling ashamed of myself. And eventually she got into the car and sat quietly next to Grandad. The social worker closed the back doors and got into the front passenger seat. Grandad wound down his window and began to say something to me. Then the driver let out this shocked howl because Gran had reached forward and grabbed his dreadlocks and was hauling his head back against the headrest. Her eyes were wild and she was showing all her teeth. The social worker tried to intervene but was hampered by her seat belt. Grandad was slow to react but at last got a grip on Gran's wrists. She let go of the driver's hair and threw herself back in her seat and started yelling.

Something in Dutch, then: "I know who you are! I'm not going with you!"

"Marijke," Grandad said. "Please, my love, what's the matter?"

"I'm not going with you! I'm staying with Tamar, here with Tamar."

The social worker said, "It's all right, Mrs Hyde. Really. You can't—"

She was cut off by Gran's scream. It was a terrible, raw sound, not feminine, not even human, and the worse thing was that it was my name she was screaming.

Grandad's head recoiled as if she had struck him physically and he stumbled out of the car. "It's you she wants," he said. "Not me. Please. Christ."

He stood with his hands open, banging them sideways against his legs, and the tears were unstoppable now. The driver had got out of the car and was rubbing the back of his head vigorously and saying "Shit, man" as quietly as he could manage.

I said, "It's okay, Grandad. I'll go with her if that's what she wants. It's okay. I don't mind."

By this time the social worker had got out too, and she said, "I don't think that's appropriate, really. It really ought to be Mr Hyde…"

"You can see what she's like," I said.

Gran was alone in the car now, sitting bolt upright, pulling against the seat belt. Her eyes were still very wild and she was turning her head from side to side, trying to work out where the stationary car was taking her, looking for familiar landmarks along the imaginary route.

"I'm sorry, I'm sorry," Grandad kept saying.

I didn't know what he was sorry for: his tears, his wife's behaviour, or something else altogether.

Eventually we decided that I would go with Gran in the car, and Grandad would follow in a taxi. We didn't have mobiles in those days, so he went back up to the flat to call for one. He was gone quite a long time. It was pretty edgy in the car, but I kept hold of Gran's hand and she stayed fairly calm, just looking about. She even gave me a quick smile, but it was that twitchy kind of smile you find yourself doing when you accidentally catch a stranger's eye on the tube. By the time Grandad came out again, the taxi was already pulling into the car park. Our car, the social work car, set off. I looked back through the rear window and Grandad was standing next to the taxi watching us go. He still had his hands hanging by his sides, open and facing forward, as if to show us and everyone else that there was nothing in them.

THE HOME WE took Gran to was over in Chiswick. River Reach, it was called, although it wasn't on the river. It was one of those huge houses originally built for Victorian millionaires, all turrets and twiddly bits of masonry and fancy brickwork. Above the front porch there was a two storey high stained-glass window. From the outside, it was a blank mosaic of lead and dirty glass. Inside, when you walked up the stairs, you could see that it showed angels carrying things – a ship's wheel, an anchor, a coil of thick rope – in the general direction of heaven. At the top was a scroll with words in very elaborate writing that I couldn't understand. Grandad said it was Latin, but he never got round to telling me what it meant.

When we went to River Reach that first time, it never crossed my mind that Gran would stay there for the rest of her life. I don't mean that I believed she would get better. We'd all given up hope of that, I think. It was just that she looked so out of place; it was impossible to think that she could ever belong there. She was so bright-eyed and smart compared to the other residents, some of whom were pretty far gone, I'm sorry to say. If you'd seen us being shown round, you'd have thought that Gran was a visiting dignitary being taken on a tour of inspection: nervous and politely interested, but not quite sure why she was there.

The day room must have been a living room once upon a time. It was huge, with tall windows overlooking the garden. There were armchairs and wheelchairs backed against the walls. Some of the men and women sitting in them were slumped like puppets whose strings had been cut. Most were staring at a big TV set next to the empty marble fireplace. One or two sat up and brightened when they saw us, perhaps thinking we might've been their relatives coming to visit. There was a powerful reek of air freshener. A door opened onto what the nurse called the sun lounge. I suppose it would have been an open terrace originally, but now it was closed in with white plastic double glazing, and full of easy chairs and house plants. A wide ramp sloped down from the sliding doors into the garden. The air was full of a sound a bit like surf coming and going: it was the heavy breathing of the Great West Road half a mile away.

"It's a shame you couldn't have been here earlier in the year," the nurse said. "The garden looks fantastic when the rhododendrons are in bloom."

"Spectacular," the social worker said. "You wouldn't believe the colours."

"That sounds nice, doesn't it, Gran?" I said, and even saying that much made me feel like a traitor.

All the way through this tour, Grandad was making little humming noises like someone quietly agreeing with everything. Except that instead of nodding his head he was shaking it from side to side.

I couldn't imagine how we were going to leave Gran without her having a monumental fit. Or without Grandad cracking up. But as it turned out, it was no trouble at all. In the corridor going along to Gran's room we met a freckly sandy-haired woman, one of the staff, but not a nurse. Gran decided that she'd known this woman all her life. She greeted her like a long-lost friend and started talking nineteen to the dozen. The freckly woman was a bit startled at first – we all were – but got hold of the situation pretty quickly. When I pulled Grandad away towards the stairs, the two of them were sitting in Gran's room, Gran in the chair chatting away in a mixture of Dutch and English, the cleaning lady or who-ever she was sitting on the bed with one plump leg crossed over the other, baffled and smiling.

She went downhill quite fast. Partly because Grandad wasn't there all the time to talk to her, I suppose. And he'd always been pretty obsessed with keeping up appearances; without his stubborn insistence on their old routines, on keeping things "normal", she just got lost. The short periods when she was clear-headed got fewer and further apart. It'll sound harsh, I suppose, but I'm sure that River Reach made her worse. Without being aware of it, probably, Gran adjusted her behaviour to fit in with the place. We all do that. Like at school: you find yourself going along with the rules automatically after a while, even though, when you stop and think about it, some of them are weird. At River Reach the rules were built around dementia. There's also the possibility that Gran found her clear periods too awful to bear. I still find it terrifying to think about that. That there might have been times when she was sane enough to understand the full horror of what was happening to her, thinking she'd been the victim of some awful mistake. Like waking from a nightmare in a strange room only to find that you're still in both.

Gran had started to forget English words long before she went to River Reach. Her English had never been perfect like Grandad's. She'd often search for the word for some-thing, clicking her fingers impatiently, then give up and use

126

the Dutch, which Grandad would translate for her. At first, the words she'd lose were slightly tricky ones, like *transfer* or *disguise*, so that was understandable. Then she started to forget ordinary words like *window* or *shower* or *cushion*. By the time I was fourteen or so, her two languages were leaking into one another continuously. I couldn't tell, of course, if what she was saying still made some sort of sense. Judging by the look I sometimes saw on Grandad's face, I don't think they did, not always. After a couple of months in the home, she seemed to have lost English completely. And I never worked out if she could still understand when she was spoken to in English, either. She would respond to me sometimes, but I had no way of knowing if it had anything to do with what I'd said. The staff at River Reach did what English people do when they speak to foreigners: talk slowly and loudly in English, and mime. Funnily enough, Gran reacted quite happily to the nurses miming at her and drawing the shapes of things in the air. She'd often look livelier, a little more aware. Younger, even. When Grandad and I visited her together, he'd translate bits and pieces of her rambling chatter for me. She spoke my name lots, and when I caught it in among the Dutch I'd ask him what she'd said. He always told me more or less the same thing.

"She says she loves you. She says she has always loved you."

Which I believed, of course, even though when she looked at me she didn't always seem to know who I was.

She started hiding food in her room. At first it was stuff we brought in for her: fruit, biscuits, cakes, that sort of thing. Then she began smuggling bits of lunch and dinner upstairs in her handbag. The staff soon caught on. They'd wait until Gran was in the day room, then go up and fish the pork chop or the omelette out of her underwear drawer or the wardrobe. Most of the time she didn't seem to notice, or

127

mind; but once, when I was there, she got very agitated. She grabbed Grandad's sleeve as soon as we arrived and hissed a stream of Dutch at him.

"What was all that about?" I asked him.

He hesitated, then said, "Your grandmother says that people are stealing from her room. She has been storing food up there, but it keeps disappearing. She says she is worried that there will not be enough to get through the winter after all."

Which was very odd; but he didn't want to say any more about it.

Then there was the business about the birds. We usually sat with Gran in the sun lounge. It was nice out there; you could almost imagine you were in a smart hotel. One day, though, Gran flatly refused to go. She was frailer by then, but she struggled like mad when we got near the door. She insisted on staying in the day room. We had to sit on three uncomfortable chairs next to the door to the hall, as far away from the windows as possible. Grandad was upset and edgy, because he hated the day room. So did I. It was too hot, the TV was usually on loud, and there were always several stroke victims staring at you out of their poor lopsided faces and forgetting to leave the room before they went to the toilet.

Anyway, we got settled, Grandad holding one of her hands and me holding the other. She wouldn't speak or do anything except watch the windows for quite a while. Eventually, gently, Grandad got her attention and she started talking. She talked more than usual that day; not that I understood a word she said. But I thought I heard her use the word *crying* several times. On the way home I asked Grandad about it.

"Crying?" he said, absently. "No, she didn't say anything about crying."

The next time I was there she refused to go out into the

sun lounge again. The same performance. So we sat in the bloody awful day room, and again I thought I heard her use the word *crying* several times. Actually, it was more like *cryin'*, without the g. Afterwards, on the way to the bus stop, I asked him again. He didn't seem to have heard me, but I knew he had, so I waited. After a bit he said, "She didn't say *crying*. She was talking about *kraaien*. The Dutch word for crows."

"What about them?"

Again it took him a long time to answer. "Marijke says that there are *kraaien* in the garden. She says they are huge and walk like men. That's why she won't go out into the sun lounge. She says that these crows are waiting to trap her. Or me."

"God," I said.

"She says that some are black and some are grey, and they have big shiny beaks. She thinks some of them have human faces concealed under their beaks, but she's not sure. They also have shiny black legs and their breasts are speckled with silver. She says they pretend not to talk to each other, but they do. They have secret ways of talking."

I suddenly felt hopeless and helpless and brimful of tears. I looked down, watching my feet move left-right-left-right on the pavement. When I looked up again, Grandad was no longer beside me. He'd stopped walking. He had both hands thrust into his coat pockets and was staring at the ground.

I turned to face him and said, "What does it mean? Do you know?"

He sniffed. "Yes, I think so. I think I've worked it out. She is talking about the Gestapo. The Gestapo and the SS."

I must have looked blank, so he said, "Nazis. Marijke is seeing Nazis in the garden. She is going backwards. She is remembering what we have tried so hard to forget. Christ help me."

He looked very old and very scared, like he had that morning outside the flat, watching the car take his wife away. Like a man waiting for a bullet to hit him. It was a February evening, and the passing traffic sloshed rainwater over the kerb.

A month later he was dead.

HOLLAND, 1944

ON SUNDAY 15TH October there were strangers among the congregation gathered in the severe and unadorned country church west of Apeldoorn. Nobody commented on them – they knew better – but there were sidelong glances, especially at those who only murmured the hymns or, worse, stayed silent during the spoken prayers. When the strangers lingered to speak to the pastor after the service, the regular churchgoers understood; they went quietly home, buttoned up against the cutting wind.

There were eight of them, these strangers, and the pastor led them into the vestry. They sat on wooden chairs that had ledges for hymn books built into the backrests. They formed a rough semicircle which had to be adjusted when they were joined by a man and a woman who had stayed outside during the service, suffering the weather because they were Roman Catholics. These two were on foreign ground; this was a sternly Protestant village where the Pope was seen as a second cousin of the devil himself.

Not all of the pastor's guests knew one another, so there was an awkward round of introductions in which most of them gave only their first names, some of which were false. Koop de Vries was one of only two people who gave their full true names; he spoke it with a kind of surly defiance.

Tamar began the meeting by reading out a personal message from Prince Bernhard. (When Dart had deciphered it, he'd presented it to Tamar with a mocking bow, like a saucy courtier in a Shakespeare play.) The message began with a loving greeting from the prince and his mother-in-law, Queen Wilhelmina; they both thought constantly of the suffering and courage of their subjects. It went on to say that despite "recent setbacks" – Koop snorted at this veiled reference to the Operation Market Garden disaster – an Allied victory in Europe was inevitable and the liberation of all the Netherlands was at hand. The prince was certain that the great Dutch virtues of hope, strength and patience would sustain his people until that longed-for moment arrived.

Tamar paused briefly and glanced around at the men and women he was supposed to unite. Some of them, including the pastor, were visibly impressed and heartened. Felix, the aristocratic local leader of the OD, looked as though he was struggling against the urge to stand to attention and sing the national anthem. The KP people, Lydia and Johan, gazed back at him stony-eyed; both were devout communists. Koop had clasped his hands behind his head and seemed to find the ceiling more interesting than anything Bernhard had to say.

Tamar cleared his throat and continued. When the great day came, the prince said, and the Allied armies surged into Holland, there would be vital and dangerous work for the resistance to do. For this reason, two things were of the utmost importance. First, he urged all resistance organizations and groups to unite under the newly formed BS, which he, Bernhard, had the honour to command. From now on, resistance activities should be coordinated by the BS commandant in each zone. He realized that this would involve difficult adjustments and compromises – "Ha!"

Johan muttered – but he begged his "valiant countrymen" to see that cooperation was the only way forward at this crucial period of their history.

Second, the prince urged all organizations to concentrate on keeping their networks intact and in a state of readiness. "Opportunist actions" which would provoke Nazi reprisals should be avoided.

And that was as far as Tamar got. It was Jaap Smedts, the other freelance agent in the room, who interrupted. He'd been fidgeting for some time.

"What's that supposed to mean, 'opportunist actions'? What other kind of actions are there? We see an opportunity, we act. That's what we do. That's what resistance means. Listen: in the last two years alone my group has derailed three Nazi trains, two bringing heavy armour in, one taking loot out. We've ambushed five convoys and blown up an arms dump and two of their wireless posts. All opportunist actions, and all bloody good ones, if you ask me."

"No one is saying they weren't," Tamar said, "but—"

"But we must look to the future," the pastor now insisted. "Which, if I may say so, is what we in the LO have always tried to do."

Koop groaned audibly, but the pastor was not deterred. He had a very personal interest in the future, in the shape of two Jewish teenagers who had lived in his loft for the past three years, not to mention an English paratroop sergeant who had been hiding in his barn for a fortnight.

"So it seems to me," he continued, "that what Prince Bernhard recommends makes good sense. We have all made sacrifices. Some of them have been noble and courageous" – and here he nodded at Jaap Smedts – "and perhaps necessary. But I'd like to remind you all that every Dutch death is a German victory, and that at the present time thousands of Dutch lives are hanging by a thread. With liberation so close, it would be madness to cut that thread by indulging in reckless and provocative activities."

That was too much for Koop. He thrust his narrow head forward like an axe. "Reckless?" he spat. "Sacrifice? What would the LO know about that, for Chrissake?"

The pastor flinched and opened his mouth, but Koop kept going. "I'll tell you what turns my stomach, and that's being told what to do by a man who scuttled off to England as soon as the Nazis turned up. Who the hell does Prince Bernhard think he is, appointing himself head of the resistance? Apart from anything else, the bugger is half German. He's got a brother in the bloody German army, for God's sake."

Felix got to his feet. His moustache writhed on his lip like a threatened caterpillar. "Damn it, man, that's treason in my book! How dare you!"

Lydia and Johan rolled their eyes and smirked at each other.

Tamar raised his hand. "Gentlemen, please! Felix, please sit down. Can we—"

But Koop hadn't finished. "And while I'm on the subject, and with all due respect to our new commandant here, he's also been out of the country for over a year. It's us who've stuck it out, risking our lives day in and day out, who should have the main say in who does what. We know the turf. As far as I'm concerned, the job's the same as it's always been, and that's killing Nazis."

Jaap, Lydia and Johan all nodded vigorously at that, and Tamar thought, Thanks a lot, you bastard.

A small bespectacled man who'd called himself Henri now spoke. "I note," he said, "that Bernhard's message suggests that the Allied advance will take place soon, and that German defeat is inevitable. But recent events don't suggest that at all. The Germans don't look whipped to me.

136

So what does 'soon' mean? And does the prince speak with any authority? I get the impression that the Brits don't take him very seriously."

Felix bristled again, but Tamar got in first. "The message comes with the full authority and support of Supreme Allied Command."

"Ah," Lydia said. "The all-conquering Americans."

"Look," Tamar said, "can we get a couple of things straight? It doesn't matter to me if the BS is under the command of Prince Bernhard or Santa bloody Claus. The fact is, it has the full backing of the British and the Americans and the Dutch government in London: I can assure you of that. And I didn't come back here to throw my weight around, either. Koop is right – most of you know the zone better than I do. Which means I can't do my job without your cooperation and advice. I think some of you have got things the wrong way round. I'm not here to tell you what to do; I'm here to help you work together, to get you what you need. Surely you can see that supply drops, communications – everything – will be more efficient if we are united."

He looked around the group. Some met his gaze, others didn't.

"And I hear what you say, Henri. I can't tell you when the Allies will cross the Rhine. It might be in a week, or a month. We might have to get through another winter before they are ready. But they will come. There can be no doubt of that. And the Nazis will go. What worries me is that they might decide to leave behind them a country of fires and corpses. They are already trying to starve us. They are destroying our sea defences and flooding our farmland. They are blowing Rotterdam to pieces. They are rounding up more and more of our people for forced labour in Germany, and the truth is that few, if any, will ever come home. Reprisals for what they call 'terrorist attacks' are getting more and more extreme.

Look at what they did over in Putten a couple of weeks ago. You must have been able to see the fires from here."

"Hang on, hang on." It was Koop again. "Are you saying we should go to ground and do nothing in case the Germans take reprisals? Is that what you came here to tell us?"

"No, I'm not saying that. Not necessarily. But it's something we should discuss."

Several people began to speak, but Tamar soldiered on. "What I am saying is that we need to save our energy and our resources for when the big battle comes. So what we need to do now is seriously consider the risks involved in any operation. If we are all dead or locked up when the Allies attack, what use are we to anyone?"

"But—"

"And," Tamar went on stubbornly, "we need to think very seriously about the question of *Todeskandidaten*, the death candidates. We must ask ourselves if shooting up a truck or blowing up a railway track is worth the deaths of ten or twenty of our comrades."

"You m-might like to know, Christiaan, that we already do a certain amount of f-f-finking about that." This was Maurice from the RVV. Anger tended to worsen his stammer.

Maurice's colleague, a tight-belted and bright-eyed woman calling herself Zena, said, "My brother is a death candidate in Amersfoort. If he were here, Commandant, he would tell you that he is not afraid to die for his country. What he has already suffered is perhaps worse than that. I am not happy that you choose to speak on his behalf."

God, he was weary. Suddenly very weary, and impatient. Not the best emotional mix for a negotiator. To Zena he said harshly, "Do you know what Patton once said? Patton, the American general? He said, 'You do not win a war by dying for your country. You win a war by making sure that some other poor bastard dies for his.'"

Jaap Smedts surprised Tamar by laughing and slapping his knee. "That's good," he said. "That's very good. I'll remember that."

"It's not only good, it's true. It's the simple truth about war. The survivors win. I can see no point in dead people being liberated."

The pastor cleared his throat. He had something to say on that subject. But Johan the communist beat him to it.

"This is all very interesting," he said, "but we cannot make decisions as a group until we actually *are* a group. Which we are not. We are several groups. If we agree to become a single organization called the BS, then we can act – or not act – together. But we have not yet agreed to unite under the command of the BS."

"So let's take a vote on it," Felix suggested. "Or is that a bit too democratic for you chaps?"

"It's not as simple as that," Lydia said. "The KP is a collective. Johan and myself are here as its representatives, not its leaders. We cannot cast a vote on a matter of such importance without consulting our comrades."

Tamar looked up at the one window that illuminated the room. It was small and bullet-shaped, criss-crossed with bars of lead, and the light within it was flat and metallic. He had a long way to go. He thought about lost souls gathering at a dark river. He thought of Marijke, how beautiful her body was inside her shapeless clothes.

It was the third Sunday in the month, so the parish curate had walked out to the asylum – the Germans had taken his bike, and he damned them to hell for it – to hold a morning service. In the kitchen, thawing his hands around his cup, he inhaled and said, "Sister Agatha, this is real tea! Incredible! I know better than to ask where you got it."

"It fell from the sky," Agatha told him, quite truthfully.

"Ah," the curate said. "Great is the power of prayer."

They gathered in the day room. The hymn singing was ragged, to say the least, which is not unusual when some members of a congregation are singing to tunes known only to themselves. Dart did not sing. He was completely tone-deaf. When he could not avoid situations involving singing, he opened and closed his mouth silently, out of consideration for others. Albert Veening spotted him doing it and grinned across at him.

When most of the worshippers were seated, the curate gave a short sermon. He took his text, he told them, from St Mark's Gospel: "If a house be divided against itself, that house cannot stand." He had a good deal to say about the perils of division at a time "when this, our house, our nation, is still besieged by the powers of darkness". There were some groans of alarm from his audience. And, the curate said, there were other kinds of division. Perhaps most dangerous of all was the divided self, in which the force of good and the force of evil were equally powerful, where love and death were locked in never-ending battle, when mind and soul were torn and sundered. Dart thought that this was an insensitive choice of topic, given the state of the congregation. He drifted a little – he hadn't had much sleep – so he didn't quite catch the bit about the love of Our Lord Jesus Christ, which makes us whole.

They spoke the Lord's Prayer, then sat more or less quietly while Sidona recited it a second time, her upturned face clenched in concentration. The curate blessed them in the name of the Father, the Son and the Holy Ghost, and Dart wondered how much ahead of schedule he could arrive at the farm without it seeming ... odd.

For as long as Marijke could remember, the house had grown smaller for the winter. When the ploughing was finished, or just after. Her grandparents had called the parlour and the sitting room "the summer rooms", although traces of darkness lingered among the glum furniture even in sun-dazed August, when baffled flies fumbled at the windows. There had always been that ritual moment in autumn when Oma removed the wedges that held the doors to those rooms open; she would stand with her hand on the brass doorknob and look into each room, and sigh and then close the door. Winter. The sad clack of a lock. The retreat into the warm kitchen, the gathering in to the wintering heart of the house.

Marijke had done that to herself, a year ago. Tamar had left in autumn, and she had closed her doors. Then she and Oma had busied themselves with the seasonal work. They had packed potatoes gently into sacks, layered carrots and beetroot with sand in the big wooden boxes in the cellar. They had gathered mushrooms and dried them above the stove, where they curled into themselves like human ears. They had picked and bottled blackberries and bilberries from the heath, purpling their fingers and lips. Marijke had cycled to town and bought – a miracle, this – a block of sugar the size of a small loaf. She had wrapped it in a cloth and hammered it to pieces on the wash-house floor, and used it to make jam from the last crop of damsons.

All of it, the gathering and preserving and storing away, was to insist that a future existed, and that somehow they would reach it and live in it. And Marijke could not quite believe this, nor want it. Not back then, not in the silent house where even the most familiar things – a chair, a cup, her bed – filled her with an unbearable sense of his absence. She had lived the year numb and mechanical, waiting to heal.

Yet despite everything – to spite her, even – the slow wheel of the seasons had revolved once more. Now, on this cold Sunday, with the easterly wind whirlpooling in the yard, she and Oma were again busy with preserving pans and glass jars, investing all over again in a future. This time, though, she wanted it, and wanted to believe in it.

And because of this she was afraid. Tamar had left for Apeldoorn the previous day, cycling away from her up the track with his left arm held high in a long farewell. Exactly – *exactly* – as he had done a year earlier, a brief six hours after the signal from London. This dreadful overlapping of then and now had frightened her so badly that her legs had lost their strength; she couldn't have run after him.

They were cutting the bruised flesh from windfall apples. Later they would stew them and store them in jars sealed with a thin layer of wax. She cut through an apple that seemed unspoiled, but found that something had burrowed to the core. Some tiny thing, some worm, had left a thin black tunnel that her knife had sliced in two.

When she heard the tinny chirrup of the bicycle bell, she thought – just for two heartbeats – that it might be him. "A week," he'd said. "Maybe a bit less." But all the same, perhaps... Then she looked at the clock and remembered.

She opened the door just as Dart raised his fist to knock. They both laughed a little awkwardly. She put her hands on his arms and kissed him lightly on both cheeks. This seemed to surprise him; he even stumbled slightly in the dark hallway.

"My God, it's cold," was the first thing he managed to say. The wind had brought tears to the corners of his eyes.

"Your face is like ice," she said. "Come into the kitchen and get warm."

Oma had already shifted the kettle onto the hottest part of the stove and now she came and kissed him too, pulling on the lapels of his coat to bring his face down to hers.

"It smells wonderful in here," Dart said. "Apples, bread ... and what's that other smell? Blackberries? You're very busy."

"It's an important time of year for us," Marijke said. "A lot depends on it. Especially this year. I don't imagine there'll be much to buy in town this winter. The Germans will take everything before we can get near it."

Oma put three cups of tea on the table and then acted something out, her head drawn back into her shoulders, making herself furtive.

Marijke translated. "Oma says that this year we will have to hide our food in different places all over the farm too. In case the German thieves come again."

Dart turned sharply to look at her. "Again? They've been here before?"

"Just once. Early in the year."

"And you're expecting them to come back?"

She shrugged. "Maybe. I don't know what to expect. For all we know, the next soldiers who knock at the door might be Americans."

He had a sudden vision of Marijke opening the door to a smiling American GI, embracing him. He blinked and it was gone. "That would be nice," he said. "God, I can hardly bend my fingers around this cup. They'd better thaw out. I can't send Morse with these claws."

"They'll be fine," she said. "You've got nearly an hour before your schedule, is that right?"

"Ah, yes. You don't mind me getting here a bit early, do you?"

"Of course not. Don't be daft. Anyway, the good thing about that room in the little barn is that it hardly ever gets really cold. I used to spend hours up there when I was a kid."

When he had gathered up his bag and coat, she followed him to the door. In the hall she said, "Tamar got off okay, by the way."

"Ah, right," Dart said. "I was going to ask."

OPERATION PEGASUS BEGAN a week later. Early in the morning of Sunday 22nd October, small groups of British soldiers began to emerge from their hiding places in the Veluwe. In borrowed civilian clothing they crept from woodsheds, chicken runs, cellars, a cemetery, a church. They followed their Dutch guides – many of them women and children – south, towards the Rhine. Not all could walk unaided.

On that same morning, two platoons of the German Wehrmacht arrived noisily in the village of Bennekom, west of Arnhem. When a large enough number of inhabitants had been herded together, the German officer in charge stood on top of his armoured car and told them that they had two hours to get their stuff together and leave. The village was being evacuated. It would be considered officially empty at eleven o'clock. He didn't actually say that Bennekom would be smashed and burned at five minutes past eleven, but the villagers got that impression. A woman with two children hiding behind her skirt asked the officer where they were meant to go. The German laughed and jerked his thumb over his shoulder at nowhere in particular. There. Somewhere else.

The expulsion of these people, who had already been picked clean by war, was a godsend for the British escapers. Instead of having to take their chances in open country and on deserted roads, they passed unnoticed among the straggled columns of the homeless. Damaged and dishevelled, anxious and carrying little or nothing, they looked entirely Dutch. The occasional German patrols who idly surveyed the refugees paid them no particular attention.

So it was that by early afternoon one hundred and twenty men had made it to their rendezvous, a logger's hut in the woods somewhere between Ede and Arnhem. They were greeted by two members of the Dutch resistance and two British officers, a lean brigadier and a madly cheerful young major. The brigadier was disguised in an ill-fitting black suit; he looked like an undertaker who'd fallen on hard times. The major wore rough farm clothes and carried, incongruously, a furled and bullet-torn umbrella. One of the Dutchmen was a heavy-set bearded man called Banjo. The other was Tamar.

After a wait that seemed longer than it was, a boy with a hunting rifle slung over his shoulder appeared on the rough track that led to the hut. He stuck two fingers into his mouth and whistled, piercingly. Soldiers who had been sitting beneath the trees got to their feet. Three elderly trucks laboured into view. Powered by charcoal gas, they wheezed and farted horribly as they manoeuvred awkwardly in the spaces between the trees. Each truck carried a great many empty sacks, as well as several containing potatoes.

The brigadier and the jaunty major divided the men into three groups and got them piled into the trucks. The drivers heaped empty sacks over the bodies and scattered potatoes on and around them. Tamar climbed into the passenger seat of the lead truck and shook hands with the driver, a middle-aged woman in overalls whose grip was as rough as tree bark. She wrestled the gear lever into first, growling, "Get in there, you bugger." The truck gasped and lurched forward; there was some muffled English swearing from the back.

Tamar had little doubt that they would run into German checkpoints before they reached Renkum. He'd talked it through with Banjo and the British officers.

"Banjo has achieved the impossible, getting these trucks for us," he said. "And the trucks themselves are our ace card, because the Germans will think we must be some sort of official convoy. There's a good chance that they'll just wave us through. There's also a chance that they won't."

"Understood," the brigadier said. "Then what?"

"Well, I'll try to bluff them. What's in our favour is that no one in his right mind would be taking three truckloads of British soldiers down to the Rhine in broad daylight."

"Absolutely," the jolly major agreed. "We've got craziness on our side. Terribly sensible, the Germans. Gives us the edge."

"So," Tamar went on, "if we are stopped, the drivers will keep the engines running. I'll do the talking. Your men must remain perfectly still, even if the backs of the trucks are opened. But if anyone starts to pull the sacks away, they must yell and scream and attack the Germans without hesitation. I know they have no weapons, but that's what they must do. Is that all right?"

"Fine," the brigadier said. "It's what they'd do anyway, I imagine. I'll go and have a chat with them."

As it turned out, there were two checkpoints. The first one, a solitary German private with his motorbike propped against a tree, made a gesture that urged them to hurry onwards, rather than stop. The second was a different matter.

Peering ahead, Tamar saw a single figure on the road: an SS trooper cradling a machine pistol. He reached over and touched the driver on her arm, and she slowed. A second

German wandered casually onto the road, lifting his rifle from his shoulder. Just off to the right was a wrecked cottage, a vehicle of some sort parked in front of it.

Tamar looked back; the other trucks were close behind. He stuck his arm out of the window and signalled to them to slow down.

The German with the machine pistol stayed where he was. He gestured to the man with the rifle, who approached Tamar's truck.

"Your papers, please."

The driver dug into her overalls, produced the little booklet and passed it through the window. The German scanned it and gave it back. Then he stepped backwards and looked at the other two trucks. In German he said, "What are you carrying and where are you going?"

She shrugged and pulled a face which said, I don't understand.

Tamar leaned across her, shoving his identity papers towards the soldier. "Potatoes," he said. *"Kartoffeln."*

The German gazed at him. Tamar saw the exhaustion in his face and made a gesture: Come here, look. He opened the door and stepped down into the road. At the corner of his vision he saw the other German do something with his machine pistol and then lift it. The trooper with the rifle walked cautiously down the blind side of the truck; while he was doing so, Tamar looked over at the half-destroyed cottage and saw the snout of a heavy machine gun poking from the fractured shutters of an upstairs window. He walked to the back of the truck and fiddled noisily with the bolts. He lowered the tailgate, speaking in German, cloaking the words in a rough Dutch accent.

"Potatoes, see? It's been a good year for them, all things considered. This truckload, *ja*, is for Arnhem. The other two for headquarters at Apeldoorn." He nudged the German.

"Nothing but the best for them, eh?"

The German stared into the truck, straight at part of an exposed foot that he didn't seem to see.

Tamar reached past him and hoisted a half-full sack onto the road. "Take these," he said. "Why should those bastards have them all? Here, take them."

The young German looked at the sack, then at Tamar. "You speak good German," he said.

"Of course!" Tamar straightened, stood stiffly like a man on a parade ground. "I was for two years in the Reich. A guest worker. Machine tools, in Essen, until my lungs packed up. You know Essen?"

The young German grimaced. "A shithole," he said. "I'm from Heidelberg."

Tamar smiled and shrugged. "Ah, yes. Heidelberg. They tell me it is very beautiful."

The German looked at Tamar and then at the slumped sack of potatoes. "All right," he said, "I'll take these. You can piss off."

"Thank you," Tamar said. *"Danke."*

He walked slowly back to the cab and climbed in.

They got to the woods above Renkum when the weakened sun was almost at the foot of the sky. The British emerged from under the sacks and spilled out. They at once began to change into their uniforms, which they had carried in their bundles and bags. They carefully packed the borrowed civilian clothes and heaped them into one of the trucks, then moved away, forming quiet groups in the deep shade of the trees. When the trucks had gone, Tamar called together the funereal brigadier, the mad young major and Banjo, and they walked through falling gold and russet leaves to the edge of the wood.

Tamar indicated markers as they went. "This is the way

we will come tonight. Remember this, the big beech tree. Remember this ditch. Here, the wooden posts with wire attached."

They came eventually to a broken gate where the woods ended and the bare fields stretched down to the Rhine.

Tamar handed his binoculars to the English brigadier. "There's a German position way over to the left, just where the river veers south. See it? Just beyond that small group of buildings. Now, track all the way to your right. The group of trees throwing the long shadow. Got that?"

"Ah, yes," the Englishman said. "There's another one. They look well settled in. What are they, do you know? Mortars? Heavy machine guns?"

"That sort of thing," Tamar said. "Now I want you to look this way a bit until you see a more or less straight line running down towards the river, through those hedges."

"Got it."

"Good. That's a drainage ditch. It's over a metre deep, and there's water at the bottom of it in some places. That's our route. It'll get us to within a hundred and fifty metres of the bank. After that, there's an open meadow, and we'll just have to take our chances."

The brigadier handed the binoculars to the major, who studied the ditch. "Looks about, what, a kilometre or more long?" he said. "Hell of a distance to crawl." He sounded as though he was looking forward to it.

"We'll set off at ten," Tamar said. "That should give us plenty of time. The hardest part will be the walk we've just taken, through the woods. It'll be pitch dark by then, with any luck, so single file all the way, okay? Each man must keep hold of the man ahead of him. Anyone who gets lost stays lost. We can't go looking for strays."

"Fair enough," the brigadier said. "What's the drill when we get to the far end of the ditch?"

"You stay where you are; I'll go down to the river. At midnight, I flash a V signal with a torch, which will tell your people over there to launch the boats. When they reach this side, I'll flash the same signal to you. Please be watching – I don't want to have to do it more than once. Then you climb out of the ditch and walk straight ahead to the water, where I'll meet you. No running. Concentrate on staying together."

"Understood," the brigadier said. He turned to the major. "Right, Digby. We'd better get back and brief the men."

"We'll be along in a minute," Tamar said. "There's a couple of things Banjo and I need to talk about."

When they were alone the two men stood staring out at the fading landscape.

"It's bloody chancy," Banjo said.

Tamar looked up at the sky where gathering sheets of cloud were streaked with a bruised red.

"Darkness and surprise, that's pretty much all we've got going for us." He grinned at Banjo. "And our luck's good. We got this far."

"Yeah. I didn't think we would. So, how do you want to do it? Are we going to be in the ditch with these guys, or d'you want me to cover one side and you the other?"

"I'll walk beside them, about ten metres this side of the ditch. You're going to stay here."

"Like hell I am," Banjo said.

"You're going to stay exactly here," Tamar said. "Because if anything goes wrong, the only thing these men can do is try to get back. And they'll need someone to cover them this end."

"Tamar, listen to me. What if you bump into a patrol down there? On your own you don't stand a chance. I'm coming with you."

Tamar said, "If it comes to a firefight in the dark, it'll not make much difference if there's one or two of us. We'd be as likely to shoot each other as anyone else. No, you're staying here. That's an order."

It was the first time he'd used those words. They sounded false and pompous, a quotation from somewhere. He half expected Banjo to laugh in his face. Instead, he shrugged and turned away to look back at the river.

"Come on," Tamar said. "Let's go."

But the other man put his hand on Tamar's arm. "Look," he said. "You might be right about our luck."

Tamar turned and saw that in the chill dusk the river had begun to conceal itself. It was exhaling a fine mist, like human breath on winter air. Already veils of vapour blurred the far bank and the low dark horizon seemed to float on shifty nothingness.

Nightmarish hours later, Tamar was down there in the hanging fog, alone, close to the invisible water. The strain of listening and staring into darkness had made his body ache and stiffen. He had simply, stupidly, not realized how noisy the business would be. Coming through the woods, the blundering and cursing file of British soldiers had sounded like a stampede of blind beasts. Then he had walked along-side the ditch, probing the night with his Sten. If there had been a German on the same track, they would have banged their faces together before they saw one another. And from the ditch there had come a continuous scrabbling and splashing and murmuring; a march of vast rats that must surely have been audible from any distance.

But, amazingly, they had made it. And now the British were slumped in the ditch behind and to the right of him, and he was wondering what the bloody hell was happening. He had lain on his belly in the dreadfully empty meadow and flashed the signal across the water. He had estimated that it would take fifteen minutes for the assault boats to cross the river; twenty-five had passed now and there was neither sign nor sound of them. He had moved a short distance westwards because the current ran that way and the boats might have drifted; he had stumbled against the stump of a wall, the remains of some small waterside building, and stayed there in its ruins. The river mist seemed to contain some sort of light within itself, because he could distinguish it from the surrounding night; but both were impenetrable. Rigid with anxiety, he repeated the signal, knowing that the timetable was unravelling. The English major might come wandering along, like a schoolmaster wondering what his boys were up to. Banjo might take it into his head to come down. The British soldiers, lying bruised and wet and lost in a drain, might do anything. Shit! Where were the boats?

He heard them before he saw them. A faint splash like a rising fish, and then another. Peering forward, he saw patches of darkness take shape in the mist. He moved out of the ruins and went towards where they might land. He heard a louder splash, and then a man was standing blackly in front of him. A suppressed voice, English.

"Hello? Ride across the river?"

Tamar tried to speak, but found that his tongue was stuck to the roof of his mouth. He sorted himself out and said, "Wait. Hold on."

He turned and Morsed the torch towards the ditch. Nothing happened at first, and then he heard a whispering that paused and resumed and then became a continuous rhythmic noise. A column of amorphous shapes appeared and grew in the darkness, and the whispering became the sound of men moving steadily through long wet grass.

The invisible man who stood beside him said, "Brilliant job, son. Ruddy brilliant. Thought we'd seen the last of these blokes. You all right for fags?"

* * *

152

In the hidden room at the Mendlo asylum, Dart paced back and forth between the couch and the blacked-out window. He stopped to check that the equipment was ready, despite knowing that it was. He broke open the Smith and Wesson revolver and removed the cartridges, turned them in his fingers and put them back again. He adjusted slightly the positions of the notepad and pencil. He sat on his chair and fingered the precise spot on his cheek where Marijke had kissed him goodbye, and carefully recreated the precise texture of her lips. He paused, frozen, when he could not remember if she'd had her eyes closed at that moment or not. The fact that he could not remember suddenly depressed him. He felt so tired and so incredibly bored that the effort of staying in the tiny room almost overwhelmed him. He went to the couch and opened the medical bag. He spilled the Benzedrine tablets onto the desk next to the transceiver and counted them, twice. There were seventy-two, and he wondered why. Because it was six dozen, of course. The bloody British, he thought, with their dozens and feet and inches and pounds and ounces and their twelve pence to the shilling and twenty shillings to the pound. Always out of step. Always in some awkward world of their own. He poured some water from the jug into the stained cup and washed two of the pills down his throat. It couldn't do any harm.

She would be asleep now. In a nightgown, nightshirt, her underwear? Curled into herself? Sprawled on her back? He sat down again and lit another cigarette. Twenty-three minutes before he could lose himself in the hiss and warble that the headphones would feed into his head. He perched the cigarette on the base of the oil lamp and felt inside the lining of his coat for the slithery sheets of code.

THERE WERE PLENTY of people in the beautiful and damaged medieval town of Deventer who deeply disliked Ruud van der Spil. On the face of it, they had good reason to. Not only was he an outsider, an Amsterdammer, but he was prospering. His bar, the Village Constable, was the only one still open for business in November 1944; and business, for Ruud, was good. Famished townspeople trudging home through the rain and early darkness were enraged by the piano music and the incredible aromas – frying pork chops, schnitzel, garlic, beer, coffee – that drifted out into the night air.

Ruud was doing good business because he was doing Nazi business. His bar faced the town hall on the opposite side of the wide expanse of the marketplace, and the town hall was the headquarters of the Nazi Party for the province. It was also the regional office of the Gestapo. Ruud's customers were almost exclusively German officers. After a hard day's work at the office or in the interrogation cells, they liked nothing better than to stroll across the square to unwind in the Village Constable. They liked the loose talk and the clatter of plates and the pools of candlelight inside the wreaths of smoke. They liked the food and the two big-breasted girls who served it. In fact, they liked the place so much that Ruud hadn't had an evening off for two and a half years. There were people in the town who wondered why the resistance didn't put a bullet through his head.

These people didn't know that Ruud was the source of the mysterious food parcels that were delivered each week to the *hofje*, the almshouse for old people. They did not know that he was the anonymous provider of the gifts of money that had kept a dozen fatherless families alive for the past several months. They had no idea that the bar's profits also financed the underground newspaper *Truth*. And they would have been astonished if they'd known that the paper was produced in Ruud's cellar, a mere hundred and twenty metres from the town hall.

"The thing about the Nazis," Ruud said, "is that they're paranoid, but they never see what's right under their noses. If they did, Hitler wouldn't wear that bloody silly little moustache."

"But what about the noise?" Tamar said. "When you're actually printing, I mean."

The two men were in the Village Constable's narrow kitchen, Tamar clutching a mug of coffee and shivering slightly in his wet clothes.

"It's not that loud," Ruud said. "It's a pretty small machine, and it's in good nick. It's right at the back of the cellar, and we've built a wall of crates and blankets around it. We used to run it in the mornings, but that was too risky. So now we do it late at night."

"What, while you're still open? When the Germans are up here?"

"Yeah. Three quarters of them are drunk as skunks by ten o'clock. I make sure of that. They make a hell of a noise, banging away at the piano and singing. That's when we run the press. You know that damned Horst Wessel Song they love? We can print fifty copies while they blubber their way through that one. Here, let me top up your coffee and we'll go down."

At the foot of the cellar steps, Ruud tugged at a dangling string and a bare electric bulb lit up. "Hey, how about that? Your luck's in. The power is on."

He led Tamar over to an ink-stained table. A metal-shaded lamp was clamped to it. It too lit up when Ruud tried the switch. "Incredible," he said. "It won't last, though. Candles and matches in the drawer over there. Paper and pencils too. Now, is this okay for you? I assume you know what you're going to write."

"More or less. When are you printing the next edition?"

"Depends. There's an old guy comes in lunchtimes, supposed to be the cleaner. He used to be a printer before the war. So I clean the place while he's down here setting up the type. If he can do it all today, we'll run it tonight. Write nice and clearly, by the way. His eyesight's not what it was. Now, how about some breakfast? Bread, eggs, sausage?"

"God, yes."

"I'll bring it down. Ten minutes."

Tamar sat and considered his task. He and Dart – and Marijke and Trixie – had worked on the article throughout the previous afternoon, and he had the text in his head. More or less. Dart had brought with him the latest signals from London and Delta Centrum. They weren't surprising, but they were shocking. Berlin's latest tactic was Nazism of the purest kind: logical, ambitious and insane. No longer content with rounding up a thousand here, a thousand there, they were going to eliminate working men from Holland entirely. The plan had the darkly poetic name of Operation Rosebranch. It worked in two ways.

First, posters went up all over towns and cities inviting volunteers to become "honoured guest workers in the

Reich". Such guest workers would be comfortably housed and well fed. In addition, their families in Holland would get preferential treatment: extra rations, winter clothing and coal, as well as half the workers' wages. A surprising number of men had volunteered. Tamar's article in *Truth* was going to be a passionate plea for others not to do the same thing.

"How can they be so bloody stupid?" Dart had asked. He'd brought with him an abridged version of a report by a Dutch clergyman who had somehow managed to talk his way into a guest workers' hostel just across the German border. The priest had found an unheated wooden shed in which two hundred and fifty men were dying of hypothermia, starvation and dysentery, lying in their own shit and vomit.

"It's not just stupidity," Trixie'd said. "People are desperate for something to hope for."

"Same thing," Dart had said.

Trixie had gazed up at him for a second or two, then said, "And not only that. A lot of these people have nowhere left to hide. Maybe they'd rather go voluntarily than be forced. Or shot."

Because that was the second phase of Operation Rosebranch. If there was an unsatisfactory response to the poster campaign, the SS would drag ten, twenty, thirty men from their homes and shoot them dead in front of their families. To encourage the others. It worked. Three and a half thousand men had been taken from Hilversum on 24th October. A fortnight later, fifty thousand – fifty, dear God – from Rotterdam. So there were three options: go, hide, die. Tamar's task was to persuade the readers of *Truth* to go for the second of these options.

Ruud came down the steps with a tray. He set it down on the table, glancing at what Tamar had written: a single sentence, crossed out. "Having trouble?"

Tamar sighed. "The first words are always hardest."

"Last words can be a bugger too," Ruud said. "Anyway, *bon appétit.*"

"Thanks, Ruud. This looks fantastic." Tamar looked up and forced a smile. "By the way, does *Truth* have a crossword?"

When Rosa was settled, Marijke said, "Is Ernst all right, do you think?"

"I doubt it," Trixie said. "He lives with old Dr Veening, six nuns and two dozen head cases in a place that gives you the creeps just looking at it. He's up half the night, most nights, with his head plugged into a radio set. He smokes too much; he doesn't get enough to eat. He's got nowhere to go except Pieter and Bibi's, and if he gets there safely he goes up into the roof and wonders if German detector cars are closing in on him. No, I shouldn't think he's all right."

"He comes here too."

"Yes, he comes here too. He comes on the bike in the rain with his arse clenched tight because he's scared. I know, because I do the same thing. And when he gets here, you send him to the barn."

"I don't send him to the barn, Trixie. He has to go there."

"You send him before you need to, and you know why. You've seen the way he looks at you."

"Trixie!"

"Come on, Marijke. Don't give me that."

"Okay, so he's lonely. Doesn't he look at you in the same way?"

"No," Trixie said, "he doesn't."

"Would you like him to?"

"I wouldn't mind." Trixie smiled. "He's quite good-looking, don't you think?"

Marijke shrugged.

"Of course you do," Trixie said. "Him and Christiaan, they look a lot like each other."

"I don't think so."

"I do."

For a short while there were only soft sounds in the kitchen: the clock's slow, dull tock, Rosa's breathing, the rain on the window.

Trixie said, "When's he next coming here? Day after tomorrow, isn't it?"

"Er, yes. I think so."

"He'll be soaked again, if it stays like this. Have you got any spare clothes you could dig out for him, so he could change into something dry?"

It was as if Marijke hadn't heard; then after a moment or two she said, "Some of Opa's old things might fit him. I suppose I should have thought of that, shouldn't I?"

Trixie shrugged. A heavier blast of rain drummed against the window. "He still doesn't know, does he?"

"Who doesn't know what?"

"Oh, Marijke, please. You know what I mean. Ernst still doesn't know about you and Christiaan."

Marijke looked away. "No. He doesn't."

Trixie shook her head. "You can say it's none of my business, if you like, but—"

"It's none of your business."

"But I think it's weird. Nuts. I mean, why hasn't Christiaan said anything? Is it against some sort of regulation, what you two are doing? Is he afraid that London would recall him if they found out?"

"I don't think so. It's not that, anyway. I think Christiaan thinks it would … get in the way."

Trixie wondered what that was supposed to mean, exactly. But she didn't ask. Instead she said, "It's not fair, though, is it?"

"Fair?"

"On Ernst. It's not fair, keeping him in the dark. Maybe I should tell him."

Marijke leaned forward. "No. You mustn't. Please."

"But—"

"I'll talk to Christiaan about it again. Please don't say anything. Not yet."

"Suit yourself," Trixie said. "But Ernst isn't stupid. He'll realize sooner or later, assuming…" She shut up, shocked that she had been about to say what should never be said. She couldn't meet her friend's eyes.

Marijke said, "Assuming they live long enough? That's what you were going to say, isn't it?" She said it quietly, flatly.

"Marijke, I—"

"It's all right. It's what we all think, anyway. It's what we never stop thinking about."

Trixie stood up and went to the window. "This bloody rain," she said. "We're going to get soaked going home."

"Why don't you stay here tonight? It would be better for Rosa." Marijke went over to Trixie and stood beside her. Seen through the streaming glass, the world outside looked warped and molten. "I'd like you to stay. I've started feeling lonely again since Christiaan came back. Doesn't make sense, does it?"

Tamar put the pencil down and read through yet again what he'd written. The passion in it, the anger, still had a hollow ring. He'd told the paper's secret readers that Operation Rosebranch was an attempt by the Germans to depopulate the Netherlands. That the Nazis, knowing defeat was inevitable, intended to leave the country crippled and castrated. He had described in brutal detail the conditions in which men who had already gone had lived and died. The promises made to guest workers and their families were a cruel ruse, an evil deception. He had repeated the pleas for non-cooperation broadcast by the Dutch government in exile. He had reminded his fellow countrymen – Dart had insisted on this bit – that volunteering to work for the Third Reich was a form of collaboration.

Tough stuff, straight stuff. But it was hopeless. It was literally hopeless; there was no hope in it. The people who read his words would hear the emptiness inside them. The choices they faced were equally deadly: go and die; resist and die; or hide, dive. And dive into what? A black and bottomless well. A night sky, without a parachute.

He sighed and added a last sentence: *Do not doubt for an instant that the hour of our deliverance is at hand.*

DART HAD NOT been told – and would not have believed – that it is possible to live in a state of constant fear and be bored at the same time. Boredom had not been among the dangers that the SOE had prepared him for. No pompous little officer had stood in front of his class and said, "Right, chaps, today we're going to learn how to deal with a particularly nasty little situation that secret agents tend to find themselves in: being bored abso-bloody-lutely rigid." It seemed to Dart this had been a serious gap in his training, because by the end of November boredom had spread a grey slime on his brain and on his soul.

He'd recognized the early symptoms: a tendency for his attention to wander when Albert or Agatha spoke to him; bouts of tiredness that had nothing to do with his lack of sleep; finding himself in a room unable to remember why he'd gone there. He knew this was dangerous. His own life, and the lives of others, depended on his nerves being as alert as the trigger hairs on a flea; but the sheer awful dullness of his everyday life was beginning to blunt and numb them.

There wasn't much he could contribute to the work of the asylum. His aborted medical training was almost irrelevant. The lunatics didn't know him or trust him, and trust was all that Albert and his staff had left to work with. So Dart stayed out of the way, or reduced himself to a fleeting, smiling presence, like a well-meaning ghost harmlessly haunting the endless corridors. He began helping Agatha and the other sisters with the work in the garden, but the ceaseless November rain soon made even that pointless.

He saw little of the dwindling winter daylight. At the end of his nocturnal radio watches he'd slip quietly back to his room through the dark murmuring house. Often, though, the steadily increasing doses of amphetamine that had sustained him through the night would still be working in him. At such times, he'd lie stubbornly rigid in his narrow bed, thinking of Marijke and trying to force her into his dreams. Then he'd awake to the terrible clamour of the alarm clock, and groggily prepare himself for a transmission or a visit from Trixie.

And all of this took place against a background of hunger, of an incessant obsession with food, food, food. Dart had discovered that a welcome side effect of Benzedrine was loss of appetite; but when its effects wore off the need to eat was sharper than ever. And the constant talk of food, of remembered meals, of fantasy meals, sometimes made the lust for it unbearable. Each day, two of the sisters gathered up the ration books and set off for town. They returned hours later with pathetic bags of mouldy vegetables, sticky grey bread, sometimes a small chunk of greasy belly pork. And the occasional horror story.

Sister Angelica said, "You know Paul Kloos, the carter? His horse died in the street, the poor old thing."

"Paul or the horse?" Albert asked.

"I beg your pardon, Doctor?"

"You said 'poor old thing', and I wondered... Never mind, Sister. What happened?"

"Well, Mr Kloos went off home to get help to carry the horse away, and when he got back..." Tears filmed the young nun's eyes. "When he got back, the meat had been cut off both the poor creature's back legs."

Albert slurped thin soup from his spoon. "There can't have been much of it," he said. "It's the only horse in town the Germans didn't bother to take."

"I was talking to Father Willem," Sister Hendrika said, "and he told me that two days ago the police were called to a house on Rose Street because the neighbours reported a terrible smell. When they went in they found that the woman's husband had died two months ago, but she'd kept the body in the back room because she was still using his ration book. She needed to, because her son-in-law was hiding in the cellar."

The sisters shuddered and crossed themselves. Dart lost interest in the soup.

Dart's trips to the Marionette House did little to lift his apathy. Just as Trixie had predicted, the guards at the Merchants' Gate checkpoint paid him less and less attention. Now, when he wheeled Bibi's heavy bike towards the barrier, the Germans didn't even leave the shelter of the archway. They stood, shapeless in their grey rain capes, and watched him struggle through the gap. They gestured dismissively if he bothered to fumble for his forged papers, and Dart would plod past without even giving them a sideways glance. They had become as much a part of his routine as he had become a part of theirs. When he thought about it at all, Dart marvelled at the memory of the terror he'd felt on that first occasion, how he'd almost fainted with fear as he'd approached the gate. Sometimes the contrast between how he felt now and how he'd felt then filled him with unease and he would lecture himself sternly on the dangers of complacency. But then the grey wet tedium of his life would overwhelm him once again. Until the next time he saw Marijke.

In reality, Sanctuary Farm was no less bleak than anywhere else. Like its neighbouring farms, it was beginning to resemble a brick island in a sea of mud, and the dimly lit kitchen was the only warm room in the whole gloomy place. In Dart's mind, though, Sanctuary was a magically bright oasis in a dismal wasteland. The ordeal of getting there only intensified the pleasure of arriving. Tamar had forbidden the use of the ambulance; there were now only ten litres of petrol concealed at the asylum, and they needed to be hoarded, in case of an emergency, until more could be stolen. So there was no option but to take the pushbike. The old waxed-canvas cape that Albert had given Dart was little protection against heavy rain driven at him by the easterly wind. He'd had to learn the trick of withdrawing into himself, of turning his body into a blind unfeeling machine that drove the cycle onwards. He would force himself to remain this numb thing until the moment Marijke opened the door to him and brushed his cheeks with her lips. Only then would he allow himself to feel the aching cold in his body, because it no longer mattered and because she might take pity on him.

On one particularly filthy day, she'd found him a set of dry clothes to change into. It was a small thing, a natural thing, to have done, but he was deeply touched that she'd thought of it. He stripped off in the wash-house and put on the heavy old work trousers and the polo-neck sweater. Marijke took his wet clothes and spread them on a clothes horse by the stove so that they would be dry by the time he left. This became a little ritual throughout those wet weeks, and the kindness of it made him almost dizzy. Putting on these other clothes made him feel that he was discarding one life – a false one, in which he had to wear a disguise – for another that was more real, more truthful.

Dart struggled to deny it, but he was glad that Tamar was away for much of this time. When they were both there, Marijke was definitely a little – what was it – edgy? Detached, somehow. That was understandable. After all, he and Tamar had business that often excluded her. And if Germans scavenging for food happened to turn up, having them both there would be hard to explain.

But there was more to it than that; he was increasingly sure of it. There could be no doubt that Marijke's behaviour towards him had changed during November. He was not imagining it. She was warmer, more attentive. As well as the dry clothes, there were other small but exhilarating developments. When he arrived, she no longer made him something to drink and then went on with what she was doing. Now she sat with him and smiled at his stories about life at the madhouse or the details of Bibi's latest dream menu. She was concerned that he was not eating enough, and always made sure there was something warm for him before he set off on the grim journey back. And once, when Trixie was there, he'd seen the two of them exchanging sly girlish looks when they thought he wasn't watching. There was no doubt that those looks had to do with him. He'd examined his memory of that brief moment over and over again, and he was sure. It had made his heart lurch. So it was not difficult to understand why there was a certain awkwardness when Tamar was there. She wouldn't want to make the other man feel envious. She was far too kind.

Late in the morning of 6th December, in his bedroom at the asylum, Dart jolted awake from a Benzedrine nightmare in which large spiders with glass legs were walking on his face. The first thing he saw was Tamar grinning down at him. When the panic had subsided, Dart understood that the brittle jangling of the spiders' legs had not been part of the dream.

Tamar was clinking together two small glasses which he held nipped in the fingers of one hand. His face was dark with stubble that folded into creases when he spoke.

"Happy *Sinterklaas*, my friend."

Dart licked his dry lips but was unable to speak straight away. He watched Tamar sit down at the foot of the bed and produce from inside his coat a slender-necked bottle of amber liquid.

"What's that?"

"Only the finest French cognac that money can't buy."

"Bloody hell. Where did you get that?"

"It's a St Nicholas's Day present from our friend in Deventer. I just got back from there."

Dart yawned and rubbed his face. "Oh, right. You were over there again, weren't you? I forgot. How is Ruud?"

"Splendid."

Tamar twisted the cork from the bottle and filled the two glasses. "Cheers," he said in English.

"Christ, wait a minute."

Dart groped on the floor beside the bed until he found a mug of water. He drank two big mouthfuls and put the mug down again. Then he chinked his glass against Tamar's and took a swig. His mouth filled with fire and honey.

"My God," he said, when he could speak.

Tamar grinned. "Now, tell me the truth. Isn't that the best cognac you've ever tasted?"

Dart thought about it while his chest filled with mellow heat. It seemed to shove the hunger down a level. "I think it's the *only* cognac I've ever tasted," he said.

Tamar laughed and leaned back against the iron foot rail of the bed. He sipped from his glass and studied Dart's face. "You look like you needed it," he said. "You look rough, if you don't mind my saying so. Have you been sleeping okay?"

Dart shrugged. "Now and again."

"What about eating?"

"Now and again. But don't talk about food, please."

"Sorry," Tamar said, "but that's exactly what I'm going to do. No, wait – were there any signals last night that I should know about?"

"Loads. But nothing top priority."

"Good." Tamar drained his glass, murmuring with pleasure. Then he lifted his left foot onto the bed and began to unlace his boot.

Dart said, "Is it really *Sinterklaas* today?"

"Yep. Not that you'd know it. I imagine if St Nicholas did try to ride that white horse of his across the sky last night he'd have been blasted to bits by German anti-aircraft fire."

Tamar grunted as the boot came off. He stuck his hand into it and pulled out the inner sole and the folded sheet of paper that he'd concealed beneath it.

"You know how British children write letters to Santa Claus telling him what they want for Christmas? Well, this is our letter to Santa. Except that our Santa is in London, not the North Pole."

Dart took the paper. It was covered with Tamar's tiny fastidious handwriting. The lines of items were separated by angled pencil strokes followed by three-letter groups that Dart recognized as the codes for local resistance organizations. He scanned the list. There were, at a quick guess, two hundred requests. Of these, there were less than a dozen asking Santa for plastic explosives, ammunition, weapons and radio equipment. All the rest were for basic food items, in very large amounts, and medicines.

Tamar said, "I had to bang a few heads together, but I've persuaded our bickering colleagues that staying alive is a fairly important part of the resistance effort. Even the hard cases like Jaap Smedts are having to admit that right now the greatest enemy we face is starvation. That tough bitch

Lydia from the KP, bless her, backed me up by pointing out that the Germans are using starvation as a weapon, and that's the way we need to look at it, as something we have to fight. So we've agreed – no more offensive actions until the new year, then we'll review the situation. Instead, we'll use all networks for food distribution. We've even agreed on where to store stuff in each area."

He refilled his glass and topped up Dart's. "Aren't you impressed?"

"Er … yes. Yes, of course. Well done. What did Koop de Vries have to say about all this?"

"He wasn't there, the awkward bastard. He'll fall into line when he finds out that everyone else has. Cheers. Oh, and it's stopped raining, by the way."

Dart scanned Tamar's list again. "This is a lot of stuff. It'll be a big drop."

"I know. We need to think about how we do it. That's one of the reasons I'm here."

"Do you think London will agree to all this? What if they say no?"

"You and I are going to send a signal they won't be able to argue with. For a start, it'll ask for twice this amount. I reckon they'll feel obliged to send us at least half. You know how sentimental the Brits are about Christmas. So come on, you lazy sod, get your trousers on and we'll go to your hidey-hole and write it. And we'll add a few treats for ourselves while we're at it. I reckon we deserve it, don't you?"

Two days before the Christmas drop, Dart began work on the ambulance. It took half an hour of stomping on a leaky foot pump to get the threadbare tyres up to an acceptable pressure. The battery was flat, so he'd spent more than an hour in the hidden room pedalling the recharger, reflecting bitterly that if he'd been on the bike, the same amount of effort would have taken him to Marijke. It was not surprising that after five weeks of almost continuous rain the distributor and the HT leads were wet. Drying them with rags didn't work, and he had to put them in the slow oven in the asylum kitchen. Later he had to do the same thing with the spark plugs, after he'd spent an hour getting the damn things free of the engine block and ripping two knuckles in the process. And after all that the engine still wouldn't start.

Dart had been shocked when Tamar told him he would be taking the ambulance to the dropping zone. It was almost unheard of for WOs to be used in operations of this sort. But, as Tamar pointed out, getting eighteen containers sorted and transported to five different distribution points would require every vehicle they could lay their hands on. It would be the biggest drop ever made into this zone.

"Why aren't *you* taking the ambulance?" Dart tried to make the question sound like a simple request for information.

"Because I'll already be there."

"Oh, right. But look, I don't know the roads."

Tamar said, "That's why you're going to have Sister Agatha riding shotgun."

"What?"

"Agatha knows the area as well as anyone. You'll be fine with her."

"But—"

"But what?"

"Well, you know. Sister Agatha isn't … she isn't supposed to be involved in this. In what we do. Is she?"

Tamar considered the question. Then he said, "Would you like to be the one who tells her what she is and isn't supposed to do?"

"Lord, no."

"Very well, then. Now, if you get stopped on the way there, you say you're on a mercy dash somewhere. You can sort out the story between yourselves. Make sure you're wearing your white coat, by the way. And bring your bag."

Dart lit a cigarette.

"When you get to the DZ, you and Agatha wait with the vehicles. Jaap Smedts's guys will be guarding them. When the reception committee has sorted the containers, we load the stuff for the asylum and the farm into the ambulance and spread a mattress over it. I get in, lie on the mattress and cover myself with a couple of blankets. I figure there's less than a one in twenty chance of us running into a checkpoint, the route we're taking. But if we do, you say you've got a patient in the back suffering from typhoid fever and you're rushing him to an isolation ward here. Tell the Germans they're welcome to check me over, but they'll need to mask their faces. Ask them if they're sure they've got access to vaccine back at their barracks, because they'll need a jab if they get close to me."

Dart tried to imagine this scenario acted out on a dark road with German machine guns pointed at his head.

"And if they don't buy it? If they decide to search us?"

"Then I'll have to shoot them."

Dart went to the small window in the wireless room and stared at the low moody sky, smoking.

"Okay?" Tamar said.

"Yes. I don't know. Christ."

Tamar looked at his friend's back for a moment or two, then said, "Another good reason for Agatha going with you is that there are Germans who are still reluctant to shoot nuns. Maybe even some who think nuns don't tell lies."

Now, leaning on the bonnet of the stubborn ambulance, Dart realized that Tamar must have discussed this lunatic scheme with Albert and Agatha before he'd discussed it with him. And that was wrong, absolutely out of order. The bastard. He slotted the crank handle through the gap in the radiator grille and heaved again. And again. Bastard!

DURING THE NIGHT the wind had swung from west to north. The morning was bright and bitingly cold; the puddles in the yard and the water in the fields glittered like shards of glass. Marijke was alone. Tamar had left for the dropping zone at daybreak. Her grandmother was still in the village of Loenen, where her cousin's daughter was recovering from the difficult birth of a son. Marijke had nursed the stove back to life with tiny doses of wood, then gone out to see if any of the chickens had managed to produce an egg. Halfway to the barn she stopped, somehow aware that she was being watched. She felt the usual flash of fear, then turned.

A woman and a child stood motionless where the track from the road came into the yard. Marijke's first thought was that they were ghosts. They were colourless, as if they had leaked all their blood. Their hair did not move in the wind. Their faces were all bones. The boy had what looked like a threadbare rug wrapped around his shoulders; the woman was supporting a bike with a warped front wheel that had no tyre.

"Can I help you?" Marijke said, and instantly felt absurd because it was something that a hotel receptionist might say.

The boy looked up at the woman as if expecting her to say something. When she didn't, he looked back at Marijke. "Please. We have a good watch. We need some food to take home."

She took them into the kitchen and the woman started to lose consciousness just inside the door, perhaps because the room was a few degrees warmer. Marijke grabbed her by the slack of her coat as she fell and managed to get her to the sagging armchair by the stove, where she slumped with her eyes closed.

The child said, "Is she dead?"

"No. Your mummy isn't dead. She's just fainted."

"She's not my mum," the child said. "I think she's my aunt."

Marijke slid the heavy kettle onto the hotplate. The woman did, in fact, look like a corpse, and Marijke felt panic rise inside her body. She turned to the boy. "You look terribly cold. Take those wet clothes off and stand close to the stove." She lifted the rug off him, but the child didn't move. She went to the cupboard and found a tablecloth. "Here. Wrap this around yourself."

Still the child didn't move. Marijke draped the tablecloth around him then reached beneath it and pulled the pathetic wet clothes off. They were, she realized, the remains of a school uniform. She hung them on the stove rail, wondering about lice. The boy stank like a rats' nest. Marijke made weak tea and poured two cups, adding a spoonful of precious sugar to each. The boy's eyes never left her. They were sunk deep in his face, like two black marbles pressed into putty.

"Have you come far?" she asked him.

He seemed to find the question difficult, so she said, "Where are you from?"

The woman spoke for the first time. "Utrecht." The word was a faint murmur.

"*Utrecht?* You've walked here from Utrecht? Dear God. How long has it taken you?"

The woman struggled to sit upright. She wrapped her hands around the cup that Marijke held out to her. "We left three days ago. Things are very bad there."

"Yes," Marijke said, "I've heard. But to have come so far…"

"There are so many of us on the roads now," the woman told her. "From Amsterdam, Rotterdam, everywhere. The farmers say they have nothing left to give us. Some of them chase us away. We have to go further and further each time."

"You've done this before?"

"Yes. We have to. We have extra people to feed." The woman had shocked herself. She shouldn't have said that. "I mean we have relatives staying," she said hurriedly. "Not, I mean…"

Marijke put a hand on the woman's arm. "It's all right. I understand."

"The tea was nice," the boy said. Wrapped in the white tablecloth, holding the cup in both hands, he looked like a shrunken priest.

Marijke filled their cups again, and when she turned back from the stove the woman had produced a man's pocket watch from somewhere inside her clothes.

"It's a good one," she said. "Real silver, the chain as well. It was my father's. Please."

Marijke could not meet the woman's eyes. "Oh, no, no. I couldn't. I don't need—"

The woman made sounds like a wounded dog. She seized Marijke's wrist and tried to stuff the watch into her hand. "Please, please. It's all we have left. We'll take anything, anything, won't we, Anton?"

The boy turned his face away.

Marijke closed the woman's hands around the watch. "No, listen. Please hush. Don't cry. I will give you something. Please stop crying. What I mean is I don't want your father's watch. Keep it."

The woman wiped her face with the wet cuff of her coat sleeve. "I'm sorry."

"It's all right. It's all right."

"No, I'm sorry, I'm sorry. It's just… I can't go back empty-handed. You've no idea how they'll look at me. I can't face it."

"When did you last eat?"

"Yesterday. A woman in a cottage gave us some boiled potatoes. There weren't enough to take home. We had to eat them all. We had to keep going."

Marijke melted a few chunks of pork fat in the skillet, then washed and sliced two potatoes and fried them with an onion. She couldn't watch them eat; it was too desperate. She went upstairs to the closet and dug out a woollen cardigan, a sweater, two pairs of socks and a heavy tweed jacket that had belonged to her grandfather. She had nothing that could replace the wretched shoes.

She returned to the kitchen to find the hunger trippers wiping the fat from the skillet with the crusts of their bread. She went down to the cellar and brought up a jar of bottled plums; the woman and the boy stared at them as if they were fat rubies looted from some fabulous treasury. When the boy had eaten his plums, he put the stones back in his mouth and sucked them. Later, when he was dressed, he took the stones from his mouth and put them in the pocket of the tweed jacket, which came down below his knees.

The woman and the child left the farm carrying unimaginable riches: a cabbage, a chunk of bacon, a bag of flour, four eggs, several potatoes and a few beetroot. And bread and cheese for the journey. The woman had asked for the bacon to be cut into several small pieces.

"If the Germans stop us," she said, "we will give them one piece. They will not think that we could have more." By then she had recovered some of her dignity. "I want you to have the watch. It is the difference between trading and begging."

Marijke shook her head. "No. And you are not beggars. I cannot believe your courage; I wish I had half as much."

"Then I will pray for you."

"Thank you. I may well need it."

She walked with them up to the road. The woman, and then the boy, shook her hand very formally.

"Look," Marijke said, "I, er, I don't know exactly how to say this, but…"

In fact, she knew exactly how to say it: by the way, this farm is the operations centre for the local resistance; my lover runs it from here; there is a wireless station in the barn; there are British guns in the house; and no matter how calm I seem I am shit-scared most of the time.

"Others, others like you. You won't tell them, will you? It's not that I don't want to help, but… It's difficult, people coming here. Do you understand?"

They looked at her with expressionless faces. Then the woman forced a smile. "Of course. I doubt I could tell any-one how to find you anyway. It's the back of beyond, this place."

Marijke stood and watched them walk away until they were lost in the broken shadows of the winter trees. She never saw them again.

Marijke fought off sleep for most of that night. She was very afraid that her dreams might be even more terrible than the black bubbles of anxiety that rose in her chest. Whenever she began to drift, unbearable images, like clips from silent horror movies, flashed into her head. Tamar caught exposed at the dropping zone, his face lit white by German torches. Tamar torn by bullets, waiting to die in a ditch. Tamar's body burning in the fiery skeleton of a car.

When at last she did fall asleep, she dreamed none of these things. She dreamed she was the starving woman from Utrecht, walking slowly and peaceably across a vast field of snow. The boy with her was her son. She knew this even though the child was so swathed in blankets that his face was invisible. Occasionally she would look back and see that their footprints had disappeared, although no snow was falling. They arrived at the gates of a great city of brightly lit towers and warm busy streets. The houses had windows of richly coloured glass. She turned to the child beside her and began to unwrap him, pulling away blanket after blanket; but when the last one dropped onto the snow there was no one and nothing inside it. She looked up and saw a crowd of people standing just inside the gates, watching her with expressionless faces.

Shortly after nine o'clock the following morning she heard the distant growl of a motor. She went to the chest under the window and took out the Sten. Then she ran to the dairy and pulled back the sacking curtain from the window. When the asylum ambulance jolted into view, she leaned her forehead against the cold wall and let out her breath.

She went outside, shouldering the gun. Dart was driving, with Trixie beside him holding Rosa on her lap. As soon as he saw her, Dart brought the ambulance to a stop and stumbled out, mimicking an old man with a bad back.

"God," he said, "they call this an ambulance, but driving it is enough to kill you."

She managed a smile for him, but her eyes were on the back of the ambulance, which was shifting and creaking on its ancient springs. When she saw Tamar's legs swing out, she felt a melting surge of relief and her smile became genuine. He was wearing a green knitted cap, its crown tweaked into a point. For a beard, he'd slit open a field dressing and teased out the white cotton wadding, then tied it around his chin. She laughed aloud because it was the worst *Sinterklaas* costume she'd ever seen. He cradled a number of packages in his arms.

"Ho ho ho!" he said. "Merry bloody Christmas! Now, feed that stove, Miss Maartens. We're starving."

During the night before Christmas Eve, winter took hold of Holland and clenched its fist. All slow water froze, and the naked trees groaned beneath their sudden heavy coats of ice. Marijke turned in her sleep, pressing herself against Tamar's back, shaping the angle of her legs to match his, seeking his warmth. When she opened her eyes she saw fern-like growths of thick frost on the inside of the window.

Later, when she and Tamar went out into the yard, the mud had solidified into frost-capped peaks and ripples that looked like mountain ranges seen from the cockpit of an aircraft. The black barbs of the hawthorn hedge were encased in melted glass. The world had become so silent and brittle that it seemed dangerous to speak. Then the chickens exploded from under the barn door, gabbling their outrage at this turn of events.

Tamar was happy. Incredible riches had fallen from the sky because he had summoned them. There had been every chance that he would die trying to gather them in, but he was alive and had returned to where his life was. This new harshness of the weather would make his work more diffi-cult, but with any luck it would hamper the German forces even more. They were pitiless and heavily armoured, but they were far from home and must by now smell defeat on the freezing air, like dinosaurs at the beginning of the ice age. He took the saw and the axe and attacked the heap of stumps and branches stacked to dry in the big barn. When he heaved the loaded wheelbarrow over to the kitchen, it jolted so heavily on the frozen ground that his teeth clacked.

Later in the morning, Marijke called him, urgently. She had already set off along the track to meet her grandmother. The old woman was a dark humped shape supporting itself on a staff; she looked like a tragic character from an ancient tale. She moved slowly and cautiously over the frozen ground. When they reached her and took her arms, she nodded her head but was too exhausted to smile. Tamar saw that where her grey hair was not covered by the woollen scarf it was filmed with ice and resembled twists of steel. She had obviously fallen at least once; the skirts of her coat were soiled down one side. He was awed by her obstinate strength, her endurance.

When they got her into the kitchen, she was too cold to sit. She leaned with her arms braced on the stove rail, glassy-eyed and breathing like an exhausted swimmer. After a while Tamar was able to lift the old haversack from her back and manoeuvre her into the armchair. Marijke made tea and kneeled in front of her grandmother.

"It's real tea, Oma, with sugar. Christiaan got it for us, and lots of other things too. We're going to be all right now. Really."

The old woman took the cup. Her fingertips were white. She looked over at Tamar. There was a blankness in her eyes, almost a lack of recognition, that disturbed him.

Marijke said, "Oma, how are things at Loenen? How are Greet and the baby?"

Julia stared into her cup, then slowly shook her head.

*　*　*

Dart had become so unused to good feelings that he'd acquired the habit of examining them like a careful shop-keeper who'd been paid with a big banknote. Test the paper between the fingers. Hold it up to the light. Squint at the customer, looking for the slightest flicker of dishonesty. But on this bitterly cold Christmas Eve afternoon the happiness was genuine.

He had survived the dreadful night of the supply drop. It had probably been a mistake to take the last of the Benzedrine before they set out, because his nerves had fizzed and popped all night like a severed power cable on a wet road. On the other hand, he had not experienced a single moment of tiredness or loss of concentration. And the two bottles of pills he'd requested had been sent, to his enormous relief. Agatha had interpreted his drug-sparked chatter as an attempt to put her at her ease. At the asylum they'd staggered out of the heavily laden ambulance and she'd embraced and kissed him, which was startling. When they'd carried in the sacks of flour and milk powder, the cans of meat and treacle and jam, the coffee, tea, sugar, he'd been greeted like a hero. In the shadowy kitchen the nuns had fluttered and pounced like magpies at a road-killed rabbit.

But all of this counted for nothing compared with their arrival at Sanctuary Farm. Marijke had been standing there to greet them and it had taken all his self-control not to cry out with joy. She'd been dressed in rough working clothes – trousers tucked into heavy boots, a frayed woollen jacket, a dark scarf up to her chin – which had made the lovely symmetry of her face more striking than ever. The Sten gun slung over her shoulder should have been grotesquely out of place. Instead it made her seem both fragile and unconquerable. He would have died to protect her. He'd stumbled out of the ambulance and she'd smiled at him. How to describe that smile? It was shy, almost, and not just private. Secretive.

Then she had been distracted by Tamar's stupid clowning, and the moment had passed. She had embraced them all in turn, saving Dart until last. She'd touched his face and said, "You need a shave." When the time had come for him to leave, she'd groaned sympathetically as his attempts to crank-start the damned ambulance failed; then when it did fire, she'd jumped up and down and clapped her hands in a wonderfully childlike display of delight.

Now, trudging and slithering along the road back to the farm, those hoarded moments of intimacy warmed Dart more than any amount of Ruud's cognac. It was possible to ride the bike for only short distances; in many places the broken road had vanished beneath sheets of muddy ice that creaked and moaned beneath his feet. The air was so cold that when he breathed through his mouth he felt an electrical pain in his teeth. He had shaved, twice, and his face felt peeled. At the burnt-out chapel he propped the bike and ran on the spot until he could feel his feet. His shoes sent ringing echoes into the distance. When he got back on the bike, the metal was so cold to his touch that it seemed to burn.

He was halfway there.

Tamar had been busy. He'd taken a billhook up onto the heath and cut down a small spruce. In the big barn he'd found a rusting oil drum and carried it into the kitchen. He brought in the tree, propped it upright in the oil drum and packed it around with sand and stones until it stood firm. When that was done, he and Marijke herded the chickens into one of the stalls in the little barn. The birds were reluctant and bad-tempered, huffed up against the cold. They formed a suspicious huddle in the corner of the stall, emitting slow, dry gargles. Marijke pointed out the oldest of the hens. Tamar moved in slowly, gently shunting the other birds out of the way with his feet. When he had the old hen penned in the corner, he stooped quickly and thrust her inside his jacket under his left arm. He soothed her by running his thumb and forefinger down her neck and over her shoulders, and when she had become calm he killed her with a quick twist and pull that separated the vertebrae of her neck just below the skull. He hugged her until the reflex spasms finished. While he plucked and gutted the bird, Marijke went back inside the house and rummaged in the cupboard under the stairs until she found the box of decorations for the Christmas tree.

When Dart, perished to the bones, gave his usual knock at the farmhouse door, no one answered. Knowing he was expected, and aching with anticipation, he fumbled at the latch with his numb claws. The door wasn't locked, and he stumbled forward into the dim and silent hall. There was a movement and an increase in light: he looked up and she was descending the stairs holding the tall oil lamp. She stopped when she saw him, four steps from the bottom. She was wearing a green belted dress and a pale cardigan patterned with small dark flowers. It was the first time he had seen her in feminine clothes. Her deep black eyes each reflected a tiny flame. Her hair was loose and a little tousled, as if she had hurried to greet him before she'd finished brushing it. His desire to touch her was so great that before he could stop himself he had held his stiffened hands out towards her. She drew in her breath, a little gasp, and stared at them.

"I..." He could not speak the next words. Instead he looked down at his hands and said, "I am so cold."

She came down to him then. "Dear God, Ernst, you must be frozen. Come into the kitchen."

She moved past him. She was, amazingly, wearing perfume: a warm flowery animal scent that hung almost visible on the cold air.

He followed her and then stopped, his senses overwhelmed, just inside the kitchen door. He had been greedily inhaling Marijke's scent, but now this was obliterated by rich aromas of cooking. The warm air in the room was laden with the smells of meat, of baking apples, of bread, and something he didn't recognize – something spiced and sweet. A delicious spasm of hunger went through him and he had to swallow saliva hurriedly so as not to dribble like a child. The table was laid with the Maartens's best china, each piece rimmed with a narrow band of gold glaze as delicate as lace. At the centre of the table two candles burned in a branched holder wreathed in holly, the berry clusters brighter than droplets of blood. The tree stood at the far end of the room on a chest covered with an old Turkish rug. Its branches were hung with slender twists of glass, like icicles, and frosted red and amber globes that glowed with blurred, reflected flames. To Dart's eyes, still tearful from the cold, the room seemed filled with threads of light like drifting cobwebs spun from gold.

Marijke stood the lamp on the dresser and lifted her arms in a gesture that was almost apologetic. "Happy Christmas, Ernst." She said it in a way that suggested she had done all this only for him, and it was inadequate.

"I don't know what to say," he said. "You… This is all so beautiful. Thank you for inviting me."

"Oh, don't be silly. You had to be here. Take your coat off. Come to the stove and warm yourself up."

They stood side by side. She lifted the lid from the bigger pan. "We're having a sort of British Christmas dinner. I think the chicken should be roasted, but it was an old bird and would have been too tough. So we're stewing it with vegetables and some herbs from the garden. Does that sound all right? It looks all right, I think. It's been cooking for hours."

She spoke more quickly than he was used to. It occurred to him that she might be as nervous as he was.

"It smells incredible," he said.

"Good. And in here, look, is this thing that we found in the supply drop."

She lifted the other lid, releasing a cloud of vapour. Dart peered in and saw something the size of a baby's head wrapped in white cloth.

"Apparently it's a traditional English Christmas pudding. Christiaan says you're supposed to steam it. For ages and ages. It smells nice, though, doesn't it? I think it's got some kind of alcohol in it."

"Ah. Yes. Rum, perhaps. I've had it before. The English have something they call custard with it. Yellow."

All of a sudden the heat and the smell of food and her irresistible nearness and the effort of talking made him so giddy that he thought he might black out, or fall against her and hold her. He went to the table and leaned heavily on it.

She turned and looked at him. "Ernst? Are you all right? You look terribly pale."

He made a huge effort to repel the darkness swarming into the edges of his vision. "I'm fine. Just the change in temperature, I think." He turned a chair so that it faced her and sat down.

"Would you like coffee? There was some in the drop."

"Yes, thank you. Coffee would be good. Christiaan is here?"

"Yes, of course. He is still upstairs." She glanced over her shoulder at him. "With Oma," she added quickly. "She's not well."

Oma. He had forgotten she existed. Not good. His world was melting, spilling over the limits of his concentration.

"Your grandmother's sick? What's wrong with her?"

She kept her back to him, fussing with the coffee pot, moving things on the stove.

"Exhaustion, mainly. She's been in Loenen, with her cousin's family. She came back yesterday and had to walk almost all the way. She should have stayed there, I told her. But there was a child born who died and she thought she shouldn't. She's caught a chill, but I think she'll be well enough to have dinner with us."

Then the door opened and Tamar came in, rubbing his hands together and grinning. Dart stood and Tamar embraced him, slapping Dart's back.

"Happy Christmas, my friend," Tamar said. "What do you think of all this?" He gestured at the table, the tree. "Good, isn't it? Did Marijke tell you we're having chicken? And English pudding? My God, we're going to eat like kings! And why not? I think we deserve it, don't you?"

His presence had tilted the delicate nervous balance in the room. The quiet intimacy of a few moments earlier had been jolted into this hearty maleness. Dart had trouble adjusting.

"Yes," he said. "I was just saying to Marijke. It's fantastic in here. How is Oma?"

"What? Oh, well, she's miserable, of course. There was a child—"

"Yes," Dart said. "Marijke told me."

"Did she? Right. Well, Oma's very upset, naturally. And the journey back was hard on her. She's got a bit of a cold, but you know Oma – tough as old boots."

Dart glanced at Marijke. It seemed to him that Tamar was being grossly offhand, but Marijke was taking it well, smiling bravely. She brought two cups of coffee to the table.

"I'll go up to her," she said. "The food is almost ready."

Dart watched her leave the room. The way her body, her legs, moved inside the green dress. He sipped his coffee, and when he raised his eyes Tamar was looking at him thoughtfully.

"Are you okay?"

"I'm fine," Dart said.

Tamar nodded, still watching Dart's face. "That was a hell of a thing, the other night. To tell you the truth, drops scare me shitless. Especially big ones like that, when there are lots of people involved. You know what I mean? Someone talks, says something in the wrong place, and you end up getting shot to pieces in a damn field in the middle of nowhere. You did very well."

"Thank you."

"Did you get everything you needed?"

Dart sipped, looking into his cup. "Yes."

Tamar nodded again, slowly, then smiled and leaned back in his chair. "I feel so good tonight," he said. "Know why?"

Dart didn't. He waited.

"It's because all this is so ... normal. Do you understand what I mean? Here, this kitchen, the food, the tree – it's like life used to be, before. And I didn't think, couldn't have imagined... You know when we jumped out of that bloody plane? It never crossed my mind that three months later you and I would be celebrating Christmas like this. Yet here we are, doing what normal people used to do in normal times. I went up to the heath and cut that tree down, and Marijke decorated it, and I thought what a mad thing we were doing while people all over the country are starving and dying. We should feel guilty, I suppose. But tonight, right now, I don't."

He reached across the table and seized Dart's wrists, startling him. "We must have a good time tonight, my friend. Because this is the most subversive thing we could be doing. This" – and here he gestured at the room again – "this is the continuation of war by other means. Joy is the true enemy of fascism. So we shall be joyous."

He has been drinking, Dart thought.

As if he had read Dart's mind, Tamar jumped up and

went to the dresser. He returned with two of Oma's china tumblers and Ruud van der Spil's cognac. Dart noticed that the level in the bottle had fallen significantly.

"Here," Tamar said, pouring large shots. "Have some of this. You still look a bit like a ghost. Cheers."

Dart drank; the liquor left a hot track through the middle of his body which felt good.

"Something else too," Tamar said, reaching into a trouser pocket. "Look at this. A Christmas present from Nicholson, I think."

It was a large buff office envelope, folded in half. The letter N was pencilled in one corner. It contained a wad of crossword puzzles clipped from newspapers.

"Thirty!" Tamar said. "Mostly from *The Times*, at a glance." He grinned happily. "Warmth, good food, something to drink and a crossword to do after dinner. We are having a little interlude in heaven, my friend."

The door opened then and Marijke and her grandmother came in. Dart stood and stooped to be kissed. The old woman was wearing a red shawl over her usual black, but this festive garment could not disguise the fact that she was frailer than before. Dart thought she had aged a good deal since he last saw her. There was a slight yellowness to the whites of her eyes and a ragged edge to her breathing; the climb down the stairs had been hard work for her. She refused to sit in the armchair, and took a seat at the table.

Tamar and Marijke busied themselves at the stove, leaving Dart to deal with Oma. She gazed absently at him for several moments, then began one of her mimes. Without Marijke to translate, Dart felt at a loss. He smiled and nodded.

"Yes, Oma," he guessed, "it is very cold. Bad weather for walking, yes. The room is beautiful, though. The food smells good. Yes, I'm very hungry."

THE CHICKEN STEW contained chunks of carrot and potato, and translucent segments of onion; the meat was slightly fibrous but good. They sucked it from the bones and wiped their plates clean with bread that Marijke had made with the British flour. Oma sat back and sighed with pleasure, or perhaps exhaustion, when she had eaten half of what was on her plate.

After a silent and contented interval, Tamar lifted the Christmas pudding from the pan. He made a comedy of unwrapping it from the hot cloth, dancing about and blowing on his fingertips. He finally got it onto a warm plate and brought it to the table; it was dark chocolatey brown and glistened stickily. Oma and Marijke peered at it with deep suspicion.

Marijke said, "If it's disgusting we can have baked apples instead."

"Of course it won't be disgusting," Tamar said. "It'll be delicious. It was probably made from the finest ingredients by the head chef of the Ritz Hotel in London, exclusively for the SOE. Do you think the RAF would send one of their planes through hellfire to deliver a nasty pudding? Now then, pass me the cognac."

Tamar filled a serving spoon and heated it in the flame of a candle. "Ruud van der Spil would probably shoot me dead if he saw me doing this with his precious booze. Here we go."

A lick of flame ran over the surface of the liquid. Tamar emptied the spoon onto the hot pudding and, for just a few seconds, it wore a transparent cloak of flickering blue fire. Marijke laughed and applauded. Oma, alarmed and wide-eyed, put her hands to her chest as if she had witnessed one of the devil's prettier tricks.

Tamar served thick wedges of the pudding into gold-edged bowls. He stared at Marijke, smiling, waiting for her to try it first. She made a comical face, then, like someone doing something brave and possibly suicidal, slid a spoonful into her mouth. The others watched and waited. Dart, tense and enraptured, saw the tip of her tongue lick traces of taste from her lips. Her eyes closed and her mouth moved thoughtfully. Then she swallowed, and carefully put the spoon down.

"Well," Tamar said, "what do you think?"

Marijke waggled her hand beside her face like someone who had been told an outrageous piece of gossip. "It is a scandal," she said, very seriously, "to have so many things in one pudding." Then she smiled delightedly. "It is incredible. Have some; have some!"

They ate, making little groans of pleasure.

"Raisins," Tamar said. "And almonds, are they?" He lifted a plump little chunk of something red from his dish. "What is this, Marijke?"

"Some sort of preserved cherry, I think. I can taste things I thought I'd never taste again."

"Nutmeg," Dart said. "Mmm … figs too. Amazing. Where did they get all this stuff? I never saw any of it in England."

"It would be wonderful with cream," Marijke sighed. "Can you imagine?"

Oma, chewing busily, waved her hand in a dismissive gesture: what they had in their dishes was sinful enough without cream.

Dart made a startled sound and the others looked at him. Frowning, he took something small and flat from his mouth.

"What have you got there, Ernst?"

Dart held the object nearer the candle. "It's a coin. British, but I've never seen one like it before." He peered at it. "It's old. The date is eighteen something."

"Ah, I know what this is. You're lucky tonight, my friend."

"Damn right. I could have choked on it."

Tamar laughed. "True. This is one of those crazy English customs. They put a little silver coin in the Christmas pudding, and the person who finds it gets to make a wish. Guaranteed to come true. Never fails."

"What a nice idea," Marijke said. "So go on, Ernst. What are you going to wish for?"

Tamar laid a hand on her wrist. "No, no. Ernst mustn't tell us. It has to be a secret wish, or it won't work."

They all watched Dart, smiling and expectant. He tried very hard not to look at Marijke, but he could not help himself. "I don't know what to wish for," he confessed.

Marijke tipped her head slightly, and in that moment Dart lost focus on everything except her face.

"Of course you do," she said. "I know what I'd wish for. I bet you'd wish for the same thing."

Her dark gaze was fixed on him, and there was no mistaking the message it contained. He had no name for the emotion that swept through him. He closed his eyes and held them tight shut until he had some control over it.

When he opened them, Tamar was grinning at him. "That was obviously a very serious wish. I hope with all my heart it comes true. Now, more, anyone?"

* * *

191

Julia Maartens went to bed not long after the meal was over. The effort of eating had tired her, and then she had a spasm of coughing that left her looking feverish. Marijke filled two stone hot-water bottles to warm the old lady's bed; then, after a slow ritual of goodnights, took her upstairs.

When the two men were alone, Tamar brought the oil lamp to the table. "Crossword?"

"Yes, why not?"

Tamar shuffled through the wad of crosswords, choosing one he liked the look of – using a selection process Dart did not understand – and found a pencil. Then he lifted the cognac bottle and looked at Dart enquiringly.

"No," Dart said. "I need to keep a clear head."

"Shit. I'd forgotten. You're on station tonight, aren't you? What time?"

"Twenty-two forty-five until midnight. Not long."

Tamar poured himself a small drink. "Okay. But the damn British. Don't they know it's Christmas?"

"Don't you know there's a war on?" Dart said, and they laughed; in England the phrase had been the everyday excuse for all sorts of lousy behaviour.

When Marijke came back down, the two men were hunched over the crossword, their heads close together. She felt excluded; they didn't look up even when she reached for the bottle and poured herself a drink. So she came round behind them and put an arm over each man's shoulder. She leaned down to them. Dart felt her hair brush his temple, breathed her perfume again.

"So," she said, "tell me how this works."

Tamar began to explain what an anagram was. Dart turned his head slightly so that he could see Marijke's hand. Her forefinger was just a few millimetres from the bare skin of his neck. Slowly, holding his breath, he raised his own fingers towards hers.

"Stop," she said. "How can I understand this? Not only is it mad, it is in English." She lifted her hands to the tops of their heads and ruffled their hair. "Come on, talk to me. Make me laugh."

Tamar sighed theatrically. "The same old story. Men engage in a peaceful, intellectual pastime, and along comes a beautiful woman and spoils everything." He pushed the crossword away and tossed the pencil down. "Go on then, Dr Lubbers – make Marijke laugh. You're the one with all the stories. Nothing interesting ever happens to me."

"That's right, Ernst," Marijke said. "You've said nothing tonight about Albert or Agatha. You must have news. How are Pieter and Bibi?"

Dart slapped his forehead. "Ach! I completely forgot. I have something to show you. It's in my bag."

He went out into the hall, and when he came back Tamar was pouring Marijke another drink.

Dart put the medical bag down on the table and opened it. "Pieter and Bibi gave me a late *Sinterklaas* present," he said.

It was a narrow box of grey cardboard with the words THE MARIONETTE HOUSE printed on the lid in green italic writing. Dart lifted the lid and took out a puppet. He held it above the table, suspended on its twisted strings from a wooden cross. The strings unwound and the figure spun in a slow blur.

Tamar said, "Hey, it's you!"

It was Dart, unmistakably. The narrow head had carved waves of hair painted black; the body wore a tweed coat with a red cross armband on one sleeve; one mitten-shaped hand was attached to a bag painted leather brown. The legs sagged inwards at the knees when the feet came to rest on the surface of the table.

Marijke's face lit up. "Oh, Ernst, what a beautiful thing! Fancy having a puppet of yourself. Aren't you flattered?" She flopped down on the chair at the head of the table and held her hands out imploringly towards the marionette. "Come on, make him walk to me."

Dart tried, but the skill of it was beyond him. The puppet moved towards her slumped and spastic, its feet dragging. He lifted it and tried again; but the hinged arms flailed and twitched and the feet clacked against the smeared pudding bowls.

Tamar, laughing, stood up. "Let me try."

He held the crosspiece and adjusted the position of his fingers, then moved his hand slowly up the table. The Dart puppet advanced towards Marijke in a jerky dance. She muffled her laughter with her hands and drew back as if something both thrilling and menacing were approaching her.

Tamar twisted his mouth to one side and imitated a poor ventriloquist. "I am a doctor. I am told there is a woman here who needs my attention."

Then in a quick movement he lifted the puppet towards Marijke's face. She caught it in her fingers and looked delightedly into its face. "Ah, Doctor, at last! Come upstairs!"

Then her laughter bubbled over, and she leaned forward. The Dart puppet collapsed onto the table. After a second or two, Dart joined in the laughter.

"Let me have a go," Marijke said, getting to her feet.

Tamar put the marionette's crosspiece in her fingers and she experimented with the strings, concentrating hard, trying not to giggle, the tip of her tongue touching her upper lip. She rocked her hand and the Dart puppet performed a slow arthritic jig while its head swivelled loosely from side to side.

"Very good!" Dart said. "Well done."

"Now," Marijke said, "I'm going to see if I can make him do a little bow."

She tipped her hand forward slightly and parted two of the strings with her fingers. The puppet folded in the middle and raised its arms.

Tamar and Dart applauded. Marijke made a little curtsy, then lowered the puppet onto the table. It slumped in a sitting position, its legs splayed.

"I think he's a very sweet little gentleman," Marijke declared. "Don't you, Ernst? Do you think Pieter would make one of me? We could make them dance together."

"I'm sure he would. I'll ask him."

Tamar reached for the bottle, but paused and turned his wrist to look at his watch.

Dart remembered. "Damn. What time is it?"

"Ten twenty."

Dart sighed heavily. "Right. I'd better think about getting organized."

Marijke pulled a long face in sympathy. "I don't think it's fair. It's Christmas."

Tamar said, "I dare say that in London there's some poor bloody signaller looking up our call sign and thinking exactly the same thing."

Marijke stood up. "Let me make you some coffee to take with you. It won't take a minute."

Dart put on his coat and wrapped the scarf around his throat. Marijke gave him coffee in a jug, and kissed him.

Then Tamar said, "I'll wait up for you. We ought to have a last drink."

Dart saw very clearly the look of displeasure that Marijke gave Tamar. There was only one way to interpret it: she did not want Tamar to be in the kitchen when Dart came back from the barn. Dart felt a surge of exhilaration so strong that for a moment he felt that, like his own marionette, he would fold and fall. It took a huge effort of will to keep his face expressionless.

"Good," he said. "I'll see you later, then."

When he stepped outside, it was as if he had been

plunged into a well of ink. He could see nothing at all. The coldness shocked him sober. He inhaled sobs of air that were like pebbles in his chest. Eventually he moved cautiously into the dark, feeling the ribs and knuckles of the ground through the soles of his shoes, hearing ice crack in diminishing ripples of sound. He hit the wall of the barn before he knew he'd reached it. Inside, he found the lamp hanging on its nail, and after a good deal of fumbling managed to get it lit. He carried the pool of yellow light up the stairs.

The fast bleeps of Morse came through the fizz of his headphones at exactly twenty-two forty-five.

He blinked in surprise when his hand wrote the *signal ends* code after just seven minutes. He waited, listening to white noise for several seconds in case there had been a mistake, then acknowledged and closed down. His vaporized breath drifted towards the lamp and disappeared. He spread the silk code sheet on the table and deciphered just the last two lines of London's message: HAPPY XMAS AND A VICTORIOUS NEW YEAR STOP NOW PISS OFF SOMEWHERE WARM SIGNAL ENDS.

Smiling, Dart disconnected the transceiver and stashed it and the battery away in the thatch behind the crippled chest of drawers. He felt a sort of giddiness, knowing that he'd be with her again so soon.

Outside the barn he stood immobile for some time, forcing himself to endure the cold and his impatience, while his sight readapted to the darkness. On other nights, he had emerged from the barn and heard the distant drone of aircraft and the continuous muffled thud of faraway explosions. Tonight the silence was absolute. He looked up. Through a sudden breach in the clouds he saw a sliver of clear sky brightly crowded with stars. Even though he was in no way superstitious, he allowed himself to see it as a portent, a sign that wishes would be granted. He closed his eyes and shuddered, perhaps because of the cold or perhaps in response to the strong thrill of anticipation that ran through him.

He felt his way to the corner of the barn and halted, puzzled. A narrow track of light lay on the ground some way ahead of him, crossing the yard. He hadn't noticed it on the way out; but then he had been staring blindly ahead, fearful of falling. It took him a few seconds to work out that it must be coming from the kitchen window. The blackout curtains had not been closed properly.

He had almost reached the safety of the farmhouse door when a perverse little notion took hold of him. He never did work out why. Perhaps he wanted to delay the pleasure of holding her and so make it more intense. Perhaps he wanted to see into that golden room from the outside, delighting in the fact that soon he would be inside it, no longer exiled. He knew that his father had sometimes done this, returning from work in the dark; he had stood outside his own window, watching his family, marvelling at the fact that he would soon be part of it again. Or maybe Dart was simply obeying a spy's instinct. For whatever reason, he made his way to the window and peered in.

The glass was studded with tiny beads of ice, and it took his eyes a couple of seconds to focus. Tamar was sitting on the same chair as before; but now Marijke was sitting on it also. She was on his lap, facing him, her legs straddling his, her hands gripping the back of the chair. The green dress had slid to the top of her thighs. Tamar was gazing into her face, which was hidden from Dart by the black tumble of her hair. Tamar's mouth moved silently. His hands were somewhere inside her clothes. Marijke took one hand from the chair and gently forced his head back, lowering her face to his. Tamar's hand appeared and pulled her hair away from their faces as if to display more clearly the way their mouths fed on each other.

Dart felt a bitter howl climbing in his throat and jammed the side of his thumb between his teeth to stifle it. He forced himself back from the window. He slipped and staggered but did not fall. When he was steady, he crossed his arms and held himself tight. He lifted his face. The stars had gone; light snow, as fine as grains of salt, swirled slowly into his vision. It looked like the sound of static in headphones. He closed his eyes.

He stood like that for a long time; he could not think what to do next because he did not want to think at all. He grew as cold as the stone cold weather.

ENGLAND, 1995

AFTER GRANDAD'S DEATH, several days passed before we could face going to the flat. The police had wanted Mum to go that same day, the day he died, and she'd put her coat on and picked up her keys before she cracked up and told them she couldn't do it.

When we did go, it was just terrible. Mum drove into the car park and headed for her usual space on the balcony side of the flats, but then she gave a sort of gasping scream and swerved away. She parked at the side of the block instead. Neither of us said anything, but we both knew why she'd done it. In the lobby two people were already waiting for the lift. When they recognized us, they pretended to change their minds and headed for the stairs.

It was dark inside the flat because the curtains across the glass balcony doors had been closed. (By Grandad? By the police?) We didn't open them. I put the lights on. We were both crying in a quiet, sniffly sort of way, but we didn't talk. Mum went over to the bureau to look for various bits of paper and documents that the solicitor had told her she'd need. I went into my bedroom to get ... well, I don't know what, really. I think at the time I just wanted to leave everything there and close the door on it. The first thing I saw was the box, this box. It was on my bed. An ordinary shoebox made of brown cardboard. It had string tied around it fastened with a tight knot. The lid had been sealed with parcel tape, and had a small white adhesive label with TAMAR written on it. I absolutely did not want to touch it.

I was still standing there staring at it when Mum came into the room.

She said, "He'd got everything ready. He must've…" She choked up. I looked at what she was holding. "See?"

There were two cardboard files, some large brown envelopes and a long thin white envelope with the word WILL printed on it. The whole lot was held together by a thick rubber band.

Then Mum saw the box. "What's that?" she said.

"I dunno."

"Is it yours? I mean, do you think—"

"I dunno," I said again. "Can we go? I want to go."

When we were in the lift, I saw she'd got the box under her arm. In the car she handed it to me, but I wouldn't take it. She looked at me for several seconds and then dropped it onto the back seat. When we got home I went straight indoors. Mum brought the box in and put it on the shelf in the hall. At some point in the evening, I took it upstairs and put it right at the back of my wardrobe. I didn't open it until nearly three months later.

Why didn't I? The reasons changed as time passed. At first, the box simply scared me. It had scared me as soon as I saw it. I had to assume that Grandad had put it on my bed just before he'd thrown himself off the balcony. Perhaps it had been the very last thing he did. Perhaps he was already naked when he put it there. If there was some connection between the box and what was going on inside his head at that moment, I really, deeply, didn't want to know about it. Also, it seemed to me that there was something, well,

202

sinister about the way the box was tied shut with two thick-nesses of string and sealed with strong tape. As if to keep something from escaping. I did get it out, just once, and when I shook it slightly I heard things shift inside with a dry, meaningless sound. Later, as I said before, my grief and hurt changed to anger. Grandad might have been over-whelmed by loss and despair, but he still had something to live for, someone who would need him even when his wife no longer knew who he was. Namely me. And killing him-self had been the cruellest possible way of telling me that I wasn't enough. A slap in the face, a punch to the heart. How dare he? That was something I found myself think-ing, often saying it out loud: how dare he? So then it was a sort of bitter stubbornness that stopped me opening the box. I refused to. If what was in there was some sort of parting gift, I didn't want it. If it was some sort of message or explanation, I didn't want to hear it. Once or twice I got close to putting it out with the rubbish.

Looking back, I'm amazed that sheer simple curios-ity didn't overcome these feelings. Because I *was* curious, of course. I thought about the box all the time, long after Mum stopped going on about it. I dreamed about it a few times. Once I dreamed it contained a severed head. I knew it was Grandad's even though it was completely wrapped in bandages. I could tell that the head was speaking because I could see the bandages over the mouth moving in and out, but I couldn't hear what it was saying. These dreams weren't really nightmares. In them I wasn't terrified. I felt sorry for the head. I wanted to help it but didn't know how.

I eventually opened the box on a hot Thursday afternoon in June. It was a daft time to choose, because I was in the mid-dle of my GCSEs. I'd sat a French exam in the morning, and I was annoyed with myself because I knew I hadn't done as well as I could've. I was alone in the house. I heated a frozen pizza in the microwave and sat down to eat it at the kitchen table, thinking about what I should have written, remembering the mistakes I'd made. For reasons I can't really explain, I decided that the box had something to do with my poor performance. That it was like a stone in my head, messing up my thinking. Halfway through the pizza I went upstairs and got the bloody thing out of the wardrobe and marched downstairs again before I could change my mind. My heart was banging. I put the box on the table and found a sharp knife in the kitchen drawer. I cut through the string and the tape and lifted the lid off.

No severed head, of course. In the order I took them out and put them on the table, the box contained: a crossword puzzle; four maps held together by a rubber band; a fat bundle of money, also bound with a rubber band; a small black and white photograph; something that looked like a handkerchief, folded up; and a thin booklet with a reddish-brown cover. That was it.

How did I feel? Disappointed? Mystified? Angry that I'd spent three months putting off opening this collection of strange bits and pieces? All of those, I think. But almost immediately I felt something else, something stronger than any of those other feelings: regret. I really wished I hadn't opened the box. Because I knew straight away that Grandad hadn't been mad when he'd put these things in it. I knew that these things fitted together in some way, and I had to find out how. I know it will sound strange, but it was as though he was in the box too. His spirit, something like that. I felt it so strongly that I wouldn't have been surprised if I'd lifted my eyes and seen him settle down at the end of the table to watch me. I regretted what I'd done because I knew that on the following day I had an English exam in the morning and a biology exam in the afternoon. And that next week

I was going to sit at a desk in the school gym taking history and maths. And that my mind wasn't going to be focused on any of it.

I spent the best part of the next two hours studying the things that Grandad had left me. I began with the money, naturally.

There were twelve fifty-pound notes, one hundred and twenty ten-pound notes, and twenty-nine fivers. I counted them twice, carefully, and added them up: one thousand, nine hundred and forty-five pounds. Mum had said that Grandad had left me some money in his will; something complicated to do with a trust, when I was eighteen. But this wasn't it, obviously. This was something else.

The crossword. It was one of those jumbo ones the papers put in at holiday times – Easter, bank holidays, that sort of thing. It was from the *Guardian* from the previous Christmas. I remembered it because it was one of the last crosswords Grandad and I had tried to do. Just about half the grid had been filled in; I recognized Grandad's neat black ink capital letters. It brought back the memories in a flood.

Mum and Grandad and I had been invited to Christmas lunch at River Reach. We'd dreaded it, but went anyway. And to be fair, the staff had done really well. The Christmas tree in the entrance hall was huge, and really beautiful, just silver and red decorations and simple white lights. The food was pretty good too, although the way some of the residents ate didn't bear much looking at. A lot of them had to be fed by their relatives or the nurses and were too distracted to work their mouths properly. There was a good deal of noise, but Gran was pretty quiet throughout the whole thing. Her eyes kept darting about, but she didn't seem to see anything to upset her. I don't think she understood what was happening, really. She almost cleared her plate, though; there were just a few sprouts, a roast potato or two and a lump of stuffing left on it when we'd all finished. But what I remember most vividly is looking over at Grandad sitting there wearing the orange paper crown from his cracker. He looked so stiff and stricken and swivel-eyed that anyone coming into the room would have taken him for one of the patients.

When we got back to our house, Mum helped Grandad off with his coat and noticed that there was a greasy stain on the side of his jacket. He looked down at it and went into the kitchen without saying anything. We watched him fish out the sausage and bits of turkey that Gran had slipped into his pocket. Later, Mum was on the phone to Andrew for about three hours, so I found the crossword, and Grandad and I sat and struggled with it. It cheered him up, that and the whisky. It was a fiendish – Grandad's word – puzzle. Several of the clues locked into other clues, so you went round and round in circles. And it turned out that it had a secret theme, *Treasure Island*. Lots of the answers were the names of characters from the story and so on. I was the one who worked that out, because we'd read the book at school the year before. Grandad had been most impressed that I'd cracked the code. All the same, we couldn't do more than half of it, and gave up in the end. So that's why I recognized it when I found it in the box.

The maps. They were all proper Ordnance Survey maps. The one on top was OS 108, and the title had my name in it: *Lower Tamar Valley & Plymouth*. The next was 112, the next 111, and the last was 126. They were all fairly new, but I could see that they had been used, or opened up at least. The creases in them weren't exactly as they would have been if they'd just come out of the shop. When I spread them out on the kitchen floor, I realized that all the maps joined up, and I found myself kneeling on a big chunk of Devon and Cornwall. The river with my name ran through all of it. For some reason I found that a bit spooky. It took me a couple of minutes to notice that there were faint pencil markings, tiny *x*s inside circles, at various places along the Tamar valley.

The photograph. It was small, about five centimetres by eight, and black and white. Old, obviously. I knew straight away where it had been taken. On the Albert Embankment, on the south bank of the Thames, there's a place where tourists are always taking pictures of each other, and sometimes politicians are interviewed for TV. That's because you get a good shot of the Houses of Parliament in the background. They were a bit out of focus in this little photo. The two men in the foreground were wearing old-fashioned army uniforms, the ones with short tunics. They were both bareheaded. I could just make out their berets rolled and tucked into their shoulder straps. The soldier on the left had one hand on the low wall of the embankment and the other in his pocket. He was looking straight at the camera. The one on the right had his arm round the other man's shoulders. He was looking away from the camera slightly, as though he'd turned to speak to someone just as the shutter had clicked.

I studied it for a while, then trudged upstairs again and rummaged about until I found the magnifying glass I used in biology. When I focused it on the photo the two soldiers jumped out at me through the thick glass. They looked alike. Both had thick dark hair cut short at the sides and rather long narrow faces. They had the kind of features that a romantic novelist might describe as "finely chiselled". Good-looking, in an old Hollywood movie sort of way. They could have been brothers. It was hard to tell how old they were. Youngish, but people somehow look older in old photographs. What I mean is that fifty years ago young people looked more like adults than we do now. And I was absolutely sure that this photo had been taken that long ago, during the war. I supposed one of these two men was Grandad, but I couldn't tell which.

I turned the photo over. There was nothing written on the back.

The handkerchief. Actually, it wasn't a handkerchief at all; it was a sheet of white silk, yellowish down the outside edges and along the creases where it had been folded. It was printed all over with row after row of letters. None of them made up words, whether you read the letters horizontally, vertically or even diagonally. They didn't seem to be anagrams, either. I gave up on it.

The booklet. It looked like it had been fished out of a dustbin of wet garbage and dried on top of a radiator. On the cover there was an eagle with its wings outstretched and its claws clutching a sort of wreath. Inside the wreath there was a Nazi swastika. Below that there was a word in what I thought was German and obviously meant identity-something. The bottom right-hand corner was wrinkled and discoloured by a dark stain.

I opened it up. At the top left of the first page there was a head and shoulders photograph, a bit smaller than the one in my passport. Black and white again, with the blurred print of a rubber stamp across the bottom corner. The man in the photo stared out at me. Lean-faced, dark-haired, with an expression that was blank but somehow defiant at the same time, like someone who'd been arrested and photographed against a police station wall. To the right of the picture there were spaces in which the man's details had been carefully written in ink, now faded. The first space had the word BOOGART in capital letters, and below that the word *Christiaan* in ordinary writing. Below that, next to the word VERKLARING, someone had written *Landarbeider*. Next down, there was a date, 19th April 1920, which I took to be his date of birth. There were other entries filled in by someone using the kind of handwriting you don't see any more. I could only guess at what they meant. Below the photo there were two fingerprints, or perhaps thumbprints. At the bottom of the page, where the brown stain had left a tidemark, there was another rubber stamp with BIJKANTOOR APELDOORN in the centre and two longer words around the edge. Next to that was a date, 21st September 1942, and a scrawled signature. The next page had a sheet of very thin paper gummed to it. The same eagle and swastika design, and underneath it, in heavy elaborate capitals, the word AUSWEIS. Then came a lot of the same stuff as before about Boogart and three more rubber stamp prints. The first was the Apeldoorn one again; the second had a sort of crest and the word ESSEN. The third one was too blurred to make out; it looked as though it had been banged onto the paper by someone in a hurry. Apart from the stain spreading up from the bottom corner, the last page was blank.

I put the London snapshot next to the photo in the identity book and stared at them both. Either one of the soldiers on the Albert Embankment could have been Boogart.

I went to the bookcase in the living room and took down the two photo albums that Mum had brought back from Gran and Grandad's flat before it was sold. There wasn't a single picture of them when they were young. The first photo was of them both sitting in the garden of our old house, with Gran holding a baby, me. Grandad didn't look much different from the way I remembered him. So that was a dead end.

I went upstairs yet again and poked about in the tragic mess I called my school work. Eventually I found a scrap of clean tracing paper. I laid it over the photograph in the booklet and carefully pencilled on a pair of glasses and a moustache. Something like a narrow-faced ghost of Grandad looked up at me.

I chewed my way through the remains of the pizza, thinking. Grandad had never said anything to me about the war. To be honest, I don't suppose I'd ever been interested enough to ask about it. I knew that he and Gran had lived in Holland and that they'd had something to do with the Dutch resistance. But when I'd read that stuff in the newspaper about him parachuting into Holland and being betrayed to the Germans and so on, I'd been amazed that in all the time I'd spent with him he'd not told me a thing about it. When I'd asked Mum, she said that she'd told the reporter all she knew, and that she'd got it from Dad, not Grandad. She didn't know anything else.

I looked at the identity booklet again. If this was Grandad's wartime identity card – and why would it have been in the box if it wasn't? – he'd once been called Christiaan Boogart. It gave me a creepy feeling. It felt like opening the door to a dark cellar and not being able to see the stairs. But if Grandad wanted to tell me who he really was, why wait until he was dead? And what did it have to do with the other stuff in the box? I started feeling angry again. I put everything back in the box and stuck it in my wardrobe again. I spent the evening trying to concentrate on *The Catcher in the Rye* for my English exam.

On Monday I came home knackered, and slumped on the sofa with a bag of crisps and gazed at the TV without really taking in what was on. I waited until six o'clock, then I went to the phone and called Yoyo.

YOYO IS MY Dutch cousin. Actually, he's not really called Yoyo and he isn't really my cousin. His proper name is Johannes, pronounced Yohannes in Dutch, and he's been called Yoyo since he was little. He's my gran's cousin's grandson or nephew, something like that. I can never remember. Mum once said that he was "a distant twig on the family tree". He showed up out of the blue just a couple of months before Grandad died. Then he came to the funeral, wearing a borrowed suit that was too short in the leg. The funeral was awful, one of those quick in and out crematorium jobs, with another hearse and two carloads of mourners queuing up behind for their turn. If Yoyo hadn't come, Mum and I and my other grandparents (who'd come down from Leicester) would have been the only family members there. He came back to the house afterwards for drinks. I had a few glasses of wine, which I wasn't used to, and ended up babbling and snivelling to Yoyo about Grandad and then Dad. Embarrassing. He was great, though. He just listened and said nice intelligent things. It was a pity I couldn't remember them the next day. We'd talked on the phone after that, and met up a couple of times. Once he took me to see some electronic Dutch band who were playing in

London. He thought they were tremendous and I thought they were crap, but we didn't fall out over it. One of the most important things about Yoyo, at least as far as I was concerned, was that he never talked down to me. He completely ignored the difference in our ages. Plus, he was very bright, and he made me laugh.

Yoyo is four years older than me, so he was nineteen, nearly twenty, when I called him that June evening in 1995. He lived in Amsterdam, studying English, but he'd got some sort of grant to spend a year at the University of London. He shared a flat down in Greenwich somewhere. It was one of his flatmates who answered the phone. When he put it down to fetch Yoyo, I could hear heavy metal music in the background. Just before Yoyo picked up the phone I heard a mumble of voices and a door slam, and the heavy metal went dead.

"Aha," he said, "the most beautiful of my cousins!"

"Shut up," I said. "Anyway, I keep telling you that you're not really my cousin."

"Yes, that's good. It means we can get married."

"Yoyo, have you been smoking weed?"

"What, on a Monday? No, of course." He managed to sound quite indignant. "Anyway, I have this very, very difficult thing to write about Sonnet 94 by Shakespeare. You know it?"

"Not that particular one," I said.

"Ah. That's too bad. I could use some help. I can't make either head or tail of it."

"It's funny you should say that," I said, "because I've got a mystery on my hands too, and I can't make head or tail of that either. I could use some help. Your help."

"Really? A mystery? What is it?"

"I can't really explain. Not over the phone, anyway. Listen, Yoyo, do you have any spare time next week?"

"Yes, I think so. What, to see you? That would be nice."

"Could you come here?"

"Er, okay. What evening?"

"Not evening. Daytime. One afternoon. Morning, even."

I could hear him thinking. "You mean when Sonia is not there? Oh, Tamar!"

"Shut up, you idiot. How about Monday? A week today. Lunchtime would be good. I'll make you a sandwich."

"Cool," he said. "How could I resist this offer? It's just a shame you live so far out."

"I don't live far out," I said. "You do."

He arrived just after half past twelve. I opened the door and he swooped down at me, kissing me on both cheeks, European style. The first thing you notice about Yoyo is how tall and thin he is. His clothes always look too big for him, as though they're suspended from coat hangers, not shoulders and hips. His hair is the colour of wet straw, and it sticks out from his head in all directions like the fur on a guinea pig. It's not deliberate, not a style statement or anything like that. It just grows that way. There's something slightly oriental about his face. He has wide cheekbones and narrow, dark, very shiny eyes.

"Okay," he said as we walked down the hall. "I've come for a mystery and a sandwich. Which is first?"

We ate sandwiches and drank Coke. He listened to what I told him without making any comment or asking any questions, just glancing now and then at the shoebox on my side of the kitchen table.

I cleared the plates away. Yoyo sat up straight and rubbed his hands together. "So, okay. Let me see what's in this mysterious box."

I slid it over to him. He opened it in a melodramatically cautious way as if he expected it to contain an angry rat.

The first item he took out was the roll of money. He weighed it in his hand and whistled. "Wow," he said, "little rich girl!" He slipped the band off and fanned the notes like a hand of cards. "How much?"

"Nearly two thousand pounds. One thousand, nine hundred and forty-five, to be precise."

"Really? You know, I don't think I have had so much cash in my hand before." He put the band back around the roll and wagged a finger at me like a teacher. "I hope you are not going to spend it all on sweets."

I gave him a Look.

The second thing he took out was the identity booklet. He pulled a face when he saw it.

"That's the main thing I need your help with," I said. "I want you to tell me what it says. You speak German, don't you?"

"Some," he said. "But this is Dutch."

"Is it?"

"Of course. You don't know the difference?"

I shook my head, and he tutted at me.

"But it's got a German swastika on the front," I said in self-defence.

"That's because this is an identity book from the war. I have seen such things before. Made by the Germans, yes, of course, but for a Dutch person, this Christiaan Boogart." He looked at the photograph. "Who is he, do you know?"

"I think he's Grandad."

Yoyo looked at me, frowning. "Your grandfather? William? Why do you think that?"

"I'll tell you in a minute." I reached across and pointed to the handwritten entries down the right-hand side of the page. "Tell me what these say."

"Okay… His name is Christiaan Boogart; his profession, *verklaring*, is farmer. No, not farmer exactly. Land worker."

"Farm labourer?"

"Yes, farm labourer, correct. Then his birth date; and the place he was born, Zutphen."

"Where's that?"

"It's in Gelderland. In the middle of the Netherlands, then a bit east. Nice place. Then next his father's name, Jakob; and his mother's name, Christiana." His finger moved down the page. "This next part is what you call, like, er … physical description details. So here is his height: one metre seventy-nine."

"What's that in English?"

"Oh shit," Yoyo said, "your crazy feet and inches? I can never work this out. It's something like six feet, a bit less. I am one metre eighty-eight."

"Okay."

"Then it says his hair colour is dark, which means nothing; he has no moustache; his eyes are brown; his face is *smal*. But this does not mean small; it is…" He mimed stretching his face longer and thinner.

"Long?" I guessed. "Narrow?"

"Yes, narrow, that's it. It also says his nose is straight." Yoyo smiled slightly. "The Nazis were very interested in the shapes of noses."

He pointed to the rubber stamp print at the bottom of the page. "This is the mark of the, ah … employment office in Apeldoorn, not so far from Zutphen."

He turned the page and studied the stuck-in sheet of paper. "Hmm… This is more difficult. *Ausweis* is a German word, meaning something like passport, but not exactly. Permit, perhaps. Then more of the same information about Christiaan Boogart. But this written here, see, is hard to read. It's all in German. Something about a hospital, but… No. I cannot read the rest of it. But look, this mark here? It says *Essen*. Essen is a place in Germany. So the plot thickens. Boogart seems to have been in Germany during the war."

He looked up; I looked blank.

"Why do you think this Christiaan Boogart is your grandfather, Tamar?"

"Grandad was Dutch, wasn't he? So he must have had another name before he was William Hyde."

"And you don't know what it was?"

"No," I said, and the look on his face made me feel stupid and lost and young. "I never asked. Why would I? And no one ever told me. He was just Grandad, right?"

Yoyo nodded slowly. "And so you think he was really this man, this Boogart, because he left you this thing in a box with your name on it, yes?"

"Yes, because it belonged to him. And because of this."

I reached over and took out the photo of the two smiling soldiers and put it down next to the booklet.

Half an hour later Yoyo lolled back in his chair and surveyed the contents of the box laid out on the table and the maps spread out on the floor. I waited.

Eventually he said, "Tamar, have you not thought of asking your grandmother about these things?"

"What would be the point? She's forgotten how to speak English. I told you that."

"Okay, so maybe I could go with you to translate."

"She doesn't make sense in Dutch either."

"But—"

"No, Yoyo. Forget it. Honestly. It would be a waste of time."

He looked at me with his eyebrows hoisted up, but all he said was, "Okay, cool."

I didn't want to show the contents of the box to Gran, that was the truth. And Yoyo knew it, of course. I just thought it would be ... dangerous. I didn't know what I meant by that. And I didn't want to talk about it, either.

So after a second or two Yoyo let out a long breath and said, "Well, if it was just the identity papers and the photo and the crossword, I would say these are only what you could call souvenirs, yes? But the silk thing and the maps and the money, these make it very complicated. They take us to what my friend Luke calls 'headache territory'. Worse than Shakespeare's Sonnet bloody 94."

"Do you want to know what I think?"

"Yes, please. By the way, you look incredibly sexy when you are being serious like this."

"Shut up. Listen, I think he put the stuff in this box very carefully. He wanted to make sure the first thing I saw was the crossword."

"Why?"

"Because we couldn't finish it. It's like saying we have unfinished business. Know what I mean? It's like saying that this, all of this, is a puzzle I'm supposed to solve."

"I had this thought also."

"Especially because of the *Treasure Island* thing," I said, hurrying now. "And the maps."

"You must go slow a little bit," Yoyo said. "I haven't read *Treasure Island*."

I took a deep breath. "It doesn't matter. But in the story there's a map showing where treasure is buried, and—"

"And these maps tell us where the treasure is? But there are lots of little crosses on them, not one. Maybe the money is the treasure."

"No, I think the money is the ship."

"I am lost now," Yoyo said, frowning. "What do you mean, the money is the ship?"

"I mean that the money is to ... to make it possible to

217

get there." Then I sank a little bit, because I wasn't at all sure what I meant.

Yoyo's fingers drummed a complex little rhythm on the table top. Then he said, "The maps are in a certain order, yes?"

"Yes."

We both looked down at them.

"They go from south to north, and what joins them together is this river that has the same name as you."

"Right."

Yoyo stood up straight and walked up and down the kitchen. "It's fantastic," he said finally.

"I know."

"You think he wants you to go there? To make a journey up this river? Is that what you think he's telling you?"

"I can't think of anything else," I said. "Can you?"

Yoyo chewed a thumbnail for a little while. Then he picked up the identity booklet. "Your grandfather was in the resistance, is that right? And you said he was dropped with a parachute into the Netherlands?"

"That's what Mum said that Dad told her, yeah."

"So, if this Christiaan Boogart person was your grandfather, and these were his identity papers, and he came from England in 1944, he must have had this with him when he arrived in Holland. But the date on the papers is 1942. There is a difference of two years."

"Is that important?" I said, feeling lost.

"Oh yes, I think so. I think that this identity thing is false. I think it was made in England. It is obvious, really. The British would not send your grandfather to Holland with his real name."

He squinted at the little snapshot again. "So yes, maybe one of these men is William Hyde, okay. But, I'm sorry, his real name was not Christiaan Boogart, I'm sure. That is not the answer to your mystery."

I knew he was right. I must have looked very dejected because Yoyo sat and took both my hands in his.

He said, "You are right and wrong at the same time. I think that for some reason your grandfather has set you a puzzle to make a mess of your head. But I think he was perhaps a mad old bugger. Old people are weird, you know. Maybe you should take all this stuff down to the bottom of the garden and put fire to it. Not the money, of course."

He tugged my hands. "Let's do it. Burn it, and I will buy you dinner. No, *you* can buy me dinner, now that you are so rich."

"No."

"Why not? Then you can just remember him the way you knew him."

"No," I said again.

"You're sure?"

"Yes," I said. "I'm sure."

Yoyo studied me with great seriousness. "Okay. Good. So what do you want to do?"

"Do you still have your car?"

"The old Saab? Of course. I came here in it."

"What are you doing in the last week of July?"

He sat back and massaged the blond stubble on his jaw, gazing at me. "Tamar, are you thinking what I think you are thinking?"

"Probably."

"You want me – us – to go together to ... where is it? Devon? Cornwall?"

I nodded. He kept his eyes on mine for several seconds, his expression very solemn. Then he slid forward off the chair and fell to his knees. He put his hands together in prayer and lifted his eyes to the ceiling.

"Thank you, Grandad," he said. "Thank you for making all my wild dreams come true."

I leaned forward and slapped the back of his ridiculous head.

I made two cups of tea and we took them outside into the hot garden. Yoyo put on his sunglasses, which were small and circular and amber-tinted; they made him look like a back-combed owl. He perched on the garden table next to the barbecue that we hadn't used since Dad left.

"You must remember two things," he said. "First, we have no idea what we are looking for. This trip will perhaps be not a treasure hunt, but a what-you-call-it – a wild goose hunt, is it?"

"I know. I've thought about that. Maybe there's nothing to find. Maybe Grandad just wanted me to go and see this river I'm named after, and that's what the money is for."

"It's a lot of money just to go to see a river."

"Yeah," I said. "It is, isn't it?"

"And it doesn't explain the other stuff in the box."

"No. What's the second thing?"

He sighed and lifted his shoulders in a sad gesture. "The second thing is that your mother will not let you do it. With me."

It's not that I hadn't thought of that, of course. I'd thought of it about three milliseconds after I'd decided to call Yoyo. I'd thought about that huge bloody obstacle almost as much as I'd thought about what was in the box. A lot more than I'd thought about biology or geography. I'd run a thousand different arguments through my head, rehearsed a thousand reasons why she should let me do it. None of them were good enough to convince me, let alone her. I was going to have to fall back on that old technique, the only technique that we can rely on in the battle with parents: nag and whinge. And when that doesn't work, nag and whinge some more. Wear them down.

"She'll be okay," I said. "I'll sort it."

Yoyo grinned at me. "She'll go through the ceiling."

"The roof," I said.

"Yes. She'll go through the ceiling and then the roof."

That was something else he was right about.

HOLLAND, 1945

On the morning of 5th January Tamar sat at the kitchen table of Sanctuary Farm. A map was spread in front of him, and the deciphered signal that had come in from London the previous night was by his right hand. The first part was clear enough, unfortunately. His requested supply drop had been postponed because of bad weather and a shortage of aircraft. There were a number of inconsistencies and contradictions in the remainder of the message; now and again Tamar would mutter to himself and utter small sounds of frustration. It seemed unlikely that London had cocked up the coding, and he had checked his own deciphering twice and found nothing wrong. If Dart were with him he'd probably see the problem in no time at all.

Dart wasn't there because Tamar had taken over responsibility for the transceiver for the time being. It had been absurd to expect Dart to struggle back and forth through the white hell of the weather. They'd agreed this on Christmas morning, but the conversation had been strangely spiky and Dart had left abruptly immediately afterwards.

It had been the first morning that Oma had been too ill to leave her bed. Dart and Marijke had spent some time with her, then Dart had come downstairs alone. He'd talked about Julia's condition in a curiously distant, matter-of-fact way. Then, just as Tamar had been about to raise the subject himself, he'd said, "I can't keep slogging out here if the weather stays like this, you know."

His tone of voice had been strange, like familiar music played in the wrong key.

Tamar said, "No, of course you can't. You could die on the road if you got caught in a snowstorm. I was going to suggest that I take over wireless operations here until the weather improves."

"Good. You've got a copy of the schedule, haven't you?"

"Yes. It's bloody ironic, though, isn't it? While Oma is sick you have the perfect excuse to come here."

Dart paused in buttoning his coat but didn't look up. "Ironic," he said. "Yes, that's one way to describe it."

And that had been it. Dart had downed most of a cup of tea and left, shoving the heavy bike up towards the road, leaving an irregular woven track that was later obliterated by afternoon snow.

The memory of that morning, their last meeting, occasionally nagged at Tamar like a torn fingernail. Still, there was probably a simple explanation for Dart's apparent ill humour: he'd been hung-over. They both had.

Tamar concentrated on the map and the coordinates again. He looked up when Marijke entered the room. She put a half-full bowl of broth and a spoon down on the table; then, without touching him, she went to the window and stood there with her arms folded. He watched her back, waiting.

"She wants a priest," Marijke said.

"Ah." He stood up to go to her.

When she heard the scrape of his chair she said, "Don't touch me. If you touch me I'll cry. And I'm not going to cry. I told her not to be so ridiculous. I pointed out that the only Catholic priest this side of Apeldoorn is Father Willem, and that he's at least as old as she is and wouldn't last ten minutes out of doors in this weather. I said that since there was no question of him coming here, she has no choice but to get better. I refuse to discuss the matter any further."

Her voice cracked on the last sentence so she tried it again. "I absolutely refuse..."

She put her hands to her face. Tamar held still. They stood like that for several long moments in the half-light of the kitchen.

Tamar said, "Can I touch you yet?"

"No."

"I want to."

She turned then and faced him. She wiped her eyes on her sleeve and folded her arms again, hugging herself.

"I'm so angry," she said. "I was all right until you came back. I'd given up. So many terrible things. Relatives, neighbours disappearing. Opa. The bloody Germans coming to ... to strip us bare. Oma's silence. *Bam, bam, bam.* Like being punched over and over again. You get numb. It doesn't hurt any more. Unless you start to hope. That's the trick, you see: you can take any amount of shit unless you start to hope."

"Marijke, come on—"

"No, listen. If you weren't here and Oma died, I'd deal with it. Because there'd be nothing more to lose. It'd be just me. But now it's different; it's worse. Because you're yet another person to lose. You do stupid, dangerous things, and every time you go away I pray in agony that you'll come back. It's unfair. Hope is pulling me to pieces. I can't stand it. I really don't think I can stand it. Can you imagine a life for me if I lose you as well?"

He said, "I really believe the war is almost over. It's all

right to hope now. Hope is … appropriate. I have no intention of dying. Or leaving. We're going to stay together."

She stretched her arms towards him, a beggar's gesture. "Listen to yourself. Don't you see?"

Two days later, in response to a signal from Amsterdam relayed through London, Tamar left the farm. He'd wrapped himself in so many clothes that when she watched him walk into the white landscape he looked like a big clumsy animal. A big clumsy circus animal pushing a bicycle.

Later that same day, Marijke, busying herself in the kitchen, heard sounds from above. The coughing was routine, and she had tuned her hearing to pick up variations in it. But this was something else. She went to the foot of the stairs. Incredibly, Oma stood looking down at her, clutching the banister. She was wrecked, red-eyed, and full of purpose.

"Oma! What are you doing out of bed? What do you want?"

The old woman wanted to be downstairs, and there was no arguing with her. She refused to sit by the stove and lowered herself onto a chair at the table. There was a coughing fit and a spell of breathing that sounded like cloth being torn. When it was over, she mimed the need for pen and paper. Marijke brought them to her, along with a mug of tea which was ignored.

Julia Maartens began to write, hunched over the paper like a schoolchild taking an examination in the presence of cheating classmates. When her sweat fell onto the paper, she blotted it carefully with her sleeve. Once, passing behind her, Marijke glanced down and saw that the letter began with the words *Forgive me, Father, for I have sinned*. She fought the desire to seize the paper and tear it apart; instead she lit the lamp because the daylight in the room was failing. When Julia had finished her confession, she folded it into an envelope which she addressed to Father Willem van Dael. With Marijke's help she got to her feet and went to the dresser. She reached up and tucked the envelope behind the brass and mahogany clock that had not worked for several years. When that was done she allowed her granddaughter to help her back to bed. It took a long time to climb the stairs. Their progress was twice halted by bouts of coughing that seemed likely to unhinge the old woman's ribs.

Before he'd left on Christmas Day, Dart had told Marijke there was a possibility that Oma would develop pneumonia. He had described the change in symptoms that would occur if that were to happen. Oma's breathing would become faster and shallower. The rattle in her chest might well turn into something more like a faint whistling; she would perhaps feel pain high in her back. Her temperature would rise and she would almost certainly be feverish and confused. Still, Dart had said, Oma was strong and the chances were that none of these things would happen. But his tone had been strangely flat, neutral; and he had not once looked Marijke in the eye. She was not reassured. Within forty-eight hours of Oma writing her confession, the changes that Dart had predicted took hold of her.

But nothing Dart said had prepared Marijke for Oma's transformation into the thin and ancient stranger who now lay in the bed. Nor was she prepared for her own sense of numb resentment. She had expected to feel pain – would have preferred it, perhaps. This hollowness felt like a lack of love or loyalty. It was familiar, though.

She had not slept in her bed since Tamar had left. Oma was worse during the nights, and Marijke had brought the quilt and a pillow from her own room and nested in the armchair beside her grandmother's bed. She dreamed incessantly, and in these dreams she was often in an unfamiliar but friendly place in which people with slow-motion mouths called her name. Because she woke frequently, these dreams crossed the border into real time. So, when she woke just before midnight on 13th January, she did not think that she had heard a real voice. Or perhaps, for the briefest moment, she hoped that she would look up and it would be him, speaking her name. She eased herself upright and the lamplight fell onto her grandmother's face. Oma's eyes were open. Her mouth moved.

"Marijke."

She was too shocked to react. Then she saw that Julia's hand was lying open on the bed. It looked too big and coarse for the pale, wasted arm it was attached to. Marijke reached over and took it in her own and somehow found herself kneeling beside the bed.

"Oma?"

She heard the old woman's tongue move stickily inside her mouth.

"Oma? Dear God. Did you say something?"

"Marijke."

It was like ventriloquism. Marijke did not remember the voice.

She said, "I'm here. I'm here."

The old woman's hand tightened its grip. Her gaze fixed on her granddaughter's face, but Marijke was not sure that the eyes could see. They were fading, like pale fish sinking deeper into a murky pool.

"Oma? Oma, stay with me. Please try to stay with me."

The mouth made small movements, then a single word which might have been "Eat."

"What? Oma, are you hungry? Shall I get you something?"

Julia Maartens moved her head on the pillow. Her eyes aimed at the dark angle of wall and ceiling above the bedroom door. "It's here," she said.

Marijke turned to look; she couldn't help herself. There was, of course, nothing there; and she was looking at nothing when her grandmother said, "Johannes."

She'd spent her last breath on the word. It ended in a soft hiss, like a puncture.

ON 19TH FEBRUARY Dart was scheduled to transmit from the Marionette House at eleven forty-eight. It worried him because he reckoned that Tamar's signal to London was too long by more than a minute. If London were to ask him to repeat, the German detector cars would have plenty of time to zero in on him. So he wouldn't repeat. Except that it would screw things up if he didn't. Jesus.

At ten thirty he put on his white coat and buttoned it, then the shabby overcoat with its red cross armband. He rubbed the lapel between his forefinger and thumb, checking the silk sheet concealed in the lining. Then he picked up the medical bag in which the transmitter crystals and the revolver were concealed and went quietly down the stairs. In the day room, his passing was ignored by two skeletal inmates who had pushed their chairs close together as if for warmth.

Propelling the heavy old bike made his emptiness much worse. It was possible not to feel it when you sat indoors doing nothing; but the slightest physical effort caused hunger to unfold itself inside the body. It was amazing, he thought, that he had the strength to move his legs at all. The cold air affected him like alcohol, and he steered an erratic course along the fractured road. He would have to get a grip on himself before he began the transmission. He would have to send very fast and make no mistakes. Yes.

His anxieties about his work were themselves a cover for what truly obsessed him.

During the bitter month of January he had brooded in the dark seclusion of his cell. It had not been a process of thinking. Rather, he had stared at the hurt in himself until it had become numb. Until it had grown a protective coating over itself, the way soft grey fur grows on mouldering food. If he had been more than usually silent and withdrawn during those weeks, it had gone largely unnoticed. All the inhabitants of the asylum seemed to have entered a state of suspended animation, as though they hoped to survive cold and hunger by dreaming themselves elsewhere. Some of the nuns now wore the same dazed and distant expression as their patients.

Eventually he had come to the conclusion that it was not her fault. She had been seduced, cynically and deliberately, by the man who should have been protecting her. Tamar had abused his position of trust. It had not been easy for Dart to accept this, because he too had trusted Tamar. Trusted him, stupidly, blindly, with his life. He'd recalled Tamar's cowardice in the plane on the night of the drop, the look of stupefied terror on his face as he stood at the hatch. He should have realized then that the man was weak. He'd been a fool to believe in him. It had come as a huge relief to Dart when he'd understood this, on a night when the blessed Benzedrine had cleared and sharpened his mind. Until then he had been misled by the image of Marijke and Tamar together in the kitchen, writhing on that chair. It had possessed and haunted him. It had tricked him into thinking that they were a single creature seeking furtive and nasty pleasures. He had tried to hate her, to see her as a tainted thing. But it wasn't like that at all, of course. When a criminal and his victim are locked together, grappling and struggling, it is not always easy to tell them apart.

By the time he returned to the farm, after the thaw, he was clear about the way he would behave towards her. He would simply pretend that nothing had happened. There would be no confrontation. She would see that his love for her had not faltered. Eventually, inevitably, she would recognize the strength of that love and turn away from Tamar's poisonous embraces. Of that he was certain. All he had to do was stay alive for her. And do something about Tamar.

But this calm resolve had been overthrown as soon as he'd arrived at the farm. Marijke had opened the door and blurted the news of her grandmother's death before he'd had a chance to speak. It had not crossed his mind that anything might have happened to Julia Maartens. He had not given the old woman a moment's thought, so he had no idea how to react. And while Marijke was pouring her grief out to him, he was falling helplessly and angrily in love all over again. She was wearing black, naturally, and it deepened her incredible eyes. He'd wanted her so much that he could not think of the proper things to say.

She'd taken him to the crude grave, and he'd been shocked. To have buried her in the potato patch, to have heaped rough stones on her! Dear God. The man was a brute. Marijke couldn't see that herself, of course; she'd been blinded by misery. He'd been so outraged that he couldn't speak, or even reach out to touch her, even though she obviously wanted him to. That had been a failure on his part, a lost opportunity, and he bitterly regretted it. Then they had gone into the house and Tamar had been there. Smiling, damn him. It had been difficult not to recoil from his greeting, knowing where those hands had been, what they had done.

Now, on the road to Mendlo, Dart shook his head to dislodge yet again the vile image of Tamar working his body against hers.

The sky was the colour of an old knife. In the ditches and in the dark and furrowed fields, small mounds of dirty snow still lingered. They looked, Dart thought, like slaughtered sheep that had been left where they had fallen. He made himself pedal faster in the hope of warming his slow blood.

The guards at the Merchants' Gate were unusually sullen. They checked Dart's papers for the first time in weeks, not looking him in the eye. There was none of the meaningless banter he'd become used to, and this made him uneasy. When he remounted the bike at the far side of the archway, he glanced back; the Germans were watching him.

He'd got as far as the junction where Canal Street met the wider avenue that led to the town hall when two Waffen-SS troopers came round the corner. One pointed at Dart and they ran towards him, the skirts of their coats flapping wildly, machine pistols slung over their shoulders.

Dart stopped. Panic rose in him like black water, threatening to shut down the valves of his heart. He imagined, as he had imagined so many times before, a cellar full of torture, a final bullet fired casually into the back of his head. His legs began to fail. Before he could topple, a hand seized the handlebars and another grabbed his arm. He looked up into the face of one of the German soldiers. It was a young face, tense and beaded with sweat.

"*Doktor?* You are a doctor?"

"I... Yes. I am. I am."

"Come with us, please. Come, *schnell*!"

They took him, running alongside the bike, past the town hall and onto Albrecht Street. He had a mad desire to say "No, stop! I must get to the puppet shop before quarter to twelve!" Seeing them approach, a woman pulled two children into a house. Dart and his escort went past them and turned into the small square called Westerplein.

It was a space shadowed by tall narrow houses. The ground floors were shops and offices, now dark and shuttered. Three houses had long since been gutted by people scavenging for firewood, their doors, shutters, window frames ripped out; they drooped like old flesh.

The first thing he saw was the corpse. Lying face down. It had been a young man, a teenager, perhaps. Its head was a mess and from it blood had spread, making a dark and sticky grid of the square cobbles. Close to the body an old man, grey-bearded and black-clad, was chanting some sort of prayer, rocking his body back and forth. Behind him a dozen or so people, adults and children, stood in two rows. Their clothes were too big for them. Their faces were as pale as bone. Some of them had their eyes open, huge eyes, as if they had seen nothing for years.

Dart thought, My God. Jews. How the hell have they stayed hidden so long?

A platoon of SS men in grey greatcoats stood in a semi-circle facing the captives. One of them had a dog, a big Alsatian, on a leash. It sat motionless, amber eyes fixed on the old man who was praying. Dart dismounted from his bike and, because he was supposed to be a doctor, he walked shakily to the corpse and kneeled beside it. Almost instantly he was yanked to his feet, but not before he saw the legs of a young girl who was standing close to the body. They were trembling out of control and a stream of urine ran down one of them into her shoe, which was a man's shoe and far bigger than her foot.

The sergeant who pulled Dart upright had teeth missing. He spoke to Dart in a fierce whisper, spraying spittle. "Not the Jew, you idiot! The major! Come!"

Dart was marched across the square to where a military staff car was parked. An officer, immaculate in field-grey uniform and polished boots, leaned against the passenger door. He was bareheaded. Close to him a trooper stood holding the officer's cap with its death's head insignia. He held it rigidly in front of him as if it were some kind of religious object that pilgrims might queue to touch. The major was so white, so pale-haired, that at first Dart took him for an albino. With his right hand he held a field dressing to the side of his head. A track of blood ran down his neck; the double zigzags of silver on his collar were smeared with it. In his left hand he held a Luger pistol.

The sergeant thrust Dart into the officer's line of vision and said, "Sir! A doctor."

The German straightened and looked into Dart's face. The only sound in the square now was the old man's chanting, and Dart was surprised that no one put a stop to it.

Dart managed to say, "What has happened, Major? How are you injured?"

The German's eyes seemed unnaturally wide open; perhaps, Dart thought, a symptom of shock. He stared at Dart for a second or two, then gestured with the gun towards the dead body.

"The little Jew rat tried to bite my ear off. He tried to bite my ear off!"

It took Dart a second to understand the words. "May I see, please?"

He took the major's hand and pulled away the wad of dressing, thinking, This is the first time I have touched a Nazi.

The ear was bleeding freely, as ears do. Where it joined the skull there was a slight rip but most of the blood was coming from the lobe, which was almost split in two. Probably the boy's canine teeth had been clamped there when the German shot him, and the flesh had torn as he fell to the ground. Dart was surprised to find himself working this out so logically; surprised that his terror allowed him to think at all.

"This will need one or two stitches, Major. I cannot do that here, of course. I would rather leave it to your own doctors. The wound is not really serious."

He was extremely startled by the officer's furious reaction to these words. Two small red patches appeared as if by magic just below the pale eyes. The voice came as a harsh whisper, a scream barely under control.

"Not serious? Not serious? What sort of damned stupid Dutch bloody doctor are you? Listen, idiot: a Jew who has lived underground like some kind of filthy little animal has bitten me. His dirty Jewish spit is in my blood. What I care about is disease, Doctor. Disease! Isn't that obvious?"

Dart had absolutely no idea what to say. He could see the little pink threads that had appeared in the German's eyes. He forced his mouth to work.

"Yes. Of course. I…" He cleared his throat. "I have swabs. And iodine. I do not have much else. Times are hard."

"Iodine? Will iodine kill the poison in Jew spit? Will it?"

"Yes," Dart said. "I'm sure it will." He fumbled with the clasps of his bag. In its false bottom was the Smith and Wesson revolver. Dear God, he thought, I want to kill this man.

He took out a swab and the iodine and painted the Nazi's ear a brownish purple. It was good to know that it hurt. While he was doing it the chanting behind him stopped. He heard the dog whine. The major sat on the running board of the car while Dart put a fresh dressing on the wound and bandaged it in place. When it was done, the major carefully examined Dart's handiwork with his fingers. If there had been a mirror available, Dart thought, the man would have spent some time studying his appearance.

By now, Dart was extremely anxious, but he did not dare look at his watch.

"Herr Major? May I go now?"

The German considered this for a moment. "No," he said. "Stay here." He took a slim metal cigarette case from his breast pocket, flicked it open and held it out to Dart. "Smoke?"

Dart took a cigarette and stood smoking it while the SS loaded the Jews into a high canvas-covered truck.

It was a surprisingly subdued business. A man who was making a low continuous moaning had to be pulled away from the dead boy, but there was little of the crying and screaming that Dart had steeled himself for. Even the children were quiet, presumably because they had not yet been separated from their parents. That, Dart knew, would happen later. Perhaps at a railway siding somewhere near Belsen or Dachau. If they lasted that long. He took a last drag on the cigarette and crushed the butt under his heel. The truck reversed and pulled out of the square. Its engine sounded sick. Dart's last sight of the ghostly faces of its passengers was through a haze of bluish exhaust.

The major returned to his car. He picked up his cap and settled into the front seat beside the driver. The sergeant and another soldier climbed into the back and sat with their weapons aimed at the sky. The major studied Dart for several seconds.

"What is your name, Doctor?"

"Lubbers. Ernst Lubbers."

"Well, Dr Lubbers. I am fortunate that you were near by. You are attached to the hospital, I presume? But I have not seen you before."

Oh shit. "Er … actually, I'm based at the asylum."

The driver had moved to start the car but the major now put out a hand to stop him.

"What? You work at the madhouse? Are you telling me that you are a psychiatrist?"

Dart forced a laugh. "Oh no, no. Not at all. I look after the general health of the patients. Also of the people here in the town. We are short of doctors. I do everything."

The man's eyelashes were incredibly white. Like a pig's, Dart thought. That was what gave him that permanently surprised expression.

"I shall remember you, Dr Lubbers."

"Thank you," Dart said stupidly.

The German gestured at the square. "One day none of this will be necessary." He sighed like a burdened man. "One day, people like you and I will live in a clean world. Do you understand what I mean? As a doctor, you will know that surgery is sometimes unavoidable. What happened here today was a medical procedure. Our children will some day thank us for having the courage to cut the infection out."

Dart said, "I understand you, Major. Really."

"And my ear will be healthy?"

"I think so." Dart could not resist leaving a germ of doubt in the man's mind. "I'm pretty sure we got to the infection in time."

The white eyelashes flickered. "I hope you are right, Doctor. It would be bad news for both of us if you were wrong." He turned to the driver. "Let's go."

Dart stepped back from the car, but the major hadn't quite finished with him.

"Dr Lubbers? The clean world I spoke about – there is a small thing you could do to help create it." He gestured with a thumb towards the centre of the square. "You could clear that up."

Unwillingly, Dart turned to look where the major had pointed, to where the dead boy still lay face down on the cobbles. As the car moved off, the town hall clock began to sound the twelve chimes of midday.

ENGLAND, 1995

"HONEST TO GOD, I still can't believe it," Yoyo yelled. "We're really on our way!"

Then he braked and we came to a dead stop in a traffic jam on the Chiswick flyover. We'd been travelling for all of fifteen minutes. It was still early in the day, but the sun was already fierce and light flashed from metal and glass all around us, from car roofs and windscreens and from the windows of office blocks. We crept at glacier speed for several miles, and by the time the traffic thinned out on the M4 and we picked up speed I was slippery with sweat.

Yoyo reached up and opened the sunroof. "So tell me," he said, "how did you do it? How did you make Sonia change her mind?"

It hadn't taken much. Just three weeks of reasonable argument, unreasonable argument, nagging and whingeing, tearful discussion, begging, throwing tantrums, sulking, being charming, and emotional blackmail.

"Just by being my sweet self," I said.

He peered at me over his amber owl-eye glasses.

"Hey, watch the road," I said. "Anyway, I'm more interested in what Mum said to you last night."

Yoyo had spent the night at our house so we could get

an early start. After dinner Mum got me clearing away and washing up while she took Yoyo into the living room for "a little chat". When he'd come back to the kitchen he'd crossed his eyes and pulled his mouth down at the corners. His ears were bright pink, as if they'd been freshly slapped.

"So come on, what did she say?"

"She gave me a big talk about safe driving and the condition of the car."

"What's wrong with it?"

"The car? Nothing, absolutely. I told her."

"What else?"

The rosy tint returned to his ears. He grinned, a bit sheepishly. "We had a most serious discussion about your birthday."

"What do you mean? My birthday isn't for ages yet."

"That is the exact point Sonia made several times. That you are not sixteen until September."

"Oh, right." I probably blushed, although I'd prefer to think I didn't.

After a pause Yoyo said, "I told her not to worry, because I am gay."

"You what? You didn't, did you? Is that what you told her?"

"Of course."

"You liar," I said, giggling. "You never."

"No, you're right. I should have said it, but I did not think of it until later."

"That's a shame," I said, then clammed up, thinking he might take it the wrong way. Or even the right way.

"Do you know what else? Your mother already made phone calls to places in Devon and Cornwall."

"What do you mean? What places?"

"The kind of places we might stay. Not hotels, these bed and breakfasts. She checked out the prices. She said to me,

'Johannes, the average price per room at this time of the year is about thirty pounds or less. So the money Tamar has got is plenty for two rooms each night.' She gave me this look she does, know what I mean?"

I knew.

"When we get back, she wants to see the…" He lifted his left hand from the wheel and clicked his fingers, searching for the word. "The reckonings."

"The bills?"

"Exactly. The bills. To make sure we have two rooms every time."

"That's cool. She can have the bloody bills," I said, hating her.

I didn't know then that we'd blow it the very first night.

I'd been a city girl all my life. Long car journeys were something I knew nothing about. I had Yoyo's road atlas on my lap, and the straightish blue lines of the motorways didn't look that long. The map took us a page or two west to Bristol, a page further south to Exeter, another to Plymouth. I had a very shaky idea of scale. The only map I really knew was the one of the London Underground, so my idea of a really long journey was from my nearest tube, Ravenscourt Park, to somewhere like Walthamstow, at the far side of the universe. The maps Grandad had left me showed hills, moors, forests, rivers that twisted like snakes. Stupidly I thought we'd start to see such exotic things quite early in our journey west – like just after Reading, maybe. I was deeply disappointed. The countryside looked hammered flat and colourless by the heat, and seemed to drift by incredibly slowly. At Bristol we crawled in dense traffic over the Avonmouth Bridge. The river below swilled like grey treacle between huge banks of cracked and crumpled mud. On the far side we ground to a halt again, locked in a mass of vehicles and traffic cones.

The Saab turned into an oven and we sat there and roasted. When I was something like medium-rare I fell asleep. I woke up when I felt the car jerk and turn. I opened my eyes and saw what could have been anywhere: a busy roundabout, billboards, an industrial estate, a high grass bank scattered with plastic bags and scraps of paper. It took me a minute to get my voice to work. My mouth felt and tasted as though a hamster had hibernated in it.

"Where are we?"

"Exeter, thank God," Yoyo said. "Motorway services. If I don't pee I will explode. And I'm starving, also."

The car park was packed with coaches, camper vans, cars towing boats, cars towing caravans, cars with racks of mountain bikes on the back, cars with surfboards on their roofs. Inside, the place was heaving and the atmosphere hit us in the face like a wave of used bathwater. We queued a lifetime for food. The muzak was a greasy orchestral version of "Summer Holiday".

Yoyo said, "If there is a canteen in hell, it is like this."

When we slid our trays along to the till, the exhausted-looking boy in the silly paper hat punched buttons and said, "Eleven pounds sixty, please."

"Incredible," I muttered, groping in my bag.

When I pulled out the wad of Grandad's cash, Yoyo murmured, "You know, it's not a good idea keeping it all in your bag like this. Someone might pinch it. Nineteen hundred and forty-five pounds is a lot of money to lose."

I stared up at him. "What? What did you say, Yoyo?"

"I just said—"

"Eleven pounds sixty, please," the boy repeated.

A melting fat man in the queue behind us said, "Come on, love, let's move it."

We found a space at the end of a table. Our neighbours were four surf boys, all with straggled bottle-blond hair, half a dozen hippy necklaces apiece and huge patchy shorts.

Yoyo got busy squirting sachets of mayonnaise onto his chips.

"I'm thick," I said, "really thick."

He looked up, licking his fingers. "What?"

"You said 'nineteen hundred and forty-five pounds'."

He looked confused. "That's right, isn't it?"

"Yeah. But didn't you wonder why it was such a weird amount? Like, why not one thousand five hundred? Or two thousand?"

Yoyo's reply was something like *"Ugh urgh-urgh"* because his mouth was full of double cheeseburger.

"It's because it's not the amount that's important," I said, "it's the number. It's a date. Nineteen forty-five."

Yoyo swallowed burger-pulp. It took a while to slide down his long thin gullet; it was like watching a cartoon of an ostrich swallowing a brick.

"Of course," he said. "Nineteen forty-five. I am as thick as you. Thicker!"

The surf boys were watching us now, grinning like bleached monkeys.

"All right, all right, it's not exactly a competition. But that's it, don't you think? The money is another, well, clue, if you like."

"Yes, I think so. And are you going to tell me what it means, Sherlock Holmes?"

"I dunno. Nineteen forty-five was the year the war ended, obviously. The year Gran and Grandad escaped and came to England, according to what was in the paper. So I s'pose this, this thing we're doing, this…"

"Adventure?" Yoyo suggested.

And I thought what a ridiculous old-fashioned word that was. Typical Yoyo. It was about right, though, no denying it.

"It must be to do with something that happened in that year."

"Brilliant," Yoyo said.

The surf boys were all ears now, leaning towards us. I turned and glowered at them. They did a sort of *"Ooh, baby"* thing and looked away, smirking.

Then I turned my death-glare onto Yoyo. "Don't take the piss unless you've got a better idea, okay?"

He stuck a mayo-coated chip in his mouth to hide what I hoped was embarrassment. "Cool," he said. "By the way, you look very sexy when you are—"

"Shut up," I said.

Not long after Exeter the motorway ended and the road split into two. Our bit, the Plymouth bit, climbed up a long hill. At the top the road levelled out and took us through a long patch of trees; and when we came out of it we could see for ever. We both said "Wow" at the same time because it was like being in a plane. Ahead and below us there were curving webs of fields and hedges between overlapping layers of blue-green hills. Far beyond it all the jagged horizon was like motionless purple smoke. I'd never seen so much landscape in one go before.

"It's beautiful, isn't it?" Yoyo said.

Well, yes, it was. But what I felt was fear. No, not fear exactly; that's too strong. Anxiety, perhaps. I'd been so tangled up in working out what Grandad was telling – or asking – me that I'd hardly given a thought to what it would actually be like, this adventure, as Yoyo had called it. And what I felt when we had that brief glimpse of huge distance was … unsafe. What made my breathing stumble was the knowledge that in all that vast countryside there wasn't a soul who knew me. I had to fight back the urge to say, "Right, we've seen it. Let's go home."

So I was glad when we hit the outskirts of Plymouth, which looked pretty much like the outskirts of anywhere else.

At the nineteenth set of lights Yoyo said, "Tamar, can we stop for the night here? I don't want to drive any more."

"Okay," I said, as coolly as I could. As if the words "stop for the night" caused me no problems at all. "I've no idea where to go, though."

Yoyo pulled over and stopped in a lay-by that had BUSES ONLY painted on it. He took the road atlas from me and flicked through to the back pages where there was a small map of the centre of Plymouth. He studied it for a minute and then craned his neck round.

"Ah," he said, "there, see? The sign says Hoe and Barbican."

"What does that mean?"

"I don't know exactly. Strange words. But look, this Hoe is green on the map and close to the sea. I would like to look at the sea."

After some ill-tempered encounters with other drivers we found a sign saying HOE PARKING. We fed the greedy ticket machine, then climbed up steps and a slope to what looked like a park. There were people lying about with half their clothes missing, and dogs panting in the shade of trees. When we got to the top of the rise, we stood there gawping. It was as if we had walked into a child's drawing, the colours of everything were so bright and simple. The green grass levelled and then fell away between beds of cartoon-coloured flowers towards the sea, which was intensely – impossibly – blue. The child artist had sketched in an island and a couple of ships for extra interest. Slap in the middle of the scene was a lighthouse painted in nice fat red and white stripes like a stick of rock. After a whole day of hot driving it was so unreal that it was ages before I could turn to look at Yoyo. He was gazing at the sea and grinning his face in half.

"Fantastic."

"Yeah. So what do we do now?"

He looked at me as if I were an alien or something. "Do?" he said. "Do? We sit and look and thank God we are not in the car still. And because I have been driving all day, you can go and find two cold drinks. Please."

Which seemed fair enough, but it took me a while. When I came back with the cans and two packets of crisps, Yoyo was flat on his back and apparently asleep. I snapped a Pepsi open and drank in the view. I saw now that the island was straight-sided and seemed to be made out of brown concrete, and that the ships parked out on the deep blue sea were warships, grey and bristling with guns and aerials.

I nudged Yoyo. "Drink? I got some crisps too. By your elbow."

He wriggled his nose and mumbled but didn't move or open his eyes. By the time I finished the Pepsi his breathing was deep and steady again. I picked his pocket for the car keys and fetched map 108 from the bag in the boot.

With the map spread out on the grass, I could see that the mouth of the Tamar was some way off, to the west of the city. It flowed into a wide stretch of water with the strange, Japanese-looking name Hamoaze. I felt edgy, restless. I looked at my watch; unbelievably, it was almost five o'clock. It was ridiculous that we had come all this way, taken an entire day, only to stop just a few miles from the Tamar, almost in sight of it. At the same time, I still felt the urge to go home, to abandon the whole thing. Now that we were on the map, the scale of everything seemed huge and impossible to deal with. I felt lonely.

"Wake up, Yoyo. Yoyo? Come on, wake up. You'll get sunburnt if you lie there much longer."

We followed a different footpath back to the car park and found ourselves looking down onto a terrace of guest houses, each with a dinky little awning over the door. The third one from the end was called The Tamar. It had a sign up saying NO VACANCIES. So did all the others, except for one called Avalon, so we went in there. The decor had a King Arthur theme; there was even a small suit of armour made of gold plastic at the foot of the stairs. We stood alone at the reception desk for a bit, and then Yoyo reached past me and shook a little brass bell that sat on the counter. When no one came, he did it again and then wandered back down the hall to a rack full of tourist leaflets.

I hissed at him to come back, and when I turned round again a woman had magically appeared behind the desk. There must have been a secret door. She was fortyish and had sunglasses pushed up into her dark hair. Her white blouse was mostly unbuttoned and I could see the top of a turquoise bikini. She gave off a strong whiff of coconut.

"Can I help you?" She had a European accent of some sort. *Help* came out as *'alp*.

"Er, yes. Hello. I was wondering, do you have two rooms for tonight?"

"For?" she asked.

I thought she'd said *four*. "No, two," I said.

She stared at me, and then her eyes slid past me towards the hall. She couldn't have seen Yoyo from her angle.

"For who? For your family?"

"Oh. No, for me and my friend. Actually, he's not my friend, he's my cousin. Sort of."

"Cousin?"

I felt my neck getting warm and realized I was blushing. I was furious with myself and that made it worse. I turned and hissed "Yoyo!" again. She leaned forward for a better view of the hall and immediately pulled back startled as Yoyo

251

appeared, looming over her with his hand outstretched. She took it cautiously, and Yoyo shook it as if she was an old friend.

"Hello! Pleased to meet you," he said, all smile and twinkle. "Yes, this is my cousin. We are here to investigate the Tamar River, which is also my cousin's name. We have come from London. I am from Holland, actually. Johannes van Zant, how do you do? As she said, we are looking for two rooms. This seems a very nice place. I like the gold soldier just here. How much is it?"

She had retreated from this barrage of words as far as the little office would let her. Her mouth opened, closed, opened again. I didn't know whether to laugh or die.

"Is no for sale," she managed finally.

"He means the room," I said. "The rooms, I mean. Each."

"Single room twenty-two pound fifty includes full English breakfast," she said. "But I doan know…"

She kept her eyes on Yoyo as she reached below the counter and brought out an impressive-looking register. I didn't think she needed to check how many vacant rooms she had. Behind her head there was a wooden board with hooks for keys, and there were only six of them.

She studied the book. "Ah, sorry. Only one double room free."

"Okay," I said quickly. "Thanks anyway. We'll try somewhere else."

"Is twin-bedded," she said. "Nice. Thirty-five pound."

"Twin-bedded?" Yoyo said. "Is that like one big bed for two, or two small ones?"

He was enjoying this, the sod. I turned away and took a deep interest in a terrible painting of a maiden chained to a rock and being menaced by a dragon. The knight in shining armour was some distance in the background. It looked to me that he was a little late showing up. When the receptionist led us upstairs, I made sure that Yoyo had a good view of my scowl.

But it was a nice room, I had to admit. It had SIR GAWAIN in fancy lettering on the outside of the door, and I was dreading more armour and whatnot inside, but it was big and cool and plain and smelled of artificial lemons. The beds were a decent three feet apart and there was a lock on the bathroom door. Yoyo went off to get the car and bring the bags up. The window looked down onto the Avalon's garden, and the receptionist was stripped to her bikini again and back on her sun lounger. She was already browner than I'd ever be.

Yoyo came back, sweaty from lugging the luggage. He dumped everything and went to the window.

"Nice view. That colour and brown skin. Perfect, I think."

"Pervert," I said.

"Not at all. I was talking only about colours. I would say the colours here are very good, not like London. Everything is clearer, somehow, isn't it?"

When Yoyo was in the shower I called Mum and lied to her.

THE NEXT MORNING we crossed the Tamar. And I hardly saw it. The traffic was a torrent that swept us onto the bridge before we could pull over.

"Yoyo, slow down! I want to look!"

He tried. From behind, a vast truck blared rage at us.

"Shit!"

On my side, the view was wrecked by the huge iron arches of the Victorian railway bridge. All I could make out were flickering glimpses of a shapeless expanse of water, boats, humps of land in the distance. I turned, straining against my seat belt to see past Yoyo, and all I saw was the side of a big white van travelling alongside. I slumped back, wailing, and then we were in Cornwall. Or, as Yoyo soon started to call it, Tamarland. We passed houses called Tamar View, Tamar Nook, Tamar Villa. We passed the Tamar Restaurant, Tamar Auto Sales, the Tamar MiniMart, Tamar Marine Services, Tamar Insurance.

Yoyo, of course, thought it was hilarious. "So cool," he said. "You are everything here! You're famous. Maybe at these places you would get, you know, what-you-call-it, discount."

"I think what I'm getting is an identity crisis," I said.

Which was a bit melodramatic, maybe, but it is pretty weird when you see your name everywhere and it's got nothing to do with you. Before this, if I heard someone say "Tamar", I could be ninety-nine per cent certain they were talking about me, not a café or a chocolate bar or something. In London, I was unique. But down here, where I was a bungalow one minute and a funeral parlour the next, I felt as though I was dissolving. I mean, if you're everywhere, you're nowhere. If you're everything, you're nothing. By the time we'd been in Tamarland for half an hour I was grumpily wondering why I'd been given such a weird name in the first place.

We stopped for petrol at a garage called Tamar Services and Body Repair, which amused Yoyo so much that he made me pose for a photo. It's here in front of me now, one of dozens he took over the next few days. I'm leaning against the side of the Saab. Yoyo had made me push my sunglasses up onto my head so that he could see my face, and because of that I look squinty and slightly bad-tempered, even though I wasn't – yet. In the background, beyond the garage, is a flat swathe of fairly uninteresting countryside. There's nothing in the picture to tell you that my river is less than a mile away.

The evening before, we'd gone out to eat and found a place where you could sit outside, on one of the quays down on the Barbican. Afterwards we wandered about for a bit, then Yoyo bought four cans of lager and two Cokes and we went back to the Avalon to have our first really close look at the maps. The faint pencil marks told us that we had to go up the west side of the Tamar, the Cornwall side; but we quickly realized that there are no roads that actually follow the river. You can't just drive up the Tamar. You can't walk up it, either. There are footpaths here and there, but for most of its twisty complicated length, the Tamar stays out of reach. Whenever a road comes anywhere near it, the river snakes and wriggles off in the opposite direction. The map showed us every bend and every detail, showed us how it curled round hills and snuck through woods; showed us how wide or narrow it was. The map had the river pinned down, yet it was shy and secretive and sneaky. It seemed like you could never get a really good look at it.

"Like you," Yoyo had said, and I'd whacked him and made him slop beer down his T-shirt.

But there were a few minor roads that crept close to the river before they retreated or petered out. Grandad's marks were at several of these points, the first one at a place called Landulph. According to the map, there was nothing much there except for a church. It was only a mile or so up from the Tamar Bridge, but the main road took us away off to the west, so we had to double back to find it. For most of the way there were high banks on both sides of the narrow lane; it was like driving down a hot green tunnel.

The church was small, quaint, picturesque. Ancient grey stone, a low tower, a gate with a roof over it. The silence was so thick that I felt as though my ears had failed. The hedge alongside the churchyard glowed with wild flowers, and I realized I didn't know the name of a single one. There was a house opposite, lurking behind evergreen trees, and no other building in sight. I couldn't imagine what a church was doing in such a remote place. Why would people come here, and when?

Well, they came when they were dead, if the churchyard was anything to go by. It was small but crowded, so crammed with headstones and crosses and crumbled angels that it was hard to pick a way through them. Bodies must have been stacked ten deep underfoot. More landfill than Landulph. Most of the headstones were scoured by erosion or smothered by lichen. They looked like slabs of grey mouldy cheese.

"Late of this perish," Yoyo said, peering at one of the few legible headstones. "What does that mean? Late for what?"

"Parish," I said, "not perish. It means… Never mind. According to the map, the footpath to the river starts down this way. Come on, Yoyo. I want to see the river, not look at bloody graves!"

We came to a stile with a board next to it telling us that we were entering a nature reserve. The board had faded pictures of the birds that lived there. It would have been more honest if it had shown the biting and bloodsucking insects, but I suppose there wasn't room on it for five million illustrations. It didn't mention the ten foot tall stinging nettles either, or the brambles and the things that slip inside your sandals and stab you in the soft flesh under your toes. After fifty metres I was ready to give up, but Yoyo was a stubborn so-and-so and wouldn't pay attention to my whimpers. So, limping and bitten and groaning, I came at last to where he took this next photo of me.

I'm sitting on the trunk of a dead tree that must have drifted down the river and got washed up here. Its roots look like the hand and fingers of a giant's skeleton. Considering it was a brilliantly hot day in the middle of summer, it's surprising there's so little colour. I remember the sky being blue, but according to Yoyo's camera it was almost white. The foreground is a beach of pale stones shrouded in seaweed that looks black in the photo. In fact, it was dark green, crunchy on top and slimy underneath. In the background there are two shades of silver. The one nearest me, the one speckled with black, is mud. The one further away is a huge expanse of flat water, as you can tell by the little flecks of colour, the sails of boats. Beyond all that you can make out the towers that the Tamar Bridge hangs from, and next to it the long ribcage of the railway bridge. You can't see the corpse of the gull that was the first thing we saw and smelled when the path ushered us onto the shore. You wouldn't know that when we emerged from the wilderness the buzzing of flies blurred into the throb of traffic crossing the bridge so that it was a moment or two before we could tell the difference. You can't trust photographs.

When he'd taken this one, Yoyo slithered over to me.

"Don't tell me this is beautiful," I said.

"I was not going to say that, actually."

"Good."

He slung a long leg over the dead tree and looked past me and then over towards the bridges and Plymouth. "It's not what you expected?"

I shrugged. "I dunno. Don't know what I expected. Something more like a proper river, I suppose. This doesn't look like a river, does it? More like a…"

I didn't know what it was like. More to the point, I didn't know what I was doing here. At that moment, I was almost convinced I'd got everything wrong. Grandad could not have meant to bring me to this bleakness.

"Let me look at the map," Yoyo said.

He studied it while I watched long-legged little birds poking their beaks into the mud.

Eventually he said, "This is not really the Tamar yet, I think. It says it is, here, but it is more like part of the sea. The sea will come in and out right up to here. And further, too. What's the word for this?"

"Tidal? Estuary? Is that what you mean?"

"Yes, I think so. So tonight, for example, this tree we are sitting on will be in the water, probably. And see that smaller bridge over there? It goes over another river which joins this one. And here and here there are other little rivers that join it also."

"So?"

"So this water is a muddle of all sorts of rivers and the

sea. Your Tamar ends here and gets mixed up with everything else and disappears."

"What are you on about?" I said nastily.

He regarded me over the top of his sunglasses. "What I'm trying to explain to my sulky little cousin is that we are doing things backwards. We are going from the end of the river to the start of the river. And endings are always sad. We are doing the sad bit first, which is wrong. Strange."

He put his hand on my shoulder and joggled me lightly. "Cheer up. The river will get more beautiful further on. It will get clearer, more like you expected, I am sure."

"I bloody hope so. This is deadly."

"Here," he said, "you see the next mark? It's just round the bend here, this tiny village."

I had to smile because I love the way he says village: *willage*.

He looked at his watch. "And I notice it has the sign which means pub."

The willage was called Cargreen and the name of the pub was even weirder: the Crooked Spaniards. It sat on a big quay that was also a car park. Yoyo had been right: the river looked a lot lovelier just this short distance further away from the estuary. Its surface rippled sky blue and silver, slicing and shuffling the reflections of the boats moored out in the deeper water. We looked upstream where the river vanished between the shoulders of the tilting hills. Yoyo took more photographs. Then we heard the rumbling of an engine and a chirpy toot. Turning, we saw a cruise boat sidling towards the quay. It carried a cargo of ancient ladies, their white and wind-fluffed heads like floral tributes on a coffin.

I thought of Gran. I wondered what she would think if she knew – if she could understand – what we were doing here. For some reason I was sure that she would be frightened. I suddenly felt very uneasy.

"Oh my God," Yoyo said, stuffing his camera into its case. "Come on, Tamar. If those old ladies get to the bar first, we'll be the same age as them before we get served."

HOLLAND, 1945

As evening closed in on 4th March, a stocky man called Paul van Os was sitting in a bar at the top of Red Lion Street in Apeldoorn. Under his coat he wore an overall stained with blood and, from the smell of him, something worse. There were two cups on the table in front of him, one containing fake coffee, the other gin from a bottle that the café's owner, Anje Mol, kept under the counter. Van Os had paid for these treats with half a kilo of fatty sausage meat which he had smuggled out of the abattoir at Epe.

For half an hour he was the only customer. The man who then came in was tall and hawkish. He came across to van Os and without speaking picked up one of the now empty cups and took it over to the counter. Mrs Mol reached into the darkness below her and brought out the gin and a second cup. The thin man made no move to pay, and it seemed that Mrs Mol did not expect him to. He stood smiling at her for a few seconds. In the light of the bar's single candle, his face resembled a primitive weapon carved from bone. Mrs Mol glanced across at van Os, shrugged slightly, and went out through the door behind the counter that led up to her living rooms.

The thin man waited until he was sure she had climbed

all the stairs, then went back to the street door and slid the bolt. He carried the two drinks to the table where the slaughterman was sitting.

"Cheers, Paul."

Van Os chinked his cup against the other man's. "Cheers, Koop. I'd almost given up on you."

"I had to come the long way round. There are bloody SS and police everywhere."

"I know," van Os said. "I got stopped twice on the way here from work." He grinned. "They don't keep me long once they get a whiff of me."

"No," Koop said. "I wouldn't fancy searching you. Dear God, Paul, you do stink." He took a sip from his cup. "Anyway, that's enough polite conversation. I understand there's something you want to talk to me about."

"Yes," van Os said. "Pork."

Two nights later, Tamar returned to Sanctuary Farm. He had been riding the knackered bike for more than five hours. His spine and crotch were in torment. His feet were wet and very cold. Every time he had seen lights or suspect shadows on the moonlit roads he had dismounted and dragged himself and the bike into wet ditches or the denser shade of trees. Crouching in such places he had held the pistol against his shoulder with both hands and struggled to steady his breathing. Twice, German motor patrols had sped past.

Throughout all this he had been reciting, memorizing, Ruud van der Spil's messages for London. Thinking about how to shorten them so Dart would not panic about the time he had to stay on air. One image had haunted his journey: Dart, frantic, his finger stabbing the Morse key, knowing the Germans were tracking his signal. Dart in the attic at the Marionette House waiting for the slam of car doors, boots on the stairs… Or at the farm. No, not the farm. He would tell Dart that there must be no more transmissions from there. The thought of Marijke being taken, of losing her, made his brain reel. Dear God, if that were to happen now, with the British and the Canadians so close…

And it was unworthy of him, but the truth was he didn't want Dart at the farm any more. The man tainted the air with his … his tetchiness. He had become both sullen and as taut as a stretched wire. You never knew how he would react. Like when he had come to the farm after the thaw and they had told him of Oma's death. He had been so distant. No sign of human sympathy at all. But at the same time it was as though he was accusing them of some sort of negligence. As if to say that it might not have happened if he'd been there, even though he'd said from the start there wasn't much he could do. The Benzedrine was part of it. Christ, the amount the man had asked London for! The signs were familiar; Tamar knew of other WOs who'd gone the same way. And the man was terribly lonely, of course. There was no mistaking the way he looked at Marijke. Or wouldn't look at her. Might he have guessed? No reason to think so. They had been careful.

Despite his exhaustion, his aching need to shape his body around Marijke's and fall asleep, Tamar was extremely cautious when he reached the farm. From the road he studied the blacked-out house closely for a full minute. Then he pushed the bike down the track, holding the revolver against his thigh. When he lifted the awful machine through the door of the big barn one of the surviving hens made an irritable noise like a rusty clock being wound up.

In the yard he put his thumb and second finger into the corners of his mouth and let out a long whistle something like an owl-call. He heard the door bolts clack and then he was in the dark hallway, holding her. They stood locked together, silently; five days had passed since they had last done this. Then Marijke freed her arms and brought his face down to hers.

She kissed him twice, then whispered, "Ernst is here." Sensing his dismay, she added quickly, "He's had a phone call."

"What?"

She took his hand. "Come. I'll heat some food for you."

The soup was thin, but it had beads of rich fat in it and, miraculously, small dumplings that glistened in the candlelight. Marijke stood with her hands on the back of Tamar's chair, urging him to eat when Dart's news threatened his appetite.

Dart paced back and forth among the shadows, smoking. "It's that crazy bastard Koop," he said. "You know the problem with him? He's got no fear. You've got to have fear in this business. It's what keeps us alive. Without fear there's no discipline, no checks; there's just damn chaos. Koop thinks this is the bloody Wild West and he's Billy the Kid."

"Who called you?" Tamar asked.

"Bobby."

"From Apeldoorn?"

"Yes."

"When was this?"

"About thirty, maybe forty minutes ago," Dart said.

Tamar put down his spoon. "I don't understand. You were at the asylum?"

"Of course."

"So how did you get here so fast?"

"I used the motorbike."

"You *what*?" Tamar glared at him.

The bike was a German courier's. It had been found in a ditch beside the Zutphen road three weeks earlier. Despite the skid, it had been in perfect working order – unlike its rider, who had come to rest ten metres from the machine with his neck broken. A couple of local amateurs had pinched it. They had some connection with Albert Veening, so they'd had the bright idea of stashing it at the asylum. Tamar had wanted rid of it. Anyone caught using it was as good as dead. That his own wireless operator had taken that risk was incredible.

Dart said defiantly, "I decided that this was an emergency. It goes without saying that I was extremely careful."

Tamar swallowed his anger with a spoonful of soup. "So what did Bobby say?"

Dart came to face Tamar across the table. "It seems that Koop knows someone who works at the abattoir at Epe. This person told Koop that three tonnes of pork are hanging there. It's for the German army, of course. God knows where it came from. Anyway, Koop ups and decides that this pork would be better used elsewhere. So he thinks it would be a good idea to steal it."

Despite himself, Tamar grinned.

"It's really not funny," Dart said. "Koop's idea is to hijack a German truck, drive it to Epe, talk his way into the abattoir and make off with the meat."

"Hijack a truck? How?"

"A roadblock," Dart said.

Tamar's spoon clattered into the almost empty bowl. "Oh no."

"Oh yes." There was a bitter note of satisfaction in Dart's voice, and Tamar heard it.

"Does Bobby know when Koop's planning to set up this roadblock?"

"Tonight. On the Arnhem road over the heath."

"Oh, dear God," Tamar said. "They're going to find themselves up against half the Wehrmacht. At least two divisions are moving up to Apeldoorn tonight and tomorrow."

"I know that," Dart said. "Which is why I came on the motorbike."

The two men stared at each other, then Dart put his hands down flat on the table and leaned towards Tamar. "You were supposed to put a stop to this kind of shit," he said.

Tamar felt as though he had been struck in the face. His own suppressed rage flared like a stoked fire. "Don't you... Do not tell me what I am supposed to do. You have no idea what I..." He lifted a hand. "Never mind. There are things that do not – must not – concern you."

"Really? I'm supposed to sit in that damned madhouse while the Germans look all over the place for me and not be concerned that cowboy operations are going on just up the road? Cowboy operations that will have the Gestapo swarming all over us. Cowboy operations *you're* supposed to prevent."

Dart's eyes were moist and there was no mistaking the hate that glittered briefly in them. Tamar saw it and recognized it. It shocked and frightened him. He was unable to speak.

It was then that Marijke went over to Dart and took his head in her hands, turning his face towards her own. She moved her right hand to his mouth and touched his lips with the tips of her fingers. When Dart forced his eyes to meet hers, she shook her head slightly and murmured "Shh" just once. It was something you might do to soothe a child, and Dart immediately became childlike. His body slumped slightly, his lower lip trembled and he released his breath in short gasps. Marijke pulled out a chair and pressed down gently on Dart's shoulders until he sat. He inhaled shakily, then rummaged in his pockets for cigarettes and lit one.

"I'm sorry," he said, letting the words out in a wreath of smoke. "I'm not losing my nerve. Don't think that. But we all know that the average life expectancy of WOs in the field is three months. I've lasted five. I feel like I'm riding my luck as it is, even without crazy bastards like Koop screwing everything up."

Marijke's hands were still on Dart's shoulders but she was watching Tamar's face.

Tamar stood up. He had that look of weary determination that was all too familiar to her. "Where's the motorbike now?"

"In the dairy," Dart said.

"How much petrol is there in the tank?"

Marijke took her hands from Dart. "Oh no," she said, shaking her head. "No, no."

Dart glanced up at her, then looked at Tamar and shrugged. "It's half full, maybe more."

Marijke moved round the table and grasped Tamar's wrists tightly. "Listen," she said. "Don't be stupid. There's not a road you could take that's safe. If the Germans catch you on that bike…" She was unable to finish the sentence.

Tamar said, "I'll go along the canal path and then take one of the tracks across the heath. I can't imagine the Germans will stray from the main road, not in armoured cars and trucks. There's just enough moon. I won't need to use the headlight. I'll be okay."

Now there was anger as well as fear in Marijke's voice. She shook his wrists. "Listen to me! We've no idea where Koop is. Are you crazy enough to think you can cruise along that road looking for him and his stupid roadblock? For all we know, he and the others might be dead by now anyway. And if they are, well…"

"Well what?"

"Well, it's too bad. We have to live. We have to carry on. Especially you. You're too important to risk your life for crazies like Koop."

Tamar opened his mouth, but before he could speak Marijke said, "You are too important to me."

So here it was, at last. Exposed. It felt to Tamar that the truth was a huge breathing presence that had entered the room, crowding it. He stared into Marijke's fierce wet eyes because he couldn't find the nerve to look at Dart. When at last he managed to, it seemed that Dart hadn't reacted at all; he hadn't even lifted his head. Now he merely reached out and carefully extinguished his cigarette in the little heart-shaped ashtray.

If Marijke was aware of what she had said there was no sign of it in her face.

Tamar cleared his throat. "I have no choice. Even if Koop and his men get away with this stunt of theirs, even if they do it without killing anyone, there'll be hell to pay. Remember what happened at Putten. Not a single German died in that ambush, but Rauter still burnt half the village and shipped six hundred people off to concentration camps. If Koop shoots up a few Germans, we'll lose a lot of people. People we need will be lined up and shot. All for a truckload of pork. I have to stop him. I have to try."

Dart, his head still lowered, said, "I have a scheduled transmission from the asylum at eight twenty. Do you by any chance want to tell me what to send?"

"I'll be back before dawn," Tamar said. "We'll go through it then."

"And if you're not?"

"If I'm not, you know what to do. Send the signal that we are blown and get the hell out."

Dart counted one and two and three in his head, then said, "And Marijke?"

Tamar said, looking into her eyes, "Take her with you."

At the kitchen door Tamar checked the Sten and gave it to Marijke while he wrapped his scarf twice around his neck and buttoned the shabby jacket.

He said to Dart, "Please go and see that everything's okay."

Reluctantly Dart took his revolver from his coat and went outside.

When she heard the outer door close, Marijke said, "I know what I said. I'm sorry. I meant it."

"It's all right. Don't worry. I suppose—"

"I beg you. Please don't go. Please, *please*, don't go."

Tamar took her face in his hands. "Marijke, you mustn't do this."

She was still holding the gun across her body, between them.

She said, "I'm pregnant."

Tamar stared at her blankly, as if she had spoken in Greek or Japanese. Everything around him seemed to sway slightly. Eventually he said the stupid thing that men always say.

"Are you sure?"

"Yes. And if you get killed now I'll never forgive you."

He kissed her on each eyelid to stop her looking at him.

Then Dart came back in. "Everything's fine," he said.

SS Lieutenant General Hanns Albin Rauter, head of internal security for Holland, was unhappy. This was by no means unusual. Indeed, Rauter considered happiness to be a form of mental deficiency. He had observed so-called pleasures such as dancing, drinking and sex, and found them stupid and grotesque. As one of very few people gifted with a cool and analytical mind, he knew that only a small number of individuals were strong enough to reject happiness and gratification in order to shape the history of the world, and he was one of them. There was nothing arrogant in this, of course. The Nazi Party and the Third Reich were an unstoppable force for good, and he was merely its servant. There was no doubt in his mind about any of these matters. However, he had a problem; one that he was trying to deal with calmly and rationally. To put it simply, his problem was that Germany was going to lose the war.

He had spent the day of 6th March at the front line, now very close to the German border. It was here, he was sure, that the final battles would have to be fought. Unless, as he fervently hoped, the Americans saw sense and joined with the Führer to defeat the barbaric Russians. Inevitably, though, Germany's armed forces would have to regroup to defend the fatherland. Protecting them as they did so might be difficult. Sabotage of road and rail routes by terrorists could be a problem, and Rauter had met senior officers to discuss this. Although he hadn't said so, he thought the Dutch resistance was crap. It was divided into all sorts of quarrelsome factions, and a good dose of public executions had taken the edge off their appetite for defiance. Also, it seemed to him, the Dutch were unlikely to rise up and take on the Wehrmacht. For one thing, they were too damn hungry – he'd seen to that. They were more likely to keep their heads down and wait for the Americans to turn up with chocolate and cigarettes. All the same, you could never be sure that some self-appointed hero wouldn't crawl out of the woodwork and blow up a vital road or bridge.

But what really bothered Rauter was that he hadn't managed to get all the Jews out. There were still several hundred of them – plus some queers and other rubbish – in the concentration camp in Westerbork. He'd been trying to get them shipped off to the east since September, but the damned trains still weren't running. And now it was probably too late. Even more worrying was that his special groups were still – *still* – finding handfuls of Jews in Amsterdam and elsewhere. Incredible. They hung on like worms in the gut. He was reconciled to the idea that he might be the last good man to leave Holland. But the idea that a Jew might emerge from its rat-hole to wave him goodbye sickened him.

Burdened by such thoughts, Rauter got into his car at dusk and was driven back to his headquarters in Didam. There, alone, he ate a large meal of soup, roast chicken and apfelstrudel. Then, drinking his coffee, Rauter made the decision that ended his career. His weekly conference in Apeldoorn with Artur von Seyss-Inquart, the Reichskommissar for the Netherlands, was scheduled for the following afternoon. In addition, he had to attend a meeting at army headquarters earlier in the day. It occurred to him that it would make sense to travel to Apeldoorn now and get a good night's sleep in his usual hotel. He was, understandably, tired.

He summoned his valet. "Run me a bath. Lay out my other uniform, and clean underwear."

"Sir."

"Then tell what's-his-name, the driver, to have the car outside at ten o'clock. And pack my laundry. I'll have it done in Apeldoorn, since no one here seems to know how to iron a shirt properly."

The car was a big BMW convertible painted a dull grey-green without markings or insignia. The roof was folded back, and a large suitcase containing Rauter's dirty washing was strapped on top of it. His orderly, Lieutenant Exner, sat in the back. Rauter was a very large man – two metres in height and weighing almost a hundred kilos – and chose to sit in the front where he had more legroom. His new driver was a young Austrian corporal recently invalided back from the Russian front, where he had lost half his right ear to frostbite. Exner passed forward one of the two Schmeisser machine pistols from the back seat. Rauter placed it across his lap. When the car pulled away, the driver had some trouble with the unfamiliar gearbox, and Rauter cursed him.

Koop and his men had been busy since nightfall. Getting across the town was no safe or simple matter. In recent days the Nazis had been behaving unpredictably. Sometimes they didn't bother to police the curfew; sometimes they had patrols on almost every street. Tonight the resistance men had been lucky. They made their rendezvous without seeing a single German.

Using the scrapyard to hide the stolen Nazi staff car had been Eddy's idea. Stealing the car had been such a brilliant thing to do, such fun, that it had taken them some time to realize the horrendous problems that came with it. Oskar's cousin, cautious Willy Vekemans, thought they should just dump it, but the others were against him. Then Eddy, who was driving, had said, "Listen. If you want to hide, do you hide in an empty place or in a crowd?"

"What are you saying?" Koop had asked.

"I'm saying that if we are going to keep this damn thing, we need a place where there are other things like it. Where it looks like it belongs."

"So what do you have in mind? A German transport depot?"

Eddy had grinned and said, "That would be perfect, but actually I was thinking about the scrapyard."

Before the war, the yard had been a tidy little family business. There'd been a petrol pump in front of the house, a couple of workshops out the back, and a small field populated by dead and cannibalized machinery. In 1941 the father and the two sons had been taken as forced labour to Germany. They had never been heard of again. The mother had struggled on for a while, then packed up and gone to live with relatives in Rotterdam. Ironically, the abandoned yard was fuller now than it had ever been. The German and Dutch police used it to dump wrecked military and civilian vehicles that obstructed key roads. Farmers used it to dispose of bits of shot-down aircraft that had landed inconveniently in their fields. There was so much wreckage that it had burst through the hedges.

So that was where the group had stashed the stolen staff car. They'd backed it into a row of wrecks, between a burnt-out three-tonne truck and an ancient high-sided van. They'd chocked up the front axle and taken the wheels off, hiding them and the battery in the smaller of the workshops. They'd draped a muddy tarpaulin over the car and, just as Eddy had said it would, it had become invisible. Later, when they had "liberated" the Waffen-SS uniforms, they'd taken those to the scrapyard too, concealing them in the workshop's roof space. The British Sten guns were kept in the empty house itself, wrapped in oilcloth under a heap of old bedding and rugs that rats had nested in and pissed on. Koop had figured that no intruder would fancy poking about in that lot, and so far he'd been correct.

Tonight's mission was the fifth time the group had used the car and the uniforms, and they had a pretty smooth routine going. Willy and Koop brought the guns and the bag of ammunition magazines out to the car, then went to watch the road. Eddy and Wim fitted the wheels and the battery while Oskar fed the tank with petrol from one of the jerrycans locked in the boot. They worked efficiently in the dark, needing only the briefest moments of torchlight. When it was done, all five men went into the workshop and transformed themselves into SS troopers. For night operations like this, it was really only necessary to wear the soft field service caps, the greatcoats and the jackboots; but Koop always insisted on the whole get-up, and no one was inclined to argue. Oskar wore the staff sergeant's uniform because his German was fluent; if talking couldn't be avoided, he would do it. He got into the front passenger seat.

Eddy pressed the starter and the engine fired on only the second attempt. "God," he said, "don't you love these German cars?"

Tamar stalled the motorbike twice on the overgrown concrete road to the canal, but by the time he was on the towpath he had mastered it. The night was less dark now, which meant he could see, but also be seen. And the bike's engine was terribly – terrifyingly – loud.

Pregnant, he thought. My God!

To the right, below him, the broken moon raced through the water.

Fifteen minutes later he cut the engine and freewheeled down the embankment onto a narrow lane that ran alongside the canal. He peered in both directions, listening. He kicked the bike back to life and rode north until he came to a track leading up to the heath. He threaded his way between clumps of gorse and stretches of bracken; in several places the thin nubbly fingers of birch trees reached out to whip him. In the open areas of pale grass and isolated pines he felt horribly exposed. When he guessed he was less than four hundred metres from the Arnhem–Apeldoorn road, he stopped and turned off the engine. He could hear nothing at all, other than the normal sounds of darkness. The light wind was in his face, so if there had been heavy German transport he would surely have heard it. Or maybe not; his hearing might have been impaired by the noise of the engine and his extreme tiredness.

He locked a magazine into the Sten and restarted the bike. The track met another, running north, parallel to the road. Tamar swung the bike onto it. He was intensely anxious now. It occurred to him that if the Germans were moving up tonight, they might well have sent scouting patrols ahead. If so, he was very likely to run into one on this track, and he would have little chance of seeing them before they shot him out of the saddle. And he had very pressing reasons for wanting to stay alive.

Hanns Rauter turned to the man in the back seat and said, "I hope you are not too cold, Exner. I know you do not share my enthusiasm for fresh air."

The lieutenant sat even more upright. "I am perfectly comfortable, Herr General, thank you."

This was not true. The suitcase perched on the back of the BMW stuck out over the rear seat. If Exner leaned back, the edge of the case tipped his cap over his eyes in a ridiculous fashion. And he didn't dare slump. The lieutenant was therefore forced to adopt an unnaturally upright position like a man struggling to control his bowels. Also, he had been dying for a cigarette for some time. But the general was a notorious non-smoker, and Exner had not dared to ask permission.

"Good," Rauter said. After a second or two he turned his head once again. "If you want to smoke, Lieutenant, please do so. It will not bother me. Another advantage of an open car."

"Thank you, sir," Exner said. He felt in his breast pocket for his cigarette case.

There were only a few bends on the road, and Oskar's opinion was that they should set up shop close to one of them. It would give any German driver less time to assess the situation. Koop's view was that a genuine roadblock would be set up on a straight stretch of road where anything coming could be seen from a long way off.

"And," Koop had said, "we are, for tonight, Germans. So we do things the way the Germans do, okay? And another thing, if we make a truck stop suddenly, the guys in it will get all twitchy and reach for their guns. But if we do it on a nice safe stretch of road, all they'll do is moan, like it's a boring routine keeping them from their food and their beds. Which means we'll just stroll up, very friendly like, and do them before they suspect a thing."

"Koop's right," Wim had said. "Let's do what they'd expect and surprise the life out of them."

Which was what they did.

Tamar left the motorbike in a small copse of tilted pines and crawled up the low slope to the road. At the top of the rise a line of ghost-white birches and rusty bracken gave him some cover. The road here ran dead straight, a grey band dissolving into the darkness.

He had imagined that by this time, twenty minutes before midnight, he would hear the sound and even see the hooded lights of the German convoy. He had hoped, although desperately, that he would find Koop's roadblock on this particularly deserted stretch. Yet the road, as far as he could tell, was empty. He had no idea what was going on. He had no idea what to do.

Something sagged inside him. It was hopeless. Marijke had been right; he had risked everything for nothing. He was exhausted. Marijke was pregnant with his child and maybe he didn't have the energy or the luck to get back to her. His back and his arse ached. His brain ached. He was almost overwhelmed by the desire for warmth and safety and sleep. He slithered back to the pines and sat against the front wheel of the bike, savouring the warmth from the engine, the Sten across his lap. He would rest for a few minutes and then begin the dangerous journey back.

His head fell forward, jerked upright, fell again. His hands slid from the gun onto the harsh carpet of pine needles. He smiled in his sleep when he heard a woodpecker drumming its beak against a distant tree.

He woke up, gasping. There was drool on his chin. Woodpecker? He stood, staggering slightly, fumbling with the Sten. It came again, on a scrap of wind: a faint rapid hammering.

Gunfire. Machine guns.

THEY'D SET THEMSELVES up on an open stretch just south of a boarded-up inn called De Woeste Hoeve. Eddy had angled the car so that the black and white cross on its side would be clearly visible to oncoming traffic. Willy, restless and anxious, had wandered a hundred metres or so down the road, so he was the first to hear the motor. He sprinted back and called to Koop.

"I don't think it's a truck. You want to get off the road?"

Koop said, "No. There's no time. Get ready."

A pair of hooded headlights came into view.

Exner had had some trouble lighting his cigarette. He'd had to bend down behind the front seats to shelter his lighter. Still hunched over, taking his first drag, he heard Rauter yell.

Eddy knew from the sound of it that it was a BMW. Lovely engine. Sweet as a baby's heartbeat. He cocked his Sten and looked across at Oskar, who was smiling as he stepped forward and raised his hand. Koop and Wim switched on the lamps, illuminating the crude HALT sign. Eddy clambered over the ditch that ran alongside the road and moved up so that he would be behind the vehicle when it stopped.

He knew that on the other side of the road Willy was doing the same thing.

Rauter knew immediately it was a trap for the simple reason that only fourteen days earlier he had issued an order cancelling all roadblocks in country areas. Without looking at the driver, he roared, "Don't stop! Drive through them!"

The young Austrian corporal was confused. Unfortunately he had not been told of the general's order regarding roadblocks. When Rauter yelled at him, he had been thinking (again) about his beautiful fiancée and whether or not she would want to marry a man with half an ear. He stamped on the pedals and caught the brakes and the accelerator at the same time. The car slewed and he fought to straighten it and bring it safely to a stop. Beside him, Rauter was struggling upright, clutching his Schmeisser in one hand and hanging onto the top of the windscreen with the other, cursing viciously.

"Shit," Oskar said. The BMW had stopped too soon, too quickly. It was maybe eighty metres away, and you couldn't guarantee hitting anything with a Sten at that range. He wasn't sure where Eddy and Willy were: beyond the car, level with it? Still ahead of it? It looked like someone was trying to get out. Someone was yelling in German.

Oskar glanced over his shoulder at Koop and Wim.

Koop said, "Walk, nice and easy. Don't run. Stay in line."

So the three of them strolled down the road.

Rauter's bulk made it difficult for him to stand up between the front seat and the dashboard. He was awkwardly upright, off balance, when he swung his machine pistol towards the three approaching silhouettes and pulled the trigger. The gun jammed.

"Exner!" he screamed. "Exner!"

Exner had been thrown forward against the driver's seat and onto the floor. Hauling himself up, bleeding from the nose, he was amazed to see the general staring white-eyed down at him, yelling, struggling with a gun. Exner got to his feet and picked up his own weapon from the floor.

"Shoot them, Exner! Shoot them!"

Exner looked ahead and saw a stop sign and three Waffen-SS men walking towards the car.

"General?"

"God damn it, Lieutenant, shoot those men!"

Baffled, Exner opened fire.

Wim, Koop and Oskar were still fifty casual metres from the BMW when they saw the flashes and heard the bullets sing off the road into the darkness. Wim went onto one knee, Koop and Oskar stood, and all three of them let rip with the Stens. The sound hammered into the night, like typewriters writing the same brilliant white word over and over again.

Off to the right of the BMW, Willy had taken the precaution of lying face down in the long damp grass on the far side of the ditch. He had no intention of being caught in the crossfire, especially with that mad sod Eddy on the opposite side of the road. By the conjunction of the moon and his good luck he was able to see clearly the silhouette of the man in the back of the car who was standing and firing at Koop and Wim and Oskar. He pushed the button of his Sten to *burst* and let off half the magazine, and the silhouette magically disappeared.

By the time Exner died, Rauter had cleared his own gun, but before he could use it the windscreen exploded into a prickling frost. He turned his face away from it and noticed that his driver had thrown himself back against his seat and was twitching like someone having a fit. Then something tore into Rauter's face and thumped into his chest and he fell sideways.

Koop and Wim and Oskar shot at the car until their magazines were empty. Then, although there was no longer any returning fire, they reloaded and fired continuously as they walked towards it, because none of them wanted to be the first to stop. When they did stop, the silence rang in their heads like a vast bell. All five men slid fresh magazines into their Stens and, at a signal from Koop, Willy and Eddy ran crouching onto the road until they were alongside the BMW. When Willy said "Now!" both men stood and aimed their guns into the car.

It was immediately obvious that the three men in it were no longer a threat to anybody. All the same, Willy moved slowly and carefully when he reached in to pick up the two machine pistols and the cigarette that smouldered on the blood-spattered back seat. He called to Koop, who went to fetch the lanterns. Eddy noted approvingly that the motor was still running, despite the hot water spewing out of the holes in the radiator. One of its headlights was intact, spilling a cone of light onto the road.

Koop trained his lantern onto the big man who was slumped across the body of the driver. His face had been opened up on one side and there were entry wounds on the front of his greatcoat. Koop studied the man's insignia and whistled softly. He opened the dead man's coat and saw the flashes on the lapels of the tunic: gold oak leaves on green panels. There was no need to look for the man's identity papers.

"Jesus," he said.

"Koop?" Eddy said. "Koop? Who is it?"

"We get out of here. Now. *Now!*"

283

Koop switched his lantern off and began to walk, almost run, back towards their car. The others followed. Eddy caught him by the arm. "What? *What?*"

"We've killed the big one," Koop said.

There was no doubt that the gunfire had come from the south. Tamar's need to get back to the farm was overwhelming. On the other hand, he had to find out what the hell was going on. It was his job to know. He stood knee-deep in the bracken gazing down the almost invisible road.

The atmosphere in the stolen staff car was weird. It was as if, Eddy thought, they were drunk. As if they were kids again, coming home far too late from a party in his father's borrowed van: that same heady mix of bravado and fear of punishment. Willy, Wim and Oskar would all talk at once, then fall silent, and then start jabbering again. Crazy mood swings.

Eddy stared fixed on the unlit road ahead, driving faster than was really safe. He felt a sudden pain in his jaw and for a mad instant wondered if he'd been shot. Then he realized that his teeth were tightly clenched. Relax, he told himself. Relax and take care of the driving.

Then Koop said, "We can't go home," and they knew it was true.

Tamar kept the bike in a low gear, its engine stumbling slightly. He was certain he was heading towards something terrible, and the desire to find it and get it over with was almost stronger than the need to be cautious. He forced his hand to stay steady on the throttle, the Sten bumping against his chest. He passed the junction to Loenen, then saw, or thought he saw, a dim light ahead. He killed the engine instantly, and wheeled the bike to the edge of the road. He propped the machine, then slithered down into the ditch and crept towards the light.

The ditch became shallower as he went forward. By the time he was able to see that the patch of brightness was a car's headlight, he was forced to bend almost double. When he guessed he was close to the light, he leaned back against the side of the ditch, listening, holding his breath. Black rags of cloud drifted across the moon. There was nothing to hear, except, perhaps, a faint spilling of water. It was quite possible, he thought, that he had crept up on a Nazi patrol; that a German was taking a leak just a metre or two away. He turned onto his belly and lifted his head until his eyes were just above the level of the road.

It was a long, low-slung car without a roof. No markings, but German, obviously. There appeared to be no one in it. Tamar listened and could hear no voices, no movement, no sound at all other than that quiet trickle. He felt around until his hand found a pebble. He threw it and ducked back down, hearing it strike metal and then skitter across the road. Nothing happened. Dragging what might be his last breath into his lungs, he stood up.

It was a BMW staff car with three dead occupants. Tamar walked around it, his flesh twitching, moving the gun restlessly. The number of bullet holes was incredible. There were two dead men in the front and one in the back. Their blood was shiny black in the moonlight. The man in the front passenger seat was lying across the driver. Both he and the one in the back were officers, or had been. As far as Tamar could make out, working by broken moonlight, there were no weapons in the car. He put his Sten down on the bonnet and used both hands to explore the big man's body. The face was pulpy and still warm, and Tamar's hands recoiled from it. He fumbled inside the man's greatcoat and found the thin wallet where the ID was. He took it to the front of the car and kneeled so that he could read the document in the dull gleam of the surviving headlight.

"Oh dearest Christ."

He stood and grabbed the Sten and blundered into the darkness back towards the motorbike. His feet slithered and he almost fell. He had slipped on spent cartridge cases; now, looking down, he could see that there were dozens, scores, of them lying on the road.

"Koop," he cried into the night. "Koop, in God's name, what have you done?"

THE HIDEOUT WAS a cluster of four wooden bungalows deep in the pine woods at the eastern fringe of the heath. Before the war, they had been the holiday homes of well-off Jewish families from Amsterdam, but these families no longer existed in any recognizable form. The houses themselves now sagged like grieving relatives. Once, the narrow lane that led to them from an obscure country road near Loenen had been tidily gravelled; now it was a couple of faint ruts either side of a meandering strip of tall grass. The labyrinth of footpaths that threaded the area had become ghostly traces. Koop and his men were among the very few people who knew them.

The group had done the buildings up in a way that made them look even more derelict than they already were. The windows had been crudely boarded up; but the gaps in the rough boards happened to provide views of all approaches, and they were wide enough for gun barrels. The holes in the shingled roofs were useful lookouts for a man armed with a machine gun. The place was fairly well stocked with food – most of it with German labels – and the group kept spare clothes there, as well as the heavy Bren gun the RAF had dropped to them eight months earlier. There were also three bicycles, all with good tyres.

It was Eddy and Wim who had first used the bungalows as a hideout. They'd slipped away there for a day or two whenever the Nazis were rounding up able-bodied men for export to Germany. Now, in the incredibly black early hours of 7th March, it was clear to all of them that they might have to stay for quite a while.

They sat on what was left of the living-room furniture in the bungalow nearest the track. The windows were blacked out with blankets taken from the abandoned bedrooms; one had a pattern of merry rabbits dressed in pyjamas. Koop had taken the candle into the decaying kitchen and come back with a bottle of schnapps, which he passed round. It had circulated twice before Eddy Dekker ended the silence.

"Well, my brave boys, what are we going to do now?"

The obvious question, and the hardest. But it broke the dam; now everybody had something to say.

"Rejoice."

"Koop, are you sure it was him? Absolutely sure?"

"Don't be so stupid. This is a disaster."

"I said, Christ, I said, I told you it wasn't a bloody truck!"

"Yeah, it was him."

"You know what? I'm glad. One of the most evil bastards to walk the earth—"

"God forgive me, but I just didn't want to stop firing."

"Koop, don't hog that bottle."

"How many did we kill tonight?"

"Three. The driver—"

"No! Let me ask this again!" It was Willy Vekemans.

Silence. Then Koop said, "Willy, don't start. We all know—"

"Yes," Willy said. "We all know. There will be reprisals. That's the word nobody has used yet. But there, I've said it. So come on. How many people have we killed tonight?"

Koop stood up, holding the schnapps. He pointed the neck of the bottle at Willy's nose.

"Listen. Do you think I haven't thought about that? Don't you think it was the first bloody thing that went through my mind when I saw it was Rauter? So don't you get all self-righteous, Willy Vekemans. It's not us who line innocent people up against the wall and shoot them. If I remember correctly, it's the bloody Nazis who do that."

"I'm not being self-righteous, Koop. I went into this tonight with my eyes open, like everybody else. We all know what Tamar told us, and we—"

"Tamar!" Koop spat the word out. "Yes, we all know what that bloody errand boy told us. *Do nothing* is what he told us. He runs off to England, has a nice break, comes back and tells us to do nothing. Well, thank you very much, Commandant. Wish you'd told us sooner. Could have saved us a lot of trouble. I could have saved us a lot of trouble if I'd shot the soft sod when he stood there in the marshes with his hands in the air."

Koop thrust the bottle into Willy's hands and threw his own arms up. "*I surrender! I surrender!* That's Tamar's message to the gallant Dutch resistance. Great, bloody great."

"Koop…"

"Hey, Koop, come on…"

Oskar raised his voice against the angry babble. "I think we should stop this right now. *Right now.* Okay. We know what we have done tonight. And what the Germans will do as a result. Personally, I think there is very little we can do to stop them. Except for one thing, of course."

Silence, then the cry of a nocturnal bird.

"We can give ourselves up. It might be enough for them."

"Don't talk so bloody daft, man." Koop's voice was harsh. "What do you want? To be a saint? A martyr? You spent too much time in Sunday school, my friend. What, we give ourselves up, the Gestapo have their fun with us, and all's square? Don't be stupid. We've just killed the top Nazi in Holland. You seriously think that our five dead bodies would make up for that? I don't think so. They'd do whatever they fancied with us, then shoot God knows how many people anyway. It'd make no difference."

Oskar said, surprisingly, "I agree with you. But I tell you this: I'm not prepared to hole up here not knowing what's going on. Someone ought to get back to Apeldoorn and find out what's happening. And since it's my suggestion, I'll go."

"No one leaves here tonight," Koop said flatly.

"Fair enough. I'll go at first light. The curfew will have ended by the time I get there. In the meantime, I think we should try to get some sleep instead of sitting around here arguing and bullshitting."

"Amen," Eddy Dekker said. "Because in the morning we're going to have to decide what to do with the car."

And that started another argument.

As dawn was breaking on 7th March, a German patrol scouting ahead of the delayed troop movement to Apeldoorn spotted a stationary car on the road ahead. The captain in command was understandably nervous, suspecting that the apparently empty and shot-up machine was a trap. He brought his armoured car to a halt two hundred metres away and studied the BMW through his field glasses. There appeared to be at least one body in it. He radioed the convoy south of him and was ordered to investigate at once and report back. The captain took two men with him and they approached the car with extreme caution.

There were an amazing number – a ridiculous number – of bullet holes in it. He recognized Rauter at once, despite the wrecked face, because the lieutenant general had pinned a medal on his chest at a parade only a week ago. Steeling himself, he pressed his hand to the left side of Rauter's neck. The flesh was very cold but below the ear there was a beat, faint as a hatching butterfly. He dashed to the armoured car and seized the mouthpiece of the radiophone from his startled driver.

Rauter was taken to the military hospital in Apeldoorn. He had several flesh wounds and a shattered jaw, but the major problem was the bullets that had penetrated his lung. All the same, they pumped blood into him and kept him alive.

In the afternoon, Rauter's deputy, Eberhardt Schongarth, went to visit his boss. As was usual by this time of day, Schongarth was fairly drunk, and he slumped into the chair beside the general's bed. He was not expecting, nor was he ready for, a conversation. So he was dreadfully surprised when Rauter spoke. Schongarth struggled to look upright and alert. Even if he had been sober, he would have found it difficult to understand what Rauter was saying. The general had lost some of the right side of his face, which was swathed in dressings, and could only speak in small groups of words punctuated by gasps.

"How many…"

Leaning closer – but not so close that Rauter would smell the booze on his breath – Schongarth said, "How many what, General?"

Rauter, heroically, managed to say, "How. Many bullet holes. In the car?"

Schongarth said, "How many? I don't know."

Rauter faded, then rallied slightly. "Count them," he mumbled. "Understand? Count them. And come. Back and tell me."

*   *   *

Schongarth returned two hours later. He sat beside the unconscious Rauter's bed impatiently, needing a drink, for almost an hour.

The general's eyes flickered and then focused. "How many?"

Schongarth said, "Two hundred and forty-three."

Rauter made a movement of his face which in other circumstances might have been a smile. "Good," he gasped. "Execute that number. Of people."

"Any particular people?"

Rauter, struggling to draw breath, said, "No. Anyone you've got."

By late evening, Eberhardt Schongarth was very drunk and extremely edgy. Obviously the best people to shoot would be death candidates, the terrorists and saboteurs taking up space in various prisons. It would be a nice clear-out. But – and he found this hard to believe – there didn't seem to be enough of them. He'd issued orders that all *Todeskandidaten* in the district were to be brought to the prison in Apeldoorn. But the total, including those already there, came to only a hundred and sixteen. Not even half – half! – the number required. He'd decided it wouldn't matter to Rauter if he went over the target. But to fail to reach it … well, he'd be in the shit and no mistake.

The answer to his problem was clear but unsatisfactory. Some of the executions would have to take place in other parts of the country. It was not a pleasing thought. He'd had the vision – it was poetic, really – of exactly two hundred and forty-three dead resisters laid out on the Arnhem to Apeldoorn road, ideally alongside the general's bullet-riddled car, and he was reluctant to abandon this elegant concept. But the logistics were daunting. Find the transport, find the escorts, to bring in extra death candidates from Amsterdam, from The Hague, from all over the place? It was impossible. To hell with it. The total was the main thing. He shouted for another bottle of wine and reached for the phone.

Lages, the chief of security in Amsterdam, was embarrassed to admit that he had only fifty-three death candidates to offer, rather than the seventy-five Schongarth wanted. But there were another six in Utrecht that he could throw in. Schongarth settled for that, and added fifty-nine to the numbers on his paper.

"And what do you want me to do with them, sir?"

"Bloody shoot them, of course," Schongarth yelled.

"Tonight, sir?"

"Whenever you damn well like," Schongarth told him, and hung up.

Almost immediately he rang back. "Lages? Ignore that last order. Wait until the morning. After the curfew ends. Eight o'clock. I want people watching, you understand? As many as possible. Make a spectacle of it."

Yes, of course, Schongarth thought. If we can't execute all the bastards in the same place, we can at least do them all at the same time.

Wolk, in Rotterdam, explained (with some difficulty) that because of attempts by the resistance to liberate his prisoners, he had transferred his death candidates to The Hague.

Schongarth called The Hague and sent a frightened security service officer to get his boss, Munt, out of bed. It was eleven o'clock by now, and Schongarth, very befuddled by drink and arithmetic, was very unpleasant to listen to. When he told Munt that he wanted eighty death candidates shot at eight o'clock the following morning, Munt got jittery. He would of course like to oblige, he said, but he had transferred most of his prisoners to the concentration camp at Amersfoort. Just the day before, in fact. Then he had to hold the telephone away from his ear while Schongarth screamed at him.

"Lissen, shithead! Your share, your quota, is eighty. Eighty, okay? I don't give a damn where you get them from. This order comes from the top, you unnerstan? The top. So just do it!"

Then the line went dead, with a bang that made Munt flinch.

Munt sat in his pyjamas and smoked two cigarettes. He'd sent forty-nine prisoners to Amersfoort, so, strictly speaking, he was thirty-one short. He phoned several of his staff officers and got them on the case. "Basically, anyone we've got locked up anywhere in the city," he told them. "Get me a list." Then, reluctantly, he dressed and called for a car to take him to the prison at Scheveningen, north of the city. He got there at midnight. He didn't have much luck. The best he could manage was eleven men (actually, some of them were boys) who had been banged up for looting. They'd have to do.

On his way back, he stopped off at the SS barracks to sort out a firing squad. He entrusted the command of it to an officer he suspected of flirting with his wife. At his headquarters he used the phone to chase up his staff. By two thirty in the morning they had, miraculously, provided him with another twenty-seven names. He wrote the word TODESKANDIDATEN at the top of the list and arranged for them to be shot along with the looters at eight o'clock sharp. He called Schongarth's office and left a message. Then he went back to bed, a relieved man. He had beaten his quota. He'd got eighty-seven.

A LL THROUGH THAT day, and well into the night, other phone lines – secret, illegal ones – had also been busy. At the asylum, Tamar made a dangerously long call to Bobby on Albert Veening's antique telephone. Later in the day, twice, Bobby called him back with news that chilled his blood.

Earlier, when a cold and pearl-grey light was filtering into the hidden room, Tamar had written a message for Dart's morning transmission to London. He made a number of mistakes in the encoding which Dart corrected, coldly and without comment. This message, when added to the ones Dart had already prepared, took the transmission time beyond the limit. When Dart protested, Tamar forcefully overruled him. Dart made a drama out of checking that his pistol was fully loaded before slamming it down on the table close to the transceiver and cramming on the headphones.

Dart was still stabbing the Morse key when Albert tapped quietly on the concealed door. Trixie was here, waiting in the conservatory. Tamar touched Dart on the shoulder without getting any acknowledgement, then followed Veening downstairs.

* * *

"My God," Trixie said. "You look terrible. Is something the matter? What's happened?"

He didn't answer, but took her by the arm and led her over to the summer house. Inside, it smelled richly of wood rot. Fingers of ivy were intruding through the broken panes. He tried to close the door but it jammed halfway.

"Trixie, would you do me a favour? Would you mind putting your arms around me and holding me very tight?"

"I thought you'd never ask." Her smile made no difference; when she held him she felt how tense he was. "Are you going to tell me?"

When he didn't answer, she pushed him away slightly in order to see his face. "It's not Marijke, is it? Oh my God, something has happened at the farm. That's why you're here."

"No," he said. "No. Marijke's fine. But listen. I want you to go there now, please. As fast as you can. Get the guns out of the house. The shed next to the dairy would be a good place for them. It's closest to the road. Anyone could have put them there. Do you understand? And Marijke needs to tidy up so there's no sign of me having been there. And I want her to check that Dart has packed everything away in the radio room. I'm sure he has, but she needs to double-check. Cigarette ends, everything. Okay?"

She hadn't taken her eyes from his face. "You're expecting a raid on the farm."

"No, but it's possible. Right now, anything's possible."

She said, "Tell me what's happened. I've a right to know."

"Rauter was shot last night. Near De Woeste Hoeve, on the Arnhem road."

"Rauter? I don't believe it!" His face told her it was true. "But I thought… My God. Who did it?"

He turned the corners of his mouth down, a grimace that could have meant anything. She understood, though.

"You're right. I don't want to know."

She moved away from him, pulling her shabby raincoat tighter around herself. She went to the door and stared out at the wet grass, the naked trees.

"Rauter," she murmured. "God help us now." Then she turned quickly to face him. "Christiaan, they're not looking for you, are they?"

"I've no reason to think so. But the Germans will turn the whole area inside out. We're all going to have to keep our heads down." He rubbed the back of his thumb across his unshaven chin, thinking. "Where's Rosa? Isn't she with you?"

"Agatha's looking after her. Why?"

"I think it would be a good idea for you to stay at the farm tonight. You and Rosa. Would you mind? I'd feel happier knowing Marijke's not alone."

"Okay."

"Thanks." He kissed her forehead. Then he sighed and said, "Right. I need to get back." He struggled to pull the door fully open. For just a second he looked like an old man. "Tell her I might not be able to get home for a while, and not to worry."

And he thought, Home. I'm not meant to call it that.

Trixie said, "I can't tell her not to worry. But I can tell her you love her, if you like."

When she'd gone, Tamar went back to the room behind the dispensary. The stale air now carried the acrid smell of burnt silk as well as cigarette smoke. Dart didn't look up when he entered. He busied himself checking and folding the silks, fiddling with the transceiver controls, closing things down.

When the silence became absurd and he could no longer bear it, Tamar said, "Mind if I open the window?"

Dart shrugged. "Sure. Be my guest." He lit another cigarette with tremulous fingers.

Tamar opened the small window halfway. He inhaled some cleaner air and turned to look at Dart. The brown bottle of Benzedrine had appeared beside the revolver on the bureau.

He said, "I realize that it's not the ideal time to tell you this, but I've decided to close down transmissions from the farm. In the circumstances I—"

He stopped because Dart held his hand up, rigid in a halt gesture, and shook his head slowly and deliberately.

"No."

Tamar closed his eyes and found that he had an immense desire not to open them again. To sleep just where he stood. Not to have this conversation...

"Dart, you can't just say no like that. I've thought carefully about it, and—"

"No," Dart said again. He sat staring at his fingers where they rested on the small black suitcase. He kept his voice more or less level. "You can't do that; you don't have the authority. I've got procedures, timetables, frequencies. Only London can change those."

"I'm sorry, but that's not the case. In the field I am authorized to make those changes. And I've made my decision."

Dart looked up now, and Tamar flinched when he saw what was in the other man's eyes.

"Oh, right. You've made your decision, have you? Well, that's just fine and dandy, isn't it? It's all right for you, for Chrissake, never in one place more than a day or two. I've got the Germans tracking me every time I send, and nowhere to go to. Do you understand?"

He got to his feet and advanced on Tamar, who folded his arms but held his ground.

"Do you *really* understand? Last week the bloody detector vans were in the town when I left. They must have been this close – *this close* – to locating me."

He held his thumb and forefinger a centimetre apart and jabbed them at Tamar's face. And although it was irrelevant, Tamar realized then that Dart had lost a lot of weight. His clothes were looser on him. The dark hair was long and oily. The unnaturally bright eyes were deeper in their sockets.

Dart's voice edged a shade closer to hysteria. "You let this shitstorm happen, and now you're telling me I can't use the farm any more? You're telling me I can't use the only safe bloody station I've got? No, *no*! You can't do that. Who the hell do you think you are?"

"Dart! Calm down, for God's sake. I know the risks you run. I do everything I can to protect you."

"Everything except let me use the only place I feel safe!"

Tamar wanted to reach out and hold him, but he couldn't bring himself to do it. "Look," he said, "you and me, we always knew the risks we were running. You said last night that you felt you were living on borrowed time. I feel the same way. But ... but I have to think about Marijke. I can't keep putting her at risk. It's not ... fair."

It was a feeble word. Childish. It brought an ugly smile to Dart's face.

"Fair, huh? All right, Commandant. Let's talk about what's fair. Let's talk about me stuck here all winter in this freezing shithole full of nutcases. Except for when I get to take a little stroll into town in order to play cat and mouse with the bloody Gestapo. Let's talk about me in this ... this tomb, sending your long-winded so-called reports when my fingers are so stiff with cold that I can't even feel the bloody key."

"Dart, I—"

"And now let's talk about you, shall we? Where are you all this time? You're tucked up in Marijke's nice warm bed with a belly full of food and your hand on her—"

"Shut up. Shut up! This conversation stops, right now."

But it didn't.

"And you know what? She deserves better."

"Dart, I'm warning you…" Tamar couldn't finish the sentence. He was dismayed to see that Dart's eyes were filling with tears.

"She deserves better. That's what's so damn well unfair. You're a death candidate, and you know it. So am I. And she deserves something better than either of us."

Tamar stared, finally speechless. Dart's last three words hung in the air like smoke.

My God, Tamar thought. Oh my God.

Oskar didn't return from Apeldoorn until well after dark. He dismounted stiffly from the bike when he was in sight of the bungalows and flashed his torch four times, then went in.

"It looks bad," he told them. "Seems they've brought men to the Apeldoorn jail from all over. Definitely from Deventer and Zwolle. A woman says she saw a truck with prisoners in the back, and one of them was her brother-in-law, and she's sure he's been held in Groningen for the last six months."

Koop said, "How many? Any idea?"

"I've been trying to figure that out. There were around fifty in Apeldoorn already, we know that. So I reckon a hundred guys, maybe more."

"Sweet Jesus," Willy murmured.

"What else?" Koop asked.

"Well, I got this second-hand, but, according to someone who knows a nurse at the hospital, all hell broke loose there first thing this morning. A military ambulance with motorcycle escorts came screaming in. The Germans herded all the Dutch staff into the canteen and shut them in, under guard. Then they emptied a ward and stuck a couple of heavies on the door. No one except the German doctors have been allowed in. Also, the operating theatre was in use this morning, but for what nobody knows. And, listen to this, that pig Schongarth was at the hospital twice today."

"Rauter," Eddy said. "Has to be."

Koop rounded on him. "Don't talk crap. The son of a bitch had more holes in him than a Swiss cheese. I looked at him. He was finished."

"The driver, then," Wim said. "Or the other guy."

"Oh, come on." Koop was exasperated now. "We emptied two magazines apiece into that car. We killed those bastards twice over. Must have done."

"So what are you saying, Koop? That Schongarth went to the hospital twice and spent two hours visiting a corpse?"

Koop shrugged and turned away.

"There's something else," Oskar said. "Something I really don't like the sound of. I knew I wasn't going to get out of town before the curfew, so I went to my aunt Anna's house for a couple of hours, to wait till it was good and dark. I was just getting ready to leave when a boy turns up. God knows how he knew I was there. Anyway, this kid lives with his grandparents right opposite the prison. He tells me that at about six o'clock, three buses – buses, mind – pulled into the yard. SS men driving them. They parked the buses up and disappeared. That's it."

A lengthy silence.

Eventually Willy said, "A hundred men. Three buses. Is anyone thinking what I'm thinking?"

"They wouldn't, would they?" Eddy said. "Not all of them."

"Hey," Koop said. "What are you on about? If they were seriously thinking about shooting everyone in the prison, why the buses? They'd do it in the yard. They'd round up half the town and make them watch. No, it's not that.

301

Anyway, a hundred guys or more? I don't think so. It's going to be something else."

"I'll tell you why the buses," Willy said. "They're going to take them down to where we shot Rauter. That's where they'll do it. And you know it." He stood up. "They'll do it tomorrow. That's why they've brought the buses there tonight. Now, if you'll excuse me, I'm going outside."

"What for?" That was Koop.

"I'm going to either throw up or pray. Probably both."

Willy was halfway to the back door when Koop called his name.

"Willy? Instead of whingeing to God, why don't you do something useful?"

"Like what?"

"Go get the Bren."

"What?"

"Go get the Bren gun. I reckon you may be right about tomorrow. But I'm not going to sit here wringing my hands while it happens. And nor are you."

SCHONGARTH'S ORDERLY WOKE him, cautiously, at six forty-five for breakfast. Coffee, brandy, a sweet pastry and the death list. Blearily Schongarth added the numbers up three times, getting three different results. But since each one was more than two hundred and forty-three he didn't give a damn. He'd done it. He thanked God and tipped the brandy into his coffee.

While it was still dark, a hundred and fifty men from Rauter's security forces began arriving at the lonely stretch of road near De Woeste Hoeve. They sealed off the area and posted guards at the inn and at the few cottages in the vicinity. They set up checkpoints on the road, north and south. Then they waited, chilled by the damp morning air. At a quarter to eight the three buses, along with two trucks, arrived from Apeldoorn. These contained a total of one hundred and sixteen captives, all of whom knew what was going to be done to them.

At almost the same time, the Amsterdam candidates were shot to death in the garden of a tea shop close to the Amstel River. There had been a short delay while members of the security police used their fists and rifle butts to assemble a satisfactory number of spectators.

Simultaneously, but without the benefit of spectators, the Amersfoort prisoners died on the rifle range outside the camp. Munt's hastily assembled thirty-eight men and boys were executed on the sand dunes near Scheveningen with the morning light in their eyes and their backs to the grey and level sea.

Koop's plan, if you could call it that, was for Willy, Eddy and himself to cycle across the heath carrying the dismantled Bren gun and two Stens. Then they'd try to take up a position overlooking the place where they'd ambushed Rauter's car. If Willy was right about what the Germans were planning, the three of them would open fire on the execution squad. The Bren was ideal for the job. It was unlikely they'd be close enough to hit anything with the Stens, but they'd make a lot of noise. With any luck, at least some of the prisoners might escape in the mayhem that ought to result. It was crude, it was desperate, and it was terrifyingly dangerous, but no one had a better idea; doing nothing was not an option.

And at first it seemed that luck was with them. By nine o'clock they'd taken up a good position just east of the road without encountering a single German. But that was because by then most of the Germans had gone.

Oscar Gerbig, head of the Apeldoorn security police, had been put in charge of the executions at De Woeste Hoeve. It was a big job, and he had approached it methodically. The prisoners would be shot in five batches of twenty and one of sixteen. They would be lined up on one side of the road, with their hands tied behind their backs – to prevent embracing and so forth – and shot by a forty-strong firing squad drawn up on the opposite side. One of the benefits of this arrangement was that five of the six groups would have to walk to their deaths past the bodies of their fellow terrorists. Before giving the order to fire, Gerbig would read out the reasons for the execution. A Dutch collaborator called Slagter would translate.

Gerbig had not, however, anticipated the singing.

At five minutes to eight, he gave the signal for the first twenty prisoners to be marched up. As the bus door was pulled open and the men stumbled out, there came a chorus of song, ragged at first, but then swelling and steadying as the prisoners in the other vehicles found their voices. Gerbig recognized the tune. The condemned men were singing a hymn by Martin Luther.

"A mighty fortress is our God,
 A bulwark never failing;
 Our helper He, amid the flood
 Of mortal ills prevailing…"

They continued singing as they were lined up to face the rifles. Gerbig had to raise his voice to make himself heard. Slagter's translation was inaudible. Irritated, Gerbig shrugged and gave the order to fire. The echoes of the volley were quickly snuffed out by the moist air.

It took about five minutes to kill each group, since some of the men needed finishing off with pistols. Only one tried to make a run for it: that was Jan Thijssen, the national leader of the Raad van Verzet, the Council of Resistance. He was easily retrieved. Weakened by torture and hunger, he managed only a few metres of the hopeless distance to the trees.

It was all done, and the hymn long silenced, by eight thirty. Gerbig got his men to arrange the bodies in an orderly line;

305

it stretched an impressive distance. On a post at the head of the row, Gerbig had a notice put up: THIS IS WHAT WE DO WITH TERRORISTS AND SABOTEURS. He left a squad of men with the bodies, and for the next hour or so they stopped all travellers along the road and forced them to read the notice and view the massacre. The display was still taking place when Koop and his companions slithered on their bellies to the edge of the tree cover and gazed at the road.

None of them was able to speak for some time. Then, muttering something the others couldn't make out, Koop took out his binoculars. He tracked slowly along the line of corpses, counting aloud, pausing occasionally to utter a string of obscenities. He'd got to forty-something when Eddy lowered his face into his hands and began to moan. Without taking his eyes from the road, Willy said softly, "May God forgive us. But I don't think He will." Then he rolled over onto his side, away from the others, and curled up like a child seeking sleep. But he turned his head fast enough when he heard the familiar sound of a Sten gun being cocked.

"Tamar! What—"

He looked so bad that Willy clammed up. An older, sicker version of the man who had fallen from the sky five months earlier. He was braced against the trunk of a silver birch, as though he could not trust his legs to support him. His Sten was aimed at a point halfway between himself and the three other men. Willy noticed that his hands were dirty, as if he had been digging in the ground with his fingers. His eyes were puffy and red-rimmed and they were fixed on Koop. When he spoke, his voice was peculiarly unemotional.

"Let me save you the trouble, de Vries. There are one hundred and sixteen bodies. And that's not all. By now there'll have been mass executions in The Hague and Amsterdam and Amersfoort. Is there any good reason why I don't shoot all three of you bastards right now?"

Koop turned onto his back and leaned up on his elbows. His right hand was not far from his own gun. He stared coldly at Tamar for a couple of seconds, then said, "Yeah. You haven't got the guts."

Willy flinched. He tried to speak, but his mouth went dry when Tamar levelled the Sten at Koop's chest. He closed his eyes, waiting for the stuttering bark of the gun.

Instead he heard Tamar say, "You're wrong, as usual. It's true I don't have the stomach for killing that you do. But the blood of those men is all over your hands. I want to kill you. I'd really like to kill you."

"Yeah," Koop said, "but like I said, you haven't got the guts."

It seemed to Willy that Tamar became, in an instant, a different and far more dangerous animal. He moved so fast that he seemed powered by an explosive force. He covered the short distance between himself and Koop faster than Willy could blink, and kicked Koop hard between the legs. Koop's arms flapped madly and he fell back, his open mouth sucking in air. The hoarse gasping was cut off when Tamar put one knee on Koop's chest and slid the muzzle of his gun into Koop's mouth.

"Tamar! Please God, don't!" Eddy cried. His voice was high-pitched.

Willy felt his heart jump in his chest, and was shocked to realize that what he felt was a sort of grim joy that punishment was here at last. He couldn't breathe, waiting for the dreadful thing that was about to happen to Koop.

But Tamar didn't pull the trigger. Instead, he took his left hand from the gun and pulled a folded sheet of paper from his jacket pocket. Then he removed the muzzle of the Sten from Koop's mouth and shoved the paper in. Koop's eyes bulged. His face was grey as ash.

Tamar said, "A list, Koop. The names of seventy-four of

the people down there on the road. You'll recognize some of them. I don't know who the others were, not yet. When I do, I'll be sure to tell you. I know where to find you."

He stood up, looking very tired again. Willy stared at Koop's wet glaring eyes in his colourless face, the list jammed in his mouth; heard him gagging on the paper. Willy thought that it would have been better if Tamar had shot him. This was worse.

"Go back to your hole," Tamar said. "Stay there until you hear from me. You are not to get involved in further actions of any sort. These are direct orders from Amsterdam. Got that? As far as I am concerned, your group no longer exists."

He eased the cocking lever of his Sten into the safety position and slung the weapon over his shoulder. He turned his back on the three men and retreated into the gloom beneath the pines. He had made no attempt to separate Koop or Eddy from their guns. When he was out of sight, Koop spat the list of the dead onto the ground.

WHEN TRIXIE WOKE up, Rosa was still asleep in her eiderdown nest beside the bed but Marijke had gone. There was birdsong, and a milky light not strong enough to throw shadows. She found Marijke in the wash-house, stooped over the sink. When Marijke noticed her she straightened up, wiped her mouth on her sleeve and forced a smile. Her eyes were watery.

"Marijke? What's the matter?"

"Nothing. I'm fine. Just felt a bit sick." She rested her back against the sink and sniffed, twice.

"Are you ill?"

"No, really. It's nothing."

Trixie stood in the doorway, arms folded, watching Marijke's face. "How long has this been going on?"

"Oh, just a day or two. I feel fine most of the time."

Trixie knew. She just knew; it made sense of things. "Marijke? Marijke, are you pregnant?"

Marijke looked down at the floor but couldn't see it because her eyes were full of tears. "Yes," she said.

Trixie walked over to Marijke and put her arms around her. After a while she said, "Why are you crying?"

Marijke said, "Why are *you* crying?"

"I don't know."

Marijke rested her cheek on the other woman's shoulder. The light from the window dazzled her through her tears.

"Yes, you do," she said. "You're crying because you're thinking what I'm thinking. That this is a terrible world to bring a child into. That this child's father is likely to be dead before it's born, that this child is going to grow up not knowing who its father was or what he did, and that I'm damned stupid to be pregnant."

"Marijke, please. Don't. I wasn't thinking that at all."

Marijke got control of her breathing. She went to the outside door where a towel hung on a hook and dried her face. "I'm sorry," she said. "I'm okay. Really. I'll make us some tea. We still have some left."

She took the big water jug from the draining board and went to the pump. "When do you think he'll be back?"

"Soon," Trixie said. "Later today, certainly."

"Perhaps."

Trixie hardened her voice a little. "No, not perhaps. He will be back."

"But that's what I'm going to think every time now, isn't it? Every time he's not here, I'm going to think I may already have said goodbye to him. I may have already touched him for the last time. How am I going to stand it?"

Trixie didn't offer an answer. She knew from experience that there wasn't one.

Marijke tried to find things to do. She made several trips with the wheelbarrow, bringing into the yard the slices of the ash tree that she and Tamar had sawn two weeks ago. The task almost exhausted her. Later she walked around the yard and the buildings, touching and moving things for no reason. Behind the house she discovered that bracken had sent new growth up through the soil: nubbly green shoots, curled like the necks of violins. Or like little green sea horses. The white sky was hung with shifting grey veils.

She went to the vegetable garden where Oma's grave was. It had been the only place where Tamar had been able to dig deep enough into the frozen ground. She remembered the grim labour of it, Tamar stubbornly hacking the narrow pit out of the hardened soil until he was chest-deep and too exhausted to dig deeper. They had covered the mound with stones pulled from the collapsing garden wall. Now thin green plant tendrils grew among those stones. She thought about pulling them out, but decided not to.

She was crossing the yard again when she sensed him; she looked up and there he was, jolting down the track, bent over the handlebars. Not riding, but being carried. He looked awful, hollowed out. It was a wonder to her that she loved someone who looked that way. She held him for a while, then led him into the kitchen. Trixie was in the old armchair by the stove, talking to Rosa about the pictures in a book. The child shrank closer to her mother's body when she saw Tamar. He slung the Sten almost carelessly on the back of a chair and sat down. Marijke put the kettle on the stove and stood with her back to the room. She was aching to look at him but did not dare to.

Trixie said, "Tell us what's happened."

Tamar looked over at her, but his eyes fixed on Rosa. He gazed at the child who was hiding her face from him.

"Tell us, Christiaan. You know you have to."

So he told them. He told them how many men there had been, how they had died, how long it had taken, the distance the bodies had stretched along the road. He told them what he knew about the killings elsewhere. When he had finished, Marijke put a mug of tea in front of him and then sat beside him. Without looking at him, she laid her right hand on his left wrist. For a long time there was no sound in the kitchen except for the soft little ticking made by the kettle as it cooled.

Rosa was disturbed by the silence. She murmured complaints, dabbing at the pages of the book. Trixie hugged her, shushing her. Then she stood, lifting the child to her chest.

"Come on, Rosa," she said. "Let's go and see what those naughty chickens are up to." On her way to the door she rested her hand briefly on Marijke's shoulder.

When the silence in the room became difficult to bear, Marijke said, "There's soup left from last night. It's not too bad."

He didn't respond for several seconds. Then he said, "You see things … sometimes you see things that make you think the rest of your life is impossible. Just seeing them damages you so much, you think, I cannot go on being human."

Marijke wrapped her fingers over his clenched fist. He didn't look at her.

"I keep thinking about the Germans in the firing squad. Killing and then killing again and again, looking at the faces… How? How did they do that? I can't … I can't even imagine. But, the thing is, if you took one of those men and stripped away the uniform, and sat him next to me, how different would we be? Would you be able to see murder on his skin? Smell murder on his breath? And not on mine?"

She could not tell if he expected an answer. She did not have one.

"I feel," he said, "I feel…" He searched for the word; the fingers of his right hand moved as if he were blind and groping for it. "Diminished. Ashamed. Because I watched all that killing, and when it was over, do you know what I wanted to do? I wanted to kill someone. Anyone. It seemed the only possible reaction to what I'd seen."

"I understand that," she said. But she was thinking, Stop this. Please stop this because I am going to have your baby. Let's talk about that, instead.

Then he did look at her, and she flinched.

"Do you?" he said. "Well, I'm glad you do, because I damn well don't. All this shit, this year-in, year-out bloody nightmare, is about difference, isn't it? We tell ourselves we're different from them. That we're not like the Nazis. But this morning, I watched while they murdered a hundred and sixteen people. So I wanted to kill *them*. The sickness in those men, those Germans? It's in me too."

She said, "Yes, it probably is. And that's why we're fighting, remember? We're fighting for the right to choose not to be evil."

He pulled his hand free of hers. "I'm not sure. I don't know if we can be good after all this."

"I don't know either, but that's not what I said."

She suddenly couldn't stay with him. She stood and he looked up at her, puzzled.

She said, "What are you going to do?"

"I don't know."

She went to the door and looked back at him. "Trixie's going back to the asylum this afternoon. Maybe there are things Ernst needs to know."

"No. Ernst knows everything."

She was halfway across the yard before it occurred to her to wonder what he'd meant.

Later they all ate the watered-down warmed-up soup, not speaking much. After Trixie had laboured up to the road, Tamar fetched the heavy splitting axe and carried it on his shoulder to the pile of wood that Marijke had lugged into the yard.

Towards the end of the afternoon, when the low red sun peered under the curtain of cloud for a last moment, she went out to him. He had formed the split chunks of ash into a flat pyramid against the wall of the barn. He had built it with great care, each wedge snug to the next. She held her arms out, palms upwards, and he loaded her with as much wood as she could carry. It smelled like the leaves of a new book.

In the kitchen she fed the stove and opened the air vent, then went into the wash-house and found her grandmother's big jam pan and the cauldron they boiled washing in. She filled them with water from the pump and heaved them up onto the stove next to the kettle. She sat in the darkening kitchen for almost half an hour, waiting for the water to heat, wondering about the life she had inside her. Was it the size of a fingernail? Less than that? It was strange that something so tiny, just a little gathering of blind cells, could make her feel so tired, so altered.

The room was warm now, and it was hard for her to get up from the old armchair. She went out to the wash-house again and lifted the zinc bathtub from the hook on the back wall and dragged it into the kitchen, positioning it on the worn rug in front of the stove. She was immediately taken back to her childhood, to a particular memory. She'd come indoors from play, after supper. It was harvest-time. How old had she been? Six? She'd had one of the new kittens, the one with gummy eyes, in her arms. Taking her shoes off in the hall, she'd heard laughter. The air in the kitchen was thickened by steam and by dusty light beamed in from the window. It smelled unusual. Her grandmother was kneeling on the floor beside the stove next to the bathtub, this bathtub, with the soapy flannel in her hand. Her grandfather was sitting in the tub, his hair wet, his pipe in his mouth, a glass of beer in his hand. His face and neck and the lower parts of his arms were a lovely colour, like sunlight on the bricks of the barn. The rest of him was white as milk. His clothes were strewn over the armchair. Both of them, Oma and Opa, looked round at her, smiling.

Happy. *Happy*. Marijke tried the word in her mouth, speaking it aloud in the shadowy kitchen. She emptied cold water from the jug into the bath and then added the boiling water from the kettle. After lighting the lamp and drawing the curtains she went outside.

He was standing by the woodpile, watching the last rooks drift slowly back to their roosts on the heath. When he heard her approach, he turned, holding out his hands for her to see. The skin on the palms was shiny, and at the base of the finger with the ring on it a blister had formed and then split. A flap of pale skin with rawness under it.

"My hands have forgotten how to do honest work," he said.

While he was taking off his boots in the hall, she heaved the cauldron and the pan from the stove and poured the hot water into the bath. She dabbled the water with her hand, checking the temperature, thinking, One day I will do this for my child. She could almost picture it, but not quite. When she looked up, her face was flushed and wet with steam and very beautiful. He stood just inside the door, looking surprised and a little awkward, but smiling. Actually smiling. He stood still while she slipped his braces over his shoulders, then she took hold of the front of the soiled shirt and led him over to the bath. She helped him undress, remembering the small starving boy who had once stood in the same place. He stepped into the tub and lowered himself, holding the handles on either side; his arms trembled, taking the weight of his body. He looked slightly absurd, like a man squeezed into a child's pedal car.

Marijke dipped the flannel into the water and lathered it with the last precious sliver of the perfumed English soap. Kneeling, she washed his back and shoulders, working the knotty muscles with her thumbs until they began to give a little. Then she folded a towel and draped it on the tub behind him. He leaned back, closing his eyes and shuddering slightly as he did so.

"Are you cold?"

"Not really. A little."

She reached across him and opened the fire door of the stove so that he would be warmed. The flamelight shimmered on his wet skin. When she turned to look at his face, his eyes were open and fiery wet. He wrapped his arms around her. She felt the heat and wetness of his body soaking into her clothes.

"I love you," she said. "Will it be enough?"

ENGLAND, 1995

At the Crooked Spaniards, Yoyo had used his shambolic charms to lure the waitress into conversation. She was a large middle-aged woman with an accent like melting butter. When we told her we were on our way to Cotehele she waxed lyrical about the place.

"Oh," she said, "it's like paradise and the Garden of Eden rolled into one."

Before we could get to this promised land, though, there was another pencil mark on Grandad's map where a side road turned down to the river and then backed away again. Halton Quay, the place was called.

It was in the middle of nowhere, but in some distant past it must have been important because the quay was built of huge blocks of yellowy-grey stone that must have been murder to bring there. The surface was worn and pitted like the sole of an old shoe. Behind the quay itself, there were two great square buildings made of the same stone. They had big arched entrances, but inside there were just a few metres of dirt floor which ended at walls of rough bare rock. The ground was littered with fag ends and beer cans. Someone, or some people, had recently lit a fire inside the first one; there was a circle of blackened stones, and a sour smell of ash. I trod on a condom.

The map showed me that we were standing on a sudden whimsical twist in the river. The Tamar looped out of sight between thick beds of reeds, their soft tufts exploding out of tall dark green stems. The water was exactly the same shade of blue as the sky.

I remember Yoyo saying, "I don't like it here much. It's ... what's the word? Spooky? Shall we go?"

And I remember feeling something similar, a sort of motionless shudder. I felt it again the following day, and then I knew what it was. Yoyo took two photos, but when he got the films developed they hadn't come out.

No shots of Halton Quay, but ten of Cotehele. These are what Yoyo calls "the paradise pictures". I fell in love with the place even before we got there. Cotehele has its own wharf, and the road takes you down there first. It's another of those twisty, green tunnel West Country lanes that don't let you see anything unless it's through a gateway in the hedge. We were almost at the wharf when I yelled "Stop!" because through one of those mean gaps I'd seen the river gleam at us. It was my first glimpse of it since Halton.

We shinned over the gate into a lush meadow that tilted steeply down towards another great swathe of crested reeds, and beyond that the Tamar made a brilliant blue arc and vanished between two low ridges of shadowed trees.

It was my real river at last: clean and high and clear and empty and slipping slowly through a landscape that cradled it. I sat down, not caring if I got grass stains on my new white shorts. Yoyo sprawled next to me and we gazed without saying anything. Away to our right, beyond a tumble of hedge, a ripening wheat field was fringed with glowing scarlet poppies. I'd never seen real poppies before, only the imitation ones made into wreaths propped against war memorials.

I felt suddenly happy. A fat, fill-your-body-up happiness; a feeling so surprising and strong that it almost stopped me breathing. Yoyo and I were miles from home and friendless, but it was as if my body was one huge smile. The feeling I had was *belonging*, and it didn't make any sense because I was a dyed in the wool city girl. But that's what it was, and it stayed with me for the rest of the afternoon.

We parked down on the wharf then wandered past the warm grey quayside buildings and up to the house itself. We paid our entrance fee and walked round to the front.

"It's not real," Yoyo said, focusing his camera on the lovely jumble of roofs and gables, of chimneys and slender arched windows.

"What do you mean?"

"It's exactly perfect." He clicked the shutter. "And nothing can be perfect. Everyone knows that."

There are level symmetrical lawns and sunken flower beds in front of the house, and then a low stone wall. When you look over it, you can't help letting out a little gasp, because the garden falls steeply down towards the river in a mad tumble of huge orange and scarlet and white flowering shrubs and unfamiliar trees. The mossy roof of an ancient stone dovecote rises from the mass of colour; as we watched, three white doves descended onto it as if they'd been expecting us. In the distance the Tamar is spanned by a viaduct, a dozen immensely tall arches of pale stone. It was built to carry the railway line from Plymouth over the Tamar, but you can almost imagine the Victorian owners of Cotehele arranging for it to be put there so that they could sit with their tea and watch the plume of train smoke cross the bridge.

Nine of the photos of that afternoon are beautiful in a picture-postcard sort of way. The National Trust could do worse than use them in their brochures. It's the other one I like best, though. Yoyo and I went down into the garden and came to a wooden open-fronted summer house, which is where I took it. The summer house is tucked in under a great cascade of leaves. It has a thatched roof, and Yoyo is standing beside one of the timber pillars that hold it up. Because the sunlight is so bright, the inside of the summer house looks as dark as a cave; and with his mussy hair and round glasses Yoyo looks like a sleepy animal who's hibernated too long and just woken up to high summer rather than early spring. He's wearing a black T-shirt with NIRVANA printed across the front in splattery red lettering. Yellow climbing roses are clinging to the pillar nearest him, almost touching his face.

We stayed inside the summer house for a long time, stretched out on the wooden bench, listening to birdsong. A few people wandered through the garden, but they were mostly silent too and looked slightly dazed, as if they were lost but didn't mind. At one point I thought Yoyo had dozed off, and I was just about to poke his foot when he spoke.

"What time is it?"

"Just after half past four," I said. "I s'pose we should think about where we're going to stay."

"We will stay here. Wouldn't it be very nice to wake up in this garden? Just imagine. Or we could hide in the house. I bet they have those historical beds, you know, with the four posts and a ceiling."

Normally this would have earned him a kick and one of my sarky remarks. But not this time, because I was so happy and because, I admit, it was a little fantasy that appealed to me too. I wanted to stay in this perfect little world. But we left the summer house at last and wandered down through the garden towards the river. We got lost and didn't care. When we accidentally found ourselves back at the car park, shadows were creeping towards the quay. The tide had turned and exposed a smooth bank of mud on the other side of the river; in the sunlight it looked like molten silver.

The car was a furnace, and we opened all the doors to let it cool. I took the map and sat on a fat wooden bollard close to the water. Then it was as if a cloud had appeared from nowhere and parked itself in front of the sun. I felt suddenly let down. Not depressed, exactly. I can only describe it as that feeling you get when you have to go back to school after a perfect holiday. Reality tugging at you, like a friend you don't really like. It was the map, I suppose. It reminded me why we were there, and of Grandad. I'd forgotten, completely forgotten. All that stuff had gone from my mind the moment I'd sat in that meadow and realized I was happy. Now it had all come back.

Yoyo saw it in my face. He squatted in front of me. "Tamar? What's the problem?"

"Nothing," I said, being pathetic.

"Come on. All of a sudden you have a long face like a horse."

"Oh, I dunno. I mean, it's lovely here and everything, perfect really, but I still don't know what we're doing. This whole thing is some sort of puzzle, we think. Right? But we haven't worked out anything. Not a single thing. I don't know what we're supposed to be looking for. I don't know if we've already missed things. I don't know why we're here."

"Mmm…" was all he said, after looking at my face for a minute. Then he put his hands on my knees to lever himself upright. He walked a few paces away and stood with his back to me, his hands in his pockets.

"If I say what I think," he said at last, "you will tell me to shut up like usual."

I probably groaned or something, but not enough to stop him. He turned and looked at me, serious.

"The first time we talked about coming here, at your house, you said maybe there wasn't anything to find. You said maybe your grandfather just wanted you to see the river with your name."

"Did I?" I'd forgotten that Yoyo had the irritating ability to remember everything you said to him.

"Yes. And now we are here, I think you were right. Part right, anyway. It's not just about having the same name. Other things are similar. What we see now is that this river is very beautiful, and so are—"

"Yoyo, don't start. I'm not in the mood."

He lifted his right hand to stop me. "Let me ask you something. Did your grandfather ever tell you that you were beautiful?"

A ridiculous question. "Of course not," I snapped. "He wasn't like that. It's not the kind of thing he would say."

Yoyo looked at the silver-blue curve of the river, the mirrored trees.

"He is telling you now," he said. He turned to me and smiled. "Better late than never, yes?"

GUNNISLAKE IS A steep little town, an avalanche of houses clinging to the Cornwall side of the Tamar valley. The town is there because of the bridge. Until the Tamar Bridge at Plymouth was built, this was the first place up the river where you could cross by road. You can tell Gunnislake was important once, long ago. You can imagine travellers being glad to get there, climbing stiffly out of their stagecoaches after being jolted across Dartmoor. The Kings Arms Hotel had been built for them. It had an arched entrance off the street, tall enough for coaches, that opened onto a cobbled yard. The stable block was now a skittle alley. Even though the holiday season was in full swing, there were several vacant rooms. The landlord gave us a good looking-over, but when Yoyo paid for our drinks with one of Grandad's fifties he became much less hostile.

For dinner I had a baked potato with chilli con carne topping. The beans were baked beans from a can, but I didn't mind that. Yoyo ate a huge slab of battered fish that stuck out over both sides of his plate. When he drenched his chips with salad cream the woman at the next table nudged her husband and they both watched.

"Rivers aren't always beautiful," I said. "It's not that simple."

"Of course. They are complicated. They go this way and that way. They are wide, then thin – no, narrow – then wide again. They are sometimes shady and secret, sometimes in the sunshine. You can swim in them and also drown in them. Sometimes they are deep and sometimes … what is the opposite word?"

"Shallow," I said.

"Exactly."

"So is that what I'm supposed to think? Is that what this is all about?"

Yoyo paused with a chip halfway to his mouth. "What?"

"That we're doing all this so I can find out that I'm … I'm twisty and … and never the same from one minute to the next? And shallow?"

He put his fork down and carefully wiped his mouth with the paper napkin.

"Listen to you," he said. "You pick up all the negative words. Let me tell you something. There are rivers you would not like to be named after. Some in Holland, well, it would be like an insult maybe. In England too, I bet. But you are Tamar, and today we saw how beautiful she – it – is. Okay, okay, I said this already, I know. And yes, those things your grandfather left you, they are complicated when you try to look at them all together. But maybe this part of it is simple. He is telling you that you are lovely. What's wrong with that?"

"He's dead, Yoyo. He killed himself."

"So? You think people stop talking to you when they are dead?"

I didn't sleep well. There were some well-thumbed trashy novels in the room and I read one of them until long after the noisy drinkers in the bar had spilled onto the street. The two rooms that Yoyo and I had been given had once been one big room, now divided by a thin wall. I could hear his bed creak. I felt very alone, knowing he was so close to me.

Above Gunnislake the Tamar squirms and wriggles and loops back on itself as though it knows it has to get to the sea but wants to put it off as long as possible. And, just like down-river, the roads couldn't get near it. We twisted and turned through the narrow lanes for ages but caught a glimpse of the river only once.

This new day was even hotter than the one before. Yoyo had appeared at breakfast wearing old black Levis with the legs cut off, which made him look taller and more stringy than ever. We drove with all the windows down and the sunroof open, but our faces still shone with sweat.

There were only two more of Grandad's marks before the Tamar ran off the edge of the map, and we were headed for the first. We'd decided we weren't in any hurry. Despite my restless night, some of the happy mood of yesterday afternoon had returned, and Yoyo was his usual laid-back self. Several times we had to reverse and cram into the hedge or a gateway to let oncoming cars pass, and he did it smilingly, waving cheerfully at the other drivers as they squeezed by. Judging from the expressions on the faces of one or two of them, they thought he was a nutter.

Grandad's mark was where a narrow lane changed its mind about meeting the river and turned away westwards. At the turn there was a dirt track leading off, with a sign saying PUBLIC BRIDLEWAY. Yoyo eased the Saab along it, avoiding the knuckly rocks that poked up through the dusty surface.

A couple of hundred metres later Yoyo parked, jamming the car tight against the hedge. I had to climb over his seat to get out. The trees met over our heads, and the path was splashes of light and shade that confused my eyes. The air was so hot it seemed to vibrate. For some reason I felt nervous, light-headed. We walked for several minutes and then came to a dead end. On either side of the path, gateways opened onto long fields of high grass. In front of us, a broken screen of tall weeds like white parasols, a line of single trees, and the sound and glitter of the Tamar. We pushed through, treading down nettles.

It was nothing like the wide waterway we'd followed the day before. It was maybe twenty metres across. The opposite bank was a tall cliff of motionless leaves. In both directions the river twisted away and disappeared. The deep silence was disturbed only by the plopping and chuckling of flowing water. It was a secretive place.

Yoyo said, "I need a pee." He turned back the way we'd come and disappeared.

Just off to my right a bed-sized slab of stone jutted into the water. I walked out onto it, grateful that it was half in the shade. On this side the river was shallow, sliding over sandy gravel that gave it the colour of pale beer. The deep-water channel was against the far bank, a dark mirror filled with warped and sliding reflections. Something made a faint splash and spread circular ripples on the surface. In the middle of the stream long trails of weed floated, like thick green hair flecked with white confetti flowers.

It was then that I felt that same chilly unease I'd felt the previous day, standing on Halton Quay; but this time, suddenly, I knew what it was.

Yoyo and I had spent lots of time wondering why Grandad had marked these particular places on the maps. Of course we had. If they were clues to something, how did they work? Were the place names some sort of code? Were there hidden meanings in Landulph or the Crooked Spaniards? If so, we hadn't found them. Yoyo showed me how map grid references worked, and we wrote down the references for one or two places and tried translating these six-figure numbers into letters, to see if they gave us words. We thought perhaps that the names or the grid references somehow related to the mysterious letters on the silk sheet. None of this got us anywhere except deeper into headache territory. We'd wondered if there were certain things in each of these places that we were supposed to find. Perhaps a special gravestone in the churchyard, a painting at Cotehele. But if that had been it, Grandad would have given us a bit more help, surely.

What I'd never considered was the possibility that he had actually visited these places. If that seems strange, I can only say that he was the kind of man who worked things out in his head or on paper, not on his feet. I just couldn't imagine him trudging up and down the Cornish countryside, not at his age. Besides, he didn't have a car, and I'd never known him to drive. I didn't even know if he had a licence. And anyway, I couldn't imagine *when* he could have come down here. He never left London, never left Gran, except once, when his doctor told him he needed a holiday. That was when the stress of Marijke's illness and her being in the nursing home had pumped his blood pressure way up. So he'd reluctantly taken himself off to Brighton for ten days. It hadn't done him much good, judging from the mood he'd been in when he got back. Apart from that, he'd not gone away anywhere for years and years. Definitely not since Dad vanished. So I'd decided that whatever the marks on the maps meant, they weren't places he'd actually been.

But as I stood chilled on warm stone with the water at my feet, I knew with absolute certainty that I'd been wrong. He had been there. I couldn't understand how or when, but he'd stood where I was standing, just as he'd stood on the worn flagstones of Halton Quay. That was what the spooky feeling was. It was him, his presence. It doesn't make sense in any normal way, I know; but I was suddenly so sure of it that I wouldn't have been surprised if he'd materialized and stood ghostly among the trees beside me. I even looked.

When I turned back to the river, a corpse had drifted into the shadowed water towards the far bank. It could have been a pale slender tree trunk, but then I saw that the branches were arms, faintly greenish in the water, and that the splintered stump was drowned hair. I stared at it for the space of a couple of missing heartbeats, and then the corpse lifted its drenched unruly head and whooped.

I yelled at him. "Yoyo! You sod! I nearly wet myself!"

"Hah! Excellent!" He arched and dived and disappeared and bobbed up again; then he turned and swam against the current, pacing himself so that he stayed in the same place.

"Come on," he called, "get in. It's great, really."

"No way! You must be mad."

"Why, can't you swim?"

I could, but only just. Two lengths of a heated swimming pool was about my limit.

"Of course I can. But I'm not getting in there. Isn't it freezing?"

"No, it's perfect."

"Well, be careful," I said. "I don't care if you drown, but I can't drive the car."

He laughed and swam towards me and got unsteadily to his feet in the shallows. The water came up to the frayed legs of his shorts. The confetti flowers wafted around his thighs. He shook his head like a dog, scattering brilliant droplets.

"Tamar, really, you should get in. Do you realize you have not put even a hand or foot into this river you are named after? You haven't touched it. It's a shame, I think."

It was a fair point. So I slid my sandals off and stepped cautiously into ankle-deep water and squealed like a kid.

"You bloody liar! It *is* freezing!"

"Of course not," he said. "It is only the, what-you-call-it, contrast. In one minute you'll get used to it."

Which was true; then it was lovely.

"Come a bit nearer," I said, "and I'll come as far as you. But no further. And no messing about, okay? I mean it. If you pull me in or anything I'll kill you."

I was almost out to him when my foot slipped and I had to grab at his arm. It was hard and cold. He held my hand and we steadied ourselves, facing into the current. He was shivering slightly despite the heat; I could feel the vibration running down into my hand. The swirls of water against my legs were delicious. I seemed to be moving forward, effortlessly. Through gaps in the trees thick beams of brilliant light tilted onto the river. Where they burned on the water the glitter was so intense that I closed my eyes. I shouldn't have done.

I suppose it was the sensation of being blind in such light that made me feel as though I was losing my balance. That, and the heat, and the hypnotic liquid murmuring of the river, and the movement of water against me. I was filled with a thrilling sickness, like vertigo, like the fear of falling from some high place and wanting to fall at the same time. I think I must have stumbled because Yoyo said my name and turned and held me by the shoulders, supporting me. I leaned against him and he had to brace his legs to steady himself. He put his arms around me. I could feel the water from his hair dripping onto mine and the water on his body soaking into my T-shirt.

After a while I said, "I'm okay now. You can let go of me."

But I didn't mean it, and he took no notice.

HOLLAND, 1945

THINGS HAPPENED SO fast and so close together that they seemed like one thing. The shock of it made Bibi Grotius draw in her breath so sharply that she almost choked on her own saliva; she had been remembering the taste of apple cake with apricot syrup. She saw two boys dash across the square from left to right. The one carrying the football called out to Trixie Greydanus. Trixie moved fast to the corner and looked down Market Street. She turned back immediately, leaned against the wall and took off her left shoe. When she looked up at Bibi's window, her mouth was open. The few people already in the square moved quickly and aimlessly like a startled shoal of fish. Three hundred metres down Prince William Street, a German heavy machine-gun carrier appeared from nowhere, howling and clouded in black exhaust, and accelerated towards the square. Someone screamed. It was just before noon on Sunday 11th March.

Bibi's cry was so hoarse that at first Dart didn't recognize it as his warning. But when he turned and saw her ashen face on the stairs he knew. His head felt suddenly full of cold blood. His body did things by itself: his legs lifted him from the yellow chair; his left hand stammered on the Morse key, sending QUG, the code for emergency shutdown; his right hand scrabbled to gather the silks, the pencil, the pad. Then his eyes fastened on the revolver and he froze, immobilized by indecision.

The four SS troopers who barged through the shop door floundered in the near darkness, colliding with delicate obstacles and each other. What light there was in the shop came from the workshop door, which Pieter had left uncurtained. So the Germans headed for that, using their rifles like scythes to smash a path through the tables, the clockwork toys, the frozen ballerinas. The surviving puppets rattled their little wooden feet against the soldiers' grey steel helmets.

Dart had reached the foot of the attic stairs when he heard the door crash open and the frantic jangling of the bell. He shrank back against the landing wall, holding the medical bag in his left hand and the revolver in his right, pressed against his leg. When the first explosion of breaking glass came, it seemed to go off inside his head. He looked down the staircase towards the workshop door. The legs and jackboots of one SS man, and then another. An order, harsh and urgent. The voice of Pieter Grotius, saying something he could not make out above the sounds of destruction. He heard someone sobbing faintly, then realized the sound was coming from his own throat.

A hand seized his arm.

Bibi dragged him into the parlour and closed the door. Stupidly he went to the window. Before Bibi pulled him away he saw, just below him, the head and shoulders of a German machine-gunner protruding from an armoured car, his weapon trained on the opposite side of the square. A number of people – was that Trixie? – were crowded together, some with their hands in the air, others huddling into shop doorways. SS troops seemed to be raiding several buildings. A young man kneeled on the cobbles with a German holding his hair. Somewhere a woman was wailing. Inside the room, Bibi was hissing at him.

"Ernst! Ernst, for God's sake! Open the bag. My leg, do my leg. Hurry!"

It was so hopeless he thought he might cry. Or laugh. He dropped the bag onto the floor and realized he still held the revolver in his other hand. Bibi saw it and swore. She grabbed it, stuffed it under the cushion on her chair and sat down. She propped her bandaged leg on the footstool and tore the safety pin from the bandage.

A loud voice from below, boots on the stairs. Dart kneeled beside Bibi, wrenched the bag open, pulled stuff, any stuff, out. Bibi leaned forward, took Dart's face in her hands and kissed him on the forehead. She fell back in the chair with tears in her eyes. Dart took hold of her ankle with his left hand and the loose end of the bandage in his right.

The door flew open.

One grey monster entered, then a second, and a third. Two with rifles; the other, the corporal, with a machine pistol. They filled the room.

"Stand up. Stand up!"

Dart looked at them over his shoulder and raised his right arm from the elbow. A shaky salute, perhaps, or a sign meaning wait. He didn't know which, just that he had done it before somewhere and it had worked. But not this time.

"Stand up! Raise your hands!"

He stayed on his knees but half turned towards them, using his hands to explain that he was in the middle of a medical procedure. The corporal stepped forward and clubbed Dart on the right-hand side of his face with a gloved fist. The crunch that Dart felt was mixed up with the sound of the other two Germans working the bolts of their rifles and Bibi's scream.

Dart collapsed sideways and somehow stopped himself from plunging head first into the glass cabinet of hollow egg-shells painted with clowns' faces. The cabinet shook and the egg-heads wobbled on their little wooden stands. His own head was full of fizzy noise like a receding wave sucking shingle from a beach. When the darkness drew back, he got himself up onto his elbows. The first thing he noticed was that his lower lip was connected to the floor by a sticky thread of blood and dribble. The second thing was a pair of highly polished boots and, above them, way, way above them, a colourless face beneath the peak of a cap with a death's head insignia.

"Ah. Dr Ludders, is it not? We have met before."

Dart wiped the mess from his mouth with his sleeve and mumbled, "Lubbers, Major. Not Ludders. Lubbers."

"Of course. Ernst Lubbers, if I remember correctly."

His face was, impossibly, more bleached out than before. Its only colour was in the rim of red below each eye and the pink scar that ran down the ragged lobe of his ear. He said, still looking down at Dart, "Who struck this man?"

After some shuffling of jackboots the SS corporal said, "Sir, he failed to obey—"

The major turned abruptly. "Corporal, we are looking for terrorists. This man is a bloody doctor. Don't you know the difference?"

"Sir." The corporal's face was a blank.

"Have you checked the rear of this building?"

"Not yet, sir."

"Do it now."

When the troopers had gone, the pale major made a leisurely inspection of the cluttered room, surveying the posters, stooping to examine a framed photograph of Pieter and Bibi Grotius posing with the infamous Jew Charlie Chaplin. He made no comment. He lifted a Russian doll from a shelf; it rattled slightly. He twisted the body and separated the two halves and took out a smaller doll, and then found another inside that one. The fifth doll, no bigger than a clothes peg, was the last and did not open. The major seemed disappointed. He went to the window and gazed out, arms folded.

"An excellent view from here," he said. "An ideal command post."

Dart's consciousness was coming and going. He wondered if it might be okay to go to sleep. Instead, he got to his feet, supporting himself on the back of Bibi's chair. She stared up at him, her eyes wet, her face almost as white as the German's.

The major turned to face them at last. "What is this woman's name, Dr Lubbers?"

"Bib... Mrs Barbara Grotius." The name came out indistinctly; his jaw somehow got in the way of his tongue. His mouth tasted of salt and something metallic.

"Grotius?"

"Yes, Major."

The German considered the name, and Dart realized that he was wondering if it sounded Jewish.

"Her husband is the dwarfish man downstairs?"

"Yes."

The major looked directly at Bibi for the first time. "And what is her problem? What are you treating her for?"

"Mrs Grotius has a leg ulcer."

"Ulcer?" The major did not seem to know the word.

"An open sore that refuses to heal," Dart said, then thought, Dear God, is he weird enough to want to see it? He tried to think. It was like scaling a cliff when all you want is to let go and fall. A voice in his head said, *Ask about the ear.*

"How is your ear, Major? The scar tissue seems healthy, from what I can see."

"It is satisfactory. It is taking a long time to heal; my wounds always do. But there was no infection."

"Good." Dart attempted a smile, which hurt. "We got to it in time, then."

The pale stare hardened.

Oh shit. I've gone too far.

The crunch of boots on broken glass, and then the corporal's voice came up the stairs. The major turned away from Dart and went to the door. Then he looked back. "I would clean myself up a bit, if I were you, Doctor. You'll frighten your patients if you turn up looking like that." Something like a smile made a brief appearance on his face. "You will have some bruising, I think."

"It's nothing, really."

"I regret your injury. The corporal overreacted, perhaps. My men are operating under unusual pressures at the present time."

Dart had no idea how to respond. He found himself nodding sympathetically, one hard-pressed professional to another. The German left the room.

Bibi's hand flew to Dart's and gripped it fiercely. Then she released it as if it were red hot. The major was speaking again.

"Dr Lubbers, would you come out here, please?"

Dart went out onto the landing. The white face seemed to hover in the gloom. Behind it, the masks watched balefully from the wall. The major gestured with his head towards the attic stairs.

"Do you know what is up there?"

"No." The word came out high-pitched and false, and Dart hurriedly made a fuss of coughing and dabbing at his mouth. "Excuse me. No. I'm sorry, I have no idea. I've never been up there."

The German peered up into the darkness. He flicked the

light switch at the foot of the stairs on and off, unsurprised when nothing happened.

Dart felt light-headed, close to hysteria. He somehow managed to force his voice into a confidential murmur. "If it's anything like the rest of the place, it'll be full of crap."

The fleeting humourless smile crossed the German's face again. He looked up into the shadows once more, hesitating. Then he turned his back on Dart and went down the stairs to the shop. "Take care of yourself, Doctor," he called.

Dart heard his curt commands, laughter, then the dying peal of the doorbell. He waited several moments and then went downstairs. He gazed dumbly at the wreckage for a long moment, then went into the workshop. Pieter Grotius was standing at his bench, holding onto it, his head lowered. The room was a shambles. His rainbow of paint pots had been raked from the shelf, and puddles of colour lay on the floor.

"Pieter? Pieter, are you all right?"

Grotius didn't look up. He began nodding his head slowly, and then the movement seemed to take over his whole body until he was rocking back and forth, his breath coming in short gasps. Dart put his hands on the little man's shoulders. They felt rigid, not made of flesh. When the rocking didn't stop, Dart didn't know what else to do. So he hoisted himself up onto the bench and sat there, his left hand still on Pieter's shoulder. After a while, there were cautious footsteps on the stairs and he heard Bibi call her husband's name. Pieter Grotius straightened and drew a long breath with a hiccup in it. When his wife appeared in the doorway, he went to meet her and the couple embraced without speaking. Bibi rested her cheek on the crown of Pieter's head. Her huge eyes met Dart's, but he could not understand what they were telling him. He felt in his coat pocket and pulled out a cigarette and his lighter. The cigarette tasted vile but he smoked it anyway, watching the pools of paint on the floor slowly

341

merge. A snake of green crept towards a spill of orange. Just as the two colours met he heard the jolly tinkle of the door-bell again and feet slushing through glass.

"Are you there? Are you all right?" Trixie's voice. She stopped in the doorway. "Jesus," she said. "The bastards."

She went to Pieter and Bibi and spread her arms around both of them. All three remained motionless and silent for some time; they looked like models for some tragic monument. Then Trixie came to Dart and looked at him, at the flesh swollen over the cheekbone, the sticky trail of blood through the stubble on his jaw.

"Ouch," she said. She raised her hand and rested it on the undamaged side of his face. "Is it bad?"

"I'll live. I can spare a few teeth."

She managed a smile. "I suppose you can. There's not much to use them on, is there?"

A little later, when the others began to clear up, Dart went upstairs to retrieve his gun and the rest of his things. He stood before the window and stared sightlessly at the now silent and empty square. Although he still could not control the trembling that ran in waves beneath his skin, his terror had given way to a sullen anger. Only four days had passed since his banishment from the farm. He had warned Tamar that this would happen. But the bastard had known anyway, and hadn't cared. Hadn't cared because all that mattered to him was keeping Dart away from Marijke while he spun his sticky web around her.

He picked up the leather bag and turned to go. His eye fell on the little puddle of blood and mucus on the floor. Then he stood motionless because he had seen, absolutely clearly, the logic of it all. Tamar had banned him from the farm and, yes, he'd known that it would greatly increase the chances of Dart being taken by the Germans. But it wasn't that Tamar didn't care. Oh no. It was what he *intended*. It was obvious, really. If their positions were reversed, if Dart was at the farm with her, not Tamar, would he want Tamar turning up all the time? Or would it be very convenient if Tamar were to disappear, permanently? Yes. By God, yes. That would be exactly – *exactly* – what he would want.

This line of reasoning could have frightened him, but it did not. He gained a certain strength from it. Because, after all, what can be imagined can be achieved.

At the head of the stairs he paused to straighten a mask that had been knocked askew.

WHILE THE SS were raiding the Marionette House, Cook Sergeant Erich Grabowski was riding a bicycle along an empty country road south of Apeldoorn. There were all sorts of reasons why he shouldn't have been. He should have been on duty, for a start. Then there was the fact that his regiment had been put on security alert as a result of that awful Nazi sod Rauter getting himself shot. It was also the case that Erich should not have taken the bike without special permission. And he definitely should not have been riding it through an area of suspected terrorist activity. Not alone, anyway, and not without his rifle.

But Erich had done a deal with another sergeant about the duty rota. He didn't give a toss about Rauter, who was just a glorified copper anyway. The bike had cost him two cans of meat. And he had never, on any of his Sunday rides, met a so-called terrorist. The people around here all seemed very peaceable. Depressed, of course, and hungry; but violent? No. And as for the rifle, what use would it be? Even with his glasses on, he'd never been any good with one. That was why they'd made him a cook. Thank God.

None of that really mattered anyway. Sergeant Grabowski would have cycled down that lonely road in spite of anything, because in a little cottage just beyond Loenen lived an agile young widow who slept with him in exchange for food. In the gas-mask canister that hung from his neck there was a can of pressed pork, and in the rolled-up rain cape strapped onto the bike's carrier there was half a kilo of margarine and a bag of flour. In the breast pockets of his tunic there was a slab of military chocolate and a pack of cigarettes. He didn't smoke, but the widow liked to.

Two kilometres north of Loenen he swung onto a narrow lane which ran alongside the heath, bypassing most of the village. The widow didn't want him seen by the neighbours. Half a kilometre from the cottage, there was a gateway and, as usual, Erich stopped there. The gate itself had gone, but the two stout posts remained. He propped the bike against one of them and did the things he always did. He took his cap off and ruffled his thinning hair to make it look more than it was. He unbuttoned his tunic and eased his back. He cupped his hands in front of his mouth and exhaled into them, sniffing to check the smell of his breath. Finally he unbuttoned his trousers and waited to pee.

That was when he noticed the tyre tracks.

They'd been made by something fairly heavy, because the tyres had pressed deep through the pine needles into the dark mud. The pattern of the tread was quite distinct. An army vehicle, of course; there wasn't any other kind. Erich scanned the surface of the lane. There were no muddy tracks on it. So whatever it was, this vehicle had gone in through the gateway, and it hadn't come out again. Odd, really. The tracks had definitely not been there last Sunday, and Erich was pretty sure that no patrols from his unit had been down this way in the past week. Nothing much went on in the camp that Cook Sergeant Grabowski didn't get to hear about.

The mystery of the tyre tracks went completely out of Erich's head very soon after his arrival at the widow's cottage. But on his way back to Apeldoorn he paused at the gateway. He studied the tracks again but didn't dismount from the bike because he had spent longer at the cottage than he had meant to. The afternoon had already shrunk to a band of steely-grey light along the western horizon, and the tyre tracks led into wet and forbidding shadows.

It was two days later that Grabowski finally found the nerve to report his discovery to his platoon commander. When Lieutenant Redler came to the field kitchen late on Tuesday afternoon he looked haggard and his uniform was mud-spattered. He wolfed down the food that Erich had kept hot for him. Then Erich handed him a mug of tea and told him. Amazingly, Redler didn't ask what in God's name the cook sergeant had been doing, poking about in the Dutch countryside fifteen kilometres from where he should have been. He simply listened, watching Grabowski through the steam rising from the mug.

When Erich had finished, Redler said, "Stay here," and walked off. He was gone for five minutes, and Erich spent the time thinking about how much he was going to miss the nimble widow. When the lieutenant returned, he led Erich into the tent behind the kitchen, put a small leather case down on the trestle table and took out a sheaf of maps. He selected one, opened it out, and said, "Show me."

While Redler and Grabowski were map-reading in the field kitchen, Dart was standing in the asylum garden watching the rooks. There had now been three consecutive days of dry sunny weather, and it occurred to him that it might soon be spring. The elms were still bare, but the rookery built among their branches was busier and more argumentative than he remembered. Were the rooks breeding? Dart was perfectly ignorant of bird behaviour, but as he watched he saw that several of the ragged black shapes returning to the trees carried twigs in their beaks. They were refurbishing last season's nests, and furiously scolding neighbours who were doing exactly the same thing. Or were they still arguing over who was going to mate with whom?

He heard someone call "Ernst!" and it took him a couple of seconds to remember that it was his name. He turned and saw Trixie Greydanus approaching.

When she was beside him she said, "Awful creatures, aren't they?"

"Are they?"

"I think so. Sinister. You always see them pecking at dead things on the road. And I hate the noise they make."

"I rather like it," Dart said. "They sound almost human sometimes."

"I think you've been keeping company with the wrong kind of humans, in that case," Trixie said. "Let me see your face."

He turned to her. The swelling over the cheekbone had gone down a little; now there was a dark indigo stain, yellow at the edges, that had spread under his eye. The right side of his top lip was still split and swollen, giving him a lopsided, sarcastic expression.

She grimaced, and then stood on her toes and kissed him on the good side of his mouth. He was so surprised that he looked at her properly for the first time in weeks. He saw that the freckles had faded, and the flesh was tighter over her jawbone. The face was narrower. The soft crescents below her eyes were now webbed with tiny creases, like the skin on cream. She looked like the older and more serious sister of the summery girl he had met all those months ago. He thought that if he were to take hold of her shoulders he would feel bone beneath the thin raincoat, that she would be easy to break.

"What was that for?"

"To kiss it better, of course. And because I think it's probably a long time since anyone kissed you."

He thought, Don't you dare feel sorry for me, damn you. But he put a smile on his face and said, "Oh, you're quite wrong there. I kiss a different nun every night."

She grinned and became younger again. "Lord, how I would love to believe you," she said. "Come on, let's walk round the garden. These birds are getting on my nerves."

She wanted to put her arm through his. Not just for his sake, although she'd never seen anyone more needy. But his hands were jammed into his coat pockets and his arms were tight against himself.

When they'd reached the first turn in the path she said, "I've just come from the farm."

"Ah," he said.

"Christiaan has a message for you."

"Yes?"

"He was very shocked by what happened at the Marionette House on Sunday. He's glad you're safe. He said you did very well."

Dart stopped walking and faced her. "Is that the message?"

Trixie was taken aback by the chill in his voice. Her smile failed her. "No, no. He says that because of what happened he is cancelling his last order to you, and that if you want to, you may return to the normal schedule in seven days' time, the twentieth. Does that make sense to you?"

"Yes." He kept his face expressionless.

"He also said that you might want to think about what happened on Sunday in a positive way. That maybe now the SS have raided Pieter and Bibi's and found nothing, it'll be safer to work from there. What do you think?"

Dart touched his wounded lip while he considered the question. "Christiaan's probably right. But I also think he hasn't thought about Pieter and Bibi. About how they must be feeling right now. And I don't think that's ... fair."

Trixie said, uncertainly, "Is that what you want me to tell him? That you don't think it's fair?"

"Yes," Dart said. "Tell him that."

WILLY VEKEMANS AWOKE not long after dawn, as he always did. There must be some sort of clock in his body, he supposed, because very little light had found its way into the boarded-up bedroom. Or maybe it was the birdsong, which was lovely and complicated here in the woods. Or maybe it was his bowels, which were terrible because of all the tinned meat they'd been living on for ... how long? A week? Today was what, Thursday? No, Wednesday. He was losing track.

Aaah, there it went again, the spasm twisting through his gut, somehow bringing with it the memory of the dead bodies lined up beside the road. Please God, no, don't let me think about that. He swung his legs off the bare mattress and felt around on the floor for his boots, then went out into the hall. In the living room two slants of light fell across Eddy Dekker, who stirred slightly on the sofa then lay still again. From the other bedroom came the irregular sound of Wim's snoring, like a summer fly bumbling against a window-pane. This worried Willy for a moment because he thought that Wim was supposed to be on watch. Or was it Koop? Yes, maybe it was Koop.

Willy unbolted the back door and opened it. The bent grass, once a lawn, was pearled with dew. Something, a fox perhaps, had left a trail through it. He carefully peeled a strip of damp wallpaper from the wall beside the door to use in the toilet and stepped out into the day. He got halfway to the little wooden privy under the trees and then stopped, spellbound. From somewhere close by a blackbird unfurled its song and spread it, like golden handwriting, on the chill morning air. It was so bright, so pure, that Willy imagined he might be able to see it if he could find the place in the sky where it was written. He lifted his face to the light and was killed by a quick burst of machine-gun fire that hit him square in the chest.

It was Koop's unbreakable rule that all five members of the group never slept in the same bungalow. He and Oskar had spent the night in the third bungalow from the track. At first they were not sure that what had shocked them awake and brought them scrambling into the hall was in fact gunfire, simply because it had stopped almost as soon as it had begun. They squatted either side of the front door, listening to a dense silence. After a very long few seconds they heard the unmistakable sound of a Sten gun firing a long burst, and then an amazing amount of answering fire from off to their left. They stole to the window of the living room and peered through a slit in the boards. They saw four SS troopers in camouflage smocks run, stooped, through the pines and bracken. The third man was lugging a Spandau machine gun. They disappeared beyond the last bungalow, off to the right. At the same time there was another outbreak of firing from the direction of the track.

Koop said, "They're going to work their way round to the back of the end bungalow. I don't think they know we're in here." His face was banded black and white by the narrow beams of light through the boards.

Oskar's breathing was shallow and rapid. His mouth was

so dry that he could only say, "Right."

Koop said, "We'll go out the back door. Then run like shit down that hedge. Get into the trees."

"Jesus, Koop."

Koop took hold of the front of Oskar's sweater and pulled him into the hall. When they got to the door, Koop eased back the bolts. Both men cocked their guns and leaned their backs against the wall. Oskar made the sign of the cross over his heart. Koop looked at him and said, "Okay?" When Oskar nodded, Koop opened the door and they stepped out into the light.

The pit had been scooped out long ago by men quarrying sand and gravel. Now it was so disguised by gorse and bracken that Koop didn't see it until he was falling into it.

The pain from the wound in his back was so intense that when he rolled to a stop he had to fight to stay conscious. The trees surrounding him revolved one way and then the other. When he'd managed to make them stay still, he realized he was lying exposed in a patch of sunlight. He dragged himself into shadow. His left leg was very difficult to move now. When he'd got himself into a sitting position with his good shoulder against a tree, he forced himself to think. He also tried to stop shaking, but couldn't.

He'd lost the bloody Sten, and he was in no condition to go looking for it. He'd never be able to climb back up that slope. Did he still have the Luger? Yes, he could feel the weight of it in his coat pocket. But so what? If it came to a shoot-out with the Germans, he'd have no chance. He was still shocked by how many of them there'd been. Oskar'd never had a hope, the poor damn idiot. He'd run down the wrong side of the hedge. God! They couldn't have missed him. His scream had come through the bushes at the same instant as the bullets. And as for Eddy and Wim and Willy... Koop had heard the flat boom of hand grenades. The SS had blown holes in the walls, for sure. Then just poured the machine-gun fire in. Dear God. He was alone now. For a terrible moment he was stricken with self-pity and on the verge of tears. It was another stab of pain in his back that brought him out of it.

What he had to think about, the really important thing, was, had he been seen? Had he made it to the hedge before the Germans came round the corner of the house? Maybe, just maybe. The bullets that had hit him were meant for Oskar, definitely, and he didn't think he'd been shot at after he'd reached the trees. And it was quiet now. Did he dare hope? It was so tempting to... No, stupid, stupid! The Germans would work out pretty damn quick that there had been five of them there, and that they were a body short. They'd look for him, all right. Shit, shit! He had to move.

He couldn't tell how far he'd come, how long he'd been dragging himself through the woods. He'd got slower, he knew that; the leg had got heavier and heavier. It was weird that it didn't hurt very much. Look at the sodding blood, though! His left trouser leg was soaked with it, and when he moved his toes he could feel the thick stickiness inside his boot. He unbuttoned his trousers. Clenching his teeth, he slid his right hand down his thigh, easing the claggy cloth away from the skin. The hole was about halfway between his knee and his hip, on the left side. It was big enough, he reckoned, for him to get his little finger into. He felt round to the inside of the thigh. No exit wound. The damn bullet was still in there. When he pulled his hand out, it was gloved in blood. He yanked his coat belt free of the loops, and with great difficulty tightened it around the top of his leg.

Standing up was murder. When he was steady, he tried to feel the wound in his back but couldn't reach it. He was unsure whether the wetness under his shirt was blood or sweat.

He now tried to get his bearings, but the lie of the land was baffling. The ground seemed to rise and fall in no particular pattern. The sun was on his left, so he was facing south. South was, he figured, the only direction he could take safely. Okay. He'd head that way and hope there'd be some easy way out of this blasted pit. Sooner or later, he'd come to somewhere he'd recognize. And then, if he could stay alive long enough, he'd find his way to the men who had betrayed him and kill them both.

The sun was setting behind a rippled bank of cloud when Tamar left the radio room, and he stood watching it for a while. In the farmhouse kitchen he sat in the old armchair and Marijke curled onto his lap, her head on his shoulder and her legs over the arm of the chair. It was the touch of his unshaven jaw against her forehead that reminded her that this was how she used to sit with her grandfather when she was a child. She remembered his smell. Cattle, woodsmoke, soap: those predictable, safe aromas. How he would pretend to groan under her weight. She felt Tamar's fingers caress the back of her head.

"Should I light the lamp?" she asked.

"Later," he said. "Don't move yet."

Dart was woken by the tapping on his bedroom door. His first act was to brush the spiders from his face, even though, as usual, there weren't any. When he managed to get the door open, Sister Hendrika was standing in the passage, cupping a little stub of candle in her hands. The flame was reflected in both lenses of her glasses so that she seemed to have eyes of fire. She took a step backwards when she saw him.

"Dr Veening would like you to come down to the kitchen," she said. "He said to ask you to bring your bag."

It took Dart several seconds to understand her words. "What time is it?"

"A little after five o'clock, Dr Lubbers."

He'd been in bed for two hours. He had no memory of falling asleep. A piece of time had simply vanished.

"What's going on, Sister?"

"I don't know. A man… Shall I wait for you?"

"No, I… I'll be down in a minute."

There was no one in the kitchen when he got there, but the stove had been lit, somehow, and a kettle and a saucepan of water were heating. Light and low voices came from the scullery, and when Dart pushed the door open he saw the body of a man lying on its side on the steel-topped table. Horribly, it looked as though Albert Veening was peeling the skin from one of its legs. Sister Agatha was bent over the man but she looked up when she heard the door creak. Dart now saw that Albert was using kitchen scissors to cut away the man's blood-soaked trousers. He looked at the dirty colourless face pressed against the table top. The eyes were closed and the mouth was open and lopsided.

Albert glanced up. "You'll know this man."

Dart could not speak, because he seemed to have walked into one of his own Benzedrine nightmares.

"Koop de Vries," Albert said. "He has at least two bullet wounds. One in the leg, but I can't see how bad it is until we clean him up a bit. He's also been hit in the back, high up, left shoulder. I'll cut the coat open in a second and we'll have a look."

Dart still couldn't bring himself to approach the table. Albert Veening looked at him curiously.

Dart said, "I don't understand. What's he doing here? How did he get here?"

Agatha said, "We don't know. Hendrika heard a noise and came down. She found him slumped outside the back door. He'd smashed a pane of glass with his elbow; I assume he hadn't the strength to get to his feet and ring the bell. Now, we'll need morphine, Ernst. And dressings and disinfectant."

"Yes, I… Of course. I've brought my things."

Dart turned and closed the door. When he looked back at the table, Koop's eyes were open, staring at him. The bloodless lips pulled back from the teeth and let out a groan of pain, or perhaps recognition. Koop's right arm moved, his hand groping at the pocket of the filthy trench coat that hung down towards the floor.

"He's awake," Albert said.

"You must lie still," Agatha murmured. "It's all right. You're safe."

Koop lifted his face from the table and mumbled something, his speech too slurred to be understood. His hand came out of the pocket with the Luger in it. His arm rose, shaking, to aim the gun at Dart, who could neither move nor speak.

"Christ Almighty!" Albert cried out.

Sister Agatha seized Koop's arm and slammed it down onto her raised thigh like someone breaking firewood. His body lifted slightly from the table as he screamed. The pistol clattered across the floor and spun, twice, at the edge of the lamplight. Koop's face made an awful damp-sounding slap as it fell back onto the table. Then he was motionless.

The others stood frozen too: Veening, open-mouthed, the blood-smeared scissors in his hand, staring at Dart; Sister Agatha with her hand pressed to her heart; Dart hypnotized by the gun. It was Sister Agatha who moved first. She pressed her fingers to the side of Koop's neck, then lifted one of his eyelids.

"God forgive me," she said. "I thought I'd killed him."

Albert said, "He'll be half out of his mind, of course. Exhaustion, loss of blood, pain. He must have thought you were the Gestapo or something."

"I suppose so," Dart said, not believing it.

He picked up the Luger and put it on the draining board next to the sink. Then he crossed to the table. The smell that arose from Koop was very bad. The slaughterhouse stink of congealed blood was mixed with something sharp and sour, like the scent a fierce animal might leave in the night to mark its territory.

When they had cut Koop's clothes away and washed his wounds, Albert said, "He may not look it, but this is a very lucky man. The bullet that sliced across his back tore some muscle and chipped the shoulder blade, but that's all. It looks worse than it is. The one in his thigh must have missed the femoral artery by less than a centimetre. If the person who shot him had aimed a little more to the left, Mr de Vries would be dead twice over."

There were so many dark calculations happening in Dart's head that he could not think of anything sensible to say. He managed to nod, as if in agreement.

Koop's shallow breathing changed. He sighed like someone dreaming something sad.

"His eyelids are moving," Agatha said. "He's regaining consciousness."

Albert Veening said, "The bullet's still in his leg, and it's deep. It'll have to come out. Do you have any surgical experience, Ernst?"

"No."

"I thought not." Veening sounded unhappy, but not surprised. "I haven't done any surgery for more than twenty years. I still have my old instruments somewhere, though." He didn't move.

Sister Agatha looked at him for perhaps three seconds before she said, "So, Albert? Go and get the damn things."

When Veening returned, Koop was shaking and mumbling even though his eyes were not open.

Agatha said, "He's lost a lot of blood and is dehydrated. I don't know if he can take enough morphine. It might well kill him."

Albert opened his leather case and took out a pair of long forceps. "I'm going to have to dig around with these," he said, "and I need new glasses. Ernst, give the poor bastard a shot, and make it a big one."

"Are you asleep, or are you pretending?"

"I'm asleep."

Marijke laughed softly, then slid her hand up his chest and nipped the lobe of his ear. "It's a beautiful morning," she said.

"I don't care. I'm still asleep anyway."

"You'd make a lousy farmer. You like your bed too much."

"Mmm … no. I like *our* bed too much."

Tamar stirred at last. He stretched, arching his back, lifting her. "Is that what I'll be? A farmer?"

She found that she could not answer. They had arrived too quickly at the checkpoint between now and the future. She didn't dare think about what might be on the other side. She didn't yet know if they would be let through.

He placed his hand on her belly. "Anyway," he said, "I think that what you're growing in here will soon put a stop to us sleeping late, don't you?"

THE FIRST TIME Koop woke up, there was the shape of a man against a square of painful light.

The second time Koop woke up, he thought he remembered who the man was, but it was like dreaming the answer to a question. Then the man turned into a black and white woman, a nun, looming over him.

The third time, he knew who the man was and that he had done something to his arm. He'd made the pain float away on a glossy white cloud. But now, when he struggled to sit up, the pain came back, like knives everywhere. His friends had died, and he'd been tortured on a metal table, that was it. There was a gun somewhere, but when he tried to feel for it his hand wouldn't move.

The man stood up and came towards him, speaking.

"Koop? Koop, why did you want to kill me?"

He looked different, Koop thought, when he could think. When the bugger had dropped out of the sky, he'd been like other agents he'd collected: well fed, excited, self-important, scared shitless. Something had happened to his face.

It took Koop some time to unglue his tongue. When he managed to speak, it was like a rook croaking. "What day is it?"

"Friday. It's, er … four o'clock. In the afternoon. You got here the night before last."

"I can't stay here."

Dart said, "Why did you try to shoot me?"

"You know damn well."

"I don't, as a matter of fact. Do you want to sit up?"

Koop rasped, "Don't you bloody touch me."

Dart sat down on the hard little chair next to the door. "The others? Eddy and the others. Are they dead?"

Koop's eyes filled with tears. It made him furious, and he turned his face to the wall. When he had control of himself he looked the other man in the eye. "It was you, you and that boyfriend of yours. I know it, you know it. If you've got any sense you'll finish me now. Because if I live I'll kill you both for what you've done, so help me God."

He tried to muster up enough saliva to spit at Dart, but all he could manage was a thick dribble that stuck to his lips. "Traitor," he gasped. "Filth. Damn you to hell." His rage seemed to exhaust him. His eyes closed.

Dart sat for almost half an hour, gazing at the unconscious man, thinking, working things out. Then he left, turning the key in the lock. In his own room, he opened the little cupboard below the washstand and took out the towel in which he'd wrapped Koop's Luger. He put the weapon in his coat pocket and went downstairs.

In the day room, Sister Juliana was playing her five-stringed guitar to half a dozen patients. One of them was Sidona. As he walked to the door he heard Juliana say, soothingly, "No, no, dear. That's not Trago. That's Dr Lubbers. You know Dr Lubbers. He's nice."

He went out through the conservatory. In the west, beyond the skeletal trees, the sky was lemon yellow, but darkness was gathering in the air. He turned right towards

the kitchen garden and stopped when he saw Albert
Veening and Sister Agatha. They were both staring vacantly
at the ground. She had been digging, but was now resting
on the handle of her spade. The lower part of Albert's face
was buried in a woollen scarf and he leaned forward inside
his oversized coat, his shoulders hunched up. He looked
like an ancient bird waiting for something edible to emerge
from the soil. Dart walked down to them. He lit a cigarette
and gave it to Albert, who took two drags before handing
it back.

"How is our patient?" Albert asked.

Dart shrugged. "Still feverish. He won't let me touch him.
His wounds will need fresh dressings. I think you or Agatha
will have to do it."

Albert reached out and Dart gave him the remains of
the cigarette.

Albert said, "Sister Agatha thinks it is unwise to keep
him here. We do not have the resources. The food."

Agatha gave him a look full of impatience. "It's not that,"
she said. "He is a danger to us."

"Just as I am," Dart said.

"Not in the same way," the nun said. "Mr de Vries is full
of hate. Poison. I can smell it on the air. And I'm not the
only one. Several of the patients have been noticeably more
disturbed since he arrived, even though none of them have
seen him. Sidona is very distressed, for example. She cannot understand why none of her good angels have visited for
the last couple of days."

"Oh, come on, Agatha," Albert protested.

"Don't 'oh come on' me, Albert. Sidona may be crazy, but
she has a good nose for evil."

Albert withdrew a little further into his scarf and coat,
like a careful tortoise. For several moments there was no
sound in the garden other than the harsh calls of the rooks.

Against the fading light their nests looked like blood clots in a web of black veins.

Dart said, "How long before he's mobile, do you think?"

Albert sighed. "Hard to tell. The wounds aren't the main problem, as long as they don't get infected. It'll be very painful for him to walk, but he could do it. He'll be extremely weak, for obvious reasons. He needs a quiet place to rest. And good food."

"Which we can't provide," Agatha said.

Dart watched the rooks. The elms were filling with their restless black shapes. "Can you think of anywhere else he could go?"

"We all know what he has done," Albert said quietly. "As a result, the poor man has become a plague virus. He delivers a death warrant to anyone who shelters him."

"Exactly," Sister Agatha said. "If the Nazis find him here, you know what will happen to us. And if they take us, what do you think will happen to our patients? They'll be sent to a place worse than hell, and die there."

After a pause, Dart said, "What about the Maartens place?"

When the garden was half filled with shadows, Tamar straightened and let the handle of the spade rest against his thigh. Close to his feet the four surviving hens dragged and stabbed at the upturned soil. The cockerel patrolled some distance away, warily twitching his head and groaning. Tamar stood watching the edge of the sky deepen from yellow to amber. He knew Marijke was there before she spoke.

"You've done well."

He turned. She had her grandmother's ancient black coat draped over her shoulders and her arms tightly folded. Tamar thought she looked fragile – something he'd never thought before.

"Yeah, not bad. What should we plant here? Potatoes?"

"We've been eating the seed potatoes for the past two weeks," Marijke said. "Hadn't you noticed?"

"Ah. What else then?"

"There's carrot seed. I don't remember what else. I haven't checked."

"Fine," he said. "We'll sow carrots."

She leaned against him, her head sideways on his chest. "Are you sure you want to do all this?"

"Yes, of course. We have to, don't we?"

"I don't know. I'm not sure if I believe we… Sometimes I wonder if it's worth it."

He wanted to touch her face, but there was soil on his hands. He took her by the shoulders and made her look at him. "It's worth it," he said. "We'll be all right."

So she smiled, and then looked away from him. "If we're going to sow, we'll have to fix these fences to keep the chickens out. We ought to clip their wings too."

"We'll do it," he said. "We'll do everything. You'll have to show me how, though. I know damn all about this business. Now, come on. Let's get inside. You look cold."

She put her left hand on his chest to stop him and looked into his eyes. "You have to promise me something," she said. "Promise me that if you have to go you'll take me with you. Don't leave me here alone. I can't do that any more."

"I won't go. I'm staying here. We're staying here together."

"Promise me anyway."

Tamar packed the transceiver away and descended the barn stairs shortly after eleven o'clock. He was almost at the door when he remembered what she'd said, what he'd promised her. He turned back and went into the loose box and hung the lantern on a harness peg. When he had lifted away the boards from the back wall, he reached down into the gap and

363

pulled out the canvas bag. He took Nurse Gertrud Berendts's fake ID over to the lamp and studied Marijke's sombre little photograph, then put the booklet into his jacket pocket with his own. Just in case.

When he crossed the yard, the night sky was a vast tracery of stars.

Dart put the tray on the low table next to the lamp, where Koop could see what it held: a small bowl of broth, a slice of pulpy bread and a glass of water. Dart took a cigarette from his packet and put that on the tray too. Then he sat down on the chair. Koop watched with rat-bright eyes.

"I didn't betray you," Dart said. He managed to keep the tone of his voice dead flat.

Koop turned his face away and said nothing.

"Think about it," Dart said. "If I wanted you dead, I'd have killed you before now. A pillow over your face while you were unconscious. An overdose of morphine. I admit I considered it. Everyone would be a lot safer if you were out of the way. Especially the people here. And I like them a lot more than I like you."

Koop's gaze rested on the food. Eventually he said, "So why didn't you?"

"Because you called me a traitor and I want to know why."

"Give me some of that water."

Dart stood and carried the glass to Koop, who took it in his right hand, which shook. Koop drank, urgently.

"Go slow," Dart warned. When Koop leaned back, breathing fast, Dart took the glass and put it back on the tray. He sat down again. "For one thing, I didn't even know where your group was hiding."

Koop lost control of himself. "Of course you bloody did! You both did!" He shook his head from side to side, gasping, struggling to hold back tears of rage. "You bastard! Why are you doing this?"

Dart waited. Then he said quietly, "I'll tell you again: I had no idea where you were."

Koop took a long breath that had a sob in it. "He said, 'I know where to find you.' *I know where to find you.* That's what the bastard said to me. So don't tell me you didn't know as well."

"He? You mean Tamar? When did he say this?"

"That morning. At De Woeste Hoeve."

"What morning? You mean the morning of the executions? You were there? You went back?"

"Yeah."

"Christ," Dart said. "What… Why were you there?"

Koop didn't answer.

"Cigarette?"

Koop shook his head stubbornly, a man nobly refusing a bribe. Then he sighed. "Yeah. Okay."

Dart lit the cigarette and put it between the fingers of Koop's right hand. Koop inhaled and coughed, and Dart could see the pain in the other man's face as the spasm pulled at the wound in his back. He held the glass of water to Koop's lips. Koop drank.

"I'm all right," he said.

"Good." Dart sat down again without taking his eyes from Koop's face. "So you were there at De Woeste Hoeve that morning. And you met Tamar. Is that right?"

Koop exhaled smoke cautiously and watched it drift into the brightness of the lamp. He faced Dart for the first time. "Are you telling me you don't know anything about this?"

Dart looked into Koop's eyes and said, "Yes, that's what I'm telling you. Tamar told me nothing about any of this."

Koop smoked the rest of the cigarette in silence. Dart picked up the tray and carried it to the bed.

"You need to eat. Think you can manage?"

Koop drank the broth straight from the bowl. When he had drained the thin liquid, he ran his tongue round the inside of the bowl to get at the solid bits. The effort of all this seemed to exhaust him, and he slumped back against the headboard with his eyes closed. Dart felt the need to hurry, now.

"Koop? Did you know Tamar was going to be there, that morning?"

"No. The bastard sneaked up on us from behind. We were looking at..." Koop's eyes opened, blinked, then stayed open, staring at the lamp. "We were watching the road. He appeared from nowhere. He stuck his bloody Sten in my mouth. *In my mouth.*"

Beautiful, Dart thought. Perfect. But go carefully. He said, "But he didn't pull the trigger. He could've blown your head off, Koop, but he didn't."

Now Koop turned his gaze on Dart, who had to force himself not to recoil. The man looked like a reptile choking on its own venom.

"Because he's a gutless bastard. He couldn't do the job himself, so he betrayed us to the bloody SS. He got them to do his dirty work, the scumbag."

Koop groaned, clenching his yellow teeth. His breathing broke up into short desperate hisses. Dart watched him suffer for perhaps a quarter of a minute before he carried the chair to the bed.

"Koop. Listen to me. Tamar didn't tell me where you and the others were. I didn't know. Do you understand what I'm saying?" Dart waited until Koop opened his eyes, then he said, "How bad is the pain?"

"Bad enough."

"I want to give you another shot of morphine. Then I need to change your dressings. Are you going to let me do that?"

Koop looked into Dart's eyes and Dart held his gaze.

"Yeah, all right," Koop said. "What happened to your face?"

When Koop had fallen asleep, Dart went to the wireless room. The corridors were intensely dark, but darkness was his element now. He walked across the dispensary and through the false cupboard as if in broad daylight. When he had closed the concealed door behind him, he went to the bureau and lit the lamp. It created a balloon of uncertain light that left the corners of the little room in deep shadow. He was full of nervous excitement but very tired, and he had that familiar prickling under his skin as if his bloodstream were full of insects. He emptied the Benzedrine bottle onto the desk and counted the tablets, even though he already knew that there were only eighteen left. He put sixteen back into the bottle and washed the other two down with a mouthful of stale water.

He sat down and took a notepad and pencil from the bureau drawer, then smoked a cigarette while staring blankly at the paper. He stubbed it out and very quickly filled three quarters of a page with random letters arranged into groups of five. When he had finished he crumpled the paper into a ball then smoothed it out flat, folded it neatly three times, and put it in his pocket.

Despite the cold, he stripped down to his shirt. He dragged one of the batteries over to the recharger and connected the leads. He climbed onto the machine and began to pedal, unsteadily at first, but then with a fast robotic rhythm. The Benzedrine took him and lifted him. Soon he was beyond the threshold of hurt and exhaustion, flying across the night towards the beacon that was Marijke Maartens. At any moment she would turn to see him. And then he would watch it dawn in her face, the joyous understanding that their love had always been inevitable.

THERE ARE CHANCE events. There are coincidences, and something people call luck. And there are happenings so perfect that they get called miracles. After the German raid on the asylum, long after, Dart decided that there had to be something else, some secret working of the world, that went beyond even the miraculous. If he hadn't fallen asleep in his room fully dressed; if, despite his exhaustion, he hadn't clicked awake at six in the morning. If the madwoman Sidona hadn't somehow got out onto the front lawn for a long-delayed appointment with her angel. If the Germans had come straight into the asylum, rather than wasting precious time positioning their machine-gunners on the road. If Koop had been unconscious, rather than struggling to his feet for some reason. If Sidona had blurted to an astute officer that there was a dark angel living in the roof. So many ifs – far too many to be dismissed as simple chance. The truth was that the world had wanted what he, Dart, wanted. He was being carried by the world's hidden mechanisms towards what he was meant to do. There could be no other reasonable explanation.

He had snapped awake because the spiders were trying to suffocate him again, only to find that this time the spiders were his own hands. He'd pushed them away and gone to the window. His normal trembling became a cold shivering as the sweat cooled on his body. Light was seeping slowly into the bottom edge of the sky and it took him some time to realize that it was raining.

He stood watching the slow growth of the dawn, and then his eye was caught by something white moving across the lawn. Sidona. The rain had plastered her white shift to her body; her breasts and belly and thighs were pinkly visible. Dart sighed and was halfway to the door when he heard Sidona begin a prolonged wail. He went back to the window to see her kneeling on the grass, arms outstretched towards the road. The SS vehicles paraded into his line of vision as if she had conjured them up: a staff car followed by two trucks, each with their canvas sides rolled up to reveal a machine-gunner and maybe eight other men peering through the rain at the female lunatic. Dart almost died of shock. He could not move. The convoy halted and now there was nothing to be heard other than the idling engines and the babble of Sidona's unearthly language. Then someone shouted, in German, and there was laughter.

Dart moved then. He grabbed the medical bag and his coat and ran to Koop's room. He wrenched at the key and shouldered the door open. Koop was standing, supporting himself on the foot rail of the bed. Dart ran at him, stooped and lifted Koop's good arm over his shoulder. Koop's balance went and his weight fell onto his wounded leg. He screamed. Dart shoved Koop's face into his shoulder to muffle the man's mouth.

"Be quiet. The Germans are here, understand? *Understand?*"

Koop's eyes were rolling, but he nodded.

They got as far as the door before Dart realized. "Shit," he moaned, on the verge of panic, of tears. He dropped the bag and put Koop's hand on the back of the chair. Koop leaned, trembling, his breathing hoarse. Dart flew across the room and ripped the sheets and blankets from the bed. He stuffed them into the bottom of the wardrobe, shoved the pillows on top of the bundle and closed the wardrobe doors as gently as his fear would let him. He eased open the door onto the corridor. It was empty.

Dart half carried, half dragged Koop to the landing on the second floor. There he had to lean on the banister, already exhausted. From below he heard a woman's voice – Agatha's? – protesting, and then a louder German voice and something crashing to the floor. He adjusted his balance and elbowed open the door that led to the back corridor. Heavy boot steps were already on the lower flight of stairs. Shouts and wailing came from a perplexing number of directions. By the time they reached the dispensary Koop's breathing had become a low persistent moaning, and Dart's terror was rising up in his chest like a thick bubble. When they were inside, he simply dropped Koop onto the floor because there was no other way he could lock the door behind them. Then he dragged Koop over to the cupboard. He saw that the leg of his pyjamas was blotched with blood and was terribly afraid that they had left a trail. If they had, they would die in the next few minutes and it was too late to do anything about it. He thought of Marijke, had a sudden brilliant vision of her. To have got this close, and still have to die… The unfairness of it almost set him snivelling like a child. Koop's head was lolling about now and his eyes seemed to have come loose.

"Don't pass out, you bastard," Dart hissed, stepping over him to yank at the hook on the cupboard wall. The concealed door swung open.

He propped Koop on the couch, slid the wooden bar across the inside of the door and stood, stooped, on shaking legs. He was drenched with sweat; he could feel it trickling down his legs and chest. He dragged in air. His lungs felt full of thorns.

Koop's face was corpse white, but his eyes had steadied. He looked around the room, and then at Dart. "It stinks in here," he said faintly.

"Shut up!"

Dart emptied the bag onto the bureau and took out the Smith and Wesson revolver. He realized that he did not know where to stand. The place he chose might very well be the place where he would die, and such a choice was impossible for him. He would have sobbed if Koop hadn't been there. In the end, he took the chair and sat on the far side of the door, opposite the couch. He put his elbows on his thighs and hung his head, the gun pointing at the floor. His gaze focused on the signet ring on his left hand. He laid the revolver between his feet and slid a fingernail into the ring, easing the engraved plate open just enough to see the tip of the cyanide capsule. The urge, the temptation, was so strong that it made him shudder. When he jerked his head up, he saw that Koop was watching him.

Dart stood and took the Luger from his coat pocket and laid it on Koop's stomach. Koop wrapped his right hand around the gun but didn't lift it. He looked up at Dart and grinned in an awful twisted way and then closed his eyes. Sprawled, bloody, holding the pistol, he looked like a police photograph of a suicide. Dart went back to his chair and picked up the Smith and Wesson. Five minutes passed like a year.

It was Koop who sensed them first. His eyes flicked open and his wolfish face turned towards the cupboard. He moved the Luger down onto his right thigh and thumbed the safety catch off. Dart felt slight vibrations in the floorboards just before he heard a faint metallic clack. He stood up. As he did so he heard the dispensary door crash open against the wall with extraordinary violence. He somehow stifled the cry that rose in his throat. There was utter silence for perhaps two seconds, then fast heavy footfalls. Voices. A question, in German. Another. Dart heard what he thought was Albert Veening's voice, and then the door into the cupboard from the dispensary was wrenched open. A bright thread of light appeared along the bottom of the inner door. A torch was being shone into the cupboard. Dart raised the revolver, holding it with both hands, aiming at where he imagined the soldier's chest to be. He was close to fainting; the edges of his vision were already dissolving. The thread of light faded, then returned, then vanished. Someone spoke in German, and then a different, louder voice gave an order. Boots hammered across the floor. The voices moved away. A second or two later the dispensary door slammed shut.

Dart slumped as if his spine had melted. He realized that his mouth was open and that he hadn't drawn breath for some time. He licked his lips, which felt as coarse and dry as scoured bone, and turned to face Koop, who was looking back at him, shaking his head, telling him not to speak or move.

They remained motionless, staring at each other, for perhaps a whole minute. Then Koop gestured with his Luger and Dart went and pressed his ear to the door, but all he could hear was the thick unsteady echo of his own heart.

The rain paused later in the morning and an uncertain grey light found its way into the wireless room. Albert Veening finished his work on Koop and straightened up. He looked a hundred years old.

"You will stay in this room, Mr de Vries," he said. "It's unlikely that the SS will be back, but I'm afraid I can't take any chances. If Ernst has to go elsewhere, Sister Agatha will take care of your needs. Now, if you'll excuse me, I have to go downstairs. This morning's visit by the German bloody army has set my patients back ten years at least. It's bedlam down there."

When he had gone, Koop looked up at the ceiling. "I can't stay in this shithole. I've got things to do."

Dart had just about managed to climb out of the pit that terror and exhaustion had dug for him. He'd taken four of the last Benzedrines, and he was waiting for them to begin their work. The early signs were there: his head was less full of clouds, and his right foot had started tapping on the floor without him telling it to. He studied Koop with an almost scientific curiosity. What the man had been through that morning should have taken him through death's door; instead, it had perked him up. There shouldn't have been any blood left in him; but there were spots of livid colour in his cheeks and a new quickness in his eyes. He fed on the things that killed other people.

Dart said, "Where's the gun? The Luger."

"Down the back of the couch. Don't try to get it off me."

"I don't intend to. How's the pain?"

Koop gave Dart a suspicious look. "I can handle it. I don't want any more of your morphine."

Dart shrugged. "Suit yourself."

He stood up, full of a restless impatience. The room was closing in. It was much smaller now that Koop was in it. Dart's mind, though, was as clear and sharp as a needle of ice, and miles and years away from this claustrophobic space. He walked to the small window and stuffed his trembling hands into his pockets. He watched the rivulets of rain running down the glass, aware of Koop watching him.

Eventually he spoke. "I have a problem."

The sound Koop made was somewhere between a snort and a laugh, which was more or less what Dart had expected. He didn't turn round.

"It has to do with you."

"Look," Koop said, "I told you. I'll be out of here soon. You don't have to worry your pretty head about me."

"That's not what I'm talking about. Where would you go, anyway?"

"None of your damn business."

"I think it might be," Dart said quietly. "You see, my problem is Tamar. What to do about Tamar."

Koop said nothing.

"The fact is, Tamar is my superior officer. He is – or was – my friend. It's also a fact that he has been acting, well, strange lately. Erratic. He says he's sick of all this. He has accused me of … things. Maybe he's having a nervous breakdown; we are operating under a lot of stress. But that's not the point. The point is that when you leave here – if you leave here – you'll try to kill him. So obviously I shouldn't let you go."

He heard Koop move on the couch now, but waited a moment or two before he turned round. Koop had the Luger in his right hand, resting it against his chest, the muzzle pointing directly at Dart. Dart's own pistol was lying on the bureau, and Koop knew it.

Dart gazed thoughtfully at the Luger for a couple of seconds and then shook his head, frowning slightly, rather like a schoolmaster deciding to ignore some piece of childish tomfoolery. He spoke in the same level tone of voice as before.

"My problem is that I believe you."

"What?"

"I believe you. I think Tamar betrayed your group. Is it okay if I sit down?"

Koop tracked him with the gun, but his harrowed face looked slack and stupefied.

Dart said, "I want to show you something." He reached into his pocket and took out the creased and folded sheet of paper. He held it out to Koop. Koop flicked his eyes at it and then back to Dart's face.

"What is it?"

"Have a look at it. Take it. Put the gun down. We both know you're not going to kill me."

Koop eventually lowered the pistol and laid it on his stomach. He took the paper but had trouble unfolding it one-handed, so Dart did it for him. Koop stared at the meaningless sequence of pencilled letters.

"It's in code," Dart said helpfully.

"I can bloody see that," Koop spat. "So what's it supposed to be?"

"It's a signal Tamar ordered me to send to London the day after you shot Rauter. We knew more or less what reprisals the Germans were planning by then. We knew about The Hague and Amsterdam and Amersfoort too, but we didn't know the numbers then, of course."

Koop looked at him.

"Ah," Dart murmured. "Sorry. You don't know, do you?"

"So tell me, damn you."

"At least another hundred people. Probably more. Almost certainly more."

The paper shook in Koop's hand, so Dart steadied it for him.

"That's basically what the first half of this is about. Down to here, see? Although to tell you the truth, I didn't understand why Tamar wanted me to send it. We'd already sent more or less the same information a few hours earlier. But he insisted. Said we had to confirm it. He was … beside himself. Almost out of control. I'd never seen him like that before."

Dart paused thoughtfully, like a man remembering sadness. "But it's the other part of the signal that matters. I refused to send it at first. Tried to talk him out of it. But like I said, he was out of control. Shouting and swearing and so forth. He said that if I didn't send it he'd shoot me for insubordination and send it himself. I don't think he would have done, though. Shoot me, I mean. As you said, it's not really his style, is it?"

Koop was now glaring silently at Dart. His eyes were moist and feverish.

"The signal goes on to say that your group is a serious and continuing hazard. It says that you personally refuse to obey orders, no matter where they're from. It says that in his opinion, Tamar's opinion, your group's reckless action may well cause deep divisions in the resistance. That much is true, by the way. Delta Centrum was baying for your blood. The last two lines of the signal are his request for authorization to disband your group using 'extreme emergency procedures' if necessary. That's what the two sequences PBUXY and RRGYQ mean."

Koop switched his hot gaze to the paper, but still didn't speak. Dart waited.

"In other words, kill us," Koop said. "Without the bullshit, that's what it means, right?"

Dart nodded. Koop turned the paper over and examined it, as if expecting to find the print of the devil's thumb in blood. "Why's it all crumpled up?"

"I was supposed to burn it," Dart said.

"Why didn't you?"

Dart looked at the floor. "I don't really know."

Koop was breathing deeply and steadily through his nose, making a faint bubbling that Dart found repulsive. "Did London reply to this?"

"Eventually," Dart said. "It came in just after four in the morning."

"And?"

"They said no. Authorization denied. They told us to await further instructions."

"Did they, by Christ? They said no? And what did pretty boy have to say about that?"

"Not much, funnily enough. He read the message twice and then burned it."

"Come on," Koop said. "You just told me he was all worked up. It must've really pissed him off."

"He'd grabbed an hour or two's sleep by then. He'd calmed down a bit."

"So he didn't say anything?"

Dart looked Koop in the eyes.

"He said something like, 'Well, things happen on the front line that London can't do anything about.' I didn't think much about it until I came down the other night and found you bleeding all over the scullery. Then I knew."

Koop stared at the wall for a full minute. There was something resembling a smile on his face when he turned to Dart again. "Veening reckons I might be able to walk unaided in a couple of days. What do you think?"

Dart thought about it. "He wants you out of here."

"I'm happy to oblige."

"I don't know," Dart said. "Your blood count must be terrible. What you really need is plenty of food. And we don't have it."

Koop grinned. "I eat like a bird," he said.

Yes, Dart thought. A vulture.

ENGLAND, 1995

IN THE EARLY afternoon of our fifth day, Yoyo and I found ourselves at the first bridge on the fourth and last map. The Tamar had dwindled to a thin blue line of small kinks and wriggles as if it had been drawn by a map-maker with a bad case of the shakes or hiccups. Little bridges stepped across it every few miles as though it wasn't there. This one, like most of the others, was narrow, ancient, made of grey mottled stone and in the middle of nowhere. Silent level farmland stretched as far as the eye could see, interrupted here and there by small gatherings of trees. My river was now only a stream, and from above you could hardly see it because it was almost smothered by the reeds and slender trees that grew on its banks.

We stopped only because Grandad had marked the place. Leaning over the parapet, we saw that there was a shady patch of grass just big enough for two people to perch their bums and dangle their feet in the water. We found our way down there and were taking our shoes off when a big grey arrow exploded out of the low darkness beneath the bridge. The shallow water churned beneath it, and when it beat its wings we felt the displaced air against our faces and fell back, alarmed. A heron. It lifted itself so slowly into the air that we thought it would stall; but at last it pulled its trailing legs into its body, folded its long neck and drifted like a primitive aircraft towards a higher bend in the stream, vanishing into the silvery-green trees.

When we clambered back up to the road, we heard the sound of an approaching vehicle and pressed ourselves against the hedge to let it pass. It was a dark blue Land-Rover coated in reddish dust. Sunlight flashed off its windscreen, making the driver invisible. We turned to walk back to the Saab but stopped and looked when we heard the other vehicle brake, its engine revving hard then falling to a soft chug. It had halted on the far side of the bridge. I thought that maybe it was the farmer who owned the land, and felt a little flicker of anxiety. But no one got out. We could see that the driver had turned in his seat to watch us. I looked at Yoyo. He shrugged and we got into our car. As soon as Yoyo started the engine the Land-Rover pulled away. By the time we'd reached the next turn in the road it was out of sight.

Just when you'd expect the Tamar to disappear altogether it swells, with a sort of *ba-boom* (if maps had soundtracks), into two big lakes. Lower Tamar Lake is a placid stretch of water where ducks trail ripples towards the bank, expecting pic-nickers to feed them bits of sandwiches. We left the Saab in the car park and followed the signs to Higher Tamar Lake. The footpath took us over a stile into a field where sheep complained about the heat; their cries were like sad people pretending to laugh. The field sloped upwards and we'd toiled halfway to the crest when we stopped to gape, amazed. A vast sloping wall of brown-stained concrete reared up out of the valley to our left. It was incredibly, brutally, out of place among the low hills and green and tawny fields. It was the dam that blocks the flow of the young river and turns the valley into a reservoir. We climbed the steps up onto it. The grey flagstones were hot beneath our feet. Halfway across we stopped to lean against the steel railings and gaze out onto the lake. The water level was low after those rainless weeks but a number of small sailing dinghies were out, seeking scraps of breeze.

"Wow," Yoyo said, opening his camera case. "What is that weird shit down there?"

I stood on tiptoe and peered over the railings. Where the wall of the dam vanished into the water, there was a jumble of rocks exactly the colour of milk chocolate. And lapping against these rocks, staining them, was a big slick of astonishingly beautiful scum. Yoyo took three pictures of it at different places along the dam. Looking at them now, they're like abstract paintings – whorls and coils and long, drifting threads of pale blue, turquoise, white and bottle green. They look like the grain in marble, swirls of molten glass, the whirling gases of a distant star. At the end of the dam there was a notice telling us what this stuff was, telling us what the photographs do not. The word TOXIC appeared more than once.

There was a picnic area and a café on the other side of the lake. We bought two tubs of ice cream and sat beneath a parasol in silence. I was happy – we both were – but I was also troubled. There was a question, or rather a small cloud of questions, hanging over the day. We had reached, you see, the last of Grandad's marks on the map. Just three miles or so north of where we were sitting was the source of the river. At least, what we reckoned was the source. Poring over the map in our room the previous night, we'd found a spring marked just where the hair-thin line of blue finally disappeared. That had to be it. And when we found it – *if* we found it – that would be the end. But unless something miraculous happened, it wouldn't mean anything at all. An end that didn't end anything, a pointless destination. We'd found out nothing. I was sure now that Grandad had made this journey and that it had been very important to him, though God knows why. And it had been important to him that I made the same journey; again, God knows why. Unless it really was for the sentimental reason that Yoyo had suggested. But that just wasn't good enough. Those damned things in Grandad's box were all connected in some way, but we'd travelled all these miles without working out how.

I'd stirred the last of my ice cream into a slush, mulling all this over. I looked up and Yoyo was watching me. He reached over and laid his hand on mine.

"Problem?" he asked. "Something is bothering you?"

"No," I said. "I'm fine. I'm happy, honestly."

Which was the truth and a lie at the same time, because my ridiculous happiness was itself part of the problem. I was afraid it would end when the journey ended. The plain fact was that by the evening – or the next day, at the latest – there would be no reason not to go back to London. Then what? The rest of the school holidays, a part-time job, then A levels maybe, then the rest of my life. And no Yoyo. He'd go back to Holland. The End. The future loomed over me like the blank wall of the Tamar dam and I didn't fancy it at all. In five days I'd become someone else, and I liked being her.

I knew that this feeling, the feeling of things coming to an end, was affecting Yoyo as well. I knew it because without saying anything we'd agreed not to talk about it. Neither of us had spoken a sentence that began with "When we get back to London…" They were the taboo words that would shatter the spell. We were sitting with empty ice-cream tubs in this rather boring place because we didn't want to say them. Sooner or later, though, one of us would have to say "Shall we go?"

It was Yoyo.

"Sure," I said, as though I'd been waiting for him.

We gathered up our stuff. I'd gone a few paces before I realized that he hadn't moved. I looked back at him. "What?"

He was staring at the car park next to the boat house.

384

Parked in the shade of a tree was a dusty blue Land-Rover.

"Is that the same one we saw at the bridge?"

He shrugged. "Maybe. No, probably. It's what farmers drive, I think. There are perhaps hundreds of them around here. It doesn't mean anything."

We walked back over the dam, pausing only briefly to look down at the beautiful gunge that polluted the water.

I'm not sure what I'd thought the "spring" that was the source of my river would be. Something like a natural fountain, maybe, a bubbling-up of crystal-clear water cupped in a niche of ancient mossy rocks. Needless to say, it isn't like that at all. It's in a bog. Not what you'd normally think of as a bog, though. Not a low swampy place. Quite the opposite. In the summer, that is. It's a high stretch of moorland covered in tall sharp-edged yellow grass and prickly stuff. According to the map, the spring itself is snug up against a country lane, but when we stopped there we realized there was no chance of getting to it. Between the lane and the moor there's a dense hedge of thorny wind-tilted trees and spiky yellow gorse. You'd be ripped to shreds if you tried to get through it. So Yoyo reversed the car until we got to a place where there was a gate and a track.

The sky seemed lower here, and was as white as paper. The heat was moist and nasty. We climbed over the gate and walked down the track until we figured we were more or less opposite the place where the spring should be. A small cloud of gnats kept us company, spiralling above our heads. We saw now that the harsh yellow grass and brambles and low spiny bushes concealed a labyrinth of ditches. In winter they'd be little streams, but in that hot dry summer not one of them contained the trickle of water that would guide us to the spring itself. We stood baffled, flapping our hands at the insects zeroing in on us. We looked down at our bare legs and skimpy trainers.

"Shit," Yoyo said poetically.

I can admit, now, that all the way up the river I'd secretly nursed the foolish idea that when we reached its source we'd be given some kind of answer. I can't remember how I'd pictured it. A magical document, a scroll of time-stained parchment in a lead casket, jammed under a rock? A letter from beyond the grave, sealed in plastic behind a veil of falling water? Something as childish as that, probably. Something from an adventure novel in which everything is revealed and tidied up in the last chapter. A key to the code. But when I stood there and saw that the end of the journey was as vague and unreachable as the beginning had been, I realized I didn't care. No, more than that: I was relieved. I didn't want an ending, didn't want to get to the full stop of our story.

Yoyo put his arm round my shoulders and I leaned into him and put my hand on his chest.

After a while I said, "Home, then?"

And it didn't seem so terrible a thing to say after all.

We walked back to the car. I was leaning on the gate, gazing back, when Yoyo nudged my arm and gestured with his head. The blue Land-Rover was parked about twenty metres in front of the Saab. The driver's door swung open and a man stepped out. He stood and watched us for a long moment and then walked towards us. He was wearing a faded denim shirt. He had the face of an old man but didn't move like one.

I heard Yoyo speak my name but his voice seemed to come from a long distance; I had that thickness inside my ears that you get on aeroplanes. And I couldn't look at him, because I was watching the other man's face and he was watching mine. He stopped just beyond the reach of my arms.

He said, "Tamar?"

The edges of my world melted.

I heard myself say, "Dad?"

TIME DOESN'T HEAL, not really. I'm no longer that fifteen-year-old girl whose world changed shape on a desolate country road. Even now, remembering her at that moment, it's as though something physically shifts inside me, pulling at a wound.

My father put his arms around me, and I held him because it was impossible not to. We may have stood like that for some time. I couldn't get into the Land-Rover with him, though. I just couldn't. So Yoyo and I followed in the Saab. Poor Yoyo; it was hard for him to drive because I couldn't let go of his left hand, even when he had to change gear. He must have been searching through his languages, desperately looking for something to say. I could only breathe in long shaky gulps, and there was nothing I could do to stop my tears. They ran down my face like rain down a window-pane. All the tears I'd never shed, all at once. A bloody river.

We drove for no more than ten minutes before the Land-Rover turned off the road through a pair of immense iron gates. A tarmac driveway curved through parkland ahead of us, and I caught a watery glimpse of a large and complicated roof. We didn't go towards it. Instead, we turned left again and parked beside a gatehouse, a quaint cottage of grey stone and fancy white-painted gables.

It's funny, isn't it, that at times of crisis we do the most ordinary things. Dad just walked to the back door of the gatehouse and said, "Come in." Then we were in a small tidy kitchen with Dad filling a kettle as if we were familiar visitors who'd popped in for a cup of tea.

If there are words for what I felt, I don't know what they are. I was so full of questions that I thought they would choke me before I could tug them out of my throat. The first one I managed was truly stupid.

"Do you live here?"

"Yes. The big house – did you see it? – it's a language school for business people. Residential. Lots of Germans, a few Japanese. I take care of the grounds and do maintenance jobs around the house. It's a beautiful old place. I'll show you round later, if you like."

He said all this very quickly, in one breath, knowing, I suppose, that if he paused I'd ask other, harder questions. I realized that I wouldn't have recognized his voice if I hadn't been looking at his face. I'd forgotten it.

The kettle built to a roar. Dad was opening cupboard doors blindly as though he didn't know where his things were kept.

"Dad? *Dad?*"

His shoulders fell. My fists were clenched; my fingernails dug into my palms. I felt Yoyo's hands on my arms.

"Dad," I said, or wailed. "Dad, for God's sake!"

He turned to face us. His eyes were wet and he couldn't seem to make up his mind what to do with his hands. In the end he stuck them under his armpits and clamped his arms tightly to his chest. The kettle clicked off, leaving a huge silence.

"I'm sorry," he said. "I know you… I know you must have so many questions. I don't know where to start."

Nor did I. I was shivering and I couldn't control it.

Dad said, "I think you might be in shock. Wait."

He took three small glasses and a bottle from a shelf and poured shots of brandy. As soon as I smelled it my mouth filled with salty saliva.

I managed to say, "Bathroom."

Dad pointed to the hallway. "Through there. Top of the stairs."

I got there somehow. A clean, almost sterile room. A bath with a plastic shower curtain. I lifted the toilet lid and threw up, twice.

When I went back down to the kitchen, Yoyo and Dad had gone. I looked around the room. Nothing in the sink, no washing up on the drainer. Tea towels neatly folded and hung on the rail of the electric cooker. A cork notice board with a few bills and business cards pinned to it, but nothing handwritten, no postcards, no photographs. A small square table, and just one chair.

I heard voices and looked out of the open window into the garden. Dad and Yoyo were sitting opposite each other at a heavy-looking picnic table, the kind that pubs have. Yoyo was talking. Dad was leaning on his elbows, his head lowered.

When I went out they both stood up as if I were the Queen or somebody. Yoyo came to meet me and put the palm of his hand gently to the side of my face. "Tamar? Are you okay?"

I nodded.

He said quietly, "This is some hell of a thing."

"I don't know if I can deal with it," I said.

"To tell the truth, I think we have no choice. This is what it was all about, the whole time. Come on."

I sat down next to Yoyo so that I could hold his hand if I needed to. Dad looked sick, despite his suntan; but perhaps that was because his face was thinner than I'd remembered.

He said, "Johannes has been telling me how you came to be here. About Mum, your gran. About your … William's death. I'm trying to take it all in."

"You didn't even know Grandad was dead?"

"No. When I saw you I thought he must have sent you here. That he'd told you where I was. Which I suppose he did, in his own twisted way."

I stared at him. I had the sensation of buckling and bending. It was a feeling that would get stronger – and worse – as the day went on.

"I don't understand," I said. "Do you mean he knew? He knew where you were all along?"

"No, no. He found me."

"What? He came to this house? You saw him?"

"Oh yes," Dad said, and there was no missing the sourness in his voice.

"When was this?"

"Last November. November the fifth, to be precise. I'd been up at the school all afternoon. Setting up a firework display. I got back here just after six and found a car outside. A hire car, from Plymouth. I couldn't see who was in it because the windows were all misted up. I was shocked to the core when it turned out to be him."

I struggled with this. Last November. Then I remembered. "He told us he'd gone to Brighton," I said.

Dad nodded, unsurprised, but said nothing.

"And he didn't tell me. He knew, he knew where you were for months, and he never told me!"

"No. I didn't think he would. Not after what happened between us."

I put my head in my hands. "I don't understand. I don't understand anything."

Dad reached across the table and took my wrists in his hands. I couldn't look at him.

"Tamar," he said, "listen, please. I suppose I knew that this would happen one day. I wanted it and dreaded it at the same time. I've missed you so much, my love. I can't tell you what it's been like."

I looked up then. There were tears in his eyes, and that was nothing like good enough.

"Don't say that. How can you say that? You left us. You left me. I thought you were bloody dead."

I pulled my arms from his grip. He clasped his hands on the table in front of him and stared down at them. Yoyo laid his palm on my back, a gentle, useless gesture. I really was all cried out by then, but my eyes felt hot and swollen.

Dad said, "I want to say sorry, but it would be…"

"What?"

He looked up. "Pathetically inadequate."

"No, Dad," I said, "it would be an insult."

"Yes."

Then there was a silence, and I couldn't bear it. "So tell me, then. Tell me why you left us." My voice didn't sound like my own.

He looked away, drawing in a long audible breath that made his shoulders rise then fall. "Yes," he said. "Yes, very well."

He took a packet of cigarettes from his shirt pocket and lit one. I didn't think I'd ever seen him smoke.

"He, William, once said to me that some of us have things, secrets, that it's best we take to our graves. That was the expression he used. And I came to believe it. Or accept it, anyway. And it's cost me more than I can say. Tell me, did he by any chance tell you how you came to be called Tamar?"

THE SUN HAD become a hazy yellow ball. Blurred shadows had gathered at the foot of the neatly clipped hedge.

"Anyway," Dad said, "we had that conversation about your name two months – no, less – before you were born. I didn't think too much about it for a long time after that. Now and again I'd try to talk to him about Holland and the war and the rest of it, but I never got anywhere. Mum, your gran, would sometimes let a few things slip, but then she'd sort of skitter away from the subject. Especially if he was there. She'd say her memories were all muddled up. Maybe they were. I don't know."

He stared down at the table, picking at the grain with a fingernail.

"Dad," I said, "what does all this have do with you … going away?"

"Everything. It has *everything* to do with it." There was a sudden fierceness in his voice which startled me. "I'm sorry. This … all this stuff goes round and round in my head all the time. All the time. I have to tell you about it in the order things happened; I can't do it any other way."

There was a look on his face that I recognized. I'd seen it on the faces of poor crazy homeless people on the streets, the ones who are desperate to tell you their tragic life stories. Dad had that same twist to his mouth, that same determination to get things said. I felt almost afraid of him. I slid my hand under the table and found Yoyo's, and he threaded his fingers tightly through mine.

I said, "Okay, Dad. I'm listening."

"It was something to do with you starting school, strange to say. It was a big thing for me. Maybe for all parents. You have this baby, and then suddenly – boom – you're dropping her off at the school gates. Time seemed to have accelerated. I was nearly forty by then; William and Marijke were well into their sixties. It started to seem like a terrible thing to me, that they would die and I would have no idea about who and what they'd been. It felt like I didn't know who I was. So I started investigating, researching, the war in Holland. For a year or two it was, well, like a sort of hobby. But it was much more difficult than I'd thought. Information was hard to come by. There was the military stuff, of course. Plenty about the battle for Arnhem, for instance. But trying to find out anything about the SOE, what it actually did, was hopeless. And every time I came up against a brick wall I got more determined to continue. As time went by I suppose I got a bit obsessive."

He took his cigarettes out again, hesitated, then decided against lighting one. "Once or twice my job took me to Holland, and I spent my free time trawling libraries, chatting up government contacts and so on. People were a bit more helpful than they were here, but I'd always find myself at a dead end sooner or later. There are still things that went on over there during the war that people don't want dug up."

Yoyo made a little grunting sound of agreement.

"I learned a lot about the period, but it was bloody laborious. I don't speak much Dutch or German, and I wasn't even sure what I was looking for, let alone where to look.

Basically all I had, you see, was the year 1944 and the name Tamar. I was forever hoping that the word would leap out at me from some dusty old file. And it didn't happen. It was like chasing shadows in fog."

He changed his mind and lit the cigarette. "Anyway, in 1988 my job changed. And as a result I found myself spending a bit of time with people from the secret services."

That made me blink. "What?" I said. "Are you telling me you were a spy or something?"

"No, no. Not really. But the department started sending me to places like Poland and Czechoslovakia, the old Iron Curtain countries. We were looking for business opportunities, future markets, that sort of thing. So I'd go over there, and when I got back I'd have to go to some anonymous office in Euston or somewhere to be interviewed by blokes in grey suits. Debriefing, they called it. They were interested in anything I'd found out about industry and technology, stuff like that."

I remembered Tweedledum and Tweedledee.

"I got quite matey with one of them. Roger. I don't suppose it was his real name. He was all right, though. Arsenal supporter, like me. So eventually I asked him if he could get his hands on SOE files. It was like I'd suggested he donate me his kidneys. But I kept on at him, and in the end he said he'd see what he could do. It was months before he got back to me. We met in a pub. He said he'd had one hell of a job finding the files, never mind getting a peep at them. But he'd done it. And what he'd found out was that everything, absolutely everything, to do with that group of agents, the Rivers group that William had been part of, had disappeared. It was as if those guys had never existed. He said he'd checked through all the Dutch section files, and although they were a bit patchy, there was at least something on all the other groups. He said it was as if someone had systematically removed the bits I was interested in. He gave me a funny look, I can tell you. He was a very suspicious man. I suppose it was a qualification for the job. He obviously thought that I might know how come those files had vanished. I didn't, then. I think I do now, though. He did tell me that the man in charge of the SOE section that would have controlled the Rivers group was a Colonel Arthur Nicholson. Later I found out that Nicholson had been killed in a car accident in Australia in 1956. There was someone else called Hendriks, who might have been English or Dutch. And it probably wasn't his real name; I never found out. So that was another dead end."

I can tell you what it was like, listening to my dad talking in that neat little garden of his. It was like listening to someone who'd been kept in a dark cellar for years. Someone who'd shaped and rehearsed the story of himself in order to stay real. I know Yoyo felt that too. So we kept quiet.

"The next time I was in Holland I put an advert in a few newspapers. The personal columns. I can't remember exactly what I said; something like *Tamar: resistance organizer 1944–45. Information sought.* Then a PO box number in Amsterdam and my London office number. Nothing. A few months later I did it again, and I got a phone call: a woman speaking perfect English with an unusual accent. Her name was Rosa Galloway. She said she might have information for me, but she was definitely suspicious. She wanted to know what my interest was. I told her that Tamar had been my father's resistance code name during the war and I was trying to trace his old comrades, which was sort of true. Then she surprised me by asking what my mother's name was. I told her, then there was a silence. I got the impression she'd covered the mouthpiece and was speaking to someone at her end. Then she said that yes, perhaps she could help me, and asked if I could come to Holland, to The Hague. Of course I said yes. We fixed a date, and a place, the bar of a hotel.

"I wangled myself a long weekend and got to The Hague early on a Friday evening. Rosa Galloway turned out to be a woman about the same age as me, very good-looking, very smartly dressed. Big brown eyes. When I commented on her excellent English, she told me that she was married to a Canadian who worked at the embassy. She'd lived in Ontario for several years. Then she told me that it was her mother who'd spotted my advert. Her name was Trixie Greydanus and she lived in a *hofje* – that's like an almshouse, an old people's home – in Delft, just south of The Hague. When she'd seen the advert she'd phoned Rosa, very agitated, because she knew who Tamar was. She'd been his courier in the resistance.

"That was an incredible moment for me. I begged Rosa to take me to Delft that evening, but she wouldn't. She said her mother was in poor health and would be too tired. In the end we agreed she would drive me there the following morning.

"The *hofje* in Delft was a beautiful old building. I was surprised to find that most of the staff were nurses. It turned out that it was, in fact, a hospice. Trixie Greydanus had cancer, although you wouldn't have known it, not at first glance. Her room had a tall narrow window, and she was sitting in a chair with her back to the light; so it took me a second or two to see what she looked like. She had the same bright chestnut-coloured eyes as Rosa. She was wearing a lot of careful make-up, and her hair was strange. Cut in a very old-fashioned style and dyed a dark blonde colour. I was a bit slow to realize that it was a wig, and that her eyebrows were painted on, not real. She was holding on tight to her chair, but I could see that her arms were trembling. I was shaky too.

"Rosa introduced us and asked me to forgive her mother for not standing to greet me because her legs were very weak. Trixie said nothing at all during this, just stared at me with those big eyes. I felt awkward. Rosa started saying something in Dutch to her mother but Trixie interrupted her.

"Rosa said, 'My mother asks when you were born, and where.'

"'October the fifth, 1945,' I said. 'In London.' Trixie nodded and said something else.

"'She asks if you've brought a photograph of your mother.'

"Which I had, of course. I'd brought three. The one that showed Marijke best was a picture I'd taken of her and William standing on the balcony of the flat the day they moved in. I gave it to her, and that's when things started getting emotional. Trixie looked at it a long time and then nodded again, and then it was like she couldn't stop nodding, and she was crying at the same time. She kept touching Marijke's face in the photo and saying the same thing over and over. I didn't need it translated.

"'No,' I said, 'she's not dead. She's not dead.'

"Rosa had her arms around her mother, trying to calm her. 'I was afraid this would happen,' she said. 'It's not good for her to get upset. The drugs she has to take sometimes make her very emotional anyway, and confused. Maybe it would be best if you left us alone for a short while.'

"So I went for a walk. It was a freezing cold day. The streets were full of people shopping and doing ordinary things. When I went back, Trixie had calmed down. She'd put fresh make-up on to cover the mess her tears had made of her face. She was trying to smile, and she started talking straight away. Rosa had to make her pause so she could fit the translations in.

"'She says she recognized your mother at once. She has hardly changed. Always such a beautiful girl. My mother had many terrible days during the war, but the day Marijke disappeared was the worst. She has never stopped thinking and, er, wondering about her. Marijke was her best friend, more like a sister. That is why she cried just now. She says she is sorry. She says you do not look like her. More like your father, perhaps, except for your hair. You have the same shape of face.'

"Sitting there, I couldn't decide whether my best bet was to wait and let Trixie Greydanus ramble on or to try to get her to answer the questions that I was desperate to ask. But before I could say anything, Trixie studied the photo again and spoke to Rosa.

"Rosa said, 'My mother asks who the man in the photograph is. Is it Marijke's husband?'

"I was taken by surprise. I laughed, I think, and said, 'That's Dad. My father. I expect he's changed a great deal since you knew him.'

"Trixie obviously understood 'father'; *vader* in Dutch is pretty much the same. She looked at me and at the photo again and said something to Rosa. Rosa glanced at me and the two of them had this fast muttered conversation, then both looked at me. Rosa opened her mouth and shut it again, and I sat there smiling at them like the idiot I was."

HOLLAND, 1945

DART AWOKE ON Sunday 18th March with a brain as busy as a pit of snakes. His mind must have been swarming in his sleep, because he could not tell the difference between dreaming and thinking.

It would all work, the mechanics of it, as long as he got the timing right. Tamar would be in the barn at two in the afternoon, making the scheduled transmission. He'd have the headphones on, so he probably wouldn't hear the ambulance anyway, but it would be best to cut the engine and coast into the yard, just to make sure... No, it was *things*, and the unpredictability of those things, that squirmed in his head. A burnt-out wire or sheared bolt in the engine of the ambulance, a cartridge jammed in a gun, an unforeseen incident on the road.

Dart pulled his legs up in the bed and locked his arms around his knees, folding into himself. A lesser man would pray for luck, but he didn't have to do that. He didn't need luck because he had inevitability. He would succeed in the same way that a river always reaches the sea no matter what tries to dam or divert it. And he'd been given Koop, his own malevolent little puppet, his instrument to use and then dispose of. There was nothing to fear.

He went to the mirror above the washstand. The bruising was now nothing more than a shadow, a trick of the light. The split in his lip had crusted over; he would have to shave very carefully tomorrow morning. He held his hands out flat. He willed the trembling to stop, and it did.

When Dart went into the kitchen, Albert Veening was sitting at the long table tapping ash from his cigarette into an empty cup. He wore a cardigan with unravelling cuffs, and looked derelict. Dart went to the stove and found something that might have been coffee in a slightly warm saucepan.

"How are things?"

"Better, I suppose," Albert said. "There are still four patients we daren't leave unattended. Sidona is the worst. She's convinced yesterday's events prove that the angels have turned against her. She believes the Nazi bastard in charge of the raid was the dark angel Trago in one of his disguises. She has it all worked out, which means that her ordinary schizophrenia has become paranoid schizophrenia. Difficult stuff to deal with, religious mania. Especially when it's so systematic. Thank God I'm an atheist."

"Have you visited our uninvited guest?"

Albert carefully stubbed out his cigarette and put the dog-end in his cardigan pocket. "Yes. I was up there half an hour ago. Can't say I enjoy treating patients who greet you by pointing a Luger at your head. Mind you, I suppose he's someone who does have reason to be paranoid."

"How is he?"

"Bloody nasty. Apart from that, he's doing surprisingly well. He's a lot stronger than he looks. Yesterday opened up his wounds, of course, but they're clean. He was on his feet when I went in this morning. He'd managed to walk around the room a few times. His temperature is normal again, which is a good sign."

Dart sat down. "Sister Agatha is right, you know. We can't keep him here."

Albert leaned back and sighed. "Actually, this is exactly where he should be. He's as crazy as a burning rat."

"Albert."

"Yes, I know."

"For one thing," Dart said, "I can't keep him in the radio room until the damn war is over."

"True. He smells, apart from anything else. I suppose we should give him a bath. Although I wouldn't want to be the one who tries it. Got any more cigarettes?"

"I'll share one."

"Thank you. Does Mr de Vries have somewhere else he can go?"

"He says he does, yes."

Albert looked up. "Not the Maartens place, is it? You mentioned that the other day and I wasn't happy about it. I wouldn't want what's-her-name, Marijke, to have to—"

"No, no. Absolutely not. That was just, you know, the first thing I thought of. No, he says he knows a safe house." Dart passed the cigarette.

Albert said, "Where?"

"He won't tell me. He says he'll direct me there."

"What do you mean?"

"He wants to go tomorrow. He wants me to take him in the ambulance."

Albert coughed smoke. "Jesus, Ernst, that's risky. Too risky. No, there has to be another way."

Dart scratched the back of his head like a man who has come, reluctantly, to a conclusion. "I don't think so. I've thought about it. And to tell you the truth, I'd rather take that risk than keep him here. As Agatha says, he puts all of us in danger. That's not right, Albert. You know it's not."

"The Germans might not come back. They didn't find anything."

Dart reached over and took the cigarette. "And that's some sort of guarantee, is it? Look, I want him out of here. I have a job to do. Koop is a loose cannon. I can't have him watching everything I do."

Albert Veening stared silently at his empty cup for some time. Dart's foot was jiggling under the table and he brought it under control.

"Okay," Albert said at last. "What time tomorrow?"

Dart shrugged. "It doesn't make much difference, as far as I can see. The afternoon is probably a bit safer than the morning. And it'll give him a few extra hours to rest up. I'll put fresh dressings on the wounds, maybe find him something to eat before he goes. Leave at one o'clockish? We'll have to make sure none of the patients see him, of course."

Albert nodded.

Dart put his hands on the table and pushed himself upright. "Fine," he said. "I'll go and tell him."

Albert looked up. "Ernst? You're a lucky man; you've lasted longer than most. You've survived two raids in less than seven days. I don't know much about the laws of probability, but I'd guess that breaks them."

"I know what you're saying, Albert. But I'm not relying on luck, believe me."

Dart went out into a day of broken light and raw wind and undertook the tedious business of servicing the ambulance. Then he went to the spider-infested gardener's shed and dug out the precious can of stolen petrol, weighing it in his hand. Fifteen litres, maybe. More than enough. He funnelled the whole lot into the tank. Without expecting anything to happen, he slotted the crank handle into place and heaved on it. It kicked back viciously twice, then on the third attempt the engine fired. A cloud of outraged birds exploded from the elms. Dart rejoiced.

When Dart backed into the radio room, Koop was sitting on the couch. His narrow bristled head and stringy neck protruded from the blankets he'd wrapped around himself; he looked like a damaged bird of prey in a filthy nest. He watched silently as Dart dropped a bundle of clothing onto the couch and set the big jug of lukewarm water, the flannel and the towel on the floor.

Koop peered down at them. "What's that for?"

"I thought you might want to get cleaned up."

Koop looked at Dart as though he'd used some unknown language. His right arm emerged from the blankets and picked through the mismatched and threadbare garments. "Classy."

"It's the best I can do," Dart said, sitting down on the chair with his back to the bureau. "Okay. Let's go through everything again. The ambulance seems—"

Koop held up a claw. "Let's *not* go through everything again," he said. "I've been stuck in this bloody cubbyhole of yours with nothing to do except go through everything again. And it occurs to me that there's a little something you haven't mentioned."

"Which is?"

"The girl."

It had been coming. Dart had been expecting it and had thought he'd be ready.

He said, "What girl? You mean the Maartens girl?"

"Yeah, the Maartens girl. Seems like we forgot to talk about her."

"She's not there. Our friend sent her to her relatives in Loenen when the shit hit the fan, after you shot Rauter. She's not a problem."

405

"How do you know she hasn't gone back?"

"She hasn't."

"How do you know?"

"It's none of your damn business how I know what I know. She's not there, okay? Do you think I'd be setting this up if she was?"

Koop's lips arranged themselves into a moist smile. "All right," he said. "If you say so. Shame, though, in a way. She's a piece, don't you think? You reckon our heroic commandant has been getting some of that? I wouldn't be surprised. I would, if I were him. I bet you would too."

The man was toxic. He fouled everything. It cost Dart an enormous effort of will not to hurl himself from the chair and crush him like a cockroach.

He said, "You might want to use some of that water to wash your mouth out."

Koop raised an eyebrow. "Ah-hmm. Didn't happen to touch a nerve there, did I, Doctor?"

Dart's foot was tapping again. "We're wasting time," he said. "Mar ... the Maartens girl is irrelevant. Let's try to keep our minds on the job, shall we?"

THE WIND DROPPED away during the night, and in the morning when Dart went shivering to the window the lawn was white with crystals of frost. When he coaxed the spluttering ambulance out onto the road just before one thirty, there was still a glittering whiteness in the shadow of the hedge. He looked through the plane trees at the great brick face of the asylum. Gerard was on the lawn, paused in his endless task of trapping clouds to watch the ambulance go by. Dart was surprised to feel a small pang of regret. He would, in spite of everything, miss the place. The nearside front wheel of the ambulance hit a pothole and the steering wheel jolted in his hands. A muffled curse came from the back.

Trixie Greydanus had interrupted her journey to Sanctuary Farm that morning to visit her grandmother's sister. The old woman had been a devoted cigar smoker all her life, and never failed to get bronchitis in the winter. This year, because she was so seriously undernourished, it looked likely that she would not survive. Trixie had done what little she could for her and was wheeling her bike back onto the road when she heard an approaching vehicle. Assuming it to be German, she retreated to the corner of the cottage to wait for it to pass.

She was very alarmed when she saw it was the asylum ambulance; and although she caught only a glimpse of the driver she was quite sure it was Ernst. Going in that direction he could only be heading for the farm, even though he was not due to go there until the following day. Did that mean there was trouble of some sort? Ought she to turn back, stay out of harm's way? She stood at the roadside for almost a minute, anxious and undecided; then she mounted the bike and set off in the direction the ambulance had taken.

Dart eased the ambulance to a halt a hundred metres before the gap in the willows and checked his watch. Koop's head appeared over the back of the passenger seat, his teeth bared. Pain had brought beads of sweat to his forehead.

"What's up? Where are we?"

"The track down to the farm is just ahead," Dart said. "It's not quite two o'clock. We'll wait. You all right?"

"Of course I'm not bloody all right. Riding in the back of this damn rattletrap would kill anyone, never mind someone with holes in him."

"You think you'll be able to walk?"

Koop's head withdrew. "I'm getting out," he said.

"What? No—" But Dart felt the wrecked springs shift. He twisted round in his seat. Koop was sitting with his good leg already out of the back and was lifting the other with his hands.

"I need to work this leg now, okay? No point falling flat on my arse when we get there."

He limped along the side of the ambulance and leaned on the bonnet, grimacing. Dart studied him: the hatchet-shaped face with its dark fur, the shabby reject clothes, the spare length of trouser belt dangling below his crotch. He seemed less than human. The world would not miss him. Dart lit his last cigarette, then took the cleaned and oiled

Smith and Wesson revolver from his bag and slipped it into his inside pocket. He took two long drags on the cigarette and held it out of the window.

"Here, finish this. Now listen: like I told you, I'm going to coast down the track with the engine off. I'll need enough speed to get us into the yard. It might be a rough ride, so brace yourself. Come on, get back in. It's time."

Marijke was at the foot of the stairs when the hall door flew open. She seized the banister because the shock threatened to topple her.

"Ernst! What…"

He looked desperate, panicky. He froze for a split second when he saw her, then grabbed her arm before she could recoil.

"Thank God. I thought I might be too late."

She opened her mouth but couldn't make a sound.

"We're getting out," Dart blurted. "Right now. We're blown. Grab whatever you need. Not much. A bag. Coat, shoes. Hurry, for God's sake. I've got the ambulance outside."

"Ernst, please, what's happened?"

"We're blown, I tell you. Betrayed. A call from Apeldoorn. Something to do with de Vries's group being taken. One of them must have talked. Koop got away. He's out on the heath somewhere. Never mind! Do as I say, Marijke. Get ready to leave, now. Where's Christiaan?"

"The barn."

She moved then, trying to shove her way past Dart. He took her by both arms and held her back. "No! I'll get him." He pulled her into a fierce and terrible embrace, then released her. She stumbled back against the wall.

"We'll be all right," he said reassuringly; for a moment it was as if they were having a different conversation altogether. Then all his mad urgency returned.

"Marijke, for pity's sake do as I say. We have no time. Get your things, now."

She fled from him up the stairs.

At seven minutes past two Tamar's headphones went dead. He shifted his gaze from the notepad to the transceiver. The needle on the voltage meter had slumped to zero. Softly cursing himself for his carelessness, he pulled the headphones off and stood up. He went to the angle of the floor and thatch and dragged out the other battery. He had connected one of the two leads when he heard what might have been a shuffling footstep below. He crouched at the open trapdoor and looked down, seeing nothing.

"Marijke? Darling, is that you?"

When no one answered he waited a second, listening, hearing nothing. He lowered his head a little way through the opening. He was torn between caution and his anxiety about the signal; he could picture the British radio operator with her pencil poised, listening to silence, imagining terrible things. He went back to the dressing table, hesitated, then picked up his revolver and put it in his jacket pocket. He descended the ladder. The small windows to his left threw angled beams of strong dusty light across the aisle. Between these shafts there were areas of dense shadow cast by the partition walls; the sequence of brilliance and darkness confused his eyes. He was in the act of taking the gun from his pocket when something moved out from between two partitions on the right of the aisle: a tilted silhouette. It lifted an arm and light fell onto the barrel of a pistol.

Dart had almost reached the barn stairs when the shots – three, maybe four – split the air. He stopped dead, filled with a dreadful joy that almost made him cry out. Then he forced himself onwards, holding the revolver out in front of him

410

with both hands. When he reached the upper floor he paused, peering through the baffling streams of light. There was a body sprawled beneath the trapdoor, half propped against the ladder. The head was thrown back over the left shoulder and Dart could not see the face. The clothes told him it was Tamar. He had obviously fallen through the hatch when Koop shot him. So Koop was still up there. Dart advanced down the aisle to within five metres of the body and stood ready to shoot him when he came down the ladder.

Interminable seconds passed during which Dart could hear nothing but his own jagged breathing. The desire to look at the corpse was almost irresistible, but he kept his eyes and the gun aimed at where the ladder disappeared into the loft.

"Koop?"

He hadn't meant to speak. The strangled whisper didn't seem like his own voice, and it was as if he were under someone else's control when he moved forward. He stood in front of Tamar's body and called again. "Koop? Koop, for Christ's sake, man! Are you all right?"

It was possible, Dart realized, just wonderfully possible that Tamar had shot Koop at the moment of his own death, that at least one of the shots had come from Tamar's gun. He looked down at the body at last and saw that yes, Tamar's revolver was lying close to the curled fingers of the right hand. He saw too that there were wet holes in the dark sweater and that the lower rungs of the ladder were slick with blood. The leather jacket was spread open and there was more blood on the lining. Two identity booklets protruded from the inside pocket.

"Koop! Can you hear me?"

Nothing. Stooping quickly, Dart took the two IDs and wiped the blood from them on his sleeve. He thumbed one open and saw Marijke's face. He stuffed the booklets into his coat pocket and again clasped the Smith and Wesson in

411

both hands and stepped back. He opened his mouth to call Koop's name again but the word died on his lips because a gun barrel jabbed into the base of his skull.

"Boo."

"Jesus! Koop, you—"

"No, don't turn round."

"What? What are you—"

"Shut up. Now, arms out straight sideways, gun in the right hand. Come on, do it!"

Dart did it.

"Slide the safety catch on and drop the gun on the floor."

The pistol thudded onto the boards and then the muzzle of the Luger was no longer pressed against Dart's head.

"Now you can turn round, sonny boy."

Dart turned. Koop's gun was aimed at the middle of Dart's face. It did not shake or waver at all. Koop's smile was yellow and his tone of voice was pleasant.

"One of the things I hate about you," he said, "is that you think I'm stupid." The Luger gestured briefly at Tamar's body. "He thought so too. But you're worse than him. You really thought I'd be stupid enough to trust you. You thought you could use me. And that upsets me."

"Are you going to kill me?"

"Yeah, I think so. Later, when you've taken me where I want to go."

He hobbled back a step and twitched the gun towards the stairs. "Let's go. Lead the way."

Dart sidled past Koop and forced his legs to take him towards the stairs. He'd gone ten paces before the unbearable injustice of it all made him unravel like a severed rope. He turned and faced Koop even though the Luger's muzzle was close to his throat. His outburst was like that of a child denied a long-promised treat. His hands beat against the sides of his thighs and ridiculous tears filled his eyes.

412

"No, no! I can't. I won't. This isn't right. It doesn't go like this! It's not—"

Koop clubbed him on the side of the face with the Luger and he went down. His head was full of wet stars and he scrabbled backwards on his hands and heels until his back hit a timber upright.

Koop swayed above him in a halo of brilliant light. The gun came up, aiming at Dart's gaping mouth.

"Damn you, then," Koop hissed. "Rot in hell."

Dart lifted his hands to ward off the bullet, and in that halted instant Koop turned away from him, staring wide-eyed to his right. The arm and the hand with the gun in it swung away. A massive rapid hammering filled the barn. Koop had a fit of grotesque movements like a jerked puppet. Soft explosions tracked across his chest and left shoulder and sent a fine spray of red matter into the bright dusty air. Above Dart's head splinters erupted from the woodwork. Koop toppled backwards; when he hit the floor he made a gargling noise and then lay still.

Dart raised his head and looked towards the stairs. He could see only the upper part of Marijke's body. Her face was a white mask painted with huge eyes. She lowered the Sten and placed it on the floor before climbing the final steps. Dart got to his knees and held his arms out to her. She ignored both him and the man she had killed, and walked, entranced, towards the body at the foot of the ladder.

Dart said, "Marijke. My love, don't."

But by then she had got there and thrown her head back, and begun to howl like an animal.

ENGLAND, 1995

DAD SAID, "TRIXIE told me the first thing that puzzled her, when she got to the farm, was that the ambulance wasn't there. She knew it had been there, because there were fresh tyre prints on the muddy parts of the track. But it wasn't now, and Ernst Lubbers couldn't have driven back towards Mendlo because she'd have met him on the road. She started to get seriously worried when she found the door to the farmhouse wide open, even though it was a cold day. She went inside and called Marijke's name several times. The kitchen stove was warm and there were two used cups and plates on the table. The bedrooms were empty. She went out into the garden, then the big barn. No sign of anyone. She was very nervous by then. She said that the silence was not like ordinary silence. When she went into the little barn, the one with the radio room in the roof, there was a funny smell, a bad smell, like *scheet*, fart. She said she somehow knew that something awful was in there, and she didn't want to climb the stairs but forced herself to. There was a Sten gun lying on the floor at the top. The trapdoor up to the loft was open. The ladder was lowered, and there was a body lying next to it. It was Christiaan Boogart."

Yoyo had been silent and as still as stone for a long

time, but now he inhaled loudly and his fingers tightened on mine. Dad's hands were clasped together. I noticed for the first time how coarse and marked they were, and that the first two fingers of his right hand were yellowed by nicotine. They were not the hands from my childhood. They belonged to a stranger. His head was lowered and I saw how thin his hair was.

"Trixie couldn't move for quite a long time. Her blood was ice, she said. She was sure, you see, that if Christiaan Boogart was dead, Marijke would be as well. She was convinced she would find her friend's body somewhere in the barn. Then it occurred to her that Christiaan might not be dead, so she made herself climb the last couple of steps and walk towards him. That's when she saw the feet. They were sticking out of one of the stalls on the right-hand side. When she drew level with them she saw that the body was a man's. She described him as looking like a tramp. She didn't know who he was. She'd never seen him before. He had terrible wounds across the front of his body, and his mouth and eyes were gaping open. He had a German pistol in his hand. The wooden partition behind him was splattered with blood. Trixie edged past him, and when she got close to Christiaan's body she knew at once that he was beyond help."

Dad stopped talking. He reached forward and picked up the stained identity booklet from the table, where I'd laid out the contents of the box. He opened it and stared at the photograph again.

"I didn't even know what he looked like," he said. "Never saw his face until today. It's so … strange."

His voice had thickened. I wanted to go over to him and hold him then, but I knew I couldn't. It was as though he had a sort of barrier around him, a barrier that he needed until he'd told us everything. So I just blinked my tears away and waited.

He took a long breath. "Trixie went up to the radio room. She said it was a dreadful thing to step over the body onto the ladder. There was blood on the rungs and it was awful, putting her feet on it. The loft was empty. The radio thing, the transceiver, was still set up. He must have been using it when it happened. So she went down again and walked the length of the barn looking in all the stalls, dreading finding Marijke in one of them. She said that when she dreams about that afternoon that's what she's doing: searching shadowy rooms along an endless corridor, expecting to find some horrible thing. When she didn't find Marijke or anything that might have explained what had happened, she rode away. She couldn't think what else to do."

Yoyo said, "Where did she go, Jan?"

"To the asylum. She was still hoping that Marijke and Lubbers might have gone back there, perhaps by some roundabout route. If they hadn't, she would have to tell Veening what she'd found. She must have been in a bad state when she got there. But she discovered who the dead tramp in the barn was. His name was de Vries. A resistance guy, but sort of an outlaw. A psycho, according to Trixie's aunt, Agatha, although I don't suppose that's the word she used. He'd shown up at the asylum with a German bullet in him, and he'd been holed up there for a few days. Veening and Agatha had been very keen to get rid of him. So Lubbers had arranged to drive de Vries to a safe house somewhere. Not the farm; Trixie said Albert Veening was sure of that. Veening thought de Vries must have put a gun to Lubbers's head and made him go there. But that's not what happened, as I now know."

Dad rubbed his eyes with the heels of his hands and then lit another cigarette. The flame of his lighter trembled.

"Anyway. Telling me all this had pretty much worn Trixie out. The poor old love looked drained. Rosa looked pretty haggard too. It had been rough on her, translating the story for me. Once or twice I'd thought she was going to refuse to continue. But I think she realized that there was a huge unburdening going on, and had decided not to interfere. When Trixie stopped talking, she sat back in the chair with her eyes closed, maybe because she was exhausted. Or maybe because she didn't want to look at me.

"I was completely baffled. I think I was still trying to believe that some sort of mad mistake had been made, that Trixie'd got the names wrong. Something was very wrong, because I knew my father wasn't dead; I'd been with him less than a week ago. Eventually I managed to stand up and go to the window. I watched a crow wander across the lawn as if it owned it. Then Rosa started to say something, I don't remember what, but stopped when Trixie sort of gasped. We both turned to her, thinking that she was in pain. But it wasn't that.

"All the time she'd been talking, Trixie had kept the photo I'd given her on her lap. Now she'd picked it up again and was staring at it. She spoke to Rosa in a low voice. Rosa didn't seem to understand. Trixie said it all again, very agitated, and her face did look as though she was hurting. She jabbed at the photo with her fingers. Rosa went quite pale and said 'Nee nee' several times. No, no. Then, in English, 'Jesus Christ, are you sure?' And then Trixie tore the picture in half. The two halves fell onto the floor on either side of her, and she clenched her fists on the arms of her chair."

"None of us spoke for what seemed an age. I had absolutely no idea what was going on. Rosa wouldn't look at me. Then she said, 'My mother needs a rest, Jan. And in a little while the nurses will be coming with her medication. Let's you and I get some fresh air.'

"It was an order, not an invitation. She walked so quickly that I had trouble keeping up. It was as if she was trying to leave me behind. We didn't speak until we reached a little park called the Prince's Garden.

"'My mother likes to come here,' Rosa said. 'I have to bring her in a wheelchair these days.'

"We walked along a path a short way and then she stopped. 'I was born in 1943 on New Year's Eve,' she said. 'I'm illegitimate. My mother has never told me who my father was. She says he was a hero, like your father.'

"'Your mother thinks she knows what really happened in that barn, doesn't she?'

"'Jan,' Rosa said, 'my mother is very ill and pumped full of drugs. She is old. All those things took place a very long time ago, when a thousand terrible things happened in Holland every day. She wasn't at that farm when those men died, she told us that. And she has never told me any of this before. Maybe she is—'

"'Please. Just tell me what she said. Tell me what she told you about my … about the man in the photograph.'

"So she did. I felt sorry for her. It must have been awful, like being forced to put a sick puppy to death or something. And I knew it was the truth, that Trixie was right. Because it made sense of everything, and because, deep down, I already knew. In the end I sat down on a bench and died."

WE SAT IN silence. When Dad lifted his face he looked dazed, almost surprised to see us there. Then he sniffed and cleared his throat and refocused. He managed a half-smile.

"Look," he said, "can I offer you a drink? Are you hungry? There's not much in the house but I'm sure we can scrape something together. I've got a bottle of wine, if you fancy some. It ought to be champagne, I suppose, but I'm afraid it isn't."

So in a stunned and clumsy way we gathered up the things on the table and went inside. Dad made me a cup of coffee and poured wine for Yoyo and himself. The living room was filled with golden light from the lowering sun, which made it more welcoming than it might have been. Dad sat in an armchair and Yoyo and I sat close to each other on the sofa.

Dad said, "All I remember about the return trip to London is that I thought I'd gone deaf. People were talking all around me but I couldn't hear them. The first thing I do remember hearing was someone saying my name. It was the announcer at the airport calling me for my flight. When I got home I stood outside the house for a long time, looking at the windows, not daring to go in. I couldn't imagine how

I could possibly behave normally. But that's what I tried to do. I kept it up for a couple of weeks, but then I started to go to pieces.

"It was unbearable, knowing what I knew. But what made it worse, much worse, was that I couldn't do anything about it without wrecking everyone else's lives. I couldn't tell anyone. Tell my mother that the man she thought had rescued her, the man she'd married and lived with for forty years, had murdered my father? My God! How could I tell Sonia? How could I stop you spending time with the bastard and not tell you why? I couldn't even tell *him* that I knew, because then what? Carry on the charade of normal family life? Sit at his table and eat Sunday bloody dinner? Besides, I didn't want to see him, couldn't bear the thought of it. I wanted to kill him. I seriously wanted to kill him. It was the only option, it seemed to me. I thought about it all the time. Worked out elaborate ways of doing it and getting away with it. It was like having a big black spider crawling around in my brain. And although I couldn't stop thinking about it, I knew I'd never do it. Because then I'd have to live with that as well."

Dad drank half his wine in one go and lit another cigarette. "I lost it completely, I'm ashamed to say. Couldn't do my job. People at the office started talking, looking at me in funny ways. Some days I'd leave home – briefcase, suit, all of that – and not get off the tube. Or just walk and end up God knows where. I started drinking quite heavily. My boss called me in, very nice at first, just 'concerned'. Then the verbal warnings, then the written variety. It got impossible to be at home too. So I invented business trips, and spent days in hotels doing nothing.

"And then one day I found myself in Paddington Station. I sat and stared at the departures board for a long time, watching the names change. When I saw that the train at platform one was going to Penzance, I bought a ticket and got on it. I don't know why. Perhaps it was just that Penzance is a nice word, or because it seemed a long way away.

"I must have slept a long time, because when I woke up and looked out of the window, all I could see was water. The train was running along right next to the sea and the light was dazzling. Then it was Plymouth, then the bridge into Cornwall. And there it was – a big sign with TAMAR on it. I don't know if it was because it was your name, my real father's name, but something sort of clicked in my head. The solution to the problem came to me. I couldn't make William Hyde disappear, but I could make myself disappear. It was a terrifying idea, and cruel, but absolutely logical. It was that or go mad. And I realized I'd started doing it already. The drinking, the hiding – I'd been trying to vanish. So I got off at the next stop and took the next train back to Plymouth, figuring that it would be easier to be invisible in a city."

I sat there in that unlived-in living room and understood that my dad had been insane. I wondered if he still was. I couldn't imagine how he could have kept all that stuff dammed up inside him all this time without being at least three parts crazy.

He said, "It turned out to be much harder to disappear than I'd imagined. The practical problems are enormous, actually. After a couple of months I was living pretty much hand to mouth. Then I had a stroke of luck. I was working in a pub down by the ferry terminal and I got talking to a man who was waiting to meet some clients off a delayed boat. It turned out to be Colin, the guy who owns this place. One thing led to another, and he offered me a job. I'd been here almost a month before I found out that it was a stone's throw from the head of the Tamar. It seemed such a beautiful coincidence. Or predestination, if you believe in that sort of thing."

I didn't know what I believed. I didn't know if it was possible to believe in anything any more.

I said, "I'm sorry, Dad. I can't get my head round all this. I mean, why didn't you just get in touch with us? Didn't you want to? Didn't you realize we were all off our heads with worry?"

"I couldn't get in touch. How could I, without explaining why I'd gone? And that was the one thing I couldn't do."

"So what were you going to do? Stay here for ever?"

"I don't know. I suppose I was waiting for Hyde, Lubbers, Dart, whoever he is – was – to die."

Hyde, Lubbers, Dart, whoever he was. Grandad.

"He is dead," I said, very cold.

The word sat there between us like a toad. Dad didn't meet my eyes. He poured more wine.

Yoyo said, "Jan, you say he came here. This is something I don't understand. How did he find you?"

"I didn't ask. It wasn't that kind of … conversation."

"What did he say?" I said. "What did he want?"

"Forgiveness." Dad's voice was so bitter. "Forgiveness. Can you imagine?"

I could. Very easily. And I thought Dad, of all people, ought to be able to.

Yoyo said, "Sorry, but I am a bit confused. You are saying that he knew you had found out these things about him?"

Dad didn't answer for a second or two, and he didn't look up at us.

"Yeah. I wrote to him. Not what you'd call a letter. A few words, several of them obscene. This was a couple of days after I got off the train in Plymouth. I'd been drinking. I was pretty dark, I suppose. I called him Lubbers, and a few other things besides. So yes, he knew." He took a long drag on his cigarette. "I suppose that's how he tracked me down. The Plymouth postmark on the letter. He'd have started from there, and … I don't know. He's a clever bastard. *Was* a clever bastard."

I thought, He came up the river. I must have said it aloud, because Dad looked at me. "What?"

I shook my head. "It doesn't matter. I want to know what he said. What did he say?"

"He admitted everything. Said he'd spent the rest of his life horrified by what he'd done, said it was like having cancer. I actually think he expected me to feel sorry for him. Christ! Then he started talking about love. How he'd always loved Mum, always loved me, loved you. Love, love, love. I wanted to strangle him. It was … appalling. Vile. And just so bloody untrue. You know how cold he was. He wouldn't know what love was if it hit him in the face."

I was tearful again, and hated myself for it. I wiped my eyes on my sleeve, hard. "You're wrong, Dad. I know you are. He did love Gran. I know because when she started going … getting ill, it broke his heart. I saw it. I was there, and you weren't. He was so…"

"Guilty."

"What?"

"Guilty. That's the word you're looking for. That's what he meant by love. He'd spent the rest of his miserable life feeling guilty. Why do you think he killed himself?"

"No, Dad. No. It wasn't like that. I know it wasn't. And Gran loved him."

"Did she?" There was a sneer in the question.

"Yes. *Yes*. I mean, she married him, didn't she? And stayed with him."

"Look, Tamar. It's not hard to figure that out, is it? She didn't know what he'd done. She believed he'd rescued her, saved her life, even, getting her out of Holland. She thought he was her lover's best friend. They got to England, where she knew nobody. Didn't even speak the language. She was

426

pregnant. She depended on him, and he exploited that. Dependence can look like love, in a certain light."

I got up. "I'm going for a walk," I said. Yoyo looked at me. "By myself," I said.

I went through into the kitchen and stopped to put on the sweatshirt I'd left there when we came in. I heard Yoyo say, "Jan, I must ask you this. Do you feel some pity at all for this man?"

And Dad said, "No, Johannes. I hope he rots in hell."

I went back to the living-room doorway and said, "Remind me again, Dad – who was it who asked you to name me after your father?"

Then I walked out into what was left of the daylight.

I went a little way up the drive and then climbed the slope that rose away from Dad's cottage. When I got to the top I could see the main house, a rambling white-faced building with lights on in several windows. Wisps of music. The big lawn had been mown in very precise light and darker green stripes: my father's work, I supposed. The sunset was perfect. Soft streamers of peach-coloured cloud hung in a blue-washed sky above distant indigo hills. It all looked no more real than flimsy scenery for a school play.

Below me, off to the right, light glittered on water. I headed that way and came to an ornamental garden with, at its centre, a large pond. A weeping willow leaned over the water, its trailing branches touching their own reflections. The air was rich with the scent of jasmine. I heard voices speaking a strange language, a series of fast broken sounds. Two men were squatting on their heels at the edge of the pond, one of them pointing at something I couldn't see. When they stood up, I saw that they were Japanese, slim men in pale short-sleeved shirts. They stood silently for a time, then one looked at his watch and spoke. They turned and walked away along a path towards the school. Where the path emerged from the garden a white marble statue stood on a pedestal: a naked goddess with an arm raised as if beckoning to the upstairs windows. As they passed her, one of the men reached up and patted her backside. When their laughter had faded I went down to the pond.

Much of it was in deep shade, but where the last light fell on the water it looked like golden oil. At first I couldn't see what the Japanese men had been looking at. Then the willow whispered, and the same breath of wind brought the little boat out of the shadow. It was smaller than the palm of my hand and woven, like basketwork, from long slender leaves. The mast was a peeled twig, the sail a small blank sheet of paper. It carried a fragile cargo of jasmine blossom and it drifted towards me, tilting but not toppling, trailing black ripples through the gold.

EPILOGUE: AMSTERDAM, 2005

IT'S TIME TO put all this stuff away. The creased English maps, a tatty fragment of silk, a photo of two young men who might have been brothers, a still unfinished crossword puzzle: the surviving items from Grandad's box. Yes, I still think of him as that, call him that. It's as real as any of his other names. The one thing that's missing – apart from the money, of course – is Christiaan Boogart's fake identity. I let Dad keep that. Whether it eases or feeds his bitterness, I couldn't really say.

The past is a dark house and we have only torches with dying batteries. It's probably best not to spend too much time in there in case the rotten floor gives way beneath our feet, like it did for Dad. Like it nearly did for me.

Yoyo said to me recently, "Love and pain, that's what families are, and they fit together like this" – he slotted the tips of our fingers together – "like cogs." Then he smiled and put a hand on my swollen belly. "And what makes these cogs turn is hope, of course."

"Or ignorance," I said.

He thought about it. "Yes, or ignorance. But hope is more reliable."

The sun has left our street now but the late day is still

warm. Through the open window I can hear, faintly, the guides' commentaries from the tourist boats gliding along the Prinsengracht. They'll have left the Anne Frank House behind them, and now the passengers will be aiming their cameras at the giant gaudy crown perched on the spire of the Westerkerk. Soon Yoyo will be home, and because it's my birthday we'll go out for something to eat. We'll probably end up at the usual place. It's just ten minutes away and I can't walk much further than that now that the Lump has got so heavy. That's what he calls it. It's what he'll say as soon as he's come in and kissed me: "How is the Lump today?"

We've still not decided what to call it if it's a boy. If it's a girl – and for some reason I'm sure it is – she'll be Marijke. That's something we agreed on from the start.

NOTES AND ACKNOWLEDGEMENTS

In part, *Tamar* is a historical novel, a mix of fact and fiction. Real events gave me the bones of the story, but I've taken liberties with them. For example, it is true that SS Lieutenant General Hanns Albin Rauter was ambushed on a country road on the night of 6th March 1945, but not by a group of men led by Koop de Vries; they exist only in the pages of this book. Likewise, you'll not find Mendlo or Sanctuary Farm on any real map.

I gathered the facts and assembled the skeleton of the story from a number of sources. Four books were especially helpful: *The Hunger Winter: Occupied Holland, 1944–45* by Henri A. van der Zee; *The SOE in the Low Countries* by M. R. D. Foot; *Secret Warfare* by Pierre Lorain; and *Between Silk and Cyanide: A Codemaker's War, 1941–1945* by Leo Marks. I based the account of Rauter's shooting and its terrible aftermath on an article by Karel Margry in volume 56 of *After the Battle*.

I am extremely grateful to the kind (and bilingual) staff

of the Netherlands Institute for War Documentation in Amsterdam; they even allowed me to work there when it was supposed to be closed.

I have an enormous and now unrepayable debt to Paul Peters, whose account of his experiences as an SOE wireless operator in occupied Holland urged me to write this novel. Not long before he died, I sat with him and his wife Marijke in their garden in Laren, Holland, and we discussed such merry topics as handguns, hunger, amphetamine dependence, suitcase transceivers, code silks and suicide pills. Marijke shared her still-vivid memories of being a teenage "hunger tripper". At one point I asked Paul what it had felt like, being "underground", living in dread of raids and Nazi detector cars. It was a stupid question, I suppose; but he considered it carefully (like a squirrel looking for the best way into a nut) and eventually said, "Boring." It was the most interesting use of the word I'd ever heard, and it gave me my way into the story.

My editor at Walker Books is Averil Whitehouse. For her creativity, diligence and patience no expression of thanks could be adequate. After working with me, it's a miracle that she's not trapping clouds with her feet or chatting to invisible angels.

Finally, an apology, if you happen to be Dutch. I've used the terms Holland and the Netherlands as though they mean the same thing. That's wrong, but it's what we British do, and I couldn't find a convenient place in the story to explain the difference.

ABOUT THE AUTHOR

Mal Peet was born in 1947 in Norfolk, England, and had many careers before he became a full-time writer. Now he is so successful a novelist that his writing is translated and known around the world.

Mal's first novel, *Keeper*, won the Branford Boase Award and a Nestlé Children's Book Prize in 2004 and was shortlisted for the *Jugendliteraturpreis* in Germany. It introduced Paul Faustino, the hard-bitten South American journalist who also features in two further novels, *The Penalty*, and *Exposure*, which won the Guardian Children's Fiction Prize in 2009. Mal's second novel, *Tamar*, in which the desperate acts of resistance fighters in Nazi-occupied Holland cast a long shadow into the future, was the winner of the 2005 Carnegie Medal and went on to win the prestigious Dutch De Gouden Lijst Award in 2011.

With his wife, Elspeth Graham, Mal also writes for younger readers. Their classic story *Cloud Tea Monkeys*, illustrated by Juan Wijngaard, was shortlisted for the 2011 Kate Greenaway Medal. Their forthcoming books for this readership, *The Mysterious Traveller* and *Night Sky Dragons*, will be illustrated by P.J. Lynch and Patrick Benson respectively.

Mal's most recent novel is *Life: An Exploded Diagram*, and he has also written several short stories for young adults. To find out more about Mal and his books, visit www.malpeet.com

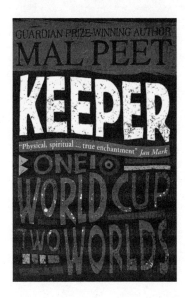

WINNER OF THE BRANFORD BOASE AWARD

In a newspaper office, Paul Faustino, South America's top sports journalist, sits opposite the man they call El Gato – the Cat – the world's greatest goalkeeper. On the table between them stands the World Cup...

In the hours that follow, El Gato tells his incredible life story – how he, a poor logger's son, learns to become a World Cup-winning goalkeeper. And the most remarkable part of this story is the man who teaches him – the mysterious Keeper, who haunts a football pitch at the heart of the claustrophobic forest.

"Mal Peet [takes] the football novel into a new league."

The Guardian

"A remarkable and absorbing story with football at its heart, but superb storytelling in its soul."

Branford Boase Award panel

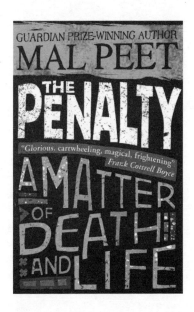

As the city of San Juan pulses to summer's sluggish beat, its teenage football prodigy El Brujito, the Little Magician, vanishes without trace.

Paul Faustino, South America's top sports journalist, is reluctantly drawn into the mystery. As a story of corruption and murder unfolds, he is forced to confront a bitter history of slavery, and the power of the occult.

"Another superb read from a master storyteller."

The Bookseller

"A sophisticated and beguiling tale of the real and spirit worlds."   ***The Times***

"Cogently constructed and elegantly written, this latest novel is teenage fiction at its best."   ***The Guardian***

**WINNER OF THE
GUARDIAN CHILDREN'S
FICTION PRIZE**

Otello: black, South America's top footballer.
Desmerelda: white, pop star daughter of a right-wing
politician.

Their sudden and controversial marriage propels them
centre stage where they burn under the media spotlight.
But celebrity attracts enemies, and some are very close to
home. When a young girl is found murdered, Paul Faustino,
South America's top sports journalist, witnesses the power
of the media in creating – and breaking – lives.

"Stunningly good, blending *Othello* with Brazilian football,
celebrity culture and the lives of slum children in a mix of
brilliance and compassion."   ***The Times***

"Peet's writing is slick, assured and sophisticated."
                                         The Irish Times

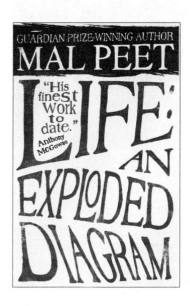

GUARDIAN PRIZE-WINNING AUTHOR
MAL PEET
"His finest Work to date."
Anthony McGowan
LIFE:
AN EXPLODED DIAGRAM

Norfolk, 1962. It's a hot summer during the Cold War. Clem, a working-class boy from a council estate, and Frankie, the daughter of a wealthy landowner, are conducting a furtive and high-risk relationship.

Meanwhile, the world's superpowers are moving towards nuclear confrontation. With the Cuban Missile Crisis looming, it seems that time is running out for Frankie and Clem. There are things they need to do before the world explodes.

"Mal Peet is like a master couturier – he stitches words together into exquisitely cut sentences."
The Sunday Telegraph

"Beautifully written and with characters you really care about." **Daily Express**

"Peet's warmth, humour and fierce intelligence are soaked into every page." **The Scotsman**

APACHE

TANYA LANDMAN

Siki is an orphan of the Black Mountain Apache. Her mother was killed by Mexicans three years ago and her father lost in an ambush the winter before that. When Siki witnesses the brutal murder of her little brother Tazhi, she vows to become an Apache warrior and avenge her brother's death.

A powerful and emotional portrayal of the Apache's struggle for survival in a hostile world.

"Apache is a magnificent account of life in a doomed tribe on the Mexican border towards the end of the 19th century: a disturbing but exhilarating experience." *The Independent*

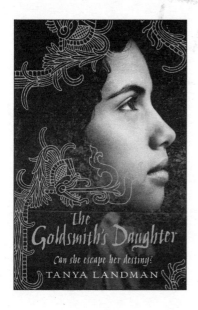

THE GOLDSMITH'S DAUGHTER

TANYA LANDMAN

In the golden city of Tenochtitlan, Emperor Montezuma rules with an iron rod and people live in fear of the gods. Itacate, a girl born under an ill-fated sky, is destined for a life of submission and domestic drudgery. But when her father, a goldsmith, discovers her talent for his craft, she starts to work as his apprentice, a secret she must keep in order to protect the lives of herself and her family. But danger awaits as Spanish strangers invade the city. And when Itacate's work comes to the emperor's attention and she falls in love with a stranger, her life takes an even more perilous turn. Can Itacate change her destiny and survive in this harsh new world?

"This is a glittering tale ... it vividly conjures up the people who had an unanswering belief in their gods and prophecies and who are eventually destroyed by the Spaniards."

Newbury Weekly News